ACCLAIM FOR JEFFERY DEAVER'S NOVELS

The Burial Hour

"Deaver is a master of plot twists, and they are abundant in this story that keeps the reader guessing about who can be trusted and what's behind the motivations of the abductor. Putting Rhyme and Sachs in unknown territory showcases a different side of their characters. Making them jump through hoops to keep international peace gives the story an extra edge. Essential for fans of the franchise."
—Associated Press

"Jeffery Deaver's forte is the diabolical puzzle mystery, and *The Burial Hour* is so devilishly tricky you can practically smell the sulfur fumes...In a bold plot twist, Deaver folds Rhyme's inquiries into a broader investigation of a humanitarian challenge shared by the whole world. Takes guts, that does."
—*New York Times Book Review*

"*The Burial Hour* proves once again Jeffery Deaver is a brilliantly intricate novelist. *The Burial Hour* is lucky number thirteen in the Lincoln Rhyme/Amelia Sachs series. Taking Rhyme and Sachs out of their New York locale appears to rejuvenate Deaver and his story. Deaver has been writing novels for many years and he has never once disappointed me. Intriguingly detailed."
—Huffington Post

"Deaver, who is a master of surprises, once again delivers an overflowing basketful of them—enough for two novels, with more to spare—while hinting at a possible new direction for Rhyme and Amelia Sachs, his partner on and off the crime scene."
—BookReporter

"Timely and relevant. Another strong entry from the always-reliable Deaver."
—Booklist

The Steel Kiss

"Deaver is a genius when it comes to manipulation and deception. Stellar plot twists are in full abundance in *The Steel Kiss*, and the story line veers in several unpredictable directions."

—Associated Press

"Deaver doesn't disappoint. With an unmatched ability to create the perfect characters... Deaver takes fans to the edge in this one and dangles them over the cliff... One of the best books of 2016."

—*Suspense Magazine*

"Darkly witty... unsettling." —*New York Times Book Review*

"Fiendishly inventive... all the usual thrills, which are worth every breathless minute."

—*Kirkus Reviews*

"The plot twists are clever and unexpected, the dialogue is colloquial and natural, and the characters... are vividly realized. Highly recommendable."

—*Booklist*

"Clever... entertaining... Convincing characters and an unexpected closing twist will remind readers why Deaver is one of today's top thriller writers." —*Publishers Weekly*

"Deaver delivers another heart-stopping thriller in his Lincoln Rhyme series... The action, suspense and horrific crimes continue unabated."

—*RT Book Reviews*

"Deaver at his best and when you are Jeffery Deaver this means the best of the best."

—*Huffington Post*

"Fans will marvel at the creative manner in which Deaver incorporates current technological and societal trends into the plots of his thrillers."

—*Library Journal*

"[*The Steel Kiss* is] like a master class in how to perfectly balance plot and character...A terrific novel."

—*Connecticut News*

"A gripping thriller...As with any thriller by Jeffery Deaver, *The Steel Kiss* is full of plot twists, misdirections, characters whose discourse is less than truthful, and contradictions that seem beyond explanation...still the reader is shocked by the final explanation, the straightening of the twists and turns of the plot. One will wonder 'How did I miss that?'"

—New York Journal of Books

"If you're looking for a pedal-to-the-floor thriller with reversals and twists, this is the novel for you."

—The Big Thrill

"Loaded from first page to (almost) last with suspense of one sort or another...*The Steel Kiss* is a terrific novel."

—BookReporter.com

Solitude Creek

"What do we truly fear, and how would we react in a crisis? Would we fall apart and claw our way to safety? Or would we help someone else? Deaver forces the reader to tackle these questions, then adds his own brand of twists to play with expectations, delivering another outstanding and unpredictable thriller."

—Associated Press

"Numerous surprises are in store for Kathryn Dance (and the reader) in bestseller Deaver's stellar fourth novel featuring the California Bureau

The Skin Collector

high energy action into novels about a brilliant criminalist...Lincoln Rhyme has become one of the genre's most iconic characters."

—*South Florida Sun Sentinel*

"Like all of his books, the storytelling is intricately plotted, with plenty of feints, misdirections and endgame twists to keep the reader guessing."

—*Raleigh News and Observer*

"For those who have never read a Deaver book, this is definitely the time to start. Once you are hooked you will find yourself searching for everything he has written in the past, and that is plenty. He is one of the premiere writers of mysteries and each and every one of his books is a reading pleasure from beginning to end. So get a copy of *The Skin Collector* and settle yourself in for hours of reading satisfaction."

—*Huffington Post*

"Another suspenseful and twist-filled entry in this always-exciting series."

—*Booklist*

"[A] page-turner full of Deaver's signature moves: frantic pacing, forensic minutiae, blindsides, gotchas and hairpin plot turns...a true return to classic form for Deaver."

—*Winnipeg Free Press*

"'Deavotees' will expect and gratefully receive the many twists and sudden turns...No one is better at narrative misdirection. Just at the point you think 'That's impossible!' Deaver demonstrates the exact opposite...Once again the depth of his research and characterisation has created a superb example of modern American Gothic."

—*The Evening Standard* (UK)

"[A] mind-bending novel with twists and turns...a masterful race-against-the-clock mystery."

—*BookPage*

"Intriguing and enjoyable... If any author could pull this off, it is Deaver. This is because he has the intelligence and skills to do anything and everything... It is a book like no other you have read."

—Huffington Post

"The premise is clever, but Deaver's ability to execute it successfully makes this experimental novel even more impressive. Revealing the ending first, he still manages to surprise with a few twists, constantly challenging readers' understanding of the story. Read it backward, forward, once or twice, to see how all the pieces fit together—just be sure to chase down this List yourself."

—*Shelf Awareness*

"An absorbing read... Deaver skillfully patches together a compelling story that is filled with his trademark twists."

—*Oklahoman*

The Kill Room

"Fast and furious...an ace thriller [by] a master magician with words."

—Associated Press

"This is Deaver at his very best and not to be missed by any thriller fan."

—*Publishers Weekly* (starred review)

"Chillingly effective... Equal parts *Marathon Man* and top-notch political thriller, this is Deaver at the top of his game. Rhyme remains the most original hero in thriller fiction today... Not to be missed."

—*Providence Sunday Journal*

THE BURIAL HOUR

ALSO BY JEFFERY DEAVER

*Featuring Lincoln Rhyme and Amelia Sachs
**Featuring Kathryn Dance

THE BURIAL HOUR

A LINCOLN RHYME NOVEL

JEFFERY DEAVER

GRAND CENTRAL
PUBLISHING
New York   Boston

Copyright © 2017 by Gunner Publications, LLC
Cover design and photo of ropes by Jerry Todd. Background photo © enviromantic/Getty Images.
Cover copyright © 2017 by Hachette Book Group, Inc.

Grand Central Publishing
Hachette Book Group
1290 Avenue of the Americas, New York, NY 10104
grandcentralpublishing.com
twitter.com/grandcentralpub

Originally published in hardcover and ebook by Grand Central Publishing in April 2017.
First Trade Paperback Edition: January 2018.

Grand Central Publishing is a division of Hachette Book Group, Inc. The Grand Central Publishing name and logo is a trademark of Hachette Book Group, Inc.

The publisher is not responsible for websites (or their content) that are not owned by the publisher.

The Hachette Speakers Bureau provides a wide range of authors for speaking events. To find out more, go to www.hachettespeakersbureau.com or call (866) 376-6591.

Library of Congress Cataloging-in-Publication Data
Names: Deaver, Jeffery, author.
Title: The burial hour : a Lincoln Rhyme novel / Jeffery Deaver.
Description: First edition. | New York : Grand Central Publishing, 2017.
Identifiers: LCCN 2016054237 | ISBN 9781455536375 (hardcover) | ISBN 9781455571178 (large print) | ISBN 9781478906636 (audio book) | ISBN 9781478906643 (audio download) | ISBN 9781455536399 (ebook)
Subjects: LCSH: Rhyme, Lincoln (Fictitious character)—Fiction. | BISAC: FICTION / Thrillers. | GSAFD: Mystery fiction. | Suspense fiction.
Classification: LCC PS3554.E1755 B85 2017 | DDC 813/.54—dc23 LC record available at https://lccn.loc.gov/2016054237

ISBNs: 978-1-5387-4544-1 (paperback), 978-1-4555-3639-9 (ebook)

Printed in the United States of America

LSC-C

10 9 8 7 6 5 4 3 2

To the memory of my friend Giorgio Faletti.
The world misses you.

THE BURIAL HOUR

AUTHOR'S NOTE

While the Italian law enforcement agencies I refer to in this novel are real, I do hope the fine members of these organizations, many of whom I've met and whose company I've enjoyed, will forgive the minor adjustments I've made to their procedures and locales, which have been necessary for the timing and plotting of the story.

And I wish to offer my particular thanks to musician and writer, translator and interpreter extraordinaire Seba Pezzani, without whose friendship, and diligence and devotion to the arts, this book could not have been written.

The winter wind blows and the night is dark;
Moans are heard in the linden-trees.
Through the gloom, white skeletons pass,
Running and leaping in their shrouds.

   —Henri Cazalis, "Danse Macabre"

THE HANGMAN'S WALTZ

CHAPTER 1

"Mommy."

"In a minute."

They trooped doggedly along the quiet street on the Upper East Side, the sun low this cool autumn morning. Red leaves, yellow leaves spiraled from sparse branches.

Mother and daughter, burdened with the baggage that children now carted to school.

In my day...

Claire was texting furiously. Her housekeeper had—wouldn't you know it?—gotten sick, no, *possibly* gotten sick, on the day of the dinner party! *The* party. And Alan had to work late. *Possibly* had to work late.

As if I could ever count on him anyway.

Ding.

The response from her friend:

Sorry, Carmellas busy tnight.

Jesus. A tearful emoji accompanied the missive. Why not type the goddamn "o" in "tonight"? Did it save you a precious millisecond? And remember apostrophes?

"But, Mommy..." A nine-year-old's singsongy tone.

"A minute, Morgynn. You heard me." Claire's voice was a benign monotone. Not the least angry, not the least peeved or piqued. Thinking of the weekly sessions: Sitting in the chair, not lying back on the couch—the good doctor didn't even have a couch in his office—Claire attacked her nemeses, the anger and impatience, and she had studiously worked to avoid snapping or shouting when her daughter was annoying (even when she behaved that way intentionally, which, Claire calculated, was easily one-quarter of the girl's waking hours).

And I'm doing a damn good job of keeping a lid on it.

Reasonable. Mature. "A minute," she repeated, sensing the girl was about to speak.

Claire slowed to a stop, flipping through her phone's address book, lost in the maelstrom of approaching disaster. It was early but the day would vanish fast and the party would be on her like a nearby Uber. Wasn't there someone, *anyone*, in the borough of Manhattan who might have decent help she could borrow to wait a party? A party for ten friggin' people! That was nothing. How hard could it be?

She debated. Her sister?

Nope. She wasn't invited.

Sally from the club?

Nope. Out of town. And a bitch, to boot.

Morgynn had slowed and Claire was aware of her daughter turning around. Had she dropped something? Apparently so. She ran back to pick it up.

Better not be her phone. She'd already broken one. The screen had cost $187 to fix.

Honestly. Children.

Then Claire was back to scrolling, praying for waitperson salvation. Look at all these names. Need to clean out this damn contact list. Don't know half these people. Don't like a good chunk of the rest. Off went another beseeching message.

The child returned to her side and said firmly, "Mommy, look—"

"Ssssh." Hissing now. But there was nothing wrong with an edge occasionally, of course, she told herself. It was a form of education. Children *had* to learn. Even the cutest of puppies needed collar-jerk correction from time to time.

Another ding of iPhone.

Another no.

Goddamn it.

Well, what about that woman that Terri from the office had used? Hispanic, or Latino... *Latina*. Whatever those people called themselves now. The cheerful woman had been the star of Terri's daughter's graduation party.

Claire found Terri's number and dialed a voice call.

"Hello?"

"Terri! It's Claire. How are you?"

A hesitation then Terri said, "Hi, there. How're you doing?"

"I'm—"

At which point Morgynn interrupted yet again. "Mommy!"

Snap. Claire spun around and glared down at the petite blonde, hair in braids, wearing a snug pink leather Armani Junior jacket. She raged, "I am on the *phone!* Are you blind? What have I told you about that? When I'm on the phone? What is so f—" Okay, watch the language, she told herself. Claire offered a labored smile. "What's so...*important*, dear?"

"I'm trying to tell you. This man back there?" The girl nodded up the street. "He came up to another man and hit him or something and pushed him in the trunk."

"*What?*"

Morgynn tossed a braid, which ended in a tiny bunny clip, off her shoulder. "He left this on the ground and then drove away." She held up a cord or thin rope. What was it?

Claire gasped. In her daughter's petite hand was a miniature hangman's noose.

Morgynn replied, "*That's* what's so—" She paused and her tiny lips curled into a smile of their own. "*Important.*"

CHAPTER 2

Greenland."

Lincoln Rhyme was staring out the parlor window of his Central Park West town house. Two objects were in his immediate field of vision: a complicated Hewlett-Packard gas chromatograph and, outside the large nineteenth-century window, a peregrine falcon. The predatory birds were not uncommon in the city, where prey was plentiful. It was rare, however, for them to nest so low. Rhyme, as unsentimental as any scientist could be—especially the criminal forensic scientist that he was—nonetheless took a curious comfort in the creatures' presence. Over the years, he'd shared his abode with a number of generations of peregrines. Mom was here at the moment, a glorious thing, sumptuously feathered in brown and gray, with beak and claws that glistened like gunmetal.

A man's calm, humorous voice filled the silence. "No. You and Amelia cannot go to Greenland."

"Why not?" Rhyme asked Thom Reston, an edge to his tone. The slim but sturdy man had been his caregiver for about as long as the line of falcons had resided outside the old structure. A quadriplegic, Rhyme was largely paralyzed south of his shoulders, and Thom was his arms and legs and considerably more. He had been fired as often as he'd quit but here he was and, both knew in their hearts, here he would remain.

"Because you need to go someplace *romantic*. Florida, California."

"Cliché, cliché, cliché. Might as well go to Niagara Falls." Rhyme scowled.

"What's wrong with that?"

"I'm not even responding."

"What does Amelia say?"

"She left it up to me. Which was irritating. Doesn't she know I have better things to think about?"

"You mentioned the Bahamas recently. You wanted to go back, you said."

"That was true at the time. It's not true any longer. Can't one change one's mind? Hardly a crime."

"What's the real reason for Greenland?"

Rhyme's face—with its prominent nose and eyes like pistol muzzles—was predatory in its own right, much like the bird's. "What do you mean by that?"

"Could it be that there's a practical reason you want to go to Greenland, a *professional* reason? A *useful* reason?"

Rhyme glanced at the single-malt scotch bottle sitting just out of reach. He was largely paralyzed, yes. But surgery and daily exercise had returned to him some ability to move his right arm and hand. Fate had helped too. The beam that had tumbled upon his neck from a crime scene many years ago and severed and crushed many nerves had left a few outlying strands intact, if injured and confused. He could grasp objects—like single-malt scotch bottles, to pick a random example—but he could not rise from his complex wheelchair to fetch them if Thom, playing nursemaid, kept them out of goddamn reach.

"Not cocktail hour yet," the aide announced, noting the arc of his boss's vision. "So, Greenland? 'Fess up."

"It's underrated. Named 'Greenland' while much of it's barren. Not the least verdant. Compare Iceland. Quite green. I like the irony."

"You're not answering."

Rhyme sighed. He disliked being transparent and hugely disliked being caught being transparent. He would appeal to truth. "It seems that the Rigspolitiet, the Danish police, have been doing rather important research into a new system of horticultural spectrographic analysis in Greenland. A lab in Nuuk. That's the capital, by the way. You can situate a sample in a much narrower geographic area than with standard systems." Rhyme's brows rose involuntarily. "Nearly the cellular level. Imagine! We think all plants are the same—"

"Not a sin of mine."

Rhyme groused, "You know what I mean. This new technique can narrow down a target area to three meters!" He repeated, "Imagine."

"I'm trying to. Greenland—no. And has Amelia actually deferred to you?"

"She will. When I tell her about the spectrograph."

"How about England? She'd love that. Is that show on still, the one she likes? *Top Gear*? I think the original is off the air but I heard there's a new version. She'd be great on it. They let people go out on the racetrack. She's always talking about driving a hundred and eighty miles an hour on the wrong side of the road."

"England?" Rhyme mocked. "You've just lost your argument. Greenland and England offer the same degree of romance."

"You'll find some disagreement there."

"Not from the Greenlanders."

Lincoln Rhyme did not travel much. The practical consequences of his disability added a layer of complication to journeys but physically, his doctors reported, there was no reason not to hit the road. His lungs were fine—he'd weaned himself off a ventilator years ago, the chest scar present but not prominent—and as long as such matters as the piss 'n' shit details—his words—and low-chafing clothing were attended to, there was little chance of being afflicted by the quad's bane: autonomic dysreflexia. A good portion of the world was disabled-accessible now—with most enterprises, from restaurants to bars to museums, offering ramps and special restrooms. (Rhyme and Sachs had shared a smile when Thom pointed out an article in the paper about a school that had recently installed a disabled ramp and bathroom; the place taught only one thing: tap dancing.)

No, much of Rhyme's reluctance to travel and his reclusiveness were simply because he was, well, a recluse. By nature. Working in his laboratory—the parlor here, filled with equipment—and teaching and writing for scientific journals appealed to him far more than tired sights polished for tourists.

But, given what was on his and Sachs's agenda in the next few weeks, a trip outside Manhattan was necessary; even he admitted that one could not honeymoon in one's own hometown.

Plans for trips to labs specializing in horticultural spectrometry, or locales of wooing romance, were, though, put on hold for the moment; the door buzzer sounded. Rhyme glanced at the security video and thought: Well.

Thom rose and returned a moment later with a middle-aged man in a camel-tan suit, which he might have slept in, though he probably hadn't. He moved slowly but with little hesitation, and Rhyme thought that pretty soon he'd be able to discard the cane, which was, however, a pretty nifty accessory. Black with a silver head in the shape of an eagle.

The man looked around the lab. "Quiet."

"Is. A few small private jobs recently. Nothing fun. Nothing exciting. Nothing since the Steel Kiss killer." A recent perpetrator had taken to sabotaging household items and public conveyances—with tragic and occasionally gruesome results.

NYPD detective Lon Sellitto, in the Major Cases Division, had been Rhyme's partner—before Rhyme had moved up to captain and taken over the Crime Scene Unit. Nowadays Sellitto would occasionally hire Rhyme to consult on cases in which special forensic expertise was needed.

"What're you looking at? Tan is all I had." Sellitto waved toward his suit.

"Daydreaming," Rhyme said. "I wasn't looking at anything."

Not true, but he hadn't been regarding either the curious color of or the savage wrinkles in the suit. He was noting, with satisfaction, that Sellitto was recovering well following the attack on him by poison, which had caused major nerve and muscle damage—hence, the cane. While the detective was always fighting his weight, Rhyme thought he looked better on the portly side, like now. The sight of a gaunt, gray Lon Sellitto had been alarming.

"Where's Amelia?" Sellitto asked.

"In court. Testifying in the *Gordon* case. On the calendar first thing. Should be over with soon. Then she was going shopping. For our trip."

"Buying herself a trousseau? What is that anyway?"

Rhyme had no idea. "Something about weddings, clothing. I don't know. But she's got a dress already. Something frilly. Blue. Or maybe pink. Today she's shopping for me. What's so goddamn funny, Lon?"

"Picturing you in a tuxedo."

"Just sweats and a shirt. Maybe a tie. I don't know."

"Tie? And you didn't complain?"

True, Rhyme had little patience for what he considered affectation. But this occasion was different. For all her edge and edginess and her need of speed and blunt firearms, her passion for tactical solutions, Sachs had a splinter of teen girl within her and she was enjoying the game of wedding planning. This included shopping for a whatever-the-hell-it-was trousseau and a romantic honeymoon, and if that pleased her, by God, Rhyme was more than happy to accommodate.

Though he really hoped he could convince her about Greenland.

"Well, tell her to shop later. I need her to run a scene. We've got a situation."

A ping resounded within Rhyme the way a submarine's sonar detects something unexpected off the port bow.

He texted Sachs and received no response. "Maybe on the stand, testifying. Tell me more."

Thom appeared in the doorway—Rhyme hadn't realized he'd left. The aide said, "Lon, coffee? Cookies? I've been baking. I've got a couple of different kinds. One is—"

"Yes, yes, yes." It was Rhyme answering. "Bring him something. Make a decision *yourself*. I want to hear his story."

Situation...

"Proceed," he told Sellitto.

"Anything chocolate," Sellitto called to Thom's back.

"Easily arranged."

"Kidnapping, Linc. Upper East Side. Apparently one adult male snatched another."

"Apparently? What requires interpretation?"

"The only wit was nine years old."

"Ah."

"Perp grabs vic, tosses him into a car trunk. Takes off."

"The girl is sure about this? Not a figment of her overactive little imagination, stoked by watching too much television, ruining her thumbs on video games, reading too many Hello Pony stories?"

"Hello Kitty. Ponies are a different book."

"Did Mommy or Daddy confirm?"

"Morgynn, the girl, was the only one who saw. But I think it's legit. She found a calling card he'd left behind." Sellitto held up his phone and displayed a photo.

At first Rhyme couldn't make out the image. It was a picture of a dark shape, thin, lying on a sidewalk.

"It's a—"

Rhyme interrupted. "Noose."

"Yep."

"Made out of?"

"Not sure. Girl said he set it on the spot where he got the vic. She picked it up but the responding set it back in the same place he'd left it, more or less."

"Great. I've never worked a scene contaminated by a nine-year-old."

"Relax, Linc. All she did was pick it up. And the responding wore gloves. Scene's secure, waiting for somebody to run it. Somebody, as in Amelia."

The noose was made out of dark material, which was stiff, since segments were not flush with the pavement, as would be the case with more limp fibers. From the size of the poured-concrete sidewalk panel, the noose was about twelve to fourteen inches long in total, the neck hoop about a third of that.

"The wit's still on scene. With Mommy. Who isn't very happy."

Neither was Rhyme. All they had to go on was a nine-year-old schoolgirl with the observational skills and perception of a . . . well, nine-year-old schoolgirl.

"The vic? Rich, politically active, connected with OC, record?"

Sellitto said, "No ID yet. Nobody reported missing. A few minutes after the snatch somebody saw a phone fly outta a car—dark sedan, nothing more. Third Avenue. Dellray's boys're running it. We find out who, we find out why. Business deal gone bad, vic has information somebody wants, or the old standby. For-profit ransom."

"Or it's a psycho. There *was* the noose, after all."

"Yeah," Sellitto said, "and the vic just happened to be WTWP."

"What?"

"Wrong time, wrong place."

Rhyme scowled once more. "Lon?"

"It's going around the department."

"Flu viruses—not viri, by the way—go around the department. Idiotic expressions do not. Or should not, at least."

Sellitto used the cane to rise to his feet and aimed his bulky form toward the tray of cookies that Thom was setting down, like a Realtor seducing prospective buyers at a condominium open house. The detective ate one, then two, then another, nodded approval. He poured himself a cup of coffee from a silver pitcher and spilled in artificial sweetener, his concession to the battle against calories being to sacrifice refined sugar for pastry.

"Good," he announced through a mouthful of cookie. "You want one? Some coffee?"

The criminalist's eyes swiveled instinctively toward the Glenmorangie, sitting golden and alluring on the high shelf.

But Lincoln Rhyme decided: No. He wanted his faculties about him. He had a feeling that the girl's observations were all too accurate, that the kidnapping had occurred just as she had described it and that the macabre calling card was a taunting message of a death soon to be.

And perhaps more after that.

He texted Amelia Sachs once again.

CHAPTER 3

A plop, as water fell from ceiling to floor.

Ten feet.

Every four seconds.

Plop, plop, plop.

The resulting sound wasn't a splash. The floor of this old, old factory, now abandoned, was scarred from the passage of metal and wooden objects, and the water didn't accumulate in pools but eased away in crevices and cuts, as patterned as an old man's face.

Plop, plop.

Moans, too, as the chill autumn breeze slipped over the mouths of ducts, pipes and vents, the way you'd blow across a bottle neck to make a hooing sound. Didn't see that much anymore, no, you didn't. Because kids used to do it mostly with soda bottles, which were now plastic, not glass. Plastic didn't work very well. Beer bottles you could use but adults didn't get any pleasure out of the hooo-hoooing sounds.

Stefan had once written a piece of music to be played on Mountain Dew bottles, each filled with a different amount of water to produce a chromatic scale of twelve notes. He had been six years old.

The tones the factory now made were a C sharp, an F, a G. There was no rhythm, as the wind was irregular. Also:

Distant traffic, a constant.

More-distant exhalations of jet airplanes.

Not distant at all: a rat skittering.

And, of course, the most captivating sound of all: the rasping breath of the man sitting in a chair in the corner of this dim storage room. Hands bound. Feet bound. Around his neck, a noose. The string Stefan had left on the sidewalk as a grisly announcement of the kidnapping was a cello string; this noose was made of two longer strings, bound together to extend the length—they were the lowest and thickest strings of an upright double bass, one of those instruments that made the happy transition from classical music to jazz. Made of mutton serosa—the lining of a sheep's intestine—these were the most expensive musical strings on the market. Each had cost $140. They produced the richest tone, and there were world-class violinists, cellists and bass players who would never think of playing a baroque piece on anything but this. Gut strings were far more temperamental than metal or nylon strings and might go out of tune at the slightest change in temperature or humidity.

For Stefan's immediate purpose, though, the strings' intolerance of humidity was irrelevant; for hanging someone, they worked just great.

The loop hung loosely around the man's neck and the tail rested on the floor.

Stefan shivered from excitement, the way any pilgrim would at the beginning of his quest. He shivered from the chill too, even though he was an insulated man—in all senses: heavyset, with long, dense curly dark hair dropping well past his ears, and full beard, and a silken pelt of chest and arm hair. And he was swathed in protective clothing too: a white sleeveless undershirt beneath a heavy dark-gray work shirt, a black waterproof jacket and dungarees, also dark gray. They were like cargo pants but not cargo pants because the place where he'd been living until recently did not permit anyone to have pockets. Stefan was thirty years old but appeared younger, thanks to the smooth, baby-fat skin.

The room these two men were in was deep within the sprawling place. He'd set it up yesterday, moving in a table and chairs he'd found in other parts of the factory. A small battery-powered light. His musical, recording and video equipment too.

The watch on his wrist revealed the time to be 10:15 a.m. He should get started. He'd been careful but you never knew about the police. Had that little girl seen more than it seemed she had? The license plate was smeared with mud but someone might have noted the first two letters. Maybe enough to track the vehicle to the long-term parking lot at JFK airport, where it had been until yesterday. Using algorithms, using deductions, using interview skills . . . they might put an identification together.

Can't have that now, can we? Have to be careful.

I am, don't worry.

Stefan believed he might have spoken these words aloud. Sometimes he wasn't sure if he *thought* his messages to Her or *spoke* them. Wasn't sure if Her responses were real or not, either.

He laid the equipment out in front of him, examining keyboards and computer, cords and plugs. Switches clicked on. Hard drives hummed, adding sound.

Plop.

Moan.

Hum.

Good.

Ah, and the rat, too.

Skitter.

As long as there were sounds, distracting sounds, seductive sounds, Stefan had a good chance of keeping the Black Screams away.

So far, so good.

And now to add one more sound, one of his own making. He played a melody on the Casio. He was not an exceptional musician but, given his love, his addiction, his obsession, he knew his way around a keyboard. He ran through the music once, then twice. These were good renditions. He tried it again.

Stefan didn't pray, as such, but he did send a thought of thanks to Her for the inspiration to pick this composition.

Now he rose and walked to the blindfolded man, who was wearing dark business slacks and a white business shirt. His jacket was on the floor.

Stefan was holding a digital recorder. "Don't say anything."

The man nodded and remained silent. Stefan gripped the noose and pulled it taut. With his other hand, he held the recorder in front of the man's mouth. The choking noise issuing from his lips was delightful. Complex, varied in tone and modulation.

Almost, you might say, musical.

CHAPTER 4

Kidnappings and other serious investigations are generally run out of the Major Cases operation at 1PP, and there was a series of conference rooms reserved for task forces running such cases in that nondescript building not far from City Hall in downtown Manhattan. Nothing high-tech, nothing sexy, nothing out of binge-worthy TV shows. Just plain rooms.

Because Lincoln Rhyme was involved, however, and his condition made commuting troublesome, his parlor—not One Police Plaza—was serving as HQ for the noose-kidnapping case.

And the Victorian-era dwelling was buzzing.

Lon Sellitto was still here, along with two additions: A slender, tidy, academic-looking middle-aged man in tweedy, blue clothes that might be called, at best, frumpy. Mel Cooper sported a pale complexion, a thinning crown and a pair of glasses that were stylish only thanks to the Harry Potter franchise. On his feet were Hush Puppies. Beige.

The other newcomer was Fred Dellray, senior special agent in the FBI's Southern District office. With skin the shade of the mahogany desk he now half sat on, half leaned against, the tall, strikingly rangy man was dressed in an outfit that you wouldn't see...well, anywhere. A dark-green jacket, an orange button-down shirt and a tie that a bird-lover might say was too canary to be true. A pocket square was purple. His slacks were modest, by comparison, navy-blue houndstooth.

While Cooper was sitting patiently on a lab stool, awaiting the evidence that Sachs was soon to return with, Dellray pushed off from the desk and paced, juggling two phone calls. The boundary between state and federal jurisdiction in criminal investigations is as gray as the East River in March but one undisputed area of joint authority is kidnapping. And for this offense, there was rarely any bickering over who wanted to run point. Saving the life of a person taken by force deflates egos fast.

Dellray disconnected one then the other phone and announced, "Maybe got ourselves an ID of the vic. Took a bit of funny-doing, putting Part A together with Part B. But s'all coming down on the pretty side of probable."

Dellray had advanced degrees—including psychology and philosophy (yes, one could philosophize as a hobby)—but he somehow fell naturally into a street patois of his own making, not gang-talk, not African American Vernacular English. It was, like his clothing and his penchant for reading Heidegger and Kant to his children, pure Dellray.

He mentioned the phone that Sellitto had told Rhyme about, the one that the kidnapper had possibly flung out the window of his car, to keep from being traced, as he sped away from the scene with the victim in the trunk.

"Our tech brain boys were all super 'cited 'bout trying to crack it—always a challenge those Apple folk give us. It's like playing *Angry Birds* to our team. When, lo and behold, there's no password! This day and age! They're prowling through the call logs, when, what happens, it rings. It's some business-soundin' fella waiting for Phone-Boy to show up for breakfast, grapefruit getting hot, oatmeal cold."

"Fred?"

"My, we are impatient this morning. Phone belongs to one Robert Ellis, head of a teensy start-up—my own description—in San Jose. In town lookin' for seed money. No record, pays his taxes. Profile's as boooooring as a corset salesman's. And when I'm saying start-up don't be thinkin' Facebook, Crap-Chat, anything sexy and lucrative. His spec-i-al-i-ty's media buying. So it's not looking like a competitor snatched him."

"Associates or family hear from the taker? About ransom?" Sellitto asked.

"Nup. Phone logs show calls to a mobile registered to a woman lives at the same address he does. So, status o' girlfriend's a solid guess. But the provider says her phone's, of all things, way, way over in Japan. Presumably in the company of said lady, one Ms. Sabrina Dillon. My ASAC called her but hasn't heard back. Other numbers aren't remarkable. Just a guy in town for business. Doesn't seem to have much else in the way of family we could find."

"Domestic issues?" Mel Cooper asked. He was a lab specialist, yes, but also an NYPD detective who'd worked cases for years.

Dellray: "Nothin' on the radar. Though, even if so, I'm thinking a bit of cheatin' nookie doesn't really make you trunk-worthy."

"True," Sellitto said.

Rhyme said, "No OC connection."

"Uh-uh. Boy is not a gangbanger, 'less they're teaching that now at UCLA. His alma mater."

Sellitto said, "So, we're leaning toward some crazy."

There was the noose, after all . . .

"May be agreeing with you there, Lon," Dellray said.

"Speculation," Rhyme grumbled. "We're wasting time."

Where the hell were Sachs and the evidence collection teams?

Cooper's computer made a cheerful noise and he looked it over.

"From your evidence folks, Fred."

Rhyme wheeled forward. The federal crime scene unit—the Physical Evidence Response Team—had analyzed the phone carefully and found no fingerprints. The perp had wiped it before pitching it out of the car.

But the techs had found some trace—smudges of dirt and, wedged invisibly into the OtterBox cover, a short, light-colored hair. Human. There was no bulb attached, so no DNA analysis was possible. It was dry and appeared to have been dyed platinum blond.

"Picture of Ellis?"

A few minutes later Cooper downloaded an image from California DMV.

A nondescript man of thirty-five. Lean face. His hair was brown.

Whose head had the paler hair come from?

The kidnapper himself?

The aforementioned Sabrina?

The door opened and Rhyme could tell that Amelia Sachs had returned. Her footfalls were distinctive. Before she even breached the doorway, he was calling, "Sachs! Let's take a look."

She entered through the archway, nodded a greeting to all. Then handed over the milk crate, containing evidence bags, to Cooper, who set them aside. He now dressed in full protective gear—booties, gloves, bonnet and splash guard, which mutually protected examiner and evidence.

He set the items out on examination tables, which were in a separate part of the parlor, away from where the others, dressed in street clothing, clustered, to avoid contamination.

The pickings were sparse. Rhyme knew this, as he'd been "with" Sachs, via video feed, as she'd walked the grid at the scene. All she'd found was the noose, random trace from where the abduction had occurred and shoe print and tire mark evidence.

But even the tiniest of substances can, in theory, lead directly to your perp's front door.

"So?" Sellitto asked. "What'd the munchkin say?"

Sachs: "I'd trade the girl—Morgynn—for two of her mothers. She'll be in politics someday. Maybe a cop. She wanted to hold my gun. Anyway, the unsub was a heavyset white male, long dark hair, full beard, wearing dark casual clothes and dark baseball cap, long bill. A little taller than me. Same age as her tennis coach, Mr. Billings, who is—I checked—thirty-one. She didn't know the kind of car except it wasn't a Tesla, which her father drives—and tells everybody he drives. Morgynn didn't catch any distinguishings, but he was wearing blue gloves."

"Damn," Rhyme muttered. "Anything else?"

"No, but this was a first. Her mother, Claire, asked if I—or somebody I knew on the force—would want to moonlight as a waitperson at a party tonight."

"What's she paying?" Sellitto asked.

In no mood for humor, Rhyme said, "First, the noose. Any prints?"

Cooper tested the cord in the fuming tent to raise invisible fingerprints and said, "A few slivers. Nothing to work with."

"What's it made out of?" Dellray asked.

"I'm checking now." Cooper looked at the material closely under a microscope—set on relatively low magnification. He then consulted a visual database.

"I can run the chromatograph but I'm sure it's proteins—collagen, keratin and fibroin. I'd say catgut."

Sellitto wrinkled his nose. "That's disgusting."

Thom was laughing. "No cats involved."

Cooper said, "That's right. It's *called* catgut but it's from sheep or goat intestines."

Sellitto said, "Why's that any *less* disgusting?"

The tech was online. He continued, "Gut was used as surgical sutures. Now the only use is musical-instrument strings. Steel and synthetic materials're more frequent nowadays, but"—he gave a shrug—"catgut is still common. Could've come from a hundred stores, concert halls and schools around the area. The length of this one? Probably from a cello."

"And the noose?" Dellray asked. "Isn't it s'posed to have thirteen coils? For bad luck?"

Rhyme didn't know about catgut, and little about musical instruments, but he was familiar with nooses. It was properly called a hangman's knot. It was not meant to tighten, like a slipknot, and choke. Death was from a snapped neck, which led to suffocation, yes, though not because the throat was closed but because signals from brain to lungs shut down. The wide knot, expertly positioned behind the left ear of the condemned, cracked the spine not far above where Rhyme's had broken.

Answering Dellray, he said, "Some had thirteen coils. Most hangmen used eight back in the day. That worked just as well. Okay, what else?"

Sachs had used a gelatin lifter and an electrostatic device to capture the shoe prints that were probably the unsub's, based on the girl's account of where he had stood and walked.

Cooper consulted a database. He said, "A Converse Con. Size ten and a half."

Naturally, a very common sneaker. Impossible to trace to a single retail source from the tread alone. Rhyme knew this about the shoe, since he was the one who had created and still helped maintain the NYPD's database of footwear.

Sachs's attempt to lift tire treads had been, on the other hand, unsuccessful. Other cars and trucks had driven in about the same path as the kidnapper's sedan, obliterating distinctive tread impressions.

Rhyme said, "I suppose we better ask. What else did the child have to say?"

Sachs described how the kidnapping had unfolded.

"A hood over the vic's head. And he went limp?" Sellitto asked. "Suffocated?"

Rhyme said, "Pretty short period of time. Drugs maybe. Chloroform—a classic. You can also use homemade concoctions."

"What color was the hood?" Cooper asked.

"Dark."

"I've got a fiber here," the tech added, looking at the evidence bag notation. "Cotton. Amelia, you rolled it up right next to where he left the noose."

Rhyme looked at the monitor on which a tuft of fiber was displayed. He had a decision to make. The intact fiber could have important evidentiary value. Say they found a hood in the possession of a suspect; he could be linked to the crime if its fibers could be associated with this one (you didn't say "matched"; only DNA and fingerprints actually matched).

That would be good for the prosecutor's case at trial. But having the fiber in its present state didn't get you any closer to discovering who the perp was and where he lived or worked. Cotton, though, was wonderfully absorbent and this tiny piece might hold very helpful clues. The problem was that they could be unlocked only with the gas chromatograph—an instrument that isolated and identified substances. And to analyze the fiber required that it be destroyed.

"Burn it, Mel. I want to know if there's anything inside."

The tech prepared the sample for the Hewlett-Packard. The whole process would take no more than twenty minutes.

In the meantime, Sellitto and Dellray checked in with their respective supervisors. There'd still been no ransom demands, and no CCTV in the area had recorded the incident or the car speeding away. Dellray then uploaded all the information they had to NCIC, the National Crime database, to see if similar incidents had been reported elsewhere. None.

Rhyme said, "Let's get a chart going."

Sachs pulled a whiteboard close and took a dry marker. "What do we call him?"

Often the month and day were used as a temporary nickname for an unknown subject. This perp would be UNSUB 920, for September 20.

But before they decided on a moniker, Cooper stirred and looked at the screen of the GC/MS computer. "Ah. You were right, Lincoln. The fiber—presumably from the hood—shows traces of chloroform. Also, olanzapine."

"Knocky-out drug?" Dellray asked. "Roofie for kidnappers?"

Cooper was typing. "A generic antipsychotic. Serious stuff."

"From our boy's medicine cabinet? Or the vic's?" Sellitto wondered aloud.

Rhyme said, "Media buyer and psychosis don't fit together felicitously. I'd vote for the perp."

Cooper took soil samples from an evidence bag marked, *Vicinity of the unsub's shoes.* "I'll GC it too." And he stepped to the chromatograph.

Dellray's phone hummed and a long finger stabbed *Answer.* "Yeah?... No...We'll take a look-see."

He said to the room, "Special agent BFF of mine, in Des Moines, was being all diligent. Had just read the NCIC wire when he got a call from some woman. She saw her son watchin' YouVid, the streaming site? Nasty stuff. Live video of a guy being strangled—in a noose. We oughta see."

Sachs walked to a laptop, which was connected via a thick, flat HDMI cable to a large monitor against a nearby wall. She typed and called up the site.

The video depicted a man in shadows. It was hard to see for sure, and he was blindfolded, but the face could have been Robert Ellis's. His head was cocked to the side—because the noose was tugging his neck upward. Ankles bound with duct tape, arms tied or taped behind his back, he stood on a wooden box, about two by two feet.

As horrific as this was, the soundtrack was just as eerie. A snippet of a human gasp had been recorded and used as the downbeat for music being played on an organ or electric keyboard. The tune was familiar, "The Blue Danube."

You could count out the time—a waltz—as *gasp*, two, three, *gasp*, two, three.

"Christ," Sellitto muttered.

How long, Rhyme wondered, could a man stand like that before collapsing or slipping off, before his legs gave way or he fainted—and fell to the noose's grip? The short fall would not, like traditional executions, break his neck, but would slowly and agonizingly strangle him to death.

As the video continued, the music began gradually to slow, as did the gasps, still keeping perfect time to the flagging music.

The image of the man began to fade too, growing darker.

At the end of the three-minute running time, the music and desperate gasps faded to silence, the image to black.

Words in blood-red type materialized on the screen—words that because they were otherwise so ordinary became unspeakably cruel.

© The Composer

CHAPTER 5

R odney?"
        Lincoln Rhyme was talking to their contact at the NYPD
Computer Crimes Unit, downtown. One Police Plaza.

Rodney Szarnek was brilliant and quirky (a geek, say no more) but also into the most obnoxious head-banging, heavy-metal rock music from your worst nightmares.

"Rodney, please!" Rhyme shouted into the speakerphone. "Make it vanish."

"Oh, sorry."

The music diminished, though it didn't vanish.

"Rodney, you're on here with a bunch of people. Speaker. Don't have time to make introductions."

"Hi, every—"

"We've got an abduction and the perp's rigged something so the vic only has a little while to live."

The music shut off completely.

"Tell me."

"Amelia's sending you a YouVid link right now. A video of the victim."

"Is it still up?" he asked.

"As far as we know. Why?"

"If there's a violent video—real life, not fake—YouVid'll probably take it down. If there're complaints or if their algorithm catches it and their vid police decide it violates TOS, terms of service, down it comes. Have somebody download and record it."

Dellray said, "Our folks're all over it. Done and done."

"Hi, Fred." A pause, then Szarnek said, "Got it…Man. Already twenty-thousand-plus views. And a ton of likes. Sick world out there. So this's that guy snatched a few hours ago? I read the wire."

"We think," Sachs said.

"Hey, Amelia. Okay. And you need the location where this was sent from. Hoping he's still alive. Okay, okay. There. I've sent the vid and an expedited request to the Warrants Desk. They'll be on the phone with a magistrate, who'll approve it ASAP. Minutes, I'm talking. I've worked with YouVid before. They're in the U.S., New Jersey, thank God, so they'll cooperate. If the server was overseas, we might never hear from them. I'll call you back as soon as I can start tracing."

They disconnected. Rhyme said to Sachs, "Get that chart going. What do we have so far?" A nod at the whiteboard. She grabbed a marker and started.

As she wrote, Rhyme turned to the computer to look at the video again. The screen changed. A red block of type came up.

This video has been removed for violation of our Terms of Service.

A moment later, though, the video arrived from Dellray's technical people, via an email. An MP4 file. Rhyme and the others viewed it again, hoping it might yield clues as to where the footage had been shot.

Nothing. A stone wall. A wooden box. Robert Ellis, the victim, struggling atop the improvised gallows.

One slip, one muscle cramp would kill him.

Sachs was finished jotting a moment later. Rhyme looked over the chart, wondering if there was anything in it that might hold clues to let them narrow down where their perp lived or worked or where he'd taken his victim to make the perverse tape.

213 EAST 86TH STREET, MANHATTAN

— Incident: Battery/kidnapping.

— MO: Perp threw hood over head (dark, possibly cotton), drugs inside to induce unconsciousness.

— Victim: Robert Ellis.
  — Single, possibly lives with Sabrina Dillon, awaiting return call from her (on business in Japan).
  — Residence in San Jose.
  — Owner of small start-up, media buying firm.
  — No criminal or national security file.
— Perpetrator:
  — Calls himself the Composer.
  — White male.
  — Age: 30 or so.
  — Approximately six feet, plus or minus.
  — Dark beard and hair, long.
  — Weight: stocky.
  — Wearing long-billed cap, dark.
  — Dark clothing, casual.
  — Shoes:
    — Likely Converse Cons, color unknown, size 10½.
  — Driving dark sedan, no tag, no make, no year.
— Profile:
  — Motive unknown.
— Evidence:
  — Victim's phone.
    — No unusual calls/calling patterns.
    — Short hair, dyed blond. No DNA.
    — No prints.
  — Noose.
    — Traditional hangman's knot.
    — Catgut, cello length.
      — Too common to source.
  — Dark cotton fiber.
    — From hood, used to subdue victim?
    — Chloroform.
    — Olanzapine, antipsychotic drug.
  — YouVid video:
    — White male (probably vic), noose around neck.

— "Blue Danube" playing, in time to gasps (vic's?).

— "© The Composer" appeared at end.

— Faded to black and silence; indication of impending death?

— Checking location where it was uploaded.

Rodney Szarnek, from Computer Crimes, called back. On the other end of the line was, thank you, only the geeky voice, no raw, wah-wah guitar licks. "Lincoln?"

"You have a location?"

"New York metro area."

Something I *don't* know, please.

"I know you're disappointed. But I can narrow it down. Maybe four, five hours."

"Too long, Rodney."

"I'm just saying. He's used proxies. That's the bad news. The good is that he doesn't really know what he's doing. He's logged onto some free VPNs, which—"

"No time for Greek," Rhyme grumbled.

"It's amateur stuff. I'm working with YouVid and we can crack it but—"

"Four hours."

"Less, I'm hoping."

"Me too." Rhyme disconnected.

"Have something else here, Lincoln." Mel Cooper was at the Hewlett-Packard gas chromatograph/mass spectrometer.

"The footprint trace? Something he stepped in?"

"Right. We have more olanzapine, the antipsychotic. But something else. Weird."

"Weird is not a chemical property, Mel. Nor is it particularly fucking helpful."

Cooper said, "Uranyl nitrate."

"Jesus," Rhyme whispered.

Dellray frowned and asked, "What, Linc? That's some pretty bad shit, I'm hearing?"

Rhyme was resting the back of his skull against the headrest of his wheelchair, staring at the ceiling. He was vaguely aware of the question.

Sellitto now: "Uranus nitrate. Is it dangerous?"

"*Uranyl*," Rhyme corrected impatiently. "Obviously it's dangerous. What would *you* call uranium salt dissolved in nitric acid?"

"Linc," Sellitto said patiently.

"It's radioactive, produces renal failure and acute tubular necrosis. It's also explosive and highly unstable. But my exclamation was positive, Lon. I'm delighted that our perp may have trod in this stuff."

Dellray said, "'Cause it's highly and extremely and deliciously rare."

"Bingo, Fred."

Rhyme explained that the substance had been used to create weapons-grade uranium for the Manhattan Project—the effort to make the first atomic bomb in World War II. While the project's engineering headquarters had been based, temporarily, in Manhattan, hence the name, most of the work in constructing the bombs had occurred elsewhere, notably Oak Ridge, Tennessee; Los Alamos, New Mexico; and Richland, in Washington State.

"But there was *some* actual construction and assembly in the New York area. A company in Bushwick, Brooklyn, made uranyl nitrate. They couldn't produce enough, though, and gave up the contract. The company's long gone but the site still has residual radiation."

"How do you—" Sellitto began.

Rhyme said smoothly, "EPA waste sites. Wonderful, Lon. Don't you *study* them? You don't *collect* them?"

A sigh. "Linc."

"I do. They tell us such wonderful things about our neighborhoods."

"Where is it?" Cooper asked.

"Well, I don't have the address *memorized*. It's an EPA waste site, designated as such. Bushwick, Brooklyn. How many could there be? Look it up!"

Only a moment later Cooper said, "Wyckoff, not far from Covert Street."

"Near Knollwood Park Cemetery," said Sachs, a Brooklyner born and bred. She stripped off her lab jacket and gloves and started out of the parlor, calling, "Lon, get a tac team together. I'll meet them there."

CHAPTER 6

S tefan froze at the sound.

A sound nearly as troubling as a Black Scream, though it was soft, meek: a beep on his mobile phone.

It told him that someone had entered the factory complex. An app was connected via Wi-Fi to a cheap security camera, mounted at the facility's entrance.

Oh, no, he thought. I'm sorry! He silently pleaded to Her not to be angry.

A glance into the next room, where Robert Ellis was balancing so precariously on the wooden crate. Then back to his phone. The webcam—high-def and color—showed a red sports car, one of those from the sixties or seventies, parked at the entrance, and a woman was climbing out. He saw a badge on the redhead's hip. Behind her, police cars were pulling up fast.

His jaw quivered. How had they gotten here, and so quickly?

He closed his eyes, at the throbbing, the ocean roar, in his head.

Not a Black Scream, not now. Please!

Move! You have to move.

He looked over his gear. None of this could be found. Stefan had been careful, but connections could be made, evidence could be discovered, and he absolutely could not afford to be stopped.

He could not, under any circumstances, disappoint Her.

I'm sorry, he repeated. But Euterpe, of course, did not reply.

Stefan stuffed his computer into his backpack, and from the canvas sports bag he'd brought he extracted two other items. A quart jar of gasoline. And a cigarette lighter.

Stefan loved fire. Absolutely loved it. Not the jerky dance of orange and black flames, not the caress of heat. No, what he loved was, not surprisingly, the sound.

His only regret was that he would not be around to hear the crackle and moan as fire turned what is into what is not.

Sachs ran to the twelve-foot-high chain link, the six uniforms behind her.

The gate was secured with a chain and an imposing padlock.

"Anybody got a breaching tool, bolt cutters?"

But these were patrol officers. They stopped speeders, defused domestics, helped out motorists, restrained mad dogs, busted street buys. Breaching tools were not among their issue gear.

She stood with her hands on her hips, gazing at the factory complex.

EPA Superfund Site
Warning—Hazardous Materials
Present in Soil and Water
NO TRESPASSING

There was no question of waiting for Emergency Service; the victim was about to hang to death. The only issue was how to get inside.

Well, one way was obvious and it would have to do. She would gladly have sacrificed her Torino but the snout of the fifty-year-old muscle car was delicate. The squad cars were mounted with push bumpers—those black battering rams that you saw in high-speed-chase videos.

"Keys," she called to a young patrol officer standing nearby, a stout African American woman. She handed them over at once. People tended to respond quickly to an Amelia Sachs demand.

"Everybody, back."

"What're you...Oh, Detective, no, you aren't. I gotta write it up, you mess up my front end."

"I'll do the footnotes." Sachs dropped into the driver's seat, went for the belt. Backed up. She shouted out the window, "Follow me and spread out and search like hell. Remember, this guy's got minutes."

If he's still alive.

"Hey, Detective. Look!" Another officer was pointing into the complex. At the end of a two-story wing of the factory a haze of white and gray mist formed into liver-colored smoke and spiraled upward fast—pushed hard by the heat from a fire. Intense heat.

"Jesus."

The unsub had tipped to them and set fire to the room where, she guessed, he'd made the video, intent on destroying the evidence.

And that meant he'd set fire to Robert Ellis too, whether or not he'd already died from hanging.

A voice shouted, "I'm calling FD."

Sachs jammed the accelerator to the floor. The Ford Interceptors weren't the gutsiest wheels on the block—punching in at 365 horses— but the hundred-foot takeoff run propelled the bulky vehicle plenty fast enough to pop the chain link like plastic and send the two sides of the gate butterflying into the air.

She continued on, the six cylinders exhaling fiercely.

The other cars were directly behind her.

In less than a minute she was at the building that was burning. There was no indication of fire in the front; the smoke was billowing from the back, though it would also be filling the interior, which Sachs and the others now had to hurry through, if they wanted to save the victim.

They had no masks or oxygen but Sachs hardly thought about that. She grabbed a Maglite from the purloined car. Drawing her Glock, she nodded to two other officers—one a short, handsome Latino man, the other a blond woman, hair in a severe ponytail.

"We can't wait. You two, with me. We go in, smoke or no."

"Sure, Detective." The woman nodded.

Sachs, the de facto commander, turned to the others. "Alonzo and

Wilkes're going up the middle with me. I want three of you around back, flanking the unsub. And somebody take wheels and circle the perimeter. He can't've gotten very far. Any vehicle, anybody, assume it's hostile."

The others left.

The blond officer, Wilkes, covered Alonzo and Sachs as they shouldered their way through the door—thank God, unlocked. She dropped to a crouch inside, sweeping with light and muzzle. Wilkes followed.

It occurred to her just as she breached the portal that the perp was probably certifiably crazy and might have decided to hang around and kill some blue, in a suicidal fit.

But no gunshots.

Listening.

No sounds.

Was Ellis dead? If so, she hoped he'd died from the hanging, not the flames.

The three now started jogging through the corridor, Sachs trying to stay oriented and keeping in mind—in general—where the smoke had been coming from. The factory was decrepit and it stank of mold. Near the entrance, the walls were decorated with graffiti, and there was a collection of used condoms, spent matches, needles and cigarette butts on the floor. Not a lot, though, and Sachs supposed that even the most desperate johns and addicts knew what a toxic-waste Superfund site was and that there were healthier places to shoot up or get a blow job.

Signs above or beside the doors: *Machine Operations. Fissile Research. Radiation Badge Testing Center—Do Not Pass Checkpoint B Without Test.*

"Funny, Detective," the man beside her said, gasping from the jog.

"What's that, Alonzo?"

"No smoke here."

True. Odd.

The black column had been quite thick, rising into the sky from a source very close. But there was no smoke directly around them.

Hell, she thought. This was a facility that had fabricated radioactive materials. Maybe at the end of this corridor they would find a thick, and impenetrable, security door, keeping the smoke out—but barring their way, as well.

They came to an L in the hallway, and paused at the juncture but only for a moment. Sachs crouched and went low, sweeping her gun forward.

Wilkes covered her again, with Alonzo going wide.

Nothing but emptiness.

Her radio crackled. "Patrol Four Eight Seven Eight. Gap in the fence in the back, K. A local outside said he saw white male, heavyset, beard, exit five minutes ago, running. Bag or backpack. Didn't see where he went or if he had wheels."

"K," Sachs whispered. "Call it in to the local precinct and ESU. Anyone in the back of the building? Source of fire?"

No one answered. But another officer radioed that the fire department had just arrived and were through the chain link.

Sachs and her colleagues continued up the dogleg of a corridor. Keep going, keep going, she told herself, breathing hard.

They were almost to the back of the wing. Ahead of them was a door. It wasn't as intimidating or impenetrable as she'd expected: just a standard wooden one and actually slightly ajar. Yet still there was no smoke, which meant there had to be another room, on the other side of this portal, sealed up, where the victim would be.

Sprinting now, Sachs ran through the doorway, pushing forward fast to find the chamber that was in flames.

And, with a breathtaking thud, she slammed directly into Robert Ellis, knocking him off the wooden box. He screamed in terror.

"Jesus Lord," she cried. Then to her backup: "In here, fast!"

She clutched Ellis around the waist and lifted hard to keep the pressure of the noose off his neck. Damn, he was heavy.

While Wilkes covered them once more—there was no certainty that the fleeing man was the perp or, if he was, that he was operating alone—Sachs and the other officer lifted Ellis up; Alonzo worked the noose off and pulled the blindfold from his eyes, which scanned the room frantically, like a terrified animal's.

Ellis was choking and sobbing. "Thank you, thank you! God, I was going to die!"

She looked around her. No fire. Here or in an adjacent room. What the hell was going on?

"You wounded, hurt?" She helped him ease to the floor.

"He was going to hang me! Christ. Who is he?" His voice was groggy. She repeated the question.

"I don't know. Not bad, I guess. My throat hurts. He dragged me around with a fucking noose around my neck. But I'm all right."

"Do you know where he went?"

"No. I couldn't see. He was in the other room, I think. That's what it sounded like. I was blindfolded most of the time."

Her radio clattered. "Portable Seven Three Eight One. Detective Sachs, K?" A woman's voice.

"Go ahead."

"We're in the back of the building. The fire's here. It's in an oil drum. Looks like he set it to burn up the evidence. Electronic stuff, papers, cloth. Gone."

Pulling on gloves, Sachs removed the duct tape binding Ellis's hands and feet. "Can you walk, Mr. Ellis? I want to clear the room here and search it."

"Yeah, sure." He was unsteady, his legs not working right, but together she and Alonzo helped him outside the building to the empty lot where the fire had been extinguished.

She glanced into the drum. Shit. The clues were ash, scorched metal and plastic globs. So this perp, the Composer, might be insane but he'd had the foresight to try to destroy the evidence.

Madness and brilliance were a very bad combination in a suspect.

She sat Ellis down on what looked like a large spool for cable. Two med techs turned the corner and she waved them over.

With bewildered eyes, Ellis scanned the scene, which seemed like a set of a bad dystopian movie. He asked, "Detective?"

"Yes?"

Muttering, Ellis said, "I was just walking down the street and next thing I knew he had this thing over my head and I was passing out. What does he want? Is he a terrorist? ISIS or something?"

"I wish I could tell you, Mr. Ellis. Fact is, we have no idea."

CHAPTER 7

He sweated.

    Palms, scalp, his hair-coated chest.

    Damp, despite the autumn chill.

Moving fast, partly to keep from being seen.

Partly because the harmony of his world had been shaken. Like kicking a spinning top.

Like hitting the wrong notes, like losing the perfect rhythm of a metronome.

Stefan was walking down a street in Queens. Manic. Armpits prickling, scalp itching. The sweat ran and ran. He'd just left the transient hotel he'd been living, well, *hiding*, in, after slipping out of the horrible, silent world where he'd been for years.

He now carted a wheelie suitcase and a computer bag. Not all his possessions, of course. But enough for now. He'd learned that, while the kidnapping had made the press, no one seemed to connect him personally to it or to composing a tune that had a very impressive if unsettling rhythm section.

His muse…She was looking out for him from Olympus, yes. But still the police had come close.

So close!

That red-haired police woman he'd seen on the webcam. If he hadn't set the thing up or if he'd missed the tone it uttered announcing their presence, he might have been captured by them and Harmony would be forever denied him.

Head down, walking quickly, fighting off a Black Scream—as he felt discord prickle his skin.

No...

He controlled it, barely.

Stefan could not help but think of the music of the spheres...

This philosophical concept moved him to his core. It was a belief that everything in the universe—planets, the sun, comets, other stars—gave off energy in the form of audible tones.

Musica mundanus, the ancients had called it.

Similar was *Musica humana*, the tones created within the human body.

And finally there was *Musica instrumentis*. Actual music played on instruments and sung.

When these tones—whether planets, the human heart, a cello performance—were in harmony, all was good. Life, love, relationships, devotion to the god of your choosing.

When the proportions were off, the cacophony was ruinous.

Now the spheres were tottering, and his chance of salvation, of rising into the state of Harmony, pure Harmony, was in jeopardy.

Stifling an urge to cry, Stefan dug into his jacket pocket and pulled a paper towel out. He mopped his face, his neck, and shoved the damp wad away.

Looking around. No eyes focused on him. No red-haired policewomen moving toward him, in four-four march time.

But that didn't mean he was safe. He circled the block twice, on foot, and stopped in the shadows near the stolen car. Finally, he could stand it no longer. He had to get away. He had to be safe.

Pausing at the car, another look around, then he set his suitcase in the backseat and the computer bag on the passenger's side in the front. He climbed in and started the engine.

The grind, the cough, the purr of cylinders.

He pulled slowly into traffic.

No one followed; no one stopped him.

He thought to Her: I'm sorry. I'll be more careful. I will.

He had to keep Her happy, pleased with him, of course. He couldn't afford to offend Euterpe. She was the one guiding him on his journey to Harmony, which, according to the music of the spheres, corresponded to Heaven, the most exalted state one could exist in. Christ had his stations of the cross, on his journey. Stefan had his too.

Euterpe, daughter of Zeus, one of the nine muses. She was, of course, the muse of music, pictured often in a robe and carrying a flute or pan pipes, a handsome face, an intelligent face, as befit the offspring of a god.

He drove around, a half-dozen blocks, until he was positive no one followed.

With his muse in mind, another thought occurred. Stefan, a distracted boy in school, had nonetheless liked mythology. He recalled that Zeus had fathered other children too, and one was Artemis, the goddess of the hunt. He couldn't remember who her mother might be, but she was different from Euterpe's; they were half sisters.

But that didn't mean the women were in harmony. Oh, not at all. In fact, now just the opposite. They were enemies.

Euterpe, guiding Stefan to Harmony.

Artemis—in the form of the red-haired policewoman—trying to stop them both.

But you won't, he thought.

And as he drove he forced away a budding Black Scream and concentrated on his next composition. He had a good piece of music in mind for his next hangman's waltz. Now all he needed was another victim, to provide the perfect bass line, in three-quarter time.

CHAPTER 8

S achs finished walking the grid and stood back to examine the scene.

The gallows was a jerry-rigged arrangement—the noose affixed to a broom handle jammed into a gap in the cinder blocks of the uranium factory wall. The wooden-box base, which Robert Ellis had been forced to stand on, was old, marked with military stencils—indecipherable numbers and letters—in faded olive-drab paint on the sides. By the time Sachs had inadvertently tackled him, he'd reported, he wasn't sure he could have stayed upright more than five minutes. He was already growing light-headed from the effort.

She walked outside, where the evidence techs were finishing up with chain-of-custody cards. There wasn't much to document; the fire'd worked real well.

She asked Robert Ellis, "You talk to Sabrina?"

"No. I haven't heard back. The time. I don't know the time in Japan." He was still bleary. The medics had pronounced him largely uninjured, as he himself had assured Sachs, but the drugs and presumably the tightened noose around his neck—to elicit gasps for the recording—had muddled his thoughts.

With disbelief in his voice Ellis said, "He kept doing it—three times or four maybe."

"Doing what?"

"Pulling the noose, recording me choking. I heard him play it back, over and over. As if the sounds I was making weren't what he wanted. He was like a musical conductor, you know. Like he could hear in his mind the sound he wanted but he wasn't getting it. He was so calculating, so cold about it."

"Did he say anything?"

"Not to me. He talked to himself. Just rambling. I couldn't hear most of it. I heard him say 'music' and 'harmony' and just weird stuff. I can't really remember exactly. I feel pretty spacey. Nothing made sense. 'Listen, listen, listen. Ah, there it is. Beautiful.' He seemed to be talking to some, I don't know, imaginary person."

"No one else was there?"

"I couldn't see—you know, the blindfold. But it was just the two of us, I'm sure. I would've heard."

What are you up to? she wondered to the Composer—it was the name they had selected for the unsub, Rhyme had told her. It seemed to fit a complex, sinister perp better than today's date.

"Still no thoughts on why he went after you?"

"I don't have any enemies, no exes. I've been with my girlfriend for years. I'm not rich, she's not rich."

Her phone buzzed. It was the officer who'd driven around the perimeter of the plant and found the witness—a boy—who reported that the Composer was fleeing. She had a brief conversation.

After disconnecting, she closed her eyes and sighed.

She called Rhyme.

"Sachs, where are you?"

"I'm almost on my way."

"*Almost.* Why *almost?*"

"The scene's done. I'm just getting the vic's statement."

"Somebody else can do that. I need the evidence."

"There's something you should know."

He must've heard the concern in her tone. Slowly he said, "Go on."

"One of the respondings was looking for more witnesses near where the unsub escaped. Didn't find anyone. But she did spot a plastic bag he must've dropped while he was running. Inside were two more miniature nooses. Looks like he's just getting started."

Rhyme's eyes scanned the treasures Sachs and the evidence collection techs had brought back.

The ECs left, one of them saying something to Rhyme. A joke. A farewell. A comment about the weather or the cleanliness of the Hewlett-Packard gas chromatograph. Who knew, who cared? He wasn't paying attention. His nose detected the whiff of burned plastic and hot metal—radiating from the destroyed evidence.

Or the evidence the perp had *tried* to destroy. In fact, water is a far more efficient contaminant than fire, though flames do remove DNA and fingerprints pretty damn well.

Oh, Mr. Composer, you tried. But let's see how successful you were.

Fred Dellray was gone. He'd been summoned to Federal Plaza unexpectedly—a confidential informant had reported an impending assassination of a U.S. attorney involved in a major drug prosecution.

Rhyme had complained: "*Impending* versus *actual*, Fred? Come on. *Our* vic has been one hundred percent certified snatched."

"Orders're orders," the agent had replied as he left.

And then, insult to injury, Dellray had just called back saying that it was a false alarm. He could get back within the hour.

"Fine, fine, fine."

Lon Sellitto was still here, presently canvassing law enforcement agencies around the country to see if there were any echoes of the Composer's MO.

None, so far.

Not that Rhyme cared about that.

Evidence. That's what he wanted.

So they began poring over what had been collected at the factory.

Here, a single Converse Con shoe print. Ten and a half.

Here, two short pale hairs that seemed identical to the one found on Ellis's cell phone.

Here, four slivers of shiny paper—photo stock, it looked like.

Here, a burned T-shirt, probably the "broom" used to obliterate marks on the floor and wipe fingerprints.

Here, gone almost completely, the dark baseball cap he'd worn. No hair, no sweat.

Here, plastic globs and metal parts—his musical keyboard and an LED light.

Here, a Baggie, one-gallon, containing two more miniature nooses, probably made of cello strings. No fingerprints. Not helpful in any way, except to tell them that he had more victims in mind.

No phone, no computer—those devices we so dearly love . . . and that betray us and our secrets so nonchalantly.

Though he'd swept, Sachs had collected plenty of dust and splinters of wood, and bits of concrete from the floor around the gallows room. The GC/MS rumbled for some time, again and again burning up samples. The results revealed traces of tobacco, as well as cocaine, heroin and pseudoephedrine—the ingredient in decongestants that was present here because of its second utility: making methamphetamine.

Sachs said, "Not a lot of traffic but the place had its crack-house attractions."

One find, more or less intact, was a scrap of paper:

CASH T

EXCHA

CONVER

TRANSAC

"*Wheel of Fortune*," Mel Cooper said.

"What's that?"

Nobody replied to Rhyme's question, as they all tried to complete the words, Thom too. Nothing, so they moved on.

The remains of the musical keyboard, presumably the one on which the Composer had recorded his eerie composition, contained a serial number. Sellitto called the manufacturer but the company, in Massachusetts, was presently closed. He'd check again in the morning, though the Composer had been so careful about so many aspects of the kidnapping that he'd surely bought the Casio with cash.

No fingerprints on it. Or anything else.

The noose that had been used to try to murder Robert Ellis was made of two gut instrument strings tied together in a carrick bend knot. This was a common knot, Rhyme knew; knowing how to tie it did not suggest any special nautical or other professional background.

The gut strings, larger versions of the calling card the schoolgirl had found, were for an upright bass. Rhyme had little hope that they'd find a clerk who'd remember a purchaser like the Composer, given their skimpy description of him...and the fact that there were thousands of musicians in the area who'd use such strings.

To break into the factory, the Composer had sliced through the chain at the gate with a bolt cutter and replaced it with his own. Both the lock and chain were generic.

The battery-powered router and Wi-Fi–enabled webcam—which had apparently alerted him to the police's arrival—were similarly untraceable.

A canvass by dozens of officers found no witnesses to follow up on the boy who'd reported that somebody resembling the Composer had fled the plant around the time of the fire.

After the information went up on the board, Rhyme wheeled in front of it.

Sachs too gazed. She called up a map of the area on one of the big-screen monitors. She tapped the place to the north of the factory, about where he'd escaped, and said absently, "Where the hell're you going?"

Sellitto, also looking over the chart, said, "He's got a car. He can drive home. He can drive to a subway and take the train, leave the car on the street. He can—"

Rhyme had a fast thought. "Sachs!"

She, Sellitto and Cooper were looking toward him. They seemed alarmed. Maybe it was his angered expression.

"What, Rhyme?"

"What you just asked."

"Where he lives."

"No, you didn't ask that. You asked where he was going?"

"Well, I meant, where's his home."

"Forget that." He scanned the chart. "Those scraps of paper you found? The photo paper?

"Right."

"Play jigsaw puzzle with them. See how they fit together."

After pulling on gloves she opened the plastic evidence envelope and arranged the slips. "They make a frame, see? Something was cut out of the middle. A perfect square."

Rhyme then consulted his computer. He asked, "One that measures fifty-one millimeters by fifty-one, by any chance?"

Sachs applied a ruler. She laughed. "Exactly."

Sellitto grunted, "How the hell'd you know that, Linc?"

"Goddamn it." He nodded at the burned triangle of paper, containing the mysterious code.

CASH T

EXCHA

CONVER

TRANSAC

More typing. Rhyme reviewed the screen and said, "Try this: 'Cash Tendered. Exchange Rate. Converted Amount. Transaction Amount.'" He nodded at the screen. "I found a receipt from a currency exchange. That's what it is. And the square cut out of the glossy paper. It's the size—"

Sellitto filled in, "A passport photo. Oh, hell."

"Exactly," Rhyme said, exhaling slowly. "Call Washington."

"DC?" Cooper asked.

"Of *course* DC. I hardly want a cup of Starbucks or a Microsoft Windows upgrade, now, do I? Tell the State Department to alert the embassies that the Composer's headed out of the country. Dellray too. Get him on the wire to the FBI offices abroad." Another scowl. "Don't know what good it'll do. No solid description or other info to give Passport Control." He shook his head in dismay. "And if he's as smart as he seems to be, he's not wasting any time. He's probably halfway to London or Rio by now."

11

IN THE FIELD OF TRUFFLES

CHAPTER 9

Could this be the place, could this be the moment he'd been waiting for?

Hoping for?

Finally, was he about to capture the devil he'd been after for months?

Ercole Benelli rolled down the window of his police vehicle, a dusty Ford SUV. American cars were common in Italy, though you didn't see many big off-roaders like this. But the nature of his work necessitated four-wheel drive and serious suspension. A bigger engine would have been nice, though Ercole had learned that budget was budget and he was thankful for what he could get. He peered through the flagging leaves of a stately magnolia, dominating this little-used country road, twenty kilometers northwest of Naples.

Youthful and taut of body, lean of face, tall and thinner than his mother had liked, Ercole played his Bausch + Lombs over the field that separated him from the abandoned structure one hundred meters away. The hour was dusk but there was enough light to see by, without using night-vision glasses. The land here was messy, carpeted with weeds and stray and struggling vegetables gone to seed. Sitting every ten meters or so, like huge, discarded toys, were parts of old machines, sheet-metal ducts and vehicle exoskeletons, which the thirty-year-old Ercole believed resembled sculpture he had once seen in an exhibit at the Centre Georges Pompidou in Paris on a long holiday weekend with his girlfriend at the time. Ercole hadn't appreciated the art. No, he had appreciated it. He hadn't *liked* it (she had, however—and passionately and tearfully—which explained much about the short life span of the romance).

He climbed from the truck, studying the building across the field again, carefully. He was squinting, though that didn't seem to improve his vision much in the autumn dusk. He kept low; his uniform and brimmed cap, boasting on the crown a fierce eagle, were gray, in contrast with the pale-buff surroundings. With the sky still illuminated he had to make sure he would not be seen.

Thinking again: Could this be his chance to snare the prey?

Was the perp inside?

Well, for certain, someone was. Ercole could see a lamp within the farmhouse, and a presence was revealed from the motion of shadow. And it was not an animal. All species have distinctive locomotion, and Ercole knew nonhuman movements very well; these shadows were from a *Homo sapiens*—unsuspecting, unconcerned—as he walked around the interior of the place. And, though the light was fading, he could still make out in the grass and a stand of old wheat what appeared to be the tread marks of a truck. Some of the vegetation had returned to near upright, suggesting to Ercole that Antonio Albini—if indeed the suspect, the *devil*, this was—had been inside for some time. The officer guessed that he had driven into the farmhouse before first light and, after a long day of unconscionable industry, planned to slip away when dusk bathed the soft hills here in deepening blue light.

Which meant soon.

Albini's modus operandi was to find such abandoned locales for his crimes but to travel to and from them only in the dark, to avoid being seen. The mastermind usually checked out his lairs ahead of time, and Ercole's exhaustive detective work had found a witness up the road, a farmworker, who'd reported that someone fitting Albini's description had examined this building two weeks ago.

"He was behaving in most suspicious ways," the grizzled man had said. "I'm certain of it." Though Ercole guessed that the conclusion was only because the worker has been speaking to a police officer. It was how he himself might have spoken to a cop when he was young and hanging out in the Spaccanapoli, or a nearby Neapolitan square, and a Carabinieri or Police of State officer would ask him, in a bored voice, if he'd seen what street thug had made off with a purse or had cleverly lifted an Omega off a careless wrist.

Whether the intruder had acted suspiciously or not, though, the farm-worker's observation was enough to follow up on, and Ercole had spent much time conducting surveillance of the farmhouse. His supervisor thought long shots like this should not take as much time as Ercole allotted to them. Still, he could behave no differently. He pursued Albini the way he would have sought the notorious serial murderer, or murderers, known as the Monster of Florence, had he been an officer in Tuscany many years ago.

Albini's crimes would not go unpunished.

Another flicker of shadow.

Now a frog called, hoping to impress a mate.

Now a tall stand of neglected wheat bent in a breeze like parishioners before a priest.

Now a head appeared in the window. And yes! It was the villain he'd worked so hard to capture. Round, porcine Antonio Albini. Ercole could see the bushy hair surrounding the bald pate. His urge was to duck, escaping the demonic gaze from under wizard's brows. The suspect was not looking outward, though. He was gazing down.

The lamps inside went dark.

And Ercole's heart twisted with dismay.

No, no! He was leaving *now*? While it was still light? Perhaps the deserted nature of the area gave him confidence that he would not be seen. Ercole had thought he would have plenty of time, after verifying the identity of the occupant, to call for backup.

So the question became this: Should he apprehend the man alone?

But, of course, he realized that it was no query at all.

He had no choice. Arresting Albini was his mission and he would now do what he needed to, at whatever risk, to snare the prey.

His hand dipped to the Beretta 9mm on his hip. He took a deep breath and continued through the field, picking his steps carefully. Ercole Benelli regularly studied the procedure books of the Carabinieri, as well as those of the Police of State and the Finance Police—not to mention the law enforcement agencies of other countries and Europol and Interpol, as well. While he had not had many opportunities to effect arrests by himself, he knew the approved techniques to stop and control a suspect.

Pausing at the relic of a harvester, then continuing on to a Stonehenge of oil drums for cover. He was listening to the thuds from inside the garage attached to the farmhouse. He knew what had made the disturbing sounds and grew all the more infuriated at Albini's crimes.

Move, now!

And with no more cover, he hurried into the driveway.

Which was when the truck, a four-wheeled Piaggio Poker van, burst from the garage, speeding directly toward him.

The young officer stood his ground.

Some seasoned criminals might think twice about killing a police officer. In Italy there was still honor among villains. But Albini?

The truck didn't stop. Would the man be persuaded by Ercole's pistol? He lifted the large black gun. Heart throbbing, breath coming fast, he aimed carefully, as he did on the range, and slid his finger off the guard to the trigger. The Beretta had a very light touch and he was careful to apply no pressure yet, but merely caress the steel curve.

This, not honor, it seemed, had the desired effect.

The ungainly truck slowed to a stop, the brakes squealing. Albini squinted and then climbed from the vehicle. The plump man stomped forward, stopped and stood with hands on hips. "Ah, ah, what are you doing?" he asked, as if genuinely confused.

"Keep your hands visible."

"Who are you?"

"I'm arresting you, Mr. Albini."

"For what?"

"You know very well. You have been dealing in counterfeit truffles."

Italy was, of course, known for truffles: the most delicate and most sought after, the white, from Piedmont, and the earthier black from Tuscany. But Campania too had a vital truffle trade—black ones from around the town of Bagnoli Irpino, near the Monti Picentini Regional

Park. These truffles were respected for their substantial taste; unlike their paler cousins from central and northern Italy, which were served only with plain eggs or pasta, Campanian fungi had the fortitude to stand up to more substantial dishes and sauces.

Albini was believed to be buying Chinese truffles—much cheaper than and inferior to the Italian—and palming them off as local to distributors and restaurants throughout Campania and Calabria, to the south. He had gone so far as to buy—or possibly steal—two expensive Lagotti Romagnolo, the traditional truffle-hunting dogs. The beasts now sat in the back of the truck, looking Ercole over cheerfully. For Albini, though, they were merely for show, since the only hunting he did for truffles was on the docks to find which warehouse held the shipments from Guangdong.

Weapon still aimed in Albini's direction, Ercole now walked to the back of the man's Piaggio Poker truck and, peeking under the canvas tarp covering a portion of the back bed, could see clearly a dozen empty shipping cartons, with Chinese characters on the side and on the bills of lading. And beside them buckets of dirt holding dozens of gray-black truffles: the thuds that Ercole had heard moments before, Albini loading the vehicle.

"You accuse me wrongly! I have done nothing illegal, Officer..." He cocked his head.

"Benelli."

"Ah, Benelli! You are perhaps an heir to the motorcycle family?" Albini's face beamed. "The shotgun family?"

The officer said nothing in response, though he was at a loss to figure out how the criminal planned to leverage a famous family connection to his advantage, had one existed, which it did not.

Then Albini grew serious. "But honestly. All I do is sell a product for which there is a need and desire and I charge a fair price. I never said they are from Campania. Has one person ever said I have made that claim?"

"Yes."

"He's a liar."

"There are dozens."

"*They*, then, are liars. To a man."

"Even so, you have no import license."

"What is the harm, though? Has anyone gotten sick? No. And, in fact, even if they are from China, they are of equal quality to those from our region. Smell them!"

"Mr. Albini, the very fact that I *cannot* smell them from here tells me they are vastly inferior."

This was certainly the case. The best truffles give off a scent that is as far-ranging as it is unique and seductive.

The crook offered what appeared to be a smile of concession. "Now, now, Officer Benelli, do you not think that most diners would have no clue as to whether they were eating truffles from Campania, from Tuscany, from Beijing, from New Jersey in America?"

Ercole didn't doubt this was true.

But still, the law was the law.

He lifted the handcuffs off his belt.

Albini said, "I have euros in my pocket. Many euros." He smiled.

"And they will be logged into evidence. Every last one of them."

"You bastard!" Albini grew agitated. "You can't do this."

"Hold your hands out."

The man's eyes were cold as they dipped to Ercole's gray uniform, scornfully focusing on the insignia on the cap and the breast of the open-necked jacket. "You? Arrest *me*? You're a cow officer. You're a rare-species officer. You're a fire warden. You're hardly a real policeman."

The first three charges, while insultingly toned, were accurate. The fourth comment slung his way was false. Ercole was a full-fledged police officer with the Italian government. He worked for the CFS, or State Forestry Corps, which was indeed charged with enforcing agricultural regulations, protecting endangered species, and preventing and fighting forest fires. It was a proud and busy law enforcement agency that dated to the early 1800s and counted more than eight thousand officers in its ranks.

"Come along, Mr. Albini. I'm taking you into custody."

The counterfeiter growled, "I have friends. I have friends in the Camorra!"

This was decidedly *not* true; yes, the crime organization, based in Campania, was involved in rackets surrounding food and wine (and, ironically, the end result thereof: garbage), but no self-respecting gang leader would invite into the fold such a small, weasely operator as Albini. Even the Camorra had standards.

"Now, come on, sir. Don't make this difficult." Ercole stepped closer. But before he could restrain the criminal, a shout of alarm rang out from the road. Indistinct words, but urgent.

Albini stepped back, out of reach; Ercole too moved away, lifting his weapon and swiveling, thinking that perhaps his assessment had been wrong and that Albini was indeed connected with the Camorra, and that there were conspirators nearby.

But he saw that the shout had come from a civilian bicyclist, a young man pedaling a racing bike toward them quickly, bounding unsteadily over the rough terrain. Finally, the cyclist gave up and dismounted, laying down his bike and jogging. He wore an almond-shell helmet, and his kit was tight blue shorts and a black-and-white Juventus football team jersey, emblazoned with the stark sans-serif *Jeep* logo.

"Officer! Officer!"

Albini started to turn. Ercole growled, "No." He lifted a finger, and the chubby man froze.

The breathless cyclist reached them, glancing at the gun and the suspect. But he paid neither any mind. His face was red and a vein prominent in his forehead. "Up the road, Officer! I saw it! It happened right in front of me. You have to come."

"What? Slow down. Take your time."

"An attack! A man was waiting at the bus stop. He was just sitting there. And another man, in a car parked nearby, he got out and, in an instant, he grabbed the man waiting for the bus and they began struggling!" He brandished his phone. "I called the police but the officer said it would be a half hour before anybody could be here. I remembered I saw your Forestry truck when I rode past. I came back to see if you were still here."

"Any weapons?"

"Not that I could see."

Ercole shook his head and closed his eyes momentarily. Jesus Christ. Why now? A glance at Albini, his face pouting innocence.

Well, he couldn't ignore an assault. A robbery? he wondered. A husband attacking his wife's lover?

A psycho, killing for pleasure?

The Monster of Florence's cousin?

He scratched his chin and considered his options. All right. He would cuff Albini and leave him in the back of the Poker, then return.

But the counterfeiter had sensed a good opportunity. He sprinted to the truck and leapt into the seat calling, "Farewell, Officer Benelli!"

"No!"

The engine started and the tiny vehicle puttered past Ercole and the bicyclist.

The officer raised the pistol.

Through the open window Albini shouted, "Ah, would you shoot me over a truffle? I do not think you will. Farewell, Mr. Pig Cop, Mr. Cow Cop, Guardian of the Endangered Muskrat! Farewell!"

Ercole's face burned with anger and shame. He shoved his pistol back into the holster and began trotting toward the Ford. He called over his shoulder to the bicyclist, "Come, get in my truck. Show me exactly. Hurry, man. Hurry!"

CHAPTER 10

T he vehicles began to arrive at the bus stop.

Two officers from the Naples Flying Squad—in a blue Police of State Alfa Romeo—as well as several in a local commune police Fiat from the closest village. The Police of State officers climbed out and one, a blond woman with her hair in a tight bun, nodded to Ercole.

Despite his despair about losing his truffle thief, and the shock of stumbling into a case of this magnitude, his heart thudded, seeing such beauty: her heart-shaped face, full lips, the fringe of wispy flaxen hair at her temples. Eye shadow the blue of her car. He thought her movie-star-worthy and noted her name was Daniela Canton. She wore no wedding ring. He surprised her when he reached out enthusiastically and shook her hand in both of his; he thought immediately that he should not have done so.

He greeted her partner with a handshake too, a gesture the young man took without a thought. Giacomo Schiller, slightly built and solemn. He had light hair and, given the last name, might have hailed from Asiago or somewhere else in the north, where many Italians were of Germanic or Austrian descent, thanks to a history of shifting borders.

Another car was here too, unmarked, driven by a uniformed officer and containing a passenger in the front seat, a man wearing a suit and tan raincoat. Detective Inspector Massimo Rossi, Ercole saw at once. Though a Forestry Corps officer, Ercole on occasion had worked with the Police of State in and around Naples, and knew of Rossi. The man, whose face was burnished with permanent stubble, it seemed, and whose head was topped with a thick pelt of black hair, side-parted, was around fifty years of age.

Resembling the actor Giancarlo Giannini—handsome, heavily browed dark eyes, thoughtful—Rossi was well known, and not just here, in Campania, but throughout all of southern Italy. He'd successfully arrested many suspects over the years, resulting in convictions of senior Camorra officials and Albanian and North African drug smugglers, as well as money launderers, burglars, wife (and husband) killers, and psychotic murderers. Ercole, whose Forestry Corps duty required him to wear a uniform, was impressed that Rossi was not a fashionista, as were some inspectors, who wore stylish designer (or, more likely, *faux*-designer) suits and dresses. Rossi wore the clothes of a journalist or insurance office worker. Modest, as tonight, his outfits were dusty and not well pressed. Ercole guessed this was to keep the suspects off guard, make them think he was slow or careless. The truth might simply be, however, that Rossi's mind was engaged in embracing cases and he didn't even notice that his look was unkempt. Then too he and his wife had five children, in whose rearing he was active, so there was little time for cultivating a trendy look.

Rossi completed a call, climbed from the car. He stretched and took in the scene: the dusty road, the unsteady bus-stop enclosure, the trees. The shadowy forest. The bicyclist.

And Ercole.

He now approached. "Forestry Officer Benelli. You have stumbled on something more than a poaching, it seems. You marked off the scene. Clever." He looked over the area around the bus stop once more. Ercole was rarely involved in crime scenes, so he carried no tape, but he had used a rope meant for rock climbing—not a hobby but an occasional necessity in his job, which included rescuing hikers and climbers.

"Yes, sir, Inspector. Yes. This is Salvatore Crovi." Ercole handed over the bicyclist's ruddy identity card.

Rossi nodded, reviewed the card, and handed it back. Crovi reiterated the story of what he'd seen: a hulking man in a dark-colored sedan, no make or model, no number plate visible. He could see little of the attacker. Wearing dark clothing and cap, the perpetrator had flung the victim to the ground. They had struggled and the bicyclist had hurried away to find Ercole. The victim was a man, dark-complexioned and bearded, wearing a pale-blue jacket.

The detective withdrew a notebook and jotted in it.

Ercole continued, "But when we arrived back, there was no one. No victim, no attacker."

"You searched?"

"Yes." Ercole pointed out a large perimeter. "All that way. Yes. He might have gotten farther. But I called out. No one answered. Mr. Crovi assisted. He went in the opposite direction."

"I saw nothing, Inspector," the bicyclist offered.

"Perhaps witnesses on a bus?" Rossi asked.

"No, sir. There have been none. I called the transit office. A bus is not due for another half hour. Oh, and I checked with the closest hospitals. No one has been admitted."

"So, maybe," Rossi said slowly, "we have a kidnapping. Though that seems curious."

A horn honked and Rossi looked up, toward a queue of cars. In the front, a sinewy, sixtyish balding man in an ancient Opel was gesturing angrily, sneering, wishing to pass. His way was blocked by Ercole's SUV. There was another car behind his, filled with a family, and this driver too began to honk. A third joined in.

Rossi asked, "Is that your Ford blocking the road?"

Ercole blushed. "Yes. I'm sorry, sir. I thought it best to protect the scene. But I'll move it now."

"No," Rossi muttered. He walked to the Opel, bent down and calmly whispered something to the driver. Even in the dark, Ercole could see that he blanched. A similar word with the driver behind him and both cars turned about quickly. The third did too, without the need for a personal visit. Ercole knew the lay of the land well here; to pick up the route on the other side of the scene would require a detour of nearly twenty kilometers.

Rossi returned to him.

Ercole added, "And, Inspector, as I was laying the rope, to preserve the scene, I found this." He walked to a spot beside the bus shelter—

little more than a sheet-metal roof supported by two poles, over a scabby bench. He pointed down at some money.

"The scuffle was here, correct?"

Crovi confirmed it was.

Ercole said, "There are eleven euros in coins and thirty Libyan dinars, in bills."

"Libyan? Hm. You said he was dark?" Rossi asked Crovi.

"Yes, sir. He could well have been North African. I would say most certainly."

Daniela Canton approached and glanced down at the money. "The Scientific Police are on their way."

The crime scene unit would lay number placards at the money and at any signs of the scuffle, take pictures of shoe prints and auto tread marks. They would then search more expertly than Ercole had.

Slowly, as if figuring out the scenario, Rossi said, "The victim was perhaps fishing for money in anticipation of the bus when the kidnapper took him and he dropped it. How else would it be scattered? Which means he didn't have a ticket. Perhaps this was an unexpected trip."

Daniela, nearby, had heard and she said, "Or, if he was illegal—a Libyan refugee—he might not have wanted to go to a ticket office."

"True." Rossi's glance rose and he broadened his examination. "The coins are here. The dinar there, a bit farther away and scattered. Let us assume he had dug out the contents of his pockets and withdrawn the money to count it out. He's attacked, the coins fall directly to the ground. The lighter dinars are carried in this breeze and float over there. Was there anything lighter yet in his hand that the wind carried?" Rossi said to Daniela and Giacomo, "Search in that direction. We should preserve it now, even before the Scientific Police arrive."

Ercole watched them pull booties and latex gloves from their pockets, don them and walk through the bushes, both playing Maglite flashlights over the ground.

Another car approached.

This was not a Police of State Flying Squad patrol car or an unmarked but a personal vehicle, a Volvo, black. The driver was a lean, unsmiling man, a dusting of short gray hair on his head. His salt-and-pepper goatee was expertly crafted and ended in a sharp point.

The car nosed to a stop and he climbed out.

Ercole Benelli recognized him too. He'd had no personal contact with the man but he owned a TV.

Dante Spiro, the senior prosecutor in Naples, wore a navy-blue sports coat and blue jeans, both close fitting. A yellow handkerchief blossomed from the breast pocket.

Fashionista...

He was not a tall man, and his deep-brown ankle boots had thick heels that boosted his height a solid inch or two. He had a dour expression and Ercole wondered if that was because he resented being interrupted at dinner, surely with a beautiful woman. Spiro, like Rossi, had had considerable success in prosecuting cases against and winning convictions of high-profile criminals. Once, two associates of a Camorra kingpin he'd put in jail had tried to kill him. He'd personally disarmed one, and had shot the other dead with the thug's own weapon.

Ercole also recalled some gossip reporter's comment that Spiro was intent on a career in politics, his eyes ultimately on Rome, though a judgeship at the World Court in The Hague might not be a bad goal either. Belgium, capital of the EU, was another destination perhaps.

Ercole noted a small book in the prosecutor's right jacket pocket. It appeared to be leather-bound, with gold-edged pages.

A diary? he wondered. He suspected it was not a Bible.

Slipping an unlit cheroot between thin lips, Spiro approached and nodded to Rossi. "Massimo."

The inspector nodded back.

"Sir," Ercole began.

Spiro ignored him and asked Rossi what had happened.

Rossi gave him the details.

"Kidnapping out here? Curious."

"I thought so too."

"Sir—" Ercole began.

Spiro waved a hand to silence him and said to the cyclist, Crovi, "The victim? You said North African. Not sub-Saharan?"

Before the man could answer, Ercole said, with a laugh, "He would *have* to be from the north. He had dinars."

Spiro, eyes on the ground where the struggle occurred, said in a soft voice, "Would not an Eskimo visiting Tripoli pay for his supper with Libyan dinars, Forestry Officer? Not in Eskimo money?"

"Eskimo? Well. I suppose. Yes, true, Prosecutor."

"And would not someone from Mali or Congo be more likely to find a meal in Libya by paying with dinars, rather than francs?"

"I'm sorry. Yes."

To Crovi: "Now. My question. Did the appearance of the victim suggest what part of Africa he was from?"

"It was not so dark, sir. I would say the features were Arab or tribal. Libyan, Tunisian, Moroccan. North African, I would say that with certainty."

"Thank you, Mr. Crovi." Then Spiro asked, "Scientific Police?"

Rossi replied, "On the way. Our office."

"Yes, probably no need to bother Rome."

Ercole knew the Naples headquarters of the Police of State had a laboratory on the ground floor. The main crime scene operation was in Rome and the trickier evidentiary analysis was performed there. He had never sent anything to either facility. Fake olive oil and misrepresented truffles were easy to spot.

Yet another vehicle arrived, a dark-blue marked police car with the word "Carabinieri" on the side.

"Ah, our friends," Rossi said wryly.

Spiro watched, chewing his cheroot. His face was devoid of any emotion.

A tall man in a pristine uniform climbed out of the passenger's seat. He wore a dark-blue jacket, and black trousers with red stripes down the sides. He surveyed the scene with a military bearing—as was appropriate, of course, since the Carabinieri, though it has jurisdiction over civilian crimes, is part of the Italian army.

Ercole marveled at the uniform and the man's posture. At his perfect hat, his insignias, his boots. He had always dreamed of being in their ranks, which he considered the elite of Italy's many police forces.

Forestry Corps had been a compromise. Helping his father tend his ill mother, Ercole would not have been able to pursue the rigorous Carabinieri training—even if he'd been accepted into the corps.

A second officer, who'd been driving, lower ranking than the first, joined them.

"Evening, Captain," Rossi called. "And Lieutenant."

The Carabiniere nodded to the inspector and Spiro. The captain said, "So, Massimo. What do you have? Anything enticing, anything plump? I see you're first on the scene."

Spiro said, "Actually, Giuseppe, *Forestry* was here first." Perhaps a joke but he was not smiling. The Carabinieri officer, however, laughed.

Was this a contest to see who would seize control of the case? The Carabiniere might have pushed, and would probably win, having a political edge over the Police of State.

As for Dante Spiro, he might harbor a personal preference for working with the Police of State, on the one hand, or for the Carabinieri, on the other, but for his career it made no difference; the prosecution would be his, no matter which police unit took control.

"Who was the victim?" Giuseppe asked.

Rossi said, "No identification yet. Some local unfortunate perhaps."

Or an Eskimo, Ercole thought but, of course, didn't even consider saying.

Rossi continued, "A good case. A press-worthy case. Kidnappings always are. Camorra? Albanians? That Tunisian gang from Scampia?" He grimaced. "I would have liked to find out, firsthand. But here you are. So, good luck to you, Giuseppe. We'll get back to Naples. Anything you need, please, let us know."

Rossi was giving away the case so easily? Ercole was surprised. But perhaps the Carabinieri wielded more power than he'd thought. Dante Spiro was looking at his phone.

Giuseppe cocked his head. "You're giving us the case?"

"Your organization is senior to us. You are senior to me. And it is clearly big. Kidnapping. Those reports you heard on the way over are wrong."

"Reports?"

Rossi paused. "The initial reports from Dispatch? Personally I think they were trying to downplay the incident."

"Massimo," Giuseppe said. "Please explain?"

"The youths, of course. That was pure speculation. I think this has to be Camorra. Or at worst Tunisian."

"Youths?" Giuseppe tried again.

"But it's not that. I'm sure."

"Still, your meaning?"

Rossi frowned. "Oh, have you not read? About the initiations?"

"No, no, I think not."

"It happens more in the north. Not in Campania." He gestured toward the scene. "That's why it could not be this."

The second Carabiniere asked, "Inspector, how does this scheme work?"

"Well, as I have read, it's university boys. The initiate must drive around, and when he sees someone he approaches on the pretense of asking directions or for change of money. Then when the victim is distracted, he is thrown in the car and driven for many kilometers and released. Pictures are taken and posted anonymously. A prank, yes, but there could be injuries. One boy in Lombardy ended up with a broken thumb."

"Broken thumb."

"Yes. And upon displaying the pictures, the perpetrators are allowed into the college club."

"Club? Not a gang?"

"No, no, no. But, again, it is the northern regions in which this is happening. Not here."

"Perhaps not yet. But kidnapping from a bus stop, way out here, nowhere close to a city center? It makes no sense."

Then a voice cut through the night: "Look what I have found." The Carabinieri lieutenant was pointing to the euros. "As he was counting out change for the bus driver."

Giuseppe walked to the rope Ercole had laid out and looked down. "Yes, so perhaps it *does* fit that category of offense."

Spiro watched silently.

"Hm. But a coincidence. Surely." Massimo Rossi nodded and stepped toward his automobile.

The Carabiniere turned to his associate and they had a quiet conversation. "Ah, Massimo, my colleague has reminded me that we have a drug operation in Positano. You are familiar?"

"Not aware of that."

"No? An interdiction planned for a few days. I think we'll need to let you have the kidnapping here."

Rossi looked concerned. "But I have no time for this, for a major criminal investigation."

"Major, is it? Pesky college boys?" Giuseppe smiled. "I will let you take all the glory, my friend. I will sign the case over to you formally back at the station."

Rossi sighed. "All right. But you do owe me."

A wink from the senior officer and they turned and left.

Spiro glanced at them departing and said to Rossi, "The Positano drug cases? They were dismissed two months ago."

"I know. As soon as he mentioned them, I knew I'd won our little contest here."

Spiro said, with a shrug, "Giuseppe's good. A solid officer. But...I prefer working for you. Army rules add layers."

Ercole realized he'd just seen a subtle chess game. Massimo Rossi had, for some reason, wanted to keep control of the case. So he had tried reverse psychology, attempting to palm off the case to the Carabiniere, who had immediately become suspicious.

If the Positano case was an illusion, so was the initiation story.

"Inspector?" Daniela Canton asked.

Rossi, Spiro and Ercole joined her.

She was pointing down to a small piece of cardboard. "It's fresh. It's likely he dropped it with the money. And it blew here. It was beside another dinar bill."

"Prepaid phone card. Good." Rossi extracted a plastic evidence bag from his pocket and placed the card inside. "We'll have Postal analyze it." To the uniformed officer he said, "Anything else?"

"No."

"Pull back then. We'll let Scientific Police search more carefully when they get here."

They returned to the road. Rossi turned to Ercole. "Thank you, Officer Benelli. Please write up a statement and then you're free to go home."

"Yes, sir. I'm happy to be of help." He nodded to the prosecutor.

Spiro said to Rossi, "We, of course, cannot assume that the dinars and phone card are the victim's. They are, probably, yes. But it could be too that the attacker had been in Libya recently."

"No, impossible." Ercole Benelli said this softly, almost a whisper. He was staring at the bus-stop bench, an ancient thing, bearing only a fraction of the paint that had been applied years ago.

"What?" Spiro snapped, staring, as if seeing Ercole for the first time.

"There would not have been enough time to go to Libya and arrive here in Italy."

"What on earth are you talking about?" Rossi muttered.

"He fled America late Monday night and arrived here yesterday, Tuesday."

Dante Spiro's voice cut like a blade. "Enough riddles. Explain yourself, Forestry Officer!"

"He's a kidnapper, though he intends to kill his victim eventually. He goes by the name 'The Composer.' He creates music videos of his victims dying."

The inspector and prosecutor—Daniela too—seemed unable to speak.

"Look." Ercole pointed to the back of the bus-stop bench.

A miniature hangman's noose hung from a beam.

CHAPTER 11

E rcole Benelli said to the others, "In the Europol alerts yesterday. A notice from the U.S. embassy in Brussels. Did you not see it?"

Spiro glared at the young officer and Ercole continued, "Well, sir, this man—they know he is a white male, though not his name—he kidnapped a victim in New York and left a noose just like this one, as a token. He tortured him. The man was about to die but was rescued just in time. The perpetrator escaped. The State Department believed he left the country but did not know where he was headed. It seems he's come to Italy."

"A copycat crime, surely." Spiro was nodding at the noose.

Ercole said quickly, "No, impossible."

"Impossible?" Spiro growled.

The young man blushed and looked down. "Ah, sir. I would say unlikely. The fact of the noose hasn't yet been released to the press. For the very reason of copycat perpetrators. Someone might have seen the video, yes, but Crovi said it was a heavyset white male in a dark outfit. And the noose? The same as the report from the NYPD about the kidnapper there. I think it must be him."

Rossi gave a chuckle. "You're a Forestry officer. Why were you reading Europol reports?"

"Interpol too. And our own Police of State and Carabinieri alerts from Rome. I always do. I might use something that I learn in my own work."

Spiro muttered, "At *Forestry*? That must happen as often as a pope's death." He kept his eyes on the blackness of the landscape. Then: "What else did this report say? The video?"

"He posted a video of the victim about to be hanged. With music playing. On a site called YouVid."

"Terrorist?" Rossi asked.

"Apparently not. The report said he is on antipsychotic medication."

"Which is obviously not doing a very good job," Daniela said.

Rossi said to Spiro, "Postal Police. I'll have them monitor the site and get ready to trace it if he posts."

"Postal Police" was an antiquated name for a state-of-the-art law enforcement division in Italy. They handled all, or most, crimes involving telecommunications and computers.

Spiro said, "Any other thoughts?"

Ercole began to speak but the prosecutor interrupted, adding, "Massimo?"

"If he is making a production of the death," the inspector said, "I won't spend much time and manpower searching for the body. Only one team. I will send most officers out to canvass and look for CCTVs in the area."

"Good."

Which cheered Ercole, since this was close to what his own suggestion would have been.

Spiro added, "I must be getting back to Naples. Good night, Massimo. Call me with any developments. I want all the reports, especially the crime scene data. And we should pursue this lead, if that's what it is." He was now looking at the noose. He shook his head and walked to his car. There, before climbing in, he paused at the driver's side, pulled the leather-bound book from his pocket and made notations. He replaced the volume, climbed into the Volvo and sped away. As his car drove off, crunching over the gravel on the shoulder, another sound filled the night. The guttural growl of a motorcycle approaching.

Several heads turned to see the gorgeous Moto Guzzi Stelvio 1200 NTX bounding along the uneven roadway. Astride was an athletic-looking man, with thick hair, clean-shaven. He wore close-fitting jeans, boots, a black shirt and a leather jacket, dark brown. On his left hip was a badge of the Police of State; on the right, a large Beretta, a Px4 .45. No-nonsense, it had been dubbed by officers who carried it, though Ercole had always thought that use of "nonsense" and *any* firearm was largely contradictory.

Ercole watched the man skid to a stop. He was Silvio De Carlo, assistant inspector, young—about Ercole's age. He strolled up to the inspector and gave a nod that was the equivalent of a salute to a commanding officer. Rossi and De Carlo began discussing the case.

The assistant was the epitome of a young Italian law enforcer— handsome, self-assured, surely smart and quick-witted. Clearly in good shape, too, and probably an ace with that powerful gun of his. Karate or, more likely, some obscure form of martial art figured in his life. Attractive to the ladies—and skilled in those arts, as well.

De Carlo was a citizen of that rarefied world alien to Ercole.

Fashionista...

Then Ercole corrected himself. He was selling De Carlo short. He'd earned his slot with the Police of State, obviously. While, as in any policing organization anywhere in the world, there would be dross at the top— officials coasting on their connections and glad-handing—a young line officer like De Carlo would only have risen on merit.

Well, Ercole decided, he himself had done his job—brought the attack to the attention of the investigators, informed them of the Composer. The truffle counterfeiter was long gone, and it was time to get home to his small flat on the Via Calibritto, in the Chiaia district. The neighborhood was far more chic than Ercole would have liked, but he'd come upon the place for a song and had spent months making it charming and comfortable: crammed full of family heirlooms and artifacts from his parents' home in the country. Besides, he had the top floor and it was a short climb up from his den to his pigeons. He was already looking forward to a coffee on the roof tonight, gazing over the lights of the city and enjoying his partial view of the park and the bay.

He could already hear the cooing of Isabella and Guillermo and Stanley.

He climbed into the front seat of his Ford. He pulled out his phone and sent several email messages. He was about to replace the unit when it sang with the tone. It was not a reply but instead a text from his superior, wondering how the operation was going.

The operation...

The capture of the truffle counterfeiter.

His heart sinking, Ercole texted he would report later.

He couldn't discuss his failure now.

The engine engaged, he pulled the seat belt strap around his chest. Did he have any food in the kitchen?

No, he believed not. Nothing that he could whip up quickly.

Perhaps he would have a pizza at one of the places on the Via Partenope. A mineral water.

Then, the short walk home.

A coffee.

His pigeons.

Isabella was nesting...

Ercole jumped at the loud rapping to his left.

He turned fast and saw Rossi's face, eyes peering at him. The inspector's head seemed oversize, as if viewed through thick glass or a depth of water. Ercole eased down the window.

"Inspector."

"Did I startle you?"

"No. Well, yes. I have not forgotten. I will prepare the report for you tomorrow. You will have it in the morning."

The inspector began to speak but his words were obscured by the growl of the Moto Guzzi engine firing up. De Carlo turned the large machine and sped off, lifting a small rooster tail of stones and dust behind him.

When the sound had faded, Rossi said, "My assistant."

"Yes, Silvio De Carlo."

"I asked him about the noose. And he knew nothing of it. Knew nothing of the case in America, the Composer." Rossi chuckled. "As I knew nothing about it. And Prosecutor Spiro knew nothing about it. But *unlike* you, Forestry Officer. Who knew very well about the case."

"I read reports, notices. That's all."

"I would like to make some temporary changes in my department."

Ercole Benelli remained silent.

"Would you be able to work with me? Be my assistant? For this case only, of course."

"*Me?*"

"Yes. Silvio will take over some of my other investigations. You will assist on the Composer case. I will call your supervisor and have you reassigned. Unless you are involved in a major investigation at the moment."

It was surely his imagination but Ercole believed a smell wafted past, not unlike the fragrance of truffles.

"No. I have cases but nothing pressing, nothing that can't be handled by other officers."

"Good. Whom should I call?"

Ercole gave his superior's name and number. "Sir, should I report to you in the morning?"

"Yes. The Questura. You know it?"

"I've been there, yes."

Rossi stepped back and looked at the field, then focused on the bus stop. "What does your instinct tell you about this man? Do you think the victim is alive?"

"As long as there's no video posted, I would say yes. Why should he change his MO because he's in a different country?"

"Perhaps you could contact the authorities in America and ask them to send us whatever information they might have about this fellow."

"I already have done that, sir."

The email he had just sent was to the New York Police and copied to Interpol.

"You have?"

"Yes. And I've taken the liberty of giving them your name."

Rossi blinked, then smiled. "Tomorrow, then."

CHAPTER 12

*S*ee Naples and die.

This was a quote from some poet.

Or someone.

The actual meaning, Stefan knew, was that once you had seen the city and had sampled all it had to offer, your bucket list was complete. There was nothing more to experience in life.

Well, for him it was the perfect quotation. Because after he was finished here—if he was successful, if he pleased Her—he would be going directly to Harmony. His life would be complete.

He was presently in his temporary residence in the region of Campania, home to Naples. It was old—as were many of the structures here. A musty smell permeated the place, mold and rot. And it was cold. But this hardly bothered him. The senses of smell and taste and touch and vision were of little interest to Stefan. His ear was the only important organ.

Stefan was in a dim room, not dissimilar to his lair back in New York. He wore jeans and a sleeveless white T-shirt, under a work shirt, dark blue. Both were tight (the meds kept his soul under control and his weight high). On his feet were running shoes. His appearance was different from what it had been in America. He'd shaved his head—common in Italy—and lost the beard and mustache. He needed to remain invisible. He was sure word would spread here, sooner or later, about the kidnapping and his "compositions."

He rose and looked out the window into the blackness.

No police cars.

No prying eyes.

No Artemises. He'd left the red-haired policewoman behind, back in America, but that didn't mean there wouldn't be another one here—or her brother god or god cousin or whoever—looking for him. He had assumed that was the case.

But all he saw was darkness and distant lights of the Italian landscape. Italy...

What a wonderful place, magical.

The home of Stradivarius stringed instruments, worth millions, occasionally stolen or left in the back of a taxi, generating *New York Post* headlines about absentminded geniuses. Appropriate at the moment, because he was winding more double-bass strings into another noose for his next composition, which he would start on shortly. Italy was, as a matter of fact, the source for the absolutely best musical strings ever made. Sheep intestine, goat, lovingly stretched and scraped. Stefan actually felt a twinge of guilt that the strings he was using for his adventure had been made in the United States.

But that was simply practical. He'd bought a supply there, concerned that a purchase here might lead the authorities to him.

Italy...

Home of the opera composers, Verdi. Puccini. Brilliant beyond reckoning.

Home of La Scala—the most perfect acoustics of any concert hall made by man.

Home of Niccolò Paganini, the famed violinist, guitarist and composer.

Stefan returned to his bench and slipped on a headset. He turned the volume up and, as he continued to twine the gut strings together and tie the noose, he listened to the sounds caressing his eardrums, his brain and his soul. Most playlists people store on iPhones or Motorolas ranged from folk to classical to pop to jazz, and everything in between. Stefan certainly had a lot of music on his hard drive. But he had far more gigabytes of pure sound. Cricket chirps, bird wings, pile drivers, steam kettles, blood coursing through veins, wind and water...He collected them from everywhere. He had millions—nearly as many as the Library of Congress's National Recording Registry.

When a mood was on him, Black Screams threatening, he sometimes grew depressed that his collection was limited to sounds dating back to merely a short time ago: the late nineteenth century. Oh, the Banū Mūsā brothers had created automated musical instruments, a water organ and a flute, in the ninth century in Baghdad, and music boxes still played the identical melodies they did when built in medieval days. But they were like music played from scores, re-creations.

Cheating.

Not the real thing.

Oh, we could marvel at a Rembrandt portrait. But it was—right?—fake. It was the artist's *conception* of the subject. If Stefan had been moved by the visual, he would have traded a hundred Dutch masters' works for a single Mathew Brady photograph. Frank Capra. Diane Arbus.

The first actual recordings of the human voice were made in the 1850s by Édouard-Léon Scott de Martinville, a French inventor, who came up with the phonautograph, yet it didn't actually capture sounds but merely made graphic representations of them, like lines of a seismograph. (Stefan was aware of rumors that de Martinville had recorded Abraham Lincoln's voice; he'd tried desperately to find if this was true and where it might be. But he'd learned that, no, the recording never happened, sending the young man into a bout of depression.) Nearly as troubling to him was the circumstance surrounding the paleophone, invented by another Frenchman, Charles Cros, twenty years later; it had the capability of creating recordings but none had ever been found. The first device to make recordings that survived to the present day was Edison's phonograph, 1878. Stefan owned every recording made by Edison.

What Stefan would have given for phonographs to have been invented two thousand years ago! Or three or four!

In his gloved hands he tested the noose, pulling it hard—though he was careful not to break the latex gloves.

On his playlist, a series of swishes came on. The sound of a knife blade being swiped against a sharpening steel. One of Stefan's favorites, and he closed his eyes to listen. Like many, if not most, sounds, this could be heard in several ways. A threat, a workman's task, a mother, preparing dinner for her children.

When this track ended, he pulled off the headphones and took another look outside.

No lights.

No Artemis.

He turned on his new Casio keyboard and began to play. Stefan knew this waltz quite well and played it from memory once, then again. Once more. In playing the third version, he began to slow the piece halfway through until, at the end, it tapered to a stop and remained a single sustained D note.

He lifted his hand off the keyboard. He played back the recording of the piece and was satisfied.

Now on to the rhythm section.

That would be easy, he thought, looking into the tiny den off the living room, where Ali Maziq, late of Tripoli, Libya, lay limp as a rag doll.

III

THE AQUEDUCT

CHAPTER 13

The Questura, the Police of State's main headquarters in Naples, at Via Medina, 75, is an impressive pale stone building in the fascist style. The letters of the word "Questura" are in a font any Latin student would recognize (the "U"s harshly carved as "V"s), and the building's architectural elements include nods to Rome (eagles, for instance).

Squinting up at the imposing structure, Ercole Benelli paused on the doorstep and straightened his gray uniform, brushing at dust. Heart thudding with a curious mixture of joy and trepidation, he stepped inside.

He approached an administrative officer, who said, "You are Benelli?"

"I... Well, yes." Surprised to have been recognized. Surprised too that Rossi was apparently still desirous of his presence.

Her unsmiling face regarded him and, upon examining his ID cards—national and Forestry—she handed him a pass, then told him a room number.

Five minutes later he entered what might be called a situation room for the kidnapping operation. It was a cramped space, the sun sliced into strips by dusty Venetian blinds. The floor was scuffed, the walls too, and a bulletin board was decorated with curling notices of new police procedures replacing old police procedures, and forthcoming assemblies... or, when he read closely, assemblies that had occurred months, or years, ago. Not so very different, Ercole thought, from the Forestry Corps facilities, the large conference room where the officers would meet before a joint raid on an olive oil adulterer, before a mountain rescue, before an assault on a forest fire.

An easel held a large white tablet with photos and notes in black marker. Another—a joke certainly—held a "Wanted" picture of a square-headed *Minecraft* character, which Ercole was aware of because he played the game with his older brother's ten-year-old son. The boy had promptly and delightedly slaughtered Ercole in a recent game; young Andrea had switched to Survival—combat—mode, without telling Uncle Ercole.

Two people were in the room. Massimo Rossi was talking to a round young woman with thick wavy black hair, shiny, and loud green-framed eyeglasses. She wore a white jacket that said *Scientific Police* on the ample breast.

Rossi looked up. "Ah, Ercole. Come in, come in. You found us all right."

"Yes, sir."

"This is Beatrice Renza. She is the forensic officer assigned to the Composer case. Ercole Benelli of the Forestry Corps. He was helpful last night. He will be joining us on a temporary basis."

The woman, in her early thirties, nodded in a distracted way.

"Sir, I have my report." Ercole handed him two yellow sheets of notes.

Beatrice looked at them, frowning. "You have no computer?"

"I do, yes. Why do you ask?"

"You have a printer?"

"Not at my home." He felt on the defensive.

"This is hard to read. You might have emailed the information to us."

He was flustered. "I could have, I suppose. But I didn't have an email address."

"The Questura website would have worked, of course." She turned back to Rossi and handed him a sheet of paper—nicely printed out—and a half-dozen photographs then said goodbye to Rossi. The woman left the situation room, without acknowledging Ercole. Fine with him; he had no time for the self-important, the smug.

Though he wished he *had* thought of typing out the report and sending it as an email attachment. Or getting a new cartridge for his printer at home.

Rossi said, "Beatrice has analyzed the evidence recovered last night at the bus stop. Could you write this onto one of those easels there? Along with your notes and mine. And tape up the crime scene photographs as well. This is how we keep track of the progress of investigations, and make connections between clues and people. Graphical analysis. Very important."

"Yes, Inspector."

He took the sheets of paper from Rossi and began to transcribe the information. Blushing, he noted that Rossi, whom one would have taken to be an old-time investigator, had printed out *his* notes via computer.

"I have heard nothing from the Americans," Rossi said. "You?"

"No. But when I contacted them, they promised to get back to us as soon as possible with full details and evidence reports. The woman I spoke with, a detective who ran the case for the New York Police Department, was quite relieved we had found the man. They were very upset he escaped their jurisdiction."

"Did she have any thoughts as to why he came here?"

"No, sir."

Rossi said, in a musing tone, "I read the other day that the Americans are worried about their exports. The economy, jobs, you understand. But exporting serial killers? They should stick with pop musicians, soft drinks and computer-generated Hollywood movies."

Ercole didn't know whether to laugh or not. He smiled. Rossi did, as well, and read texts. The young officer moved slowly in front of the easel as he transcribed the notes and pinned up photos. A gangly man, he was far more comfortable in the woods and on rock faces than in restaurants, shops and living rooms (hence, his favorite "perch" in the city: the table and chair outside his pigeon coop on the apartment building's roof). His parts—arms, legs, elbows, knees, all of which hummed like a tuned machine out of doors—grew awkward and rebellious in places like this.

He now backed up to examine the chart and bumped into Silvio De Carlo, Rossi's assistant, who had stepped unseen into the room to hand a file to Rossi. The handsome, perfectly assembled young officer didn't glare but—this was worse—offered a patient smile as if Ercole were a child who had accidentally left a blackberry gelato stain on someone's laundered sleeve.

De Carlo, he was sure, would resent this awkward interloper, taking some shine away from his role as Rossi's favored protégé.

"The Postal Police are monitoring YouVid?" Ercole asked Rossi after De Carlo had walked, smoothly and with supreme self-confidence, from the room.

"Yes, yes. But it's a chore. Thousands of videos uploaded every hour. People would rather watch such time-wasting things than read or converse."

Someone else entered the room. Ercole was pleased to see it was the woman Flying Squad officer from last night: Daniela Canton, the stunning blonde. Such a beautiful face, he thought again, elfin. Her eye shadow was that appealing cerulean tint he remembered from last night, a color you didn't see much in fashion nowadays. It told him that she would be the sort to go her own way, make her own style. He noted too that this was the extent of her makeup. No lipstick or mascara. Her blue blouse fit tightly over her voluptuous figure. The slacks were taut too.

"Inspector." She looked up, with a friendly expression, at Ercole. Apparently the brash offering of his hands last night had not put her off.

"Officer Canton. What have you learned?" Rossi asked.

"Though the case had the earmark of a Camorra snatch, it seems unlikely they were involved. Not according to my contacts."

Her contacts? Ercole wondered. Daniela was a member of the Flying Squad. One would think Camorra cases were handled by those higher up.

Rossi said, "I appreciate your looking. But it didn't seem likely our gamers were involved."

Gamers . . .

The word was a slang reference to the gang, whose name was a blend of *Capo*, as in "head," and *morra*, a street game played in old Naples.

She added, "But I cannot say for certain. You know how they operate. So quiet, so secretive."

"Of course."

The Camorra was composed of a number of individual cells, with one group not necessarily knowing what the others were up to.

Then she said, "But for what it's worth, sir, there are rumors of some particularly troublesome 'Ndràngheta gang member who's come to the Naples area recently. Nothing specific but I thought you should know."

This caught Rossi's attention.

Italy was known for several organized crime operations: the Mafia in Sicily, the Camorra in and around Naples, the Sacra Corona Unita in Puglia, the southeast of Italy. But perhaps the most dangerous, and the one with the broadest reach—including such places as Scotland and New York—was the 'Ndràngheta, based in Calabria, a region south of Naples.

"Curious for one of them to come here." The group was a rival to the Camorra.

"It is, yes, sir."

"Can you follow up on that too?"

Daniela said, "I'll try." She turned to Ercole and seemed suddenly to remember him, eyeing his gray Forestry Corps uniform. "Yes, from last night."

"Ercole." So her smile a moment ago was not one of recognition.

"Daniela."

He didn't dare offer his hand again. Just a cool-guy nod. A nod worthy of Silvio De Carlo.

Silence for a moment.

Ercole blurted, "You would like a water?"

And as if she didn't know what mineral water might be, he gestured toward the inspector's San Pellegrino, which stood open on the edge of the table.

And struck it, sending the liter bottle cartwheeling to the floor. Being carbonated, it evacuated most of the contents in seconds.

"Oh, no, oh, I'm so sorry..."

Rossi gave a chuckle. Daniela tilted a perplexed look toward Ercole, who crouched and began mopping furiously with paper towels he pulled from a roll in the corner of the room.

"I..." the blushing man stammered. "What have I done? I'm sorry, Inspector. Did I get any on you, Officer Canton?"

Daniela said, "It's no harm."

Ercole continued to mop.

Daniela left the situation room.

As Ercole's eyes followed her, from his kneeling position on the floor, he noted someone else appear in the doorway. It was Dante Spiro, the prosecutor.

The man was looking past Ercole, as if the young officer were not even present. He greeted Rossi and examined the board. He absently slipped into his side pocket the leather book Ercole recognized from last night. He put away a pen too. He'd been jotting something in the volume.

Today Spiro wore black slacks and a tight brown jacket with a yellow pocket square, a white shirt. No tie. He set a briefcase on a desk in the corner, which apparently he had commandeered as his own, and Ercole guessed he would be a frequent visitor. The man's office—Procura della Repubblica Presso il Tribunale di Napoli—was on the Via Costantino Grimaldi, across the street from the criminal courts. It was not far from the Questura here, a ten-minute drive.

"Prosecutor Spiro," he said, still mopping.

A glance at Ercole, then a frown, wondering, clearly, who he was.

"Anything more, Massimo?" Spiro asked Rossi.

"Beatrice's run the evidence. Ercole has written it up, along with his and my notes." A nod at the paper on the easel.

"Who?"

Rossi gestured toward Ercole, who was dropping a soaked paper towel into the trash bin.

"The Forestry officer from last night."

"Oh." It was clear that Spiro had mistaken him for a janitor.

"Sir, I am pleased to see you again." Ercole smiled but lost the grin when Spiro ignored him once more.

"What of the phone card?" Spiro asked.

"Postal said they should have information within the hour. And they are still monitoring the websites for video uploads. There has been nothing yet. And Ercole anticipates we should hear more from the Americans soon."

"Does he now?" Spiro asked wryly. He took a cheroot from his pocket and slipped the end into his mouth. He did not light the stick. He gazed at the board.

ABDUCTION, BUS STOP, VIA DEL FRASSO, NEAR COMMUNE OF D'ABRUZZO

— Victim:

    — Unknown. Libyan or with Libyan connections? Likely North African. Refugee? Approximate age: 30–40. Light weight. Bearded. Dark hair.

— Perpetrator:

    — Witness didn't see clearly, but possibly American, white male, early to mid-30s. Beard, long bushy hair. (Information from New York City Police Department.)

    — Dark clothing, dark cap.

    — Known as the Composer. (Information from New York City Police Department.)

    — Checking flight manifests for travel to Rome, Naples. Elsewhere? Negative so far.

— Vehicle:

    — Dark sedan. Make and model unknown, but wheelbase consistent with large vehicle: American, German?

    — Tire tread mark Michelin 205/55R16 91H.

— Physical Evidence:

    — Trace of human blood (AB positive), in sample of propylene glycol, triethanolamine, nitrosamines, sodium lauryl sulfate.

    — DNA results, negative for matches in:

        — United Kingdom: National DNA Database (NDNAD).

        — United States: Combined DNA Index System (CODIS).

        — Interpol: DNA Gateway.

        — Prüm Treaty Database.

        — Italian National Database.

    — Nitrogen compounds—ammonia, urea and uric acid—hydrogen, oxygen, phosphates, sulfates, carbon dioxide. As well as: C_8H_7N (indole), 4-Methyl-2,3-benzopyrrole (skatole), and sulfhydryl (thiol), suspended with paper fibers. Desiccated. Old.

    — Decomposing bits of polymer cis-1,4-polyisoprene, thermoset (vulcanized). Translucent. Quite old.

    — *Bartonella elizabethae* bacteria.

    — Thirty-two hairs—animal. Dog shedding? Awaiting Scientific Police analysis as to what type of animal.

    — Lead.

- Shavings of Fe (iron), rust on one side (see photo).
- Limestone.
- Phone card, purchased at Arrozo Tabaccaio, Naples. No CCTV, cash sale.
    - Awaiting analysis from Postal Police.
- Fingerprints:
    - No match in Eurodac, Interpol, Europol or Italy; IAFIS (America); Ident1 (UK).
- Footprints:
    - Victim apparently in Nike running shoes, size 42.
    - Perpetrator apparently in Converse Cons, size 45.
- Blood, other fluid: See above.
- Cash, €11 and 30 dinars (Libyan).
- Miniature hangman's noose, made out of a musical instrument string— probably cello. About 36 centimeters long. (Similar to noose in New York kidnapping, according to NYPD.)
- Witness Account:
    - Witness on bicycle was approaching the bus stop, where the victim was standing. He noted that the dark vehicle was parked nearby, about ten meters away at the side of the road. Behind bushes. Suspect was possibly waiting for the victim, or drove up and hid after victim arrived. Suddenly he assaulted victim. A struggle ensued. No observed provocation. Witness then departed to find police assistance. (Information on witness on file; see Inspector Rossi.)
- Canvass: No one, other than the bicyclist, saw the incident or a vehicle.
- CCTV: None for 10km radius.
- Reports of missing persons: None.
- No apparent Camorra or other organized crime connection.
- Possible 'Ndràngheta operative in area, but no connection to the kidnapping verified.
- No known motive.
- Americans will supply analysis from crime scene in New York City.
- Postal Police are monitoring YouVid, prepared to trace, if suspect uploads video of the victim.

"Beatrice has done her typically solid job," Spiro said.

"Yes. She's good."

The prosecutor seemed to sway slightly as he stared at the writing. "What is that word?"

"Bacteria, sir."

"I can hardly make it out. Write more carefully." Then he scanned the photographs. Spiro mused, "So we have this American psycho who has come here on vacation to prey outside his usual hunting grounds. What patterns can we see?"

"Patterns?" Ercole said, smiling. He mopped a bit more water and rose.

The lean man, with the most intense black eyes that Ercole had ever seen, turned slowly. "I'm sorry?" Though Spiro was shorter, Ercole felt he was looking up into the prosecutor's eyes.

"Well, sir, I am not sure about that."

"'Not sure, not sure.' Tell me what you mean." His voice boomed. "I'm quite curious. You're not sure about something? What might you not be sure about?"

Ercole was no longer smiling. Blushing, he swallowed. "Well, sir, with respect, how can there be any patterns? He's picking his victims at random."

"Explain."

"Well, it's obvious. He finds a victim in New York City, a businessman apparently, according to the Europol report. Then he flees to Italy and selects, it seems, a foreigner of limited means at a rural bus stop." He gave a laugh. "I see no pattern there."

"'See no pattern, see no pattern.'" Spiro tasted the words as if trying a suspect wine. He paced slowly, studying the chart.

Ercole gulped once more and looked to Rossi, who tossed an amused glance toward both men.

"What do you do with the fact, Forestry Officer—"

"Benelli."

"—that the kidnapper's car was parked by the desolate roadside and the kidnapper was waiting in the bushes? Does that not suggest design?"

"It's not clear when the kidnapper arrived. It might have been before or after the victim did. I would suggest, at best, there's a design to kidnap *a* victim, but not necessarily *this* victim. So, pattern? I'm not sure I see one."

Spiro glanced at his watch, a large gold model. Ercole could not detect the brand. He said to Rossi, "I have a meeting upstairs, with another in-spector. Let me know about any videos. Oh, and Forestry Officer?"

"Yes, sir."

"Your name is Ercole, right?"

"It is."

At last, he recognizes me. And he is going to concede my observation about patterns. Ercole felt victorious.

"From mythology."

His name was the Italian version of "Hercules," the Roman god.

"My father enjoyed ancient lore and—"

"You are familiar with the twelve labors that Hercules was required to complete?"

"Yes, yes!" Ercole laughed. "As an act of penance, in the service of King Eurystheus."

"You're falling behind in yours."

"My..."

"Your labors."

Silence.

Looking away from the man's fierce eyes, Ercole said, "I'm sorry, sir?"

Spiro pointed. "You missed some water there. You wouldn't want it to seep under the tile, now, would you? The gods would not be pleased."

Ercole glanced down. Tight-lipped for a moment, and furious that he could not control the reddening of his face. "I will get right to it, sir."

As Spiro left, Ercole dropped to his knees. He happened to glance up and see just outside the doorway Rossi's protégé Silvio De Carlo, looking in. The handsome officer would have witnessed the entire dressing-down—and the order to complete mopping, the implication being that Ercole was not even a competent janitor, let alone investigator. His face a blank mask, De Carlo moved on.

Ercole said to Rossi, "What have I done, Inspector? I was merely stat-ing what seemed logical from the facts. I could see no pattern. A crime in New York, a crime in the hills of Campania."

"Ah, you committed the crime of blinders."

"Blinders. What is that?"

"It's a subtle psychological condition that inexperienced investigators fall victim to. You had already—on the basis of very preliminary evidence—reached the conclusion that this was a random crime. But by embracing that theory you will be disinclined to expand your investigative horizons and consider that the Composer might have acted out of design to target these particular people and that we can discover a pattern to his acts that will help us apprehend him.

"Is it possible to see a pattern at this point? Of course not. Does Prosecutor Spiro think it likely? Of course not. But there is no one I know with a mind that is more expansive than his. He will take in all the facts, making no judgment, long after others have drawn conclusions. Often, he is right and the others are not."

"Open mind."

"Yes. Open mind. The most important asset an investigator can have. So, we will not vote on patterns or no patterns at this point."

"I'll remember that, Inspector. Thank you."

Ercole glanced down at the puddle on the tile floor once more. He'd used all the paper towels. He stepped outside and strode past De Carlo, who was texting on his mobile. My God, the man is completely in vogue, from hair coiffure to polished shoes. Ercole ignored his glance and continued down the hall to the men's room to fetch more towels.

As he was returning, he noted Daniela Canton up the hall, finishing a conversation with her fellow officer, the blond, Giacomo Schiller. After he had walked away Ercole hid the paper towels behind his back and, after a hesitation, approached. "Excuse me. May I ask a question?"

"Yes, of course, Officer..."

"Call me Ercole, please."

She nodded.

He asked, "Prosecutor Spiro." A whisper. "Is he always so stern?"

"No, no, no," she said.

"Ah."

"Usually he is far less polite than he was in there."

Ercole lifted an eyebrow. "You heard him?"

"We all did."

Ercole closed his eyes momentarily. Oh, my. "And he can be worse? Is that true?"

"Oh, yes. He's formidable. A smart man, there's no doubt. But he tolerates no errors—in fact or in judgment—by others. Be careful not to anger him." She lowered her voice. "Did you see that book in his pocket? The leather one."

"Yes."

"He's never without it. People say it's a notebook in which he writes down the names of people who have crossed him or are incompetent and will damage his future."

Ercole recalled seeing the prosecutor on RAI television not long ago, smoothly fielding questions about his plans for a career in politics.

"He wrote down something just now, as he was leaving!"

She was uncomfortable. "Perhaps it was just a coincidence." Her beautiful blue eyes scanned his face. "In any event, be careful, Officer."

"I will. Thank you. You are very kind and I—"

"Ercole!" a voice shouted from up the hall.

Gasping, he turned to see Inspector Massimo Rossi storming from the situation room. It was odd, and unnerving, to see the otherwise placid man so agitated.

Had the Postal Police reported that the Composer uploaded a video?

Had someone found the body of the Libyan?

"Excuse me." He turned from Daniela.

"Ercole," she said.

He paused and looked back.

She pointed at the floor. He had dropped the paper towels.

"Oh." He bent and retrieved them then ran up the hall to Rossi.

The inspector said, "It seems the information you requested from America about the kidnapping has arrived."

Ercole was confused; the expression on Rossi's face was even more troubled than a moment ago. "And isn't that good for us, sir?"

"It most certainly is *not*. Come with me."

CHAPTER 14

Lincoln Rhyme looked around the well-worn lobby of Naples police headquarters.

Though he'd never been here, the building was infinitely familiar; law enforcement doesn't need translation.

People came and went, officers in several, no, *many*, different styles of uniforms—most of which were spiffier and more regal than the U.S. equivalent. Some plainclothes officers, wearing badges on hips or lanyards. And civilians too. Victims, witnesses, attorneys.

Busy. Like Naples outside, Naples inside was hectic.

He studied the architecture once more.

Thom said to Rhyme and Sachs, "Prewar."

It occurred to Rhyme that in Italy the phrase would, in most people's minds, refer to the Second World War. Unlike America for the past eighty years, Italy had not regularly dotted the globe with tanks and infantry and drones.

Thom followed his boss's eyes and said, "Fascist era. You know that Italy was the birthplace of fascism? World War One. Then Mussolini took up the standard."

Rhyme had not known that. But, then, by his own admission, he knew very little that was not related to criminalistics. If a fact didn't help him solve a case, it was a nonfact. He did, however, know the origin of the word. He shared this now. "The word 'fascist' comes from 'fasces.' The

ceremonial bundle of sticks carried by bodyguards to signify power in Roman officials."

"As in speak softly, and carry a big one?" Sachs asked.

Clever. But Lincoln Rhyme was not in the mood for clever. He was
in the mood to get on with the unusual, and infuriating, case against the
Composer.

Ah, at last.

Two men, focusing on the Americans, appeared in the hallway, one in
his fifties, rumpled and solidly built, sporting a mustache. He wore a dark
suit, white shirt and tie. With him was a tall younger man, around thirty,
in a gray uniform with insignia on the breast and shoulder. They shared a
glance and moved quickly toward the trio.

"You are Lincoln Rhyme," said the older. His English was heavily accented but clear.

"And this is Detective Amelia Sachs. And Thom Reston."

As planned, she proffered her gold badge. Not as imposing as fasces,
it was nonetheless *some* indicia of authority.

Even in the short period he'd been in Italy—about three hours—
Rhyme had noted a great deal of hugging and cheek kissing. Man-
woman, woman-woman, man-man. Now, not even a hand was
offered—at least not by the older cop, the one in charge, of course.
He merely nodded, his face stiff with wariness. The younger stepped
forward, palm out, but, seeing his superior's reticence, eased back
quickly.

"I am Inspector Massimo Rossi. The Police of State. You are coming
from New York here, all the way?"

"Yes."

The young man's eyes radiated awe, as if he were seeing a living uni-
corn. "I am Ercole Benelli."

Curious name, pronounced *AIR-colay*.

He continued, "I am honored to meet such an esteemed figure as
you. And to meet you in person, Signorina Sachs." His English was
better and less accented than Rossi's. Generational, probably. Rhyme
suspected YouTube and American TV occupied more of the younger
officer's time.

Rossi said, "Let us go upstairs." He added, as if he needed to, "For the moment."

They rose in silence to the third floor—it would be the fourth in America; Rhyme had read in the guidebook on the way here that in Europe the ground floor was counted as zero, not one.

Out of the elevator, as they made their way down a well-lit corridor, Ercole asked, "You flew on a commercial flight?"

"No. I had access to a private jet."

"A private jet? From America!" Ercole whistled.

Thom chuckled. "It's not ours. A lawyer Lincoln helped in a case recently lent it to us. The crew is flying clients of his to depositions around Europe for the next ten days. We were going to use it for other plans but then this arose."

Greenland, Rhyme thought. Or some other suitable honeymoon site. He didn't, however, share this with the police officer.

At the reference to the duration of their visit—ten days, as opposed to one, or a portion of one—Rossi cocked his head and didn't seem pleased. Rhyme had known from the moment he and Sachs had looked at each other, following Ercole's email about the Composer's presence in Italy, and decided to come here, they would not be welcome. So he was pleased that Thom had fired off the ten-day line; nothing wrong with getting the Italians used to the idea that they were not to be scooted away too fast.

Sachs said to Ercole, "You speak English well."

"Thank you. I have studied from the time I was a *ragazzo*, a boy. You speak Italian?"

"No."

"But you do! That is Italian for 'no.'"

No one smiled and he fell silent, blushing.

Rhyme looked around him, noting again how familiar the place seemed, little different from the Big Building—One Police Plaza, in New York. Harried detectives and uniforms, some joking, some scowling, some bored. Directives from on high posted on bulletin boards and taped directly to the walls. Computers, a year or so past state-of-the-art. Phones ringing—more mobiles in use than landlines.

Only the language was different.

Well, that and another distinction: There were no paper coffee cups, as you'd find littering the desks of American cops. No fast-food bags either. Apparently the Italians avoided this sloppy practice. All to the good. When he'd been head of NYPD forensics, Rhyme had once fired a technician who was examining slides of evidence while he chomped on a Big Mac. "Contamination!" he'd shouted. "Get out."

Rossi led them into a conference room of about ten by twenty feet. It contained a battered table, four chairs, a filing cabinet and a laptop. Against the wall easels held pads of newsprint, covered with handwritten notes and photos. These were just like his own evidence charts, though paper, rather than whiteboards. While there were words he couldn't make out, many items on the list of physical evidence were understandable.

"Mr. Rhyme," Rossi began.

"Captain," Ercole said quickly. "He retired as captain from the NYPD." Then seemed to decide he should not be correcting his superior. A blush.

Rhyme gave a dismissing gesture with his working arm. "No matter."

"Forgive me," Rossi continued, apparently genuinely troubled by this lapse. "Captain Rhyme."

"He is now a consultant," Ercole added, "I have read about him. He often works with Detective Sachs here. That is correct too?"

"Yes," she said.

A cheerleader, like this Ercole, was not a bad idea, Rhyme thought. He was curious about the man. He had both a confidence *and* a rookie's air about him. And Rhyme had seen throughout the building no gray uniforms like his. There's a story here.

Sachs tapped her shoulder bag. "We have the results of the evidence analysis at the two crime scenes involving the Composer in New York. Crime scene photos, footprints and so on."

Rossi said, "Yes. We were looking forward to receiving it. Have you gathered any more information since you spoke to Officer Benelli?"

"Nothing definitive," Sachs said. "We could find nothing about the source of the musical strings he used for the nooses. His keyboard was purchased with cash from a large retailer. There are no fingerprints anywhere. Or, at best, small fragments that aren't helpful."

Rhyme added, "Our FBI is looking at manifests for flights here."

"We have done so too, with no success. But flight manifests would be, what do you say, a long shot. With no picture, no passport number? And your Composer could have flown into a dozen airports in the EU and moved over borders without any record. Rented or stolen a car in Amsterdam or Geneva and driven. I assume you considered he might not have left from a New York–area airport. Perhaps Washington, Philadelphia...even Atlanta on Delta. Hartsfield is the busiest airport in the world, I have learned."

Well, Rossi was at the top of his game.

"Yes, we considered that," Rhyme said.

Rossi asked, "He's American, you think?"

"It's our assumption but we aren't sure."

Ercole asked, "Why would a serial killer leave the country and come here to kill?"

Sachs said, "The Composer isn't a serial killer."

Ercole nodded. "No, he hasn't killed, that's true. You saved the victim. And we have not found the abducted man's body here."

Rossi: "Detective Sachs doesn't mean that, Ercole."

"No, Inspector, you're right. A serial killer is a rare and specific criminal profile. In males the motives're sexual in nature usually, or nonsexual sadism. And while there's ritualistic behavior, that's limited in most cases to binding or arranging the victims in certain ways or leaving fetishes at the scene or taking trophies, postmortem. The behavior doesn't rise to the Composer's level of elaborate staging—the videos, the noose, the music. He's a *multiple* perpetrator."

Silence flowed into the room. Then Rossi spoke. "We thank you for your insights and assistance."

"In whatever humble way we can," Rhyme said. Not very humbly.

"And in coming all this way to deliver to us that file." Not very subtly.

Then Rossi looked him over. "You, Captain Rhyme, I think, are not used to perpetrators, *come si dice?* Absconsioning?"

"Absconding," Ercole corrected his boss. Then froze, blushing once more.

"No, I am not," Rhyme said. Dramatically, perhaps overly so. Though he believed the delivery was appropriate since his impression was that Rossi, too, was a cop who would not do well with absconsioning perpetrators.

"You are hoping for extradition," Rossi said. "After we catch him."

"I hadn't thought that far," Rhyme lied.

"No?" Rossi brushed at his mustache. "Whether the trial is here or in America, that is a decision for the court, not for me or for you. *Allora*, I appreciate what you've done, Captain Rhyme. The effort. It must be taxing." He avoided a glance at the wheelchair. "But now you have delivered your report I cannot see how you can be of further help. You are a crime scene expert but we have crime scene experts here."

"Your Scientific Police."

"Ah, you know of them?"

"I lectured at the main facility in Rome years ago."

"I do hate to disappoint you, and you, as well, Signorina Sachs. But, once again, I see little you can offer other than that." He nodded to her bag. "And there are practical issues. Officer Benelli and I speak serviceable English but most others involved in the case do not. I must add too that Naples is not a very..." He sought a word. "...*accessible* city. For someone like you."

"I've noticed." Rhyme shrugged, a gesture he was fully capable of.

Silence, again.

Broken at last by Rhyme: "Translation is easy, thanks to Google. And regarding mobility: In New York, I don't get out to crime scenes much. No need. I leave that to my Sachs and other officers. They return like bees with nectar. And we concoct the honey together. Forgive the metaphor. But what can it possibly hurt, Inspector, for us to hang around? We'll be sounding boards for ideas."

"Sounding board" seemed to confuse him.

Ercole translated.

Rossi paused then said, "This that you are proposing, it is irregular and we are not people who are well with irregularness."

At that moment Rhyme was aware of a person striding into the room. He swiveled the chair around to see a lean man of slight build in a stylish jacket and slacks, pointy boots, balding and salt-and-pepper goatee. His eyes were narrow and tiny. The word "demonic" came to mind. He looked over Sachs and Rhyme and said, "No. No sounding boards. There will be no consulting, no assistance at all. That is out of the question." His accent was thicker than Rossi's and Ercole's but his grammar and syntax were perfect. This told Rhyme he read English frequently but probably had not been to America or the UK often and watched little English-language media.

The man turned to Ercole and fired off a question in Italian.

Flustered, blushing, the young officer muttered defensively, obviously a denial. Rhyme guessed the question was: "Did you ask them to come?"

Rossi said, "Captain Rhyme, Detective Sachs, and Signor Reston, this is Prosecutor Spiro. He is investigating the case with us."

"Investigating?"

Rossi was silent for a moment, considering Rhyme's question, it seemed. "Ah, yes. From what I know, it is different in America. Here, in Italy, prosecutors function as policemen, in some ways. *Procuratore* Spiro and I are the lead investigators in the Composer case. Working together."

Spiro's dark eyes lasered into Rhyme's. "Our tasks are to identify this man, to ascertain where he is hiding in Italy and where he is keeping the victim, and to marshal evidence to be used at the trial when we capture him. As to the first, you clearly cannot help because you have failed to identify him in your country. The second? You know nothing of Italy so even your expertise in evidence would offer little help. And as to the third, it is not in your interest to assist in a trial *here*, as you wish to extradite the suspect back to America for trial *there*. So, you see, your involvement would at best be unhelpful and at worst a conflict of interest. I thank you for the courtesy of providing us with your files. But now you must leave, Mr. Rhyme."

Ercole started to blurt, "It is *Capitano*—"

Spiro shut him off with a glare. "*Che cosa?*"

"Nothing, *Procuratore*. Forgive me."

"So, you must leave."

Apparently prosecutors—or *this* prosecutor, at least—carried more authority than police inspectors when it came to investigations. Rhyme sensed no disagreement on the part of Rossi. He nodded to Sachs. She dug into the shoulder bag and handed the inspector a thick file. Rossi flipped through it. On the top were photos of the evidence and profile charts.

He nodded and handed them to Ercole. "Put this information on the board, Officer."

Spiro said, "Do you need assistance getting to the airport?"

Rhyme said, "We'll handle our departure arrangements, thank you."

"He has a private jet," Ercole said, still awestruck.

Spiro's mouth tightened, approaching a sneer.

The three Americans turned and headed to the door, Ercole escorting them—as Rossi's nod had instructed.

Just before they left, though, Rhyme stopped and pivoted back. "If I can offer an observation or two?"

Spiro was stone-faced but Rossi nodded. "Please."

"Does *fette di metallo* mean 'bits of metal'?" Rhyme's eyes were on the chart.

Spiro's and Rossi's eyes swiveled to one another's. "'Slices,' yes."

"*Fibre di carta* is 'paper fibers'?"

"That is correct."

"Hm. All right. The Composer has changed his appearance. He's shaved his beard and I am fairly certain his head as well. He has the victim hidden in a very old location, and it's deep underground. It's most likely urban, rather than rural. The building is not now accessible to the public and hasn't been for some time but it once was. It's in a neighborhood where prostitutes used to work. They still might. That I couldn't tell you."

Ercole, he noted, was staring at him as if mesmerized.

Rhyme continued, "And one more thing: He won't use YouVid again. He uses proxies to hide his IP address but he's not good at it and I'm sure he's smart enough to know that. So he'll expect your computer people, and YouVid security, to be onto him. You should start monitoring *other* upload sites. And tell your tactical people to be ready to move quickly. The victim doesn't have much time at all." As he turned his chair toward the door he said, "Goodbye now. I mean, arrivederci."

CHAPTER 15

A m I dead?

And in Jannah?

Ali Maziq could honestly not say. He believed he had been a good man and a good Muslim all his life, and he thought that he had earned a place in Paradise. Perhaps not the highest place, Firdaws, reserved for prophets and martyrs and the most devout, but certainly in a respectable locale.

Yet...yet...

How could Heaven be so cold, so damp, so shadowy?

Alarm coursed through his body and he shivered, only partly from the chill. Was he in al-Nar?

Perhaps he had gotten everything wrong, and had been dispatched straight to Hell. He tried to think back to his most recent memory. Someone appearing fast, someone strong and large. Then something was pulled over his head, muffling the screams.

After that? Flashes of light. Some strange words. Some music.

And now this...Cold, damp, dark, only faint illumination from above.

Yes, yes, it could be. Not Jannah but al-Nar.

He had a vague sense that perhaps this *was* Hell, yes. Because perhaps he had *not* lived such a fine life, after all. He had *not* been so good. He'd done evil. He couldn't recall what specifically but something.

Perhaps that was what Hell was: an eternity of discomfort spent in a state of believing you had sinned but not knowing exactly how.

Then his mind kicked in, his rational, educated mind. No, he couldn't be dead. He was in pain. And he knew that if Allah, praise be to Him, had sent him to al-Nar, he would be feeling pain far worse than this. If he were in Jannah, he would be feeling no pain at all but merely the glory of God, praise be to Him.

So, the answer was that he wasn't dead.

Which led to: So, then, where?

Vague memories tumbled through his thoughts. Memories, or maybe constructions of his own imagination. Why can't I think more clearly? Why can I remember so little?

Images. Lying on the ground, smelling grass. The taste of food. The satisfaction of water in his mouth. Good cold water and bad tea. Olives. A man's hands on his shoulders.

Strong. The big man. Everything going dark.

Music. Western music.

He coughed and his throat hurt. It stung badly. He'd been choked perhaps. The lack of air had hurt his memory. His head ached too. Maybe a fall had jumbled his thoughts.

Ali Maziq gave up trying to figure out what had happened.

He focused on where he was and how to escape.

Squinting, he could discern that he was sitting in a chair—*bound* into a chair—in a cylindrical room that measured about six or seven meters across, stone walls, no ceiling. Above was merely a dim emptiness, from which the very faint illumination came. The floor, also stone, was pitted and scarred.

And what exactly did this room remind him of?

What? What?

Ah, a memory trickled from a dim recess in his mind, and he was picturing a class trip to a museum in Tripoli: the burial chamber for a Carthaginian holy man.

A brief recent memory flickered again: sipping cold water, eating olives, drinking tea that was sour, made from water shot out of a cappuccino machine steamer, residue of milk in the brew.

With somebody?

Then the bus stop. Something had happened at a bus stop.

What country am I in? Libya?

No, he didn't think so.

But I am certainly in a burial chamber...

The room was silent except for the drip of water somewhere in the chamber.

He was gagged, a piece of cloth in his mouth, which was covered with tape. Still, he tried calling for help—in Arabic. Even if he were elsewhere and a different language was spoken, he hoped the tone of his voice would draw rescuers.

But the gag was efficient and he made hardly any sound whatsoever.

Ali now gasped in shock as there was sudden pressure against his windpipe. What could this be? He couldn't see clearly and he had no use of his hands but by twisting his head from side to side and analyzing the sensation, he realized that his head was in a hoop of what seemed to be thin twine. It had just grown slightly tauter.

He looked up and to the right.

And then he saw it—the device meant to kill him!

The cord around his neck traveled upward, to a rod stuck into the wall, then over another rod and down to a bucket. The pail was under an old rusted pipe, from which water dripped.

Oh, no, no! God protect me, praise be to Him!

He now understood the source of the sounds. Slowly the drops of water were filling the bucket. As it grew heavier, it tugged the noose tighter.

The size of the bucket suggested that it would hold easily a half-dozen liters. Ali didn't know how many kilos that represented. But he suspected that the person who had created this horrible machine did. And that his calculation was accurate enough to make certain that—for reasons only God knew, praise be to Him—the bucket would soon be more than heavy enough to choke Ali to death.

Ah, wait! Are those footsteps?

When his breathing slowed, he listened carefully.

Had someone heard him?

But, no, the sound was only the slow *plick, plick, plick* of water leaching from the ancient pipe and dropping into the bucket.

The noose tugged upward once more, and Ali Maziq's muffled pleas for help echoed softly throughout his burial chamber.

CHAPTER 16

H m, was sure I'd get a ticket." Thom's handsome face was perplexed.

The three Americans were outside the police station and the aide was staring at the disabled-accessible van he'd leased online and picked up at Naples airport a few hours ago. The battered, dusty vehicle, a modified Mercedes Sprinter, sat more on the sidewalk than in a parking place. It had been the only spot he'd been able to find near the Questura.

Sachs surveyed the chaotic traffic zipping past and said, "Naples doesn't seem like a place that bothers much with parking tickets. Wish we saw that more in Manhattan."

"Wait here. I'll bring the van over."

"No, I'd like something to drink."

"Too much alcohol isn't good when you've been flying. The pressurization."

This concern, Rhyme was convinced, was a complete fiction. True, a quadriplegic's system is more sensitive than that of a person who isn't disabled, and stress on the body *can* be a problem. The confused nervous system, conspiring with an equally perplexed cardiovascular network, can sometimes send the blood pressure through the roof, which could result in stroke, additional neuro damage and death, if not treated quickly. Rhyme supposed the cabin pressure might in rare cases lead to this condition—autonomic dysreflexia—but blaming alcohol consumption for increased risk was, he was convinced, a shabby ploy to get him to cut down.

He said as much now.

Thom fired back, "I read about it in a study."

"Anyway, I was referring to *coffee*. Besides, what's the hurry? The pilots've gone on to London to ferry those witnesses to Amsterdam. They can't just turn around and fly us back to America. We're spending the night in Naples."

"We'll go to the hotel. Maybe later. A glass of wine. Small."

They had a reservation for a two-bedroom suite at a place Thom had found near the water. "Accessible and romantic," the aide had said, drawing an eye roll from Rhyme.

Then, looking around him, Rhyme said, "Coffee then? I *am* tired. Look. There's a café." He nodded across the street, Via Medina.

Sachs was watching a low, glistening sports car growl past. Of its make, model and horsepower, Rhyme had no clue. But to catch her attention it must have been quite a machine. Her eyes turned back to Rhyme. She said in an edgy voice, "Jurisdictional pissing contests."

Rhyme smiled. Her mind was still on the case.

She continued, "Feds versus state in the U.S. Here, Italy versus America. It happens everywhere, looks like. This is bullshit, Rhyme."

"Is, yes."

"You don't look that upset."

"Hm."

She glanced back at the building. "We need to stop this guy. Damn it. Well, we can still help them from New York. I'll call Rossi when we get back home. He seemed reasonable. More reasonable, at least, than the other one. The prosecutor."

Rhyme said, "I like the name: Dante Spiro. Coffee?" he repeated.

As they headed for the place, which seemed to specialize in pastry and gelato, Thom said to Rhyme, "You're tired, you should have tiramisu. The dessert, you know. It means 'pick me up' in Italian. Like tea in England— gives you energy in the afternoon. Remember, 'coffee' here is what we call espresso. Then there's cappuccino and latte and Americano, which is espresso with hot water, served in a larger cup."

The hostess found a space for them outside, near a metal divider, separating the tables from the rest of the sidewalk. It was covered with a painted banner, probably red when it was installed, now faded pink. It bore the word "Cinzano."

The server, a laconic woman, mid-twenties, in a dark skirt and white blouse, approached and asked for their order in broken English.

Sachs and Thom ordered cappuccino and the aide a vanilla gelato as well. She turned to Rhyme, who said, "*Per favore, una grappa grande.*"

"*Sì.*"

She vanished before Thom could protest. Sachs laughed. The aide muttered, "You tricked me. It's an ice cream parlor. Who knew they had a liquor license?"

Rhyme said, "I like Italy."

"And where did you learn the Italian? How do you even know what grappa is?"

"Frommer's guide to Italy," Rhyme said. "I put *my* time on the plane to good use. You were sleeping, I noticed."

"Which you should have been doing too."

The beverages came and, with his right hand, Rhyme lifted the glass and sipped. "It's...refreshing. I would say an acquired taste."

Thom reached for it. "If you don't like it..."

Rhyme moved his hand away. "I need a chance to complete my acquisition."

The server was nearby and had overheard. She said, "Ah, we are not having the best grappa here." Her tone was apologetic. "But go to a bigger restaurant and they will offer more and betterer grappa. Distillato too. It is like grappa. You must have them both. The best are from Barolo, in Piemonte, and Veneto. The north. But that is my opinion. Where is it are you visiting from?"

"New York."

"Ah, New York!" Eyes shining. "The Manhattan?"

"Yes," Sachs said.

"I will go someday. I have been to Disney with my family. In Florida. Someday I will go to New York. I want to skate on the ice at Rockefeller Center. It is possible doing that all the time?"

"Only the winter," Thom said.

"*Allora,* thank you!"

Rhyme took another sip of grappa. This taste was mellower but he was now determined to try one of the better varieties. His eyes remained where they had largely been, on the front of police headquarters. He finished the sip and had another.

Thom, clearly enjoying his dessert and coffee, said, with a suspicious look in his eyes, "You seem a lot better now. Less tired."

"Yes. Miraculous."

"Though impatient about something."

True, he was.

"About—?"

"About that," Rhyme said as Sachs's phone hummed.

She frowned. "No caller ID."

"Answer. We know who it is."

"We do?"

"And on speaker."

She pressed the screen and said, "Hello?"

"Detective Sachs?"

"Yes."

"Yes, yes. I am Massimo Rossi."

"Pay," Rhyme said to Thom, finishing the grappa.

"And, Captain Rhyme?" Rossi asked.

"Inspector."

"I hoped I might catch you nearby."

"A café, across the street. Having some grappa."

A pause. "Well, I must tell you that the Composer's video has been uploaded. You were correct. Not on YouVid. It was on NowChat."

"When?" Rhyme asked.

"The time stamp was twenty minutes ago."

"Ah."

Rossi said, "Please, Captain Rhyme. I think you are not the sort of man to play games. Clearly not. I have discussed the matter with Prosecutor Spiro and we were, to say the least, impressed at your observations."

"Deductions, not observations."

"Yes, of course. *Allora*, we decided we might ask you, changing our ideas, if you would in fact be willing to—"

"We'll be in your offices in five minutes."

CHAPTER 17

At Rhyme's suggestion—insistent suggestion—the situation room was moved from upstairs to a larger conference room in the basement, near the Scientific Police laboratory.

The lab was efficiently constructed. There was a sterile area, where trace was extracted and analyzed, and a larger section for fingerprints, tread and shoe prints and other work where contamination would not be a risk. The conference room opened onto this latter part of the lab.

Rhyme, Sachs and Thom were here with Rossi and the tall, rangy Ercole Benelli.

Two others were present, uniformed officers, though in blue outfits, different from Ercole's—the light gray. They were a young patrolman, Giacomo Schiller, and his apparent partner, Daniela Canton. Both blond—she darker than he—they were serious of expression and attentive to Rossi, who spoke to them like a grandfather, kindly but one you made sure to obey. They were, Rossi explained, with the Flying Squad—which corresponded, Rhyme deduced, to the patrol officers assigned to squad cars, Remote Mobile Patrols in NYPD jargon.

Rhyme asked, "And Dante Spiro?"

"*Procuratore* Spiro had other matters to attend to."

So the temperamental man had reluctantly agreed to let the Americans return but wanted nothing to do with them. Fine with Rhyme. He was not quite sure about this Italian arrangement of the district attorney's active involvement in the investigation. It probably wasn't a conflict of interest—and Spiro seemed sharp enough. No, Rhyme's objection could be summed up in a dreaded cliché: too many cooks.

Ercole was setting up the easels and charts, and translating from Italian to English. In the doorway, advising him, was round, no-nonsense Beatrice Renza, a senior analyst in the lab.

Her name, Rhyme learned, was pronounced *Bee-a-TREE-chay*. Italian took some getting used to, certainly, but was far more melodic than blunt English.

She spoke to Ercole in clipped, rapid Italian and he grimaced and responded testily, apparently to some objection about a translation or characterization of something he was writing. She rolled her eyes, behind elaborate glasses, then stepped forward to take the marker from him and make a correction.

Schoolmarm, Rhyme thought, but then, so'm I. He was admiring her professional style. And her skill in extracting the evidence. The breakdown of the trace was excellent.

Daniela and Giacomo finished setting up a large laptop. She nodded to Rossi, who said, "Here is the video."

Giacomo tapped keys and the screen came to life.

In lightly accented English, Daniela said, "The site had taken down the video. It's against their policy to show graphic violence. In Italy that can be a crime. But at our request they sent a copy to us."

"Were there comments by viewers on the page where it was posted?" Sachs asked. "About the video?"

Rossi explained, "We hoped too what you are suggesting, yes. That the Composer might respond to a comment and we might learn more. But that has not been the case. The video site has left the page up—again at our request—without the video. And Giacomo here is monitoring comments. But he has remained silent, the Composer."

The young man gave a sour laugh. "It is a sad state. The comments mostly are people angry that the video is down. The audience wants to see a man die." He nodded toward the computer. "*Ecco*."

They all stared at the screen.

The video showed a dimly lit room, walls apparently damp, dotted with mold. The gagged victim—a slim man, dark-complexioned, with a beard—sat in a chair, a thin noose around his neck. The cord—another musical-instrument string—disappeared up out of the scene. It was not very tight. The man was unconscious, breathing slowly. The video, like the one in New York, included only music, played on a keyboard, presumably a new Casio or something similar.

This tune too was in three-four waltz time. And, as in the earlier video, the downbeat was a man's gasp and, as the visual grew darker, the music and inhalations grew slower.

"*Cristo*," Ercole whispered, though he had presumably seen it at least once before. He looked toward Daniela, who regarded the video impassively. Ercole cleared his throat and put on a stoic face.

The music was familiar but Rhyme couldn't place it. He mentioned this.

The others seemed surprised. It was Thom who said, "'The Waltz of the Flowers.' *Nutcracker.*"

"Oh." Rhyme listened to jazz occasionally; there was something intriguing about how improvisation could find a home in the mathematical absolute of a musical composition (it was how he approached crime scene work). But in general, music, like most arts, was largely a waste of time to Lincoln Rhyme.

The victim stirred as dirt or stones trickled onto his shoulder, from the wall or ceiling, but did not come to. The screen grew dimmer, the music slower. Finally, it went black and the soundtrack ended.

The perverse copyright notice came up on the screen.

Rhyme asked, "Metadata?" Information embedded in pictures and videos about the work itself: type of camera, focal length, date and time, speed and aperture settings, sometimes even the GPS location. This had been removed from the New York video, but perhaps the Composer failed to do so here.

Rossi said, "None. The Postal Police said it was re-encoded and all the data stripped out."

"Postal Police?"

"It is our telecommunications arm."

Rossi stared at the black screen for a moment. "How much time do you think we have?"

Rhyme shook his head. Any suggestion would be simply a guess, a waste of effort.

Sachs mused, "How does the gallows work? Something off camera will pull the noose up, a weight or something."

They looked at the video for any clue but saw nothing.

"Well, let us move now. See if we can solve this puzzle. Captain Rhyme—"

"How did I draw my conclusions I told you about?"

"Yes. That's where we should start."

Nodding toward the now-translated chart, Rhyme said, "The trace, of course. Now, the substances paired with the propylene glycol are shaving cream. With the blood, it's a reasonable conclusion that he cut himself shaving. To change his appearance as much as he can, he'd lose the hair and beard. The shaved-head look seems popular here in Italy.

"Now, the indole, skatole and thiol are excrement." A glance toward the chart once more. "Those're shit. With the paper fiber? Human shit, of course. No other creatures I know wipe. It's old shit, quite old, desiccated. You can see in the picture—and of several different types. See the color and texture variations? I would speculate there is a sewer nearby, one that might not have been used for some time.

"The animal hairs are from a rat. It's shedding because it's scratching; it has a skin irritation—the bartonella bacteria are causing that. The particular strain is the one that most commonly infects rats. Rats and sewers, well, you find them everywhere but more often in cities than smaller towns. So, urban setting."

"*Bene,*" said Beatrice Renza.

"The iron shavings tell me the Composer cut a lock or chain to get access to the place. Iron isn't used much anymore—most locks are steel—so it's old. With the rust on only one side—you can see it there, that photo—it was recently cut."

Rossi said, "You suggested it used to have public access, in the past."

"Yes, because of the rubber."

"The rubber?" Ercole asked. He seemed to be memorizing all that Rhyme said.

"What else would be vulcanized? Translucent, decomposing shreds. Vulcanized rubber."

It was Beatrice who nodded. "They are the old condoms, might it not be?"

"Exactly. Hardly a romantic trysting place, with the rat neighbors, and sewers, but perfect for streetwalkers." Rhyme shrugged. "They're bold deductions. But we have a man who's about to be strangled to death. I don't think we have time to be timid. So, what does this tell you about where the victim might be? Underground in Naples? Of course, a deserted area."

Rossi said, "Not many of those here. We are a very crowded city."

Beatrice said, "And Naples has more underground passages and walkways than any other city in Italy. Perhaps than Europe. Kilometers after kilometers."

Ercole disagreed. "But not so many where access is in deserted places."

The lab analyst muttered to him, "No, I think many. We must find other ways to narrow these concerns down."

Rhyme said, "A map. There has to be a map of underground locations."

"Historical documents," Daniela offered.

With a smile, Ercole said to her, "Yes, of course. From a library or a college or a historical society."

Rhyme turned to him and his eyebrow rose.

Ercole hesitated and said, "Is that wrong? It was just a suggestion."

Rossi said, "I think, Ercole, that Captain Rhyme is not questioning your thought—which is a good, if obvious, one—but your delay in *providing* such maps."

"Oh, yes, yes, of course."

Sachs told him, "Go online. We don't have time for you to prowl though libraries like *The Da Vinci Code*."

Must have been a book, Rhyme supposed. Or movie.

Sachs asked Beatrice, "You mentioned the underground passages here. Are there walking tours?"

"Yes," she replied. "My sister's children, we are going on such tours. Several, three times."

"Ercole," Rhyme called, "download all those tour routes too."

"Yes, I will. You mean so that we can eliminate those areas from our underground search. Of course he would avoid places with tourists."

"I want to orient myself. A map of the city. We need a map."

Rossi spoke to Daniela, who vanished then returned a moment later with a large foldout map. She taped it to the wall.

"How are we coming, Ercole?"

"I...There are quite a few underground areas of the city. I didn't realize how—*come si dice*—how extensive the passages are."

"As I was saying," Beatrice offered to Ercole.

"Some are contradictory. Indicated on one map but not another."

"I would think certain underground areas will have been filled in, construction," Rossi said. To Rhyme, Sachs and Thom he said, "This is a problem in Italy. A real estate man wishes to build an office or apartments and as soon as the excavation is started, a Roman or—here often—a Greek ruin is discovered, and all construction comes to a stopping."

"Give me something to work with, Ercole. We need to get on this."

"I have some, a few passageways, old buildings, grain storage warehouses, even some caves that are promising." He looked up. "How do I print?" he asked Daniela.

"Here." She leaned over him. She typed and a moment later, the Hewlett-Packard in the corner came to life. Rhyme didn't know why he was surprised—perhaps because he was in an ancient city, looking at ancient maps; wireless printing routers seemed out of place.

Sachs fished the pages from the tray and handed them to Daniela. Rhyme instructed, "Draw the passages on the map."

"*Tutti?* All of them?"

"Except the ones that seem to be bricked off."

In her firm, swift strokes, she outlined the networks.

Rhyme said, "Now add public works. Sewers. But just the older ones, from historical maps. Old shit, remember? And open, not enclosed, pipes. The Composer *stepped* in the trace."

The young officer began a new search. The maps Ercole found were obviously incomplete but they showed some sewage sluices that had been in operation in the eighteenth and nineteenth centuries. Daniela put these on the map.

"Okay, now eliminate the walking-tour routes," Rhyme instructed.

Ercole printed out the website information from "Underground

Naples, See History Up Close!" and a half-dozen others. Daniela noted the routes and marked off any that coincided with the passageways and sewers they'd found.

Still, miles and miles of places to stash the victim remained.

Rossi said, "And an area where prostitutes worked, you were suggesting?" He looked at Giacomo, who gazed at the map and said, "I have patrolled—you would say in vice squad—many of the areas where working women and men are found, the Spanish Quarters, Piazza Garibaldi, Corso Umberto, Gianturco, Piazzale Tecchio—the San Paolo stadium, Via Terracina, Fuorigrotta, Agnano and Corso Lucci. These are active now. The Domiziana—or now Domitiana—area, north and west of Naples, was known historically for prostitution, and still is. But it's very congested and the population is mostly immigrant. It would be hard for the Composer to get his victim there. And no underground passages are nearby."

Rhyme said, "Circle the first areas you have mentioned, Officer."

Giacomo took the marker from Daniela and did so.

This narrowed down the number of passageways and chambers to about two dozen.

"What are they exactly," Sachs asked.

Rossi said, "Roman roads and alleyways and sidewalks before they were built over. Tunnels for delivery of merchandise to avoid the congested streets. Water reservoirs and aqueducts. Grain warehouses."

"Water?"

"Yes. The Romans built the best water delivery *infrastruttura* in the world."

Then Rhyme called, "Beatrice, you found limestone and lead?"

She didn't understand, and Ercole translated.

"Sì. Yes, we did. There it is, you can see."

"Were the old Roman aqueducts limestone?"

"Yes, they were and, as you are suggesting, I believe, the pipes...shifting the water, transporting the water to the fountains and the homes and the buildings, were lead. Now replaced, of course, for healthy reasons."

"Ercole, maps of Roman water supplies?"

This document was readily available in the historical archives.

Ercole handed the printout to Daniela. He pointed to the document and said, "Here I have ten Roman water-holding chambers in the areas we have marked. They are like large wells or silos, round. These were connected to aqueducts coming into the city from the north and west. Some of them are large municipal reservoirs, twenty by twenty meters, and some are those serving smaller areas or individual homes, much smaller. When the supply of water became more modern, and pumping stations were created, many of these reservoirs were converted to warehouses and storerooms. Doors and windows were carved into the walls."

Daniela marked them.

Rhyme: "I want to see the video again."

The image came onto the screen once more. "Look at the wall, the stone. Is it a water reservoir?"

"It might be." Ercole shrugged. "Carved stone. Stained with what might be water marks. And if converted, it could have had a doorway cut for access. There, that shadow suggests there is a doorway."

Sachs said, "We've narrowed it to nine or ten locations. Can we do a search of them all? Get a hundred officers?"

Rossi seemed uncomfortable. "We do not have the resources I would like." He explained that there'd just been reports of potential terror attacks in Italy and other parts of Europe recently and many officers had been pulled off non-terror crimes.

Rhyme had the video played once more: the stone, the noose, the unconscious victim, his chest rising slowly, the trickle of dust, the—

"Ah. Look at that." His voice was a whisper. But everyone in the room turned to him immediately. He grimaced. "I saw it before but didn't think a damn thing of it."

"What, Rhyme?"

"The dust and pebbles, falling from the wall."

Sachs and Ercole spoke simultaneously. She: "Subway!" He: "*Rete Metropolitana!*"

"A train's shaking the walls. Ercole, quick, what lines run through the areas we've marked?"

He called up a subway system schematic on the laptop. Looking it over, Daniela drew the transit lines on their working map.

"There!" Rossi called. "That water reservoir, the small one."

It was a room about twenty by twenty feet, at the end of an aqueduct. It was accessed by a passageway that ran to a street by a square on Viale Margherita.

Giacomo added, "I know that area. That reservoir would be in the basement of an old building, now abandoned. Prostitutes could have used the passages years ago, yes."

"Abandoned," Rhyme said. "So the doors might be sealed with the lock and chain the Composer cut through; that's the rust and the slices of metal."

"I'll call the SCO," Rossi said.

Daniela offered: "Servizio Centrale Operativo. Our SWAT force."

Rossi spoke for several minutes, giving firm orders then hung up. "The central office is assembling a team."

Sachs met Rhyme's eyes. He nodded.

She asked, "How far away is that?" She stabbed the map, the entrance around which Daniela had drawn a red circle.

"No more than a few kilometers from us."

"I'm going," Sachs announced.

After a brief hesitation Rossi said, "Yes, certainly." He looked to Giacomo and Daniela, and the three had a brief conversation in Italian.

Rossi translated, "Their vehicle is with other officers. Ercole, you drive Detective Sachs."

"Me?"

"You."

As they started for the door, Rhyme said, "Give her a weapon."

"What?" Rossi asked.

"I don't want her in the field without a weapon."

"That's irregular."

We are not people who are well with irregularness . . .

"She's an NYPD detective and a competitive shooter."

Rossi considered the request. Then he said, "I am not aware of the agreement we have with the United States but I authorized gendarmes in pursuit of a criminal from France to enter Campania armed. I will do the same now." He vanished and returned a few minutes later with a plastic pistol container. He jotted the number from the case onto a form and opened it. "This is a—"

"Beretta ninety-six," she said. "The A-one. Forty caliber." She took it and pointed it downward, moving the slide slightly to verify it was empty. She took two black magazines and the box of ammunition that Rossi had also brought.

"Sign here. And where it says 'Rank,' and 'Affiliation'—those words there—write something illegible. But please, Detective Sachs, do not shoot anyone if you can avoid it."

"I'll do my best."

She scrawled where he'd indicated, slipped in a mag and worked the slide to chamber a round. Then, making sure it was on safe, she tucked the weapon into her back waistband. She hurried to the door.

Ercole looked from Daniela to Rossi. "Should I—?"

Rhyme said, "Go! You should *go*."

CHAPTER 18

That's *it*?" Amelia Sachs asked as they ran from the Questura. "That's your car?"

"Yes, yes." Ercole was beside a small, boxy vehicle called a Mégane, soft blue, dusty and dinged. He began to walk to her side and open the door for her.

"I'm fine." She waved him off. "Let's go."

The young officer climbed into the driver's seat and she dropped into the passenger's.

"It's not much, I'm sorry to say." He gave a rueful smile. "The Flying Squad actually had two Lamborghinis. One was in an accident a few years ago so I'm not sure if they still have both of them. It's a marked police car. What a—"

"We should move."

"Of course."

He started the engine. He put the shifter in first, signaled to the left and looked over his shoulder, waiting for a gap in traffic.

Sachs said, "I'll drive."

"What?"

She slipped the shifter into neutral and yanked up on the brake, then leapt out.

Ercole said, "I should ask, do you have a license? There are probably forms to be filled out. I suppose—"

Then she was at the left-hand door, pulling it open. He climbed out.

She said, "You can navigate." Ercole scurried around the car and dropped into the other seat and she settled into the right, not needing to adjust the seat's position; he was taller and it was as far back as it might go.

She glanced at him. "Seat belt."

"Oh. Here, no one cares." A chuckle. "And they never give you a ticket."

"Put it on."

"All right. I will—"

Just as it clicked, she slammed the gears into first, fed the engine a slug of gas and popped the clutch, darting into a minuscule gap in traffic. One car swerved and another braked. Both honked. She didn't bother to look back.

"*Mamma mia,*" Ercole whispered.

"Where do I go?"

"Straight on this road for a kilometer."

"Where're your lights?"

"There." He pointed to a switch. The headlights.

"No, I mean the flashers. You have blue here, in Italy?"

"Blue? Oh, police lights? I don't have them—" He gasped as she zipped into a space between a truck and a trio of motorcyclists. "This is my personal car."

"Ah. And how much horsepower? Eighty?"

Ercole said, "No, no, it's closer to a hundred, one ten, in fact."

Be still my heart, she thought, but said nothing. Amelia Sachs would never tarnish anyone's image of his own wheels.

"You don't have flashers in your personal cars?"

"The Police of State might. Inspector Rossi and Daniela. I am, as you know, with the Forestry Corps. We do not. At least none of the officers I work with do. Oh, we are to turn soon."

"Which street and which way?"

"Left. That one up there. But I didn't prepare. I am sorry. I don't think we can get over in time."

They got over in time.

And took the ninety degrees in a screaming second gear. He gasped.

"Next turn?"

"Half a kilometer, to the right. Via Letizia."

He inhaled harshly as she accelerated to eighty kph, weaving into and out of all four lanes.

"Will they reimburse you, the Police of State?"

"It's only a few euros for the mileage, hardly worth the effort of the forms."

She'd been referring to repairing the transmission but decided not to bring that up. Anyway, how much damage could a hundred horses do to a tranny?

"Here is the turn."

Via Letizia...

The road grew congested. Rear ends and brake lights loomed.

She was skidding to a stop, using both brakes, inches from the jam.

A blast of horn. Nobody moved.

"Hold your badge up," she told him.

His smile said the gesture would do no good.

She hit the horn again and guided the car over the curb and along the sidewalk. Furious faces turned toward her, though the expressions of some of the younger men switched from indignant anger to amusement and even admiration when they noted the insane driver was a beautiful redhead.

She breached the intersection and turned as Ercole had instructed. Then roared forward.

"Call," she instructed. "See if the—what's the name of your tac outfit again?"

"Tac?"

"Sorry. Tactical. See where they are."

"Oh, SCO." He pulled out his phone and placed a call. Like most of the conversations she'd heard so far, this one unfolded lightning-fast. It ended with a clipped, "*Ciao, ciao, ciao, ciao...*" He gripped the dash as she shot between two trucks and said, "They're assembled and on the way. It should be fifteen minutes."

"How far are we?"

"*Cinque.* I mean—"

"Five." Sachs was grimacing. "Can't somebody be there any faster?

We'll need a breaching team. The Composer would have locked the door-way or gate again. He did that in New York."

"They'll probably think of that."

"Tell them anyway."

Another call. And she could tell from the tone, if not the words, that there was nothing to do to expedite the arrival of the tactical force.

"They have hammers and cutters and a torch."

A fast shift, fourth to second. She punched the accelerator. The en-gine howled.

A phrase of her father's came to mind. A bylaw of her life.

When you move they can't getcha...

But just then: A blond teenager, his long curls flying in the breeze, steered a peppy orange scooter through a stoplight, oblivious to any traffic.

"Shit."

In a blur of appendages, Sachs used the gears, the foot brake and the hand brake to decelerate and then skid around the Honda, missing the kid by inches. He didn't even notice. Sachs saw he wore earbuds.

Then first gear, and they were on their way once more.

"Left here." Ercole was shouting over the screams of his laboring engine.

It was a narrow street they were speeding along. Residential—no stores. Pale laundry hung above them like flags. Then into a square around a tiny anemic park, on whose scarred benches sat a half-dozen older men and women, a younger woman with a baby carriage and two children playing with scruffy dogs. It was a deserted area and the Com-poser could easily have slipped the victim out of his car and underground without anyone's seeing.

"There, that's it," he announced, pointing to a shabby wooden doorway in the abandoned building Giacomo Schiller had referred to. This, like all the building façades nearby, was covered with graffiti. You could just make out the faded sign: *Non Entrare.*

Sachs brought the Mégane to a stop twenty feet from the door, leaving room for the tactical officers and ambulance. She hurried out. Ercole was close behind her.

Jogging again. But carefully. Sachs kept a close monitor on her legs—she suffered from arthritis, which had become so severe she'd nearly been sidelined from her beloved profession. Surgery had removed much, if not all, of the pain. Still, she always stayed mindful. The body can betray at any moment. But now, all functioned smoothly.

"You're new to this, right? To entry."

"Entry?"

That answered the question.

She'd learned enough. "First, we secure the site, make it safe from hostiles. It doesn't help the victim, even if he's seconds away from dying, if we die too. Okay?"

"Sì."

"When it's clear, we try to save him, CPR, open airways if we can, apply pressure to stop bleeding, though I don't think blood loss is going to be a problem. After that we secure the crime scene to preserve evidence."

"All right...Ah, no!"

"What?"

"I forgot the booties. For our shoes. You are supposed to—"

"We don't wear those now. They're too slippery. Here."

She dug into her pocket and handed him rubber bands. "On the ball of your feet."

"You carry those with you?"

They both donned the elastic.

"Gloves?" he asked. "Latex gloves."

Sachs smiled. "No. Not in tactical situations."

The door, she was surprised to see, was barred with the cheapest of locks and a hasp that was affixed to the wooden door and frame with small screws.

She dug into her pocket and the switchblade was in her hand. Ercole's eyes went wide. Sachs smiled to herself as the thought occurred that the weapon was Italian—a Frank Beltrame stiletto, a four-inch blade, staghorn handle. She flicked it open and in one deft move pulled the bracket away from the wood, then tucked the knife away.

Holding her finger to her lips, she studied Ercole's nervous, sweaty face. Some of the consternation was from the harrowing drive; the source of the remainder was clear. He was willing, but he was not battle-tested. "Stay behind me," she whispered.

"Yes, yes." Which came out more as a breath than words.

She pulled a halogen flashlight from her pocket, a tiny but powerful thousand-lumen model. A Fenix PD35.

Ercole squinted, surely thinking: Rubber bands, flashlight, flick-blade knife? These Americans certainly came prepared.

A nod toward the door.

His Adam's apple bobbed.

She pushed inside, raising the light and the gun.

There was a startling crash; the door had struck a table, spilling a large bottle of San Pellegrino mineral water.

"He's here!" Ercole whispered.

"Not necessarily. But assume he is. He may have set up the table to warn him somebody breached. We have to go fast."

The entryway atmosphere was pungent, the walls covered with graffiti. It resembled a cave in some wilderness, rather than a man-made structure. A stairway led down two flights. They went slowly. The halogen would give them away but it was their only source of illumination. A fall down these steep stones could be fatal.

"Listen," she said, pausing at the bottom. She believed she'd heard a moan or grunt. But then nothing.

They found themselves in an old brick tunnel about eight feet wide. The aqueduct, a square-bottomed trough about two feet across, ran through the middle. It was largely dry, though old iron pipes overhead— the ceiling was six feet above them—dripped water.

Ercole pointed to their left. "The reservoir would be there, if the map is correct."

A rumbling began in the distance and grew in volume. The floor shook. Sachs supposed that it was the subway, nearby, she recalled from the map, but it also occurred to her that Naples was not so very far from Mount Vesuvius, whose volcano she'd read might erupt at any time. Volcanoes equal earthquakes, even the smallest of which might pin her under rubble—and leaving her to die the worst death imaginable. Claustrophobia was her big fear.

But the roaring rose to a crescendo, then faded.

Subway. Okay.

They arrived at a fork, the tunnel splitting into three branches, each with its own aqueduct.

"Where?"

"I am sorry. I do not know. This part was not on the map."

Pick one, she thought.

And then she saw that the left branch of the tunnel contained not only an aqueduct but a terracotta pipe, largely broken. Probably an old sewer drain. She was recalling the scatological trace from the Composer's shoes. "This way." She began along the damp floor, the smell of mold tickling her throat and reminding her of the uranium-processing factory in Brooklyn, site of the Composer's first murder attempt.

Where are you? she thought to the victim. Where?

They pressed on, walking carefully in the aqueduct until the tunnel ended—in a large, dingy basement, lit dimly from airshafts and from fissures in the ceiling. The aqueduct continued on arched columns to a round stone cylindrical structure, twenty feet across, twenty high. There was no ceiling. A door had been cut into the side.

"That's it," Ercole whispered. "The reservoir."

They climbed off the aqueduct and down stone stairs to the floor, about ten feet below.

Yes, she could hear a gasping sound from inside. Sachs motioned Ercole to cover the aqueduct they'd come down and the other doorways that opened off the basement. He understood and drew his pistol. His awkward grip told her he rarely shot. But he checked that a round was chambered and the safety catch off. And he was aware of where the muzzle was pointed. Good enough.

A deep breath, another.

Then she spun around the corner, keeping low, and played the light through the room.

The victim was fifteen feet from her, sitting taped in a rickety chair, straining to keep his head raised against the upward tension of the noose. She saw clearly now the mechanism the Composer had rigged—the deadly bass strings running up to a wooden rod hammered into a crack in the wall above the victim's head, then to another rod and finally down to a bucket filling with water. The weight in the pail would eventually tug the noose tight enough to strangle him.

He squinted his eyes closed against the brilliance of the flashlight.

The room had no other doors and it was clear that the Composer wasn't present.

"Come inside, cover the door!" she barked.

"Sì!"

She holstered her weapon and ran to the man, who was sobbing. She pulled the gag out of his mouth.

"Saedumi, saedumi!"

"You'll be okay." Wondering how much English he spoke.

She had gloves with her but didn't bother now. Beatrice could print her later to eliminate her friction ridges. She gripped the noose and pulled down, which lifted the bucket, and then she slipped the noose over his head. Slowly she lowered the bucket. Before it reached the floor, though, the stick wedged into a gap between the stones gave way and the pail fell to the floor.

Hell. The water would contaminate any trace on the stone.

But nothing to do now. She turned to the poor man and examined him. His panicked eyes stared from her to the tape binding his arms up to the ceiling and back to her.

"You'll be okay. An ambulance is coming. You understand? English?"

He nodded. "Yes, yes."

He didn't look badly hurt. Now that he was okay, Sachs pulled on latex gloves. She removed her switchblade once more, hit the button. It sprang open. The man recoiled.

"It's all right." She cut the tape and freed his hands, then feet.

The victim's eyes were wide and unfocused. He rambled in Arabic.

"What's your name?" Sachs asked. She repeated the question in Arabic. All NYPD officers in Major Cases who had occasion to work counterterrorism knew a half-dozen words and phrases.

"Ali. Ali Maziq."

"Are you injured anywhere, Mr. Maziq?"

"My throat. It is my throat." He took to rambling again and his eyes darted once more.

Ercole said, "He doesn't seem too injured."

"No."

"He is, it seems, quite disoriented, though."

Tied up by a madman and nearly hanged in an old Roman ruin? No surprises there.

"Let's get him upstairs."

CHAPTER 19

T he tactical team arrived.

A dozen SCO officers. They appeared in deadly earnest and were fully confident as they scanned the area and gripped their weapons like true craftsmen.

Sachs stopped them at the entrance. She was wearing the NYPD shield on her belt, gold for detective, which gave her some authority, ambiguous though it might be. The commander asked, "FBI?" A thick accent.

"Like that," she said. Which seemed to satisfy him.

The man was large of body and large of head, which was covered with a fringe of curly red hair, about the same shade as hers. He nodded to her and said, "Michelangelo Frasca."

"Amelia Sachs."

He vigorously shook her hand.

She gestured past him to the arriving medical team, a burly man and a woman nearly as imposing—they might have been siblings—and they sat Maziq on a gurney and took his vitals. The medic spent a moment examining the red ligature mark and said something in Italian to his partner and then to Sachs: "Is okay, is good. In physicalness. His mind, very groggy. Drunk I would say if he was not Muslim. Maybe it is being drugs the assaulted used." They assisted Maziq into the back of the ambulance and had a conversation with Ercole.

The young officer spoke at length to Michelangelo, presumably about what had happened. He gestured toward the entrance.

"I have told them where to search and that the killer may still be nearby."

Sachs noted that the men wore black gloves, so she wasn't worried about fingerprints, and hoods, which would prevent hair contamination. She dug into her pocket and handed Michelangelo a dozen rubber bands.

He looked at her quizzically.

"*Fai così,*" Ercole said, pointing to his feet.

The commander nodded and his eyes seemed impressed. "*Per le nostre impronte.*"

"*Sì.*"

"*Buono!*" A laugh. "*Americana.*"

"Tell them to walk quickly through the entrance room, where we found the table and water bottle, and to avoid the chamber where we got the victim. That's where most of the evidence will be and we don't want it contaminated any more."

Ercole relayed the information, and the big man nodded. He then quickly deployed his troops.

She heard voices behind them. A large crowd had gathered—among them reporters, calling questions. The police ignored the journalists. Uniformed officers strung yellow tape, as in America, and kept back the crowd.

Another van arrived, large and white. The words *Polizia Scientifica* were on the side. Two men and a woman climbed out and walked to the double doors in the back, opened them. They dressed in white Tyvek jumpsuits, the name of the unit on the right breast and the words *Spray Guard* over the left. They approached a uniformed officer, who pointed to Sachs and Ercole. The three approached and spoke with Ercole, who, she could tell from his gestures, told them about the scene. The woman glanced at Sachs once or twice during the lengthy explanation.

Sachs said, "If I can borrow a suit, I'll search with them. I can show them exactly where—"

A man's voice interrupted her. "That is not necessary."

Sachs turned to see the prosecutor, Dante Spiro. He was approaching from behind a clutch of uniformed officers and cars. One officer leapt forward and lifted the yellow tape for him, high so that Spiro did not have to bow down.

"*Procuratore*," Ercole began.

The man cut him off with a stream of Italian.

The young officer said nothing but looked down and nodded every few seconds as Spiro continued to speak to him.

Ercole said something, nodding to Maziq, sitting in the back of the ambulance now, looking much better.

Again, Spiro shot words his way, clearly unhappy.

"*Sì, Procuratore.*"

Then the young officer turned to her. "He says we can leave now."

"I'd like to search with the team."

"No, that is not possible," Spiro said.

"I'm a crime scene officer by profession."

Michelangelo appeared in the dim doorway. He spotted Spiro and approached. He spoke to him for a moment.

Ercole translated. "They have finished the search. No sign of the Composer. They've gone down all the aqueducts and searched all the rooms in the basement. There is a supply tunnel that leads to the subway station. No sign he was anywhere there."

"The building above the basement." She nodded to the structure behind them.

Michelangelo said, "Is sealed off with concretes. No entrance is possible from *sotto terra*."

As the woman forensic officer walked past her she said, with a smile, "We're going to step the grid."

Sachs blinked.

"Yes, we know who you are. We use *Ispettore* Lincoln Rhyme's book in our lessons. It is not in Italian but we took turns translating. You are both an inspiration. Welcome to Italy!"

They vanished through the doorway.

Spiro fired another dozen sentences to Ercole, then walked off toward the ancient doorway, pulling on his own blue latex gloves.

Ercole translated, "*Procuratore* Spiro appreciates your assistance and your offer to help with the scene but he thinks it would be best, for continuity's sake, if the investigation is conducted by Italian law enforcement."

Sachs decided that to push the matter further would merely embarrass

Ercole. He looked desperately to the Mégane and lifted a hand to her shoulder, as if to direct her toward it. Her glance at him had the effect of lowering the limb as if it were in free fall, and she knew he would never try to usher her anywhere again.

As they approached the car he looked tentatively at the driver's seat.

Sachs said, "You drive."

To Ercole's great relief.

She handed him the keys.

Once she and Ercole were settled and the engine running, she asked, "That line you gave me about continuity? Is that what Spiro really said?"

Ercole was blushing and concentrating on getting the car in first gear. "It was a rough translation."

"Ercole?"

He swallowed. "He said I was to get the woman—that is, you—out of the scene immediately, and if I let her—that is, again, you—talk to any officers again, much less the press, without his permission, he would have my job. Here, and in my own unit of Forestry."

Sachs nodded. Then asked, "Was 'woman' the word he really used?"

After a pause: "No, it was not." He signaled, let up on the clutch, then pulled gingerly into the street surrounding the square, as if his frail grandmother were sitting in the backseat.

CHAPTER 20

S tunned.

That was Rhyme's impression of Ali Maziq.

In the situation room at police headquarters Rhyme was watching the kidnap victim through open doorways, across the hall, an empty ground-floor office.

The scrawny man sat in a chair, clutching a bottle of Aranciata San Pellegrino soda. He'd already drunk one of the orange beverages, and several small drops dotted his beard. His face was gaunt—though this would be his natural state, Rhyme supposed, since his ordeal had been only a day or so in length. Dark circles under his eyes. Prominent ears and nose . . . and that impressive mass of wiry black hair that wholly enveloped his scalp and lower face.

Rossi, Ercole and Sachs were with Rhyme. There was little for Thom to do at the moment, so he'd left to check into the hotel and make sure the disabled accessibility was as the place claimed.

For a half hour, Maziq been interviewed by a Police of State officer, who was fluent in Arabic and English.

Sachs had wanted to be present, or to conduct her own interview, but Rossi had declined her request. Dante Spiro would have been behind that.

Finally, the officer concluded the interview and joined the others. He handed Rossi his notes, then returned to the office across the hall. He spoke to Maziq, who still seemed bewildered. He slowly rose and followed the officer down the corridor. He clutched his orange soda as if it were a lucky charm.

Rossi said, "He will stay here in protective custody for the time being. He is remaining in a, how do you say, a state? Confused state. Better that we keep an eye on him. And, with the Composer still out in the world, we do not know for certain that Maziq is safe. There is, of course, no motive that we can see."

"Who is he?" Sachs asked.

"He is an asylum-seeker from Libya. One of so many. He came here on a ship that crashed." He frowned and spoke to Ercole, who said, "Beached."

"Sì. *Beached* in Baia a week ago, a resort area northwest of Naples. He and forty others arrived there and were arrested. They had good fortune. The weather was good. They survived, all of them. That very day a ship sank off Lampedusa and a dozen died."

Sachs said, "If he'd been arrested why was he out in the countryside?"

"A very good question," Rossi said. "Perhaps it is helpful to explain our situation in Italy with regard to refugees. You are aware of the immigrants coming out of Syria, inundating Turkey and Greece and Macedonia?"

Current events held little interest for Rhyme, but the plight of refugees in the Middle East was everywhere in the news. He'd actually just read an article about the subject on the long flight from the United States.

"We have a similar problem here. It's a long, dangerous journey to Italy from Syria but a less long trip from Egypt, Libya and Tunisia. Libya is an utterly failed state; after the Arab Spring it became a land of civil war, with extremists on the rise. ISIS and other groups. There is terrible poverty too, in addition to the political turmoil. Adding to the problem, the drought and famine in sub-Saharan Africa are driving refugees from the south into Libya, which can hardly accommodate them. So human smugglers—who are also rapists and thieves—charge huge sums to ferry people to Lampedusa, which I mentioned. It is Italy's closest island to Africa." He sighed. "I used to vacation with my family in there, when I was a boy. Now I would never take my own children. So, the smugglers bring the poorer asylum-seekers there. Others, if they pay a premium, will be taken to the mainland—like Maziq—in hopes they can avoid arrest.

"But, like him, most are caught, though it is an overwhelming challenge for the army, navy and the police." He looked toward Rhyme. "It has not touched your country as much. But here it is a crisis of great proportions."

The article Rhyme had read on the plane was about a conference presently under way in Rome, on the refugee situation. The attendees, from all over the world, were looking for ways to balance the humanitarian need to help the unfortunates, on the one hand, and the concerns about economic hardship and security in the destination countries, on the other. Among the emergency measures under consideration, the story said, the U.S. Congress was considering a bill to allow 150,000 immigrants into the country, and Italy itself was soon to vote on a measure to relax deportation laws, though both proposals were controversial and were being met with strong opposition.

"Ali Maziq is typical of these people. Under the Dublin Regulation on asylum seeking, he was required to apply for asylum in the country of entry—Italy. He was run through Eurodac, and—"

"Dactylosopy?" Rhyme asked. The technical term for fingerprinting.

It was Ercole who answered, "Yes, that is correct. Refugees are fingerprinted and undergo a background check."

Rossi continued, "So, this is Maziq's situation. He passed the initial review—no criminal or terrorist connections. If so, he would have been deported immediately. But he was cleared so he was removed from the intake camp and placed in a secondary site. These are hotels or old military barracks. They can slip out, as many do, but if they don't return they will be deported to their home country when caught.

"Maziq was staying in a residence hotel in Naples. Not a very pleasant place but serviceable. As for the events leading up to the kidnapping, he himself has no memory of what happened. The interviewer was inclined to believe him, because of the trauma of the kidnapping—the drugs and the lack of oxygen. But Daniela canvassed the hotel and a fellow refugee said Maziq told him he was planning on taking a bus to meet someone for dinner near D'Abruzzo. It's a small town in the countryside."

Sachs said, "We should find that guy he ate with and talk to him. *He* might have seen the Composer. Maybe tailing Maziq."

Rossi said, "There is a possibility about that. The Postal Police have analyzed the data from the phone card found where he was kidnapped. It is surely his, rather than the Composer's. He used a prepaid mobile, as all refugees do. Just before he was kidnapped he made calls to other prepaids—in Naples, in Libya and to an Italian town in the north, Bolzano, not far from the border. The Postal Police believe they can correlate the pings. You understand?"

"Yes," Rhyme said. "To find out where he was when he was at dinner."

"Precisely. They will let me know soon."

Sachs asked, "What does he have to say?"

"He remembers very little. He believes he was blindfolded much of the time. He awoke in the reservoir and his kidnapper was gone."

Unsmiling Beatrice—as womanly round as a Botticelli model—walked from the laboratory to the situation room.

"*Ecco.*" She held up a few printouts.

Ercole picked up a Sharpie and stepped to the board. She shook her head, adamantly, and took the marker from his hand. She glanced at Rossi and spoke.

Ercole frowned, while Rossi laughed. He explained, "She has said the Forestry officer's handwriting is not the best. He will read the results of the Scientific Police's analysis in English and she will write it on our chart. He will assist her in translation."

As the man read from the sheets, the woman's stubby fingers skittered over the pad on the easel in, yes, it was true, quite elegant handwriting.

"THE COMPOSER" KIDNAPPING, VIALE MARGHERITA, 22, NAPLES

— Site: Roman aqueduct reservoir.

— Victim: Ali Maziq.

    — Refugee, temporarily housed at Paradise Hotel, Naples.

— Minor injuries to neck and throat from strangulation.

— Minor dehydration.

— Disorientation and memory loss from drugs and lack of oxygen.

— Trace from clothing of Victim:

    — Variant of drug, amobarbital.

    — Residue of liquid chloroform.

    — Clay-based dirt, source unknown.

— Footprints:

    — Victim's.

    — Converse Cons, Size 45, same as at other scenes.

— Bottle, containing water. No source determined.

— Nokia phone, prepaid mobile (sent to Postal Police for analysis), EID number indicates bought for cash two days ago at tobacco store on Viale Emanuele. Phone short-circuited in water spill upon entry to site. SIM card revealed five calls earlier in day from one number, prepaid, no longer active.

    — DNA on phone (sweat, most likely).

      — Matches that of Composer.

— Trace of olanzapine, antipsychotic drug.

— Small amount of sodium chloride, propylene glycol, mineral oil, glyceryl monostearate, polyoxyethelene stearate, stearyl alcohol, calcium chloride, potassium chloride, methylparaben, butylparaben.

— Duct tape. No source determined.

— Cotton cloth, used as gag. No source determined.

— Noose, made of two musical instrument strings, E string for double-bass instrument. Similar to noose from crime scene in New York used on victim Robert Ellis.

— Bucket, common. No source determined.

— Lock and hasp, barring front door. Common. No source determined.

— Wooden rod, improvised gallows. Common. No source determined.

— No fingerprints, other than Victim's. Smudge marks suggest latex gloves.

— Related: Uploaded video on NowChat video posting service, four minutes, three seconds, depicting Victim, noose. Music playing: "Waltz of the Flowers" from *The Nutcracker* and human gasping (possibly Victim's).

    — Postal Police attempting to trace upload, but use of proxies and virtual private networks is slowing search.

Beatrice then taped up a dozen crime scene photographs of the water reservoir where Maziq had been held, as well as the entryway to the old building, the aqueduct and the musty brick basement.

Ercole stared at the pictures of the reservoir, which seemed to depict a medieval torture chamber. "A grim place."

Rhyme said nothing to the Forestry officer but scanned the chart. "Well, I mentioned crazy. I didn't see how right I was."

"What is that you mean, Captain Rhyme?"

"You see the sodium chloride, propylene glycol and so on?"

"Yes. What is that?"

"Electroconductive jelly. It's applied to the skin for electroconvulsive shock treatments for psychotics. Rare nowadays."

"Could the Composer be seeing a mental doctor here?" Ercole asked. "For those treatments?"

"No, no," Rhyme said. "The procedure takes time in the hospital. It's probably from the same place where the Composer got the antipsychotic drug: a U.S. hospital. He's functioning well enough, so I'd guess he had the treatment a few days before the New York attack. And what's amobarbital? Another antipsychotic?"

Sachs said, "I'll check the NYPD database." A moment later she reported, "It's a fast-acting sedative to combat panic attacks. It was developed a hundred years ago in Germany as a truth serum—it didn't work for that but doctors found it had a side effect of quickly calming agitated or aggressive subjects."

Many bipolar and schizophrenic patients, Rhyme knew from past cases, were often racked with anxiety.

Another figure stepped slowly into the doorway. It was Dante Spiro, who scanned everyone with an expressionless face.

"*Procuratore*," Ercole said.

The prosecutor cocked his head and wrote something in his leatherbound book.

For some reason, Ercole Benelli witnessed this with concern, Rhyme noted.

Spiro slipped the book away and reviewed the evidence chart. He said only, "English. Ah."

Then he turned to Sachs and Rhyme. "Now. Your involvement in this case is to be limited to these four walls. Are you in agreement, Inspector?" A nod toward Rossi.

"Of course. Yes."

"Mr. Rhyme, you are here by our grace. You have no authority to investigate a crime in this country. Your contributions to analyzing the evidence will be appreciated, if they prove helpful. As they have, and I acknowledge that. And any thoughts you might have about the Composer's frame of mind will be taken into account too. But beyond that, no. Am I understood?"

"Perfectly," Rhyme muttered.

"Now one more thing I wish to say. On a subject that has been raised before. Extradition. *You* have lost jurisdiction over the Composer and his crimes in America, while we have gained it. You will wish to try for extradition but I will fight it most strenuously." He eyed them for a moment. "Let me please give you a lesson in the law, Mr. Rhyme and Detective Sachs. Imagine a town in Italy called Cioccie del Lupo. The name is a joke, you see. It's not a real place. It means Wolf Tits."

"Romulus and Remus, the founding of Rome myth," Rhyme said. His voice was bored because *he* was bored. He stared at the newsprint pads on the easel.

Ercole said, "The twins, suckling on a wolf."

Rhyme corrected, absently, "The female *suckles*, the baby *sucks*."

"Oh. I didn't—"

Spiro cut Ercole short with a glare and continued to Rhyme: "The legal lesson is this: Lawyers from America do not win cases in Cioccie del Lupo. Lawyers from Cioccie del Lupo win cases in Cioccie de Lupo. And you are Americans firmly in the city center of Cioccie del Lupo at the moment. You will not win an extradition, so it will be better for you if that thought vanishes from your mind."

Rhyme said, "Maybe we should concentrate on catching him. Don't you think?"

Spiro said nothing but slowly withdrew his phone and sent a text or email.

Rossi stirred a bit, uneasy at the exchange.

Ercole said, "*Procuratore*, Inspector, I have a thought and I would like to pursue it."

After a moment Spiro put his phone away and lifted an eyebrow toward the young man. "*Sì?*"

"We should set up surveillance at the place where we found Maziq. The entrance to the aqueduct."

"Surveillance?"

"Yes. Of course." Ercole was smiling at Spiro's apparent inability to see what was obvious to him. "There has been no press announcement. The police have left the area. There is tape on the door, but you must get close to see that. He might return to the scene of the crime and when he gets within the area, slap! We can arrest him. When I was there I noted hiding places across the street where one could remain concealed."

"You don't think that would be a waste of our resources—which we know are more limited than I would hope for."

Another grin. "Not at all. Waste? How do you see that?"

Spiro flung his arm in the air. "Why do I even bother? Is that what you do in the woods, as a Forestry officer? Disguise yourself as a stag, a bear? And wait for a poacher?"

"I just was . . ." Then Italian trickled from his mouth.

Rhyme glanced at the doorway and noted that another officer stood in the hallway, watching the exchange. He was a handsome young man, dressed quite stylishly. He was studying Ercole's blushing face with a neutral expression.

"I simply thought it made sense, sir."

Rhyme decided to end the mystery. "He will not be back."

"No?"

"No," Spiro said. "Tell him why, Mr. Rhyme."

"Because of the water that spilled when you and Sachs opened the door."

"I do not understand."

"Do you see what the water drenched?"

Ercole looked toward the pictures. "The phone."

"The Composer set up the table and the items on it very carefully. Anyone opening the door—especially quickly—would knock the bottle of water over, shorting out the phone."

Ercole closed his eyes briefly. "Yes, of course. The Composer would call every fifteen minutes or so and as long as the mobile rang he knew no one was there. When he called and it was dead, he would realize that someone had breached the door. And it was unsafe to return. So simple, yet I missed it."

Spiro cast a glance down his nose at Ercole. Then he asked, "Where is Maziq now?"

"A protective cell," Rossi said. "Here."

"Forestry Officer," Spiro said.

"Yes, sir?"

"Make yourself useful and find our Arabic-speaking officer. I am interested in that substance, the electroconductive gel."

"*Allora . . .*" Ercole fell silent.

"What do you wish to say?"

The officer cleared his throat.

Rhyme broke in again. "Our supposition was that it was from the Composer. He's taking antipsychotic drugs, so we assumed he'd undergone ECS treatment."

Spiro replied, "That is logical. But it's not impossible that Maziq was being treated in Libya for a condition. And I would like to eliminate that as a possibility."

Rhyme nodded, for it was a theory that he had not considered, and it was a valid one.

"*Sì, Procuratore.*"

"And that other substance, amobarbital?" Spiro gazed at the chart.

Sachs told him it was a sedative the Composer took to ward off panic attacks.

"See if Maziq has ever taken that too."

"I will go now," Ercole said.

"Then go."

After he'd left, Rhyme said, "Prosecutor Spiro. It's rare that someone knows the raw ingredients of electroconductive gel." Rhyme had concluded that's what the ingredients were, before the prosecutor had arrived.

"Is it?" Spiro asked absently. His eyes were on the chart. "We learn many things in this curious business of ours, don't we?"

Stepping outside the situation room, Ercole Benelli nearly ran directly into Silvio De Carlo, Rossi's favorite boy.

The Stylista, the Fashionista of the Police of State.

Mamma mia. And now I will endure the comments.

Will De Carlo snidely remark on my mopping up spilled mineral water too, or just the most recent dressing-down by Spiro?

More Forestry Corps comments?

Zucchini Cop. Pig Cop...

Ercole thought for a moment about walking past the young man, who was again dressed in clothing that Ercole not only couldn't afford but wouldn't have had the taste to select, even if he'd been given the run of a Ferragamo warehouse. But then he decided, No. No running. As when he was young and boys would torment him about his gangly build and clumsiness at sports he'd learned that it was best to confront them, even if you ended up with a bloody nose or split lip.

He looked De Carlo in the eye. "Silvio."

"Ercole."

"Your cases going well?"

But the assistant inspector wasn't interested in small talk. He looked past Ercole and up and down the corridor. His rich brown eyes settled on the Forestry officer once more. He said, "You have been lucky."

"Lucky?"

"With Dante Spiro. The offenses you have committed..."

Offenses?

"...have not been so serious. He might have cut your legs out from underneath you. Stuck you like a pig."

Ah, a reference to the Forestry Corps.

De Carlo continued, "Yet you received what amounted to a slap with a glove."

Ercole said nothing but waited for the insult, the sneer, the condescension, not knowing what form it might take.

How would he respond?

It hardly mattered; whatever he said it would backfire. He would make a buffoon of himself. As always with the Silvio De Carlos of the world.

But then the officer continued, "If you want to survive this experience, if you want to move from Forestry into Police of State, as I suspect you do—and this might be your only opportunity—you must learn how to work with Dante Spiro. Do you swim, Ercole?"

"I...yes."

"In the sea?"

"Of course."

They were in Naples. Every boy could swim in the sea.

De Carlo said, "So you know riptides. You never fight them, because you can't win. You let them take you where they will and then, slowly, gently you swim diagonally back to shore. Dante Spiro is a riptide. With Spiro, you never fight him. That is to say, contradict him. You never question him. You agree. You suggest he is brilliant. If you have an idea that you feel must be pursued and is at odds with him then you must find a way to achieve your goal obliquely. Either in a way that he can't learn about, or one that seems—*seems*, mind you—compatible with his thinking. Do you understand?"

Ercole did understand the words but he would need time to translate them to practical effect. This was a very different way of policing than he was used to.

For the moment he said, "Yes, I do."

"Good. Fortunately, you're under the wing of a kinder—and equally talented—man. Massimo Rossi will protect you to the extent he can. He and Spiro are peers and respect each other. But he can't save you if you fling yourself into the lion's mouth. As you seem inclined to do."

"Thank you for this."

"Yes." De Carlo turned and started to walk away then looked back. "Your shirt."

Ercole looked down at the cream-colored shirt he had pulled on this morning beneath his gray uniform jacket. He hadn't realized the jacket was unzipped.

"Armani? Or one of his protégés perhaps?" De Carlo asked.

"I dressed quickly. I don't know the label, I'm afraid."

"Ah, well, it is quite fine."

Ercole could tell that these words were not ironic and that De Carlo truly admired the shirt.

He offered his thanks. Pointedly he did not add that the shirt had been stitched together not in Milan but in a Vietnamese factory and was sold not in a boutique in the chic Vomero district of Naples but from a cart on the rough and rugged avenue known as the Spaccanapoli by an Albanian vendor. The negotiated price was four euros.

They shook hands and the assistant inspector wandered off, pulling an iPhone, in a stylish case, from a stylish back pocket.

CHAPTER 21

Not in Kansas anymore.

Walking down the residential portion of this Neapolitan street—dinnertime and therefore not so crowded—Garry Soames thought of this clichéd line from *The Wizard of Oz*. And then he whispered it aloud, glancing at a young brunette, long, long hair, long legs, conversing on a cell phone, passing by. It was a certain type of look, and she returned it in a certain way, eyes not exactly lingering, but remaining upon his sculpted Midwest American face a fraction of a second longer than a phone talker would do otherwise.

Then the woman, the epitome of southern Italian élan, and her swaying, sexy stride, were gone.

Damn. Nice.

Garry continued on. His eyes then slipped to two more young women, chatting, dressed as sharply—and as tactically—as any hot girl on the Upper East Side in Manhattan.

Unlike Woman One, a moment ago, *they* both ignored him but Garry didn't care. He was in a very good mood. And what twenty-three-year-old wouldn't be, having exchanged his home state of Missouri (sorta, kinda like Kansas) for Italy (Oz without the flying monkeys)?

The athletic young man—built like a running back—hitched his heavy backpack higher on his shoulder and turned the corner that would take him to his apartment on Corso Umberto I. His head hurt slightly—a bit too much Vermentino and (Heaven help him!) cheap grappa at his early supper a half hour ago.

But he'd earned it, finishing his class assignments early in the afternoon and then wandering the streets, practicing his Italian. Slowly, he was learning the language, which had at first seemed overwhelming, largely because of the concept of gender. Carpets were boys, tables were girls.

And accents! Just the other day he'd raised eyebrows and earned laughs when, at a restaurant, he'd ordered penises with tomato sauce; the word for male genitalia was dangerously close to penne, the pasta (and to the word for bread too).

Little by little, though, he was learning the language, learning the culture.

Poco a poco . . .

Feeling good, yes.

Though he would have to rein in the late-night parties. Too much drinking. Too many women. Well, no, *that* was an oxymoron; one could not have too many women. But one could have too many possessive and temperamental and needy women.

The kind that he, naturally, ended up bedding all too often.

Naples was far safer than parts of his hometown of St. Louis but instinct told him he probably shouldn't sleep over in strangers' apartments quite so much, waking to the girl, bleary-eyed, staring at him uncertainly, muttering things. Then asking him to leave.

Just control it, he told himself.

Thinking specifically of Valentina, a few weeks ago.

What was her last name?

Yes, Morelli. Valentina Morelli. Ah, such beautiful, sexy brown eyes . . . which had turned far less beautiful and far more chilling when he'd balked at what he'd apparently suggested as they lay in bed. It seemed he'd told her—thank you, Mr. *Vino*—that she could come to the United States with him, and they could see San Diego together. Or San Jose. Or somewhere.

She'd become a raging she-wolf and flung a bottle (the expensive Super-Tuscan, but empty, thank God) into his bathroom mirror, shattering both.

She'd muttered words to him in Italian. It seemed like a curse.

So. Just be more careful.

"Spend the year in Europe, kiddo," his father had told him, upon his departure from Lambert Field. "Enjoy, graduate at the bottom of your class. Experience life!" The tall man—an older version of Garry, with silver in his blond hair—had then lowered his voice: "But. You do a single milligram of coke or pot and you're on your own. You end up in a Naples jail, all you'll get from us is postcards, and probably not even that."

And Garry could truthfully tell his father that he'd never tried any coke and he'd never tried any pot.

There was plenty else to amuse him.

Like Valentina. (San Diego? Really? He'd used *that* as a come-on line?) Or Ariella. Or Toni.

Then he thought of Frieda.

The Dutch girl he'd met at Natalia's party on Monday. Yes, picturing them being on the roof, her beautiful hair dipping onto his shoulder, her firm breast against his arm, her damp lips against his.

"You are, I am saying, a pretty boy, isn't it? You are the football player?"

"Your football or mine?"

Which broke her up.

"Foot…ball…" Her mouth on his again. Above them spanned the Neapolitan evening, milky with million stars. He and this beautiful Dutch girl, blond and tasting of mint, alone in a deserted alcove of the roof.

Her eyelids closing…

And Garry looking down at her, thinking: Sorry, sorry, sorry…It's out of my hands. I can't control it.

Now he shuddered and closed his eyes and didn't want to think about Frieda again.

Garry's mood grew dark, and he decided that, hell, he'd open up a new grappa when he got home.

Frieda…

Shit.

Approaching the doorway of the old flat. It was a shabby two-story place, on a quiet stretch of road. The building had probably been a single-family at one point but then converted into a two-unit apartment. He lived in the basement.

He paused and found his key. Then Garry was startled by two people walking up to him. He was cautious. He'd been mugged once already. An ambiguous threat; two skinny but mean-eyed men had asked to borrow money. He'd given it up, along with his watch, which they hadn't asked for but had happily taken.

But then he saw that these two were police officers—middle-aged, stocky both of them, a man and woman, in the blue uniforms of the Police of State.

Still, of course, his guard was up.

"Yes?"

Speaking good English, the woman asked, "You are Garry Soames?"

"I am."

"May I see your passport?"

In Italy, everyone was required to carry—and produce upon demand— a passport or identity card. It rankled the civil libertarian within him but he complied without protest.

She read it. And slipped it into her own pocket.

"Hey."

"You were at a party Monday night, in the flat of Natalia Garelli."

His memories of just a few moments ago.

"I . . . well, yes. I was."

"You were there all night?"

"What's all night?"

"When were you there?"

"I don't know, from maybe ten p.m. until three or so. What's this all about?"

"Mr. Soames," the man said, his accent thicker than his partner's. "We are putting you under arrest for certain events that occurred at that party. I would like you to present your hands."

"My—"

Steel cuffs appeared.

He hesitated.

The male cop: "Please, sir. I would recommend you do this."

The woman lifted the backpack off his shoulder and began to look through it.

"You can't do that!"

She ignored him and continued to rummage.

The man cuffed him.

The woman completed the search of his bag and said nothing. The man searched his pockets, taking his wallet and leaving everything else. He found three unopened condoms and held them up. The two officers shared a look. Everything the man took he placed in an evidence bag.

Each taking an arm, they led him up the street to an unmarked car.

"What's this all about?" he repeated stridently. They were silent. "I haven't done anything!" He switched to Italian and said, in a desperate voice, "*Non ho fatto niente di sbagliato!*"

Still no response. He snapped, "*Qual è il crimine?*"

"The charge is battery and rape. It is my duty to inform you that, as you are now under arrest, you have the right to an attorney and an interpreter. Signor, please, get into the car."

CHAPTER 22

Rhyme and Sachs examined the evidence chart that Beatrice and Ercole had assembled.

Rossi and Spiro stood behind them, also scanning, scanning, scanning.

Beatrice had done a solid job, isolating and identifying the materials.

"Do you have a geological database?" Rhyme asked Rossi. "Where we can narrow the source of that clay-based soil?"

Rossi summoned the woman from the crime lab.

When posed the question, Beatrice answered. The inspector's translation: "She has compared the soil with a number of samples but it is common with those found in hundreds of areas and can't be narrowed down more."

Rhyme asked, "Can we canvass stores that would sell duct tape, wooden rods and buckets?"

Rossi and Spiro regarded each other with amusement. It was for Rossi to say, "That is beyond our resources."

"Well, at least can we see if the tobacco store where he bought the phone has a video camera?"

The inspector said, "Daniela and Giacomo have that assignment, yes."

Ercole Benelli appeared in the doorway and entered cautiously, almost as if worried he'd be physically assaulted by Dante Spiro.

"Sir, no, Ali Maziq has not had electroconvulsive treatment. He does not know what that is. And he has taken no medication. Well, I am not accurate. He takes Tylenol for his pains."

"That's not relevant, Forestry Officer."

"No, of course, *Procuratore*."

Spiro said, "Electroconvulsive, antipsychotic drugs, anti-anxiety drugs. So the Composer was surely a patient at some mental facility recently. Have you searched mental hospitals?"

Rhyme wondered if the question was calculated to be a barb to counter what he might perceive as Rhyme's criticism of the Italians' inability to search for the sources for the wooden rod, tape and bucket, which it was not.

"There are too many hospitals and doctors to check. And the theft of a small amount of the sedative wouldn't be reported in the national database. Our NCIC shows no similar crimes. Ever."

Beyond our resources...

Spiro regarded the evidence chart. "And no clue as to where he's holed up."

Surprised at the old-time American expression.

"Holed up?" Ercole asked tentatively.

"Where he's staying. Where he took the victim right after the kidnapping."

"It wasn't there, at the aqueduct?"

"No," Spiro said and offered nothing more.

Rhyme explained, "He hadn't peed. Or defecated." He knew this because either Sachs or the medical team would have observed and reported if he'd done so. "The Composer has a base of operation in or near Naples. He videoed Maziq in the aqueduct reservoir room but he assembled and uploaded the video from somewhere else. Maybe something there will tell us where. Maybe not." A nod toward the chart.

Rossi answered his mobile and had a conversation. After he disconnected, he said, "That was my colleague with the Postal Police. They have completed the analysis of Maziq's phone card. They have significantly narrowed the area where he made calls within the hour before he was kidnapped at the bus stop. They center on a cellular phone tower about ten kilometers northeast of the town of D'Abruzzo."

Spiro said to Rossi, "I know nothing about the area. Why would the Composer be hunting that far from downtown? *Allora.* Can your officers get out there, Massimo? Tomorrow?"

"Possibly. Not, however, until later. Daniela and Giacomo will be canvassing here. Why don't we send Ercole?"

"Him?" Spiro looked his way. "Have you ever canvassed before?"

"I've interviewed suspects and witnesses. Many times."

Rhyme wondered if the prosecutor would make some cruel comment about canvassing wildlife. But the man merely shrugged. "Yes, all right."

"I will do it, *sì.*" Ercole paused, glancing to the room where Maziq had been interviewed. "Can you assign an Arabic speaker to come with me? Perhaps the officer who spoke with him earlier?"

Rossi asked, "Arabic, why?"

"Because of what you said, *Procuratore.*"

"Me?"

"Yes, just now. Why would he go all that distance if there was not a Muslim community there? He doesn't speak Italian. I would guess he met with an Arabic speaker."

Spiro considered this. "Perhaps."

But Rossi said, "Our translators, Marco and Federica, are busy solidly." To Rhyme: "Our greatest lack, *one* of our greatest lacks, is Arabic interpreters, given the refugee flood."

The young officer frowned. To Sachs he said, "You were speaking Arabic."

"Me? Oh, I—"

"You were quite proficient," Ercole said quickly. Then to Rossi, "She was speaking to Maziq." To Sachs he said, "Perhaps you could assist." Then he grew stern. "Only for that purpose. You translate for me, and say nothing else."

Sachs blinked.

Rhyme reflected that there was something faintly comical about the gentle young man trying to sound like a prickly, lecturing father.

Ercole said to the prosecutor, "I recall what you said, *Procuratore.* She will translate only, and if anyone were to ask, that is what I will tell them. But I think it is important, if you agree, to find this dinner companion of Maziq. Or find evidence the Composer might have left or witnesses who saw him. Perhaps this will lead to establishing the pattern you were speaking of."

"But under no circumstances—"

"Will she utter a word to the press."

"Correct."

Spiro looked from Ercole to Sachs. He said, "On that condition. Complete silence other than to interpret the Forestry officer's words. If there is no need, you will remain in the car."

"Fine."

Spiro walked to the doorway. There he paused and turned back to Sachs. "*Hal tatahaddath alearabia?*"

She eyed him evenly. "*Nem fielaan.*"

Spiro met her gaze for a moment, then pulled a lighter from his pocket and, clutching it and his cheroot together, continued into the corridor.

Rhyme suspected that with those two exchanges, the prosecutor had used up a good portion of his entire Arabic vocabulary. He knew Sachs's numbered about two dozen words.

He swiveled to see Thom standing in the doorway.

"And we're going to the hotel," the aide said firmly.

"I need—"

"You need rest."

"There are a dozen unanswered questions."

"I'll unplug the controller and push you to the van."

The chair weighed close to a hundred pounds. But Rhyme knew Thom was fully capable of doing just what he'd threatened.

A grimace. "Fine, fine, fine." He turned the chair and headed out into the hallway, leaving it to Sachs to say good night for both of them.

CHAPTER 23

Close to 11 p.m.

Stefan was driving outside Naples, edgy. Anxious. He wanted to start the next composition. He *needed* to start the next composition.

Wiping sweat, wiping. Stuffing the tissues into his pocket. So very careful to avoid that DNA crap.

He was aware of noises, of course, always. But tonight they didn't calm him or dull the anxiety: the car's hum, the shush of rubber on asphalt, the two dozen tones from one dozen insects, an owl, no two. An airplane overhead, imposing its imperial growl over everything else.

Evenings are best for listening: The cool damp air lifts sounds from ground and trees, sounds you'd never otherwise hear, and carries them to you like the Wise Men's gifts.

Stefan was careful to drive the speed limit—he had no license, and the vehicle was stolen. But there were no daughters, or sons, of Greek gods close on his trail. A Police of State car passed him. A Carabinieri car passed him. Neither driver paid him, or anyone else on the crowded road, any mind.

The meds humming through his system, and his muse, Euterpe, hovering in his heart, helped, but still he remained unsteady. Shaky-hand, sweaty-skin.

As for his most recent participant in the composer's art, Ali Maziq, he thought nothing at all. The skinny little creature no longer existed to Stefan. He'd played his part in Stefan's journey to Harmony—and a fine contribution he had been.

He hummed a bit of "The Waltz of the Flowers."

Gasp, two, three, *gasp,* two, three...

The car rose to the crest of a hill and he pulled onto the weedy shoulder and stopped. He gazed over the fields of Capodichino. This district, now a suburb of Naples, had been the site of a heroic battle: the Neapolitans against the Nazi occupiers on the third day of the famed—and successful—uprising known as the Four Days of Naples in 1943.

These fields were home to Naples airport and a number of businesses, small factories and warehouses. Modest residences too.

And here you would find something else, something that insistently drew the gaze of any passerby: the Capodichino Reception Center, one of the largest refugee camps in Italy. It was many acres in size and filled with orderly rows of blue plasticized tents, *Ministero dell'Interno* emblazoned in stark white letters on the roofs.

The camp was surrounded by an eight-foot fence topped with barbed wire, though it was flimsy and little-patrolled, Stefan noted. Even now, so late, the place was bustling. Many, many people milled about, or sat or squatted. He had heard that all the camps in Italy were vastly overcrowded, security inadequate.

All of which was great for Stefan, of course. A chaotic hunting ground is a good hunting ground.

Having verified that there were few guards, in vehicles or on foot, patrolling the roads surrounding the camp, he now pulled back onto the road and maneuvered his old Mercedes forward. He parked not far away from the main entrance, climbed out. He walked closer, mixing with a cluster of lethargic reporters, probably backgrounding human interest pieces. Protesters too. Most placards he didn't understand but several were in English.

Go Back Home!

Scanning the camp: It was even more crowded than when he'd first been here, just recently. But otherwise, little had changed: Men in taqiyah or kufi skullcaps. Nearly all the women were in hijabs or wearing other head coverings. A few of the arrivals had suitcases but most carried cloth or plastic bags, filled with their only remaining possessions in the world. Some clutched the thick quilted blankets they would have been given by the Italian navy, after their human smugglers' boats had been interdicted—or after they'd been fished from the Mediterranean. A few still held orange life vests, also given out by the military and NGOs and, occasionally, the smugglers themselves (at least those worried that drowned customers were bad for business).

Many of the refugees were families. The second-most populous group seemed to be single men. There were hundreds upon hundreds of children. Some playing, cheerful. Most sullen, bewildered.

And exhausted.

The soldiers and police officers were plentiful and, given the many different uniforms, must have come from a number of branches of government. They seemed weary and stern but appeared to treat the refugees well. None of them paid the least attention to Stefan, just like the other day.

Chaos.

Hunting ground...

Something caught his eye. Stefan could see a man slipping out at the far end of the fence, through a slit cut vertically in the link. Was he escaping? But, watching, he noticed the man stroll nonchalantly up to one of a dozen vendors ringing the camp, selling food, clothing and personal items. He made a purchase and then returned.

Yes, the camp security was porous.

Stefan bought food from one of these stands, a Middle Eastern dish. It was tasty but he had little appetite. He simply wanted some calories for the energy. He ate as he walked up and down the roadway along the camp. He then returned to the main gate.

Soon a large panel truck arrived, its precious cargo yet more refugees, with varying degrees of dark skin and wearing garb typical of North Africa, he supposed. Some too, he guessed, would be from Syria, though the journey over so many kilometers of rough sea—to the western shore of Italy—seemed unimaginable.

He heard, in his mind's ear, the creak of boards of the frail ships, the thump of the Zodiac boat pontoons, the unsteady stutter of struggling motors, the cries of babies, the slap of waves, the call of birds, the hiss and flutter of wind. Eyes closed, shivering as he was momentarily overwhelmed by hearing sounds he could not hear. He calmed and wiped the sweat, putting away the tissue. See, he thought to Her, I'm being careful.

Always, for his muse.

The thirty-odd refugees disembarked from the newly arrived truck and stood near the entrance to the camp, under the eyes of two guards. No machine guns. Just white leather holsters containing pistols on lanyards. They were directing the arrivees into a processing station— a long, low table where four aid workers sat, over clipboards and laptops.

Stefan moved closer yet. It was so crowded that no one paid him any mind. He was near to a couple who stood sullen and exhausted looking— nearly as tired as the two-year-old child asleep in the mother's arms. They stepped to the table and the husband—they wore wedding rings—said, "Khaled Jabril." A nod to his wife. "Fatima." Then he brushed the child's hair. "Muna."

"I'm Rania Tasso," said the woman they stood before. Heads nodded, but no hands were shaken.

Khaled was dressed Western—jeans and a counterfeit Hugo Boss T-shirt. Fatima was scarfed and wore a long-sleeve tunic, but was also in jeans. They both had running shoes. The little girl was in a costume, yellow. Some Disney character.

The woman reviewing their passports, Rania, had dark-red hair, done in a double braid, down to the small of her back. The radio on her hip and badge dangling from her neck meant she was an employee of the organization. After some minutes of watching her, Stefan decided she was very senior, perhaps the director of the camp. She was attractive. Her nose was Romanesque and her skin an olive shade that suggested her Italian ancestry was mixed with Greek or perhaps Tunisian.

The refugees answered questions. And, oh my, Stefan did not like

Fatima's voice one bit. "Vocal fry," the tone was called—a condition afflicting more women than men, he believed. A rasping, growling quality to the voice.

She spoke more words.

Oh, he didn't like that sound at all.

Rania typed some data into the computer. She wrote some information—in Arabic—on a three-by-five card and handed it to Fatima, who then asked some questions. She was frowning. It was almost as if she, here by the grace of the country, were interviewing Rania about *her* intentions and worth.

The director answered patiently.

Fatima began to speak again, but her husband, Khaled, spoke softly to her—he had quite the pleasant baritone. Fatima fell silent and nodded. She said something else, which Stefan took to be words of apology.

Then the exchange was over and, clutching a backpack, two large plastic bags and their child, the couple vanished into the camp, directed down a long row to the back of the place.

Suddenly, and surprisingly, music swelled. Middle Eastern music. The sound came from the front of one of the tents, where a clutch of young men had set up a CD player. The music of the Arab world was curious. Not thematic, not narrative, it lacked the familiar timings and progressions of the West. This was like a tone poem, repetitive but in its own way pleasing. Seductive. Almost sensual.

If Ali Maziq's gasps provided the beat for Stefan's waltz, this music would be the buzz and hum of the body.

In any event, the music calmed him and stubbed out a budding Black Scream. The flow of sweat seemed to lessen.

Fatima paused in mid-step and aimed her beautiful but witchy face toward the cluster of young men. She frowned and spoke to them—in her sizzling voice.

Looking awkward, one shut the radio off.

So, not only did she cackle when she spoke, but she disliked music.

Euterpe would not like her.

And it was never wise to incur the anger of a muse. You thought they were charming, you thought they were delicate creatures who lived quietly in the sequestered world of art and culture, lounging about on Olympus. But they were, of course, the daughters of Olympus's most powerful and ruthless god.

THE LAND OF NO HOPE

CHAPTER 24

A melia Sachs was downstairs in the lobby of the hotel where they were staying, the Grand Hotel di Napoli.

Quite the place. The design was, she believed it was called, rococo. Gold-and-red wallpaper, flecked velvet, elaborate armoires, glass-fronted, filled with ceramics and silver and gold and ivory artifacts like ink wells, fans and key fobs. On the walls were paintings of Vesuvius—some depicting eruptions and some not. The artist might have applied brush to canvas on this very spot; looking east and south, one could see the sullen, dusky-brown pyramid. It seemed gentle, not the least imposing or ominous—but then, Sachs reflected, wasn't that the case with many killers?

Also on the walls of the Grand Hotel were photos of the famous, presumably guests or diners: Frank Sinatra and Dean Martin, Faye Dunaway, Jimmy Carter, Sophia Loren, Marcello Mastroianni, Harrison Ford, Madonna, Johnny Depp, and dozens of others, actors, musicians and politicians. Sachs recognized perhaps half of them.

"Breakfast, Signorina?" The clerk behind the desk was smiling.

"No, *grazie*." She was still on U.S. time, which meant her body was clocking in about 2 a.m. Besides, she'd stuck her head into the breakfast room, to get a glass of orange juice, and been overwhelmed by the spread. There was enough food for an entire day's calories. She wouldn't know where to begin.

At exactly nine, Ercole Benelli pulled up in front of the hotel. Via

Partenope was largely pedestrian but no one stopped the lanky man, dressed in his gray uniform, even if his vehicle was the well-worn baby-blue Mégane, missing any insignia, except for a bumper sticker with a silhouette of a bird on it. Curious.

She stepped outside into the heat and was rewarded with a spectacular view of the bay and, directly in front of the hotel, a castle, no less.

Ercole started to get out, keys in hand, but she waved him back into the driver's seat, and a look of relief spread over his face. No need for Formula One driving today.

She was amused to see a tube of Dramamine sitting in the cup holder. It had not been there yesterday.

Sachs took off her black jacket, revealing a beige blouse, tucked into black jeans, and dropped the Beretta into her shoulder bag, which she set on the floor.

They belted in. Ercole signaled—though his was the only car on the road—and steered into the crowded, chaotic streets of Naples.

"The hotel, she is nice?"

"Yes, very."

"It is quite famous. You saw the people who have stayed there?"

"Yes. It's a landmark, I assume. Nineteenth century?"

"Oh, no, no. There are certainly old buildings here—as you and I know from the ruins where Ali Maziq was held. But many of the wood and stone structures on the surface were destroyed."

"The war?"

"Yes, yes. Naples was the most bombed Italian city in World War Two. Maybe in all of Europe. I do not know that. More than two hundred air strikes. You understand, one thing I am worried about: You know I do not expect you to be my translator."

"That was a bit odd."

"Yes, yes. I know the area well. I know the countryside outside of Naples like my hand's back. And I know there are no Arab-speaking communities there. But, you see, I think this is an important possibility of a lead."

"Lincoln and I do too."

"But I am not up to the task. I don't know the questions to ask and the places to look. But you do. This is your specialty. And so I needed you."

"You played Spiro."

"Played?"

"Tricked."

His long face tightened. "I suppose I did. Someone, another officer, told me Spiro needs to be flattered and his opinions, however wrong, must be respected. That is what I did. Or I tried to do. I am not used to such games."

"It worked out. Thank you."

"Yes."

"Just as well. I only know a few Arabic phrases—like the one I answered Dante with. And then: 'Can I see some ID?' and 'Drop the weapon, hands in the air.'"

"Let us hope we don't need the last one of those."

They drove for ten minutes in silence. The landscape grew from densely urban to a mix of factories and warehouses and residences, then finally to farmland and small villages dusty and dull in the hazy autumn sun. Ercole piloted the car with great care. Sachs was making every effort to avoid even the appearance of impatience. The Mégane hovered just under the limit of ninety kph, about sixty mph. They were regularly being passed by cars—and even trucks—going much faster. One driver—in a Mini Cooper—seemed to be going twice their speed.

They passed a sprawling farm, which, for some reason, took Ercole's attention.

"Ah, look there. I will have to come back to that place."

She glanced to the left, where he was gesturing—with both hands. She'd noted that this seemed to be an Italian habit. However fast the ride, however congested the roads, drivers seemed unable to grip the wheel with both hands—sometimes not even with one—when having a conversation.

Sachs studied the farm. Pigs, she noted, were the most populous animals in the spread he was indicating, a rambling two acres of low buildings and a lot of mud. A powerful, disgusting smell swept into the car.

She noted Ercole was genuinely troubled.

"Part of my job is to monitor the condition of farm animals. And from a rapid glance it appears to me that those swine are kept in poor quarters."

To Sachs, they were pigs in mud.

"The farmer will have to improve their situation. Proper drainage and sewage. Healthy for the people, of course, and better for the animals. They have souls too. I firmly believe this."

They drove through the town of D'Abruzzo—Ercole explained that this was not to be confused with Abruzzo, a region of Italy east of Rome. She wasn't sure why he thought she'd make the mistake but thanked him anyway. They then continued into the rolling farmland and fallow ground where the Postal Police had reported that Ali Maziq's phone had been used.

Sachs had a map, on which was a large circled area, encompassing six small towns or clusters of stores, cafés, restaurants and bars where Maziq and his colleague might have met. She held it up for him. He nodded and pointed out one. "We're closest to there. In twenty minutes."

They drove along the two-lane road. Ercole spoke about any topics that came to mind: His pigeons, which he kept for no reason other than that he liked the cooing sound they made and the thrill of racing them. (Ah, the bumper sticker now made sense.) His modest apartment in a pleasant part of Naples, his family—two siblings, older brother and younger, both of whom were married—and his nephews, in particular. He talked reverently about his mother and father; they'd both passed away.

"*Allora*, may I ask? You and *Capitano* Rhyme, you will be married soon?"

"Yes."

"That is nice. When, do you think?"

"It was going to be within the next couple of weeks. Until the Composer. That delayed things."

Sachs told Ercole that Rhyme had been talking about Greenland for their honeymoon.

"That is true? Odd. I have seen pictures of the place. It is somewhat barren. I would recommend Italy. We have Cinque Terre, Positano—not so very far from here. Florence. Piemonte, Lago di Como. Courmayeur is where I would be married. It is where Monte Bianco is located, near the border, north. Ah, so beautiful."

"Are you seeing anyone?"

She had observed the admiring looks he'd shot toward Daniela Canton, and she wondered if they'd known each other before the Composer case. She seemed smart, if a bit serious; she certainly was gorgeous.

"No, no, not at the moment. It is one regret. That my mother did not see me married."

"You're young."

He shrugged. "I have other interests at the moment."

Ercole then launched into a discussion of his career and his desire to get into the Police of State or, even better, the Carabinieri. She asked the difference, and it seemed the latter was a military police organization, though it had jurisdiction over civil crimes, as well. Then there was the Financial Police, which covered crimes involving immigration as well as financial irregularities. This didn't appeal to him. He wanted to be a street cop, an investigator.

"Like you," he said, blushing and smiling.

It was clear that he saw the Composer case as an entry into that world.

He asked her too about policing in New York City, and she told him about her career—from fashion model to NYPD. And about her father, a beat patrol officer all his life.

"Ah, like father like daughter!" Ercole's eyes shone.

"Yes."

Soon they came to the first village on the list and began canvassing. It was a slow process. They would go into a restaurant or bar, approach the server or owner and Ercole would flash a picture of Maziq and ask if they had seen him on Wednesday night. The first time this happened, a lengthy and intense conversation ensued. Sachs took this as a good sign, thinking that the person he was speaking to had provided a lead.

As they returned to the car, she asked, "So he saw Maziq?"

"Who, the waiter? No, no, no."

"What were you talking about?"

"The government is desiring to build a new road nearby and that will improve business. He was saying that sales have been down lately. Even with the depressed price of gasoline, people don't seem to be taking trips out into the countryside because the old road can get washed out, even in a small rainstorm. And—"

"Ercole, we really should move along."

He closed his eyes briefly and nodded. "Oh. Yes, of course." Then he smiled. "In Italy, we enjoy our conversations."

Over the next two hours they hit eighteen establishments. The results were negative.

Just after noon they finished interviewing people in one small town and marked it off the list. Ercole looked at his watch. "I would say, we will have lunch."

She looked around the small intersection. "I could use a sandwich, sure."

"*Un panino, sì.* Possibly."

"Where can we get one to go? Coffee too."

"To go?"

"To take with us."

He seemed confused. "We . . . Well, we do not do that in Italy. Not in Campania, at least. No, nowhere that I know of in Italy. We will sit down. It won't take long." He nodded to a restaurant whose owner they had just interviewed. "That is good?"

"Looks fine to me."

They sat outside at a table covered by a vinyl sheet that depicted miniature Eiffel Towers, though French food did not appear on the menu.

"We should start with mozzarella. That's what Naples is known for— pizza, too. We invented it. Whatever they say in Brooklyn."

She blinked. "I'm sorry?"

"An article I read. A restaurant in Brooklyn in New York claimed to have created pizza."

"Where I live."

"No!" He was delighted to learn this. "Well, I bring no offense."

"None taken."

He ordered for them. Yes, fresh mozzarella to start and then pasta with *ragù*. He had a glass of red wine and she got an Americano coffee, which the waitress thought curious—apparently it was a beverage intended for *after* the meal.

Before the cheese, though, an antipasto plate, which they hadn't ordered, appeared, meats sliced microscopically thin and sausages. Bread too. And the drinks.

She ate a bite of the meat, then more. Salty and explosive with flavor. A moment later the mozzarella cheese came—not slices but a ball the size of a navel orange. One for each of them. She stared. "You eat it all?"

Ercole, already halfway through his, laughed at the nonsensical question. She ate some—it *was* the best she'd ever had, and she said so—and then pushed the plate away.

"You don't care for it, after all?"

"Ercole, it's too much. I usually have coffee and a half bagel for lunch."

"To go." He shook his head, winking. "That is unhealthy for you." His eyes glowed. "Ah, here, the pasta." Two plates arrived. "This is ziti, which we're famous for in Campania. It is made from our hard flour, but the very finely milled variety, *semolina rimacinata*. Topped with local *ragù*. The pasta is broken by hand before cooking. The gnocchi here would be good too—it's how we get around our Campanian disdain for potatoes—but that's a heavy dish for lunch."

"You must cook," Sachs said.

"Me?" He seemed amused. "No, no, no. But everyone in Campania knows food. You just...you just do."

The sauce was rich and dense and dressed with just a bit of meat cooked down to tenderness. And there wasn't too much; it didn't overwhelm the pasta, which had a richness and flavor of its own.

They ate in silence for a few moments.

Sachs asked, "What else do you do in...what's your organization called?"

"In English you would say Corps of Forestry of the State. CFS. We do many things. There are thousands of us officers. Fight forest fires—though I myself do not do that. We have a large fleet of aircraft. Helicopters, too, for rescues of climbers and skiers. Agricultural product regulation. Italy takes its food and wine very seriously. You know truffles?"

"The chocolates, sure."

A pause, as he processed her response. "Ah, no, no, no. Truffles, fungi. Mushrooms."

"Oh, right, the ones pigs hunt for."

"Dogs are better. There's a special breed that's used. They are very expensive and prized for their fine noses. I've run several cases of Lagotti Romagnolo kidnappings by truffle hunters."

"Must be tough. I mean, without a paw print database."

He laughed. "They say humor does not cross borders but that is quite funny. And, as a serious matter, it's a shame there is no such thing. Some owners put chips in their dogs, microchips, though I've heard that's not always safe."

He proceeded to explain about how white truffles from the north of Italy and black from central and south were extremely valuable, though the former more so. A single truffle could be worth a thousand euros.

He continued to tell her a story about his search for a local truffle counterfeiter, passing off Chinese varieties for Italian. "A travesty!" The Composer case had derailed his hunt. A grimace. "The *furfante* . . . the villain escaped. Six months of work gone." He scowled and finished his wine in a single gulp.

He received a text, read it, then replied.

Sachs lifted an eyebrow.

"Ah, not about the case. My friend. The pigeons I mentioned, he and I race them together. There is a race soon. Do you know anything about birds, Detective Sachs?"

"Amelia."

The only ones she had experience with were the generations of peregrine falcons that had nested outside Lincoln Rhyme's Central Park West town house. They were beautiful, striking and perhaps the most efficient and ruthless predator, pound for pound, in the world.

And their favorite meal was the fat, oblivious pigeons of New York City.

She said, "No, Ercole. Not a thing."

"I have Racing Homers. Mine compete at fifty to a hundred kilometers." A nod to the phone. "My friend and I have a team. It can be quite exciting. Very competitive. Some people complain that the pigeons are at risk. There are hawks, bad weather, man-made obstacles. But I would rather be a pigeon on a mission than one that sits all day on a statue of Garibaldi."

She chuckled. "That'd be my choice too."

Pigeon on a mission...

They'd taken a long-enough break. Sachs called for the check. He absolutely refused to let her pay.

They resumed their own mission.

And, curiously, the delay for lunch—the delicious lunch—paid off.

At the next town, they stopped at a restaurant in which the server had just come on duty; had they not taken their meal in the previous town they would have missed her. The waitress in Ristorante San Giancarlo was a slim blonde, with her grandmother's flip hairstyle and very up-to-date tats. She looked at the picture Sachs proffered of Ali Maziq and she nodded. Ercole translated: "The man in the picture was dining with a man who was Italian, though not from Campania, she believes. She herself is Serbian so she couldn't place the accent but it was not like the people in this region talk."

"Did she know him? Had she seen him before?"

"No," she said to Sachs, and spoke some more in Italian.

Ercole explained, telling Sachs that Maziq seemed uncomfortable the whole meal, looking around. The men spoke English but would fall silent when she approached. Maziq's companion—she didn't think they were friends—was "not so very nice." The big man, with a dark complexion and thick dark hair, complained that his soup was cold. Which it was not. And said the bill was wrong. Which it was not. His dark suit was dusty and he smoked foul cigarettes, not caring who was offended.

"They paid with a credit card?" Sachs asked, hoping.

"No," the waitress responded. "Euros. And they gave no tip, of course." A sour pout.

Sachs asked how they had arrived but the server wasn't sure. They had just walked in, from up the road.

Sachs inquired, "Did anyone seem to be interested in them? Anyone in a black car?"

She understood the English. "*Da!* I mean to say, yes." Her eyes widened. "Fascinated that you would be speaking of that."

She returned to Italian.

Ercole said, "Halfway through the meal a large black or dark-blue car drove by and slowed suddenly, as if the driver took an interest in the restaurant. She was thinking that she might be having rich tourists as customers. But no. He drove on."

"The driver might have seen them?"

"Yes," the waitress said. "Possible. The two men I am been talking about, they were outside. That *tavola*, table, there."

Sachs looked up and down the quiet street. On the other side of the road was a tree-filled lot and, behind that, farmland. "You said they fell silent but did you hear them say anything?"

After a conversation with the waitress, Ercole explained, "She did hear them mention Trenitalia—the national train service. She believed the Italian said 'you,' meaning Maziq, would have a six-hour trip and Maziq seemed discouraged by that. Six hours—that means he would be going north." He smiled. "We are not such a big country. They could almost be at the northern border in that time."

The woman had nothing more to add and seemed disappointed that they didn't want a second lunch. The tortellini was the best in southern Italy, she promised.

So, the Composer was cruising the streets looking for a likely target— an immigrant, possibly. And he had seen Maziq. What then? She scanned the hazy street, dead quiet. And then gestured for Ercole to follow her. They crossed the road and ducked through the stand of trees and bushes bordering the empty lot opposite the restaurant.

She pointed. They were looking at the tire treads of a car with a large wheelbase. The markings seemed similar to those of the Michelins from the bus-stop kidnapping. The vehicle had pulled into the back of the vacant lot and parked. The ground here was sparse grass and dank earth, and it was easy to see where the driver had gotten out and walked to the passenger's side—which faced the line of trees and bushes and, beyond, the very table where Maziq and his unpleasant companion had sat. It appeared that the Composer had opened the passenger's door and sat, facing outward, toward the diners, the door open.

"He liked the looks of his prey," Ercole said. "He sat here and spied on Maziq."

"So it seems," she said, walking up to the trees, through which she could see the tortellini restaurant clearly.

She pulled on latex gloves and told Ercole to do the same, which he did. She handed him rubber bands but he shook his head and produced a handful from his pocket. She smiled at his foresight.

"Take pictures of the impressions—shoes and tread marks."

He did so, shooting from a number of different angles.

"Beatrice Renza? Is she good?"

"As a forensic officer? I never met her until the other day. Again, I am new to the Police of State. But Beatrice seems good, yes. Though she is aloof. And...Is it a word: attitudinal?"

"Yep."

"Not like Daniela," Ercole said wistfully.

"You think photos will be enough for her to type the tread marks, or should we call a forensic team in?"

"I think the photos will do for her. She will browbeat them into submission."

Sachs laughed. "And scoop up samples of the dirt where he stood and sat."

"Yes, I will."

She handed him some empty bags. But he had already produced some of his own from his uniform pocket.

She squinted back toward the restaurant. "And something else?"

"What, Detective? Amelia."

She said, "You're a Forestry officer. Do you by any chance have a saw in the trunk of your car?"

"As a matter of fact, I have three."

CHAPTER 25

C os'è quello?"

Rhyme could translate that one for himself. In fact, he was wondering the same thing.

Ercole, who was carting in the—presumably—item of evidence, answered, "It's St. John's bread. You might know it as a carob tree. *Ceratonia siliqua.*" The object was foliage, about five feet tall, four branches joined to a single trunk. It had been sawn off at the base.

In gloved hands Ercole also carried a large plastic bag containing smaller bags, filled with dirt and grass.

They were in the situation room once more. Sachs accompanied Ercole. Massimo Rossi and earnest, unsmiling forensic officer Beatrice Renza were present too. Though it was an odd piece of evidence, the woman regarded the large foliage with the same clinical detachment as she might a bullet casing or latent friction ridge lift.

Rhyme noted that Sachs's hands were glove-free—in keeping with her limited role as translator. Or the *appearance* of her limited role.

Ercole continued enthusiastically, "It is quite an interesting plant. Of course, the beans are used to make carob powder, like chocolate. The name 'carob,' I find most interesting, is the source for the word 'carat,' as per the measuring unit for diamonds."

"Forestry Officer, I do not care about its esteemed place in the pantheon of plants," Spiro growled. "Could you be more responsive to my question?" He slipped into his pocket the slim book he'd been jotting notes in, the book he was never without.

Ercole regarded the book with concern once again, it seemed, and answered quickly, "I found a place where the Composer was spying on Ali Maziq and the man he had dinner with."

"You found him, this Arabic speaker?" Spiro asked.

"No. But I learned he's Italian, though most likely not Campanian," Ercole continued, with a glance toward Beatrice. "The pictures I uploaded?"

The forensic officer answered, "I will say that the shoe prints were not dissimilar to those left by the kidnapper in New York and at the bus stop where Maziq was kidnapped. Converse Cons, most likely. And the tire treads too are indicative of the same model as at the bus stop. The Michelins."

Spoken like a true criminalist, though under these circumstances Rhyme would not have objected to a bolder conclusion, like: *Sì*, it was his shoes and his car.

Rossi asked the location of the restaurant exactly and Ercole answered. Rossi walked to a map and marked it. He said, "There are not bus routes there. So, following dinner, the colleague, or someone else, would have driven Maziq to the bus stop. The Composer followed."

Ercole explained that the vehicle had driven past the restaurant and slowed, probably as he saw Maziq and his colleague dining outside. He then drove around the corner, parked and spied on them. "I took samples of the dirt and grass from where he stood and sat." He nodded down at the bags and handed them to Beatrice, who took them in her gloved hands.

They had a brief conversation in Italian, a small argument clearly, which ended with Beatrice shaking her head and Ercole grimacing. She stepped into the lab.

Speaking through the branches, his face only partly visible, Ercole continued, "And from the footprints, it seems that he walked to the bushes to get a good look at the restaurant. I am hoping he pushed them aside to see Maziq."

Rossi pulled out his phone. "I will call an officer guarding Ali Maziq.

We perhaps can find if what you learned helps out his memory." He placed the call and, head down, had a conversation.

Gesturing to the large, bushy branch Ercole held in front of him, Spiro said, "Do something with that, Forestry Officer. It is as if I am speaking to a tree."

"Of course, *Procuratore*." He took it into the lab and returned with some notes that, he explained, Beatrice had given him. Apparently concerned that his handwriting was not in vogue, here in the Questura, Ercole dictated; Sachs wrote.

Vantage Point Across Road from Ristorante San Giancarlo, 13km from D'Abruzzo

- Ali Maziq, Composer kidnap victim, met with colleague, 1 hour prior to kidnapping.
- Companion:
    - ID unknown.
    - Italian most likely. Not from Campania. Large. Dark-complexioned. Black hair. Wearing dark suit, dusty. Smoked foul cigarettes. Described as surly.
- English was spoken. But they tried not to speak in front of the waitress.
    - Reference to Trenitalia journey, six hours.
- Dark car (black, blue) drove past at some point. Slowed, possibly to examine Maziq and Companion.
- Shoe prints at vantage point: Converse Cons, Size 45, same as at other scenes.
- Michelin 205/55R16 91H tread marks found in vantage point.
- Trace recovered at vantage point.
    - Presently being analyzed.
- Branches recovered at vantage point.
    - Presently being examined for trace and fingerprints.

Rossi disconnected his call and looked over the chart. His face bore a wry smile. "No, Signor Maziq still remembers nothing of the day or so before the kidnapping. Or claims he doesn't. But I think perhaps it is less due to the Composer's drugs and the suffocation than to a typical criminal's amnesia."

"How's that?" Rhyme asked.

"As I mentioned, leaving a refugee camp briefly is not considered a serious offense. But leaving the country of first landfall is. And that's what Maziq was trying to do, it appears."

Spiro added, "Yes, now the phone calls on Maziq's mobile to and from Bolzano make sense. That is in the South Tyrol—very far north in Italy, close to the Austrian border. And about six hours on Trenitalia from here. It would be a good way station for an immigrant desiring to slip out of Italy and into northern European cities, where there are better opportunities for refugees than Italy. This man he dined with? Another human smuggler arranging to spirit Maziq out of the country, north. For a substantial fee, of course. This is a serious crime and, accordingly, he remembers nothing of it."

Rhyme noted Ercole's face brighten as he glanced toward the doorway. The blond Flying Squad officer Daniela Canton walked briskly into the room, her posture perfect.

"Officer," Spiro said.

She spoke to those assembled in Italian and Ercole translated for the Americans. "She and Giacomo have canvassed for witnesses and looked for CCTVs around the site of the kidnapping, Viale Margherita. They found nothing. One person thinks he saw a black car late at night but nothing else about it. And the *tabaccaio* where the Composer purchased the Nokia—the one to alert him that the aqueduct facility had been breached? No camera and the clerks have no memory of who it might have been."

Daniela left the room, Ercole's gaze following like a puppy, and then he turned back.

Sachs said, "So, the Composer is driving around the countryside, looking for a potential target. He sees Maziq and decides to kidnap him. But why, though? Why him?"

"I have a thought," Ercole said, speaking hesitantly.

Rossi asked, "And what might that be?"

A glance at Spiro. "It takes into account your interest in patterns, *Procuratore*."

"How?" the prosecutor muttered.

172 / JEFFERY DEAVER

"We've found the drugs, the evidence of electroconvulsive treatment. We know the Composer's psychotic. Schizophrenia is one of the common forms of psychosis. These patients truly believe they are doing good— sometimes the work of God or alien beings or mythological figures. Now, on the surface, Maziq and Robert Ellis are very different. A refugee in Italy and a businessman in New York. But the Composer might have become convinced that they are reincarnations of some evil figures."

Spiro asked, "Mussolini? Billy the Kid? Hitler?"

"Yes, yes, just so. He is justified in killing them to rid the world of their evil. Or to get revenge on behalf of a deity or spirit."

"And the music? The video?"

"Perhaps so other demons or villains will see. And flee back to hell."

"If they have good Internet servers," Spiro muttered. "You must have much free time in Forestry, Ercole, to study such subjects."

He blushed and responded, "*Procuratore*, this particular fact about criminal psychosis I learned last night. Doing some, *come si dice?*" A frown. "Doing homework."

"Mythological figures enlisting the Composer to rid the world of evil." Spiro frowned, gazing at the newsprint sheet. "I think we have not yet stumbled upon a pattern that satisfies me." He regarded his elaborate watch. "I have a call to Rome I must make."

Without another word he turned and left the situation room, pulling a cheroot from his pocket.

Rhyme's phone hummed with a text. He assumed it was Thom, who had taken a few hours off and was seeing the sights in Naples. But he saw immediately that he was wrong. The text was lengthy and, after reading it, he nodded to Sachs. She took the phone and frowned.

"What do you think of this, Rhyme?"

"What do I think?" He scowled. "I think: Why the hell now?"

CHAPTER 26

Greeting Lincoln Rhyme proved troublesome for some people. Such as Charlotte McKenzie.

Should you offer a hand and risk embarrassing a "patient" unable to reciprocate? Should you not, and embarrass anyway by suggesting you don't want to touch a person who's different?

Rhyme could not have cared less, so he had no reaction when, after an awkward glance at the chair, the woman simply nodded and said with a stilted smile that they should keep their distance; she had a cold.

This was a common excuse.

Rhyme, Sachs and Thom were meeting with McKenzie in the U.S. consulate, a white, functional five-story shoe box of a building, near Naples Bay. They'd showed their passports to the U.S. Marines downstairs and been ushered up to the top floor.

"Mr. Rhyme," the woman said. "Captain?"

"Lincoln."

"Yes. Lincoln." McKenzie was about fifty-five, with a doughy, grandmotherly face, powdered but otherwise largely makeup-free. Her light hair was short, in the style he believed favored by some famous British actress whose name he could not recall.

McKenzie opened a file folder. "Thank you so much for seeing me. Let me explain. I'm a legal liaison officer with the State Department. We work with citizens who've run into legal problems in foreign countries.

I'm based in Rome but a situation's come up in Naples and I flew down here to look into it. I'm hoping you might be able to help."

"How did you know we were here?" Sachs asked.

"That case, the serial killer? An FBI update went to the embassy and all the consular offices. What's his name, the killer?" she asked.

"We don't know. We're calling him the Composer."

She offered a concerned furrow of brow. "That's right. Bizarre. Kidnapping and that music video. But you saved the victim yesterday, I read. Is he all right?"

"Yes," Rhyme said quickly, preempting Sachs and Thom, who might be inclined to explain further.

"How's it working out with the Police of State? Or is it Carabinieri?"

"Police of State. Working well enough." Rhyme fell silent and only the lack of a timepiece prevented him from glancing at a wristwatch. He had to convey impatience by a studied lack of interest. But this he was very good at.

McKenzie may have noticed. She got to it. "Well, I'm sure you're pressed. So thanks for coming in. Your reputation is significant, Lincoln. You're maybe the best forensic officer in the U.S."

U.S. only? he thought, unreasonably offended. He said nothing but offered a cool smile.

She said, "Here's our problem. An American student attending Federico the Second, the University of Naples, has been arrested for sexual assault. His name's Garry Soames. He and the victim—she's known in the police documents as Frieda S.—were at a party here in town. She's a first-term student from Amsterdam. At some point she passed out and was assaulted." McKenzie looked up, to the doorway. "Ah, here. Elena will be able to tell us more."

Two others entered the office. The first was a woman in her forties, of athletic build, her hair pinned into a bun, taut, though errant strands escaped. She wore glasses with complex metal-and-tortoiseshell frames, the sort you'd see in upscale fashion mags. (He thought of Beatrice Renza's eyewear.) Her outfit was a charcoal-gray pin-striped suit with a dark-blue blouse, open at the neck. Beside her was a short, slim man, in a conservative suit, also gray, though lighter. He had thinning blondish hair.

He might have been thirty or fifty. His skin was so pale Rhyme thought at first he was a person with albinism, though, no, it seemed that he just didn't get outside very much.

"This is Elena Cinelli," McKenzie said.

In slightly accented English the woman said, "I'm an Italian attorney. I specialize in defending foreigners who've been accused of crimes here. Charlotte contacted me about Garry's situation. His family has retained me."

The pale man said, "Captain Rhyme, Detective Sachs. I'm Daryl Mulbry. I'm with the community and public relations office here at the consulate." The inflected tones situated his roots somewhere in the Carolinas, or possibly Tennessee. Seeing that Rhyme's right arm functioned, Mulbry extended his hand and they shook. (Rhyme now tempered his criticism of Charlotte McKenzie, who was dabbing her nose and then fighting down a sneeze; apparently she did have a reason for not shaking anyone's hand—gimps included.)

Mulbry greeted Thom too. And he lifted an eyebrow to McKenzie— apparently at her win on getting Rhyme into the office, undoubtedly to pitch a request his way.

We'll see about that.

"Please," McKenzie said, gesturing to a coffee table. Rhyme wheeled close and everyone else sat around it. "I was just filling in our visitors about the arrest. You can explain, Signorina Cinelli, better than I could."

Cinelli reiterated some of what McKenzie had said, then: "Garry and the victim were drinking quite a bit and becoming romantic and—to seek privacy—went upstairs to the roof. The victim says she remembers going up there but soon passed out. The next thing she recalls, it is waking hours later on the roof of an adjoining building, having been sexually assaulted. Garry admits they were up there but when Frieda grew tired he left her and returned downstairs. There were, from time to time, others on the roof—at a place where people were smoking—but the adjoining roof, where the attack occurred, is not visible from there. No one saw or heard the actual attack."

Sachs asked, "Why was Garry implicated?"

"The police received an anonymous call that he seemed to have mixed something into the victim's wineglass. We haven't been able to find out who this person is. On the basis of that call, the police searched his flat and found traces of a date-rape drug. Like roofie?"

"I'm familiar," Rhyme said.

"And a blood test after the attack revealed that Frieda S. had the same drug in her bloodstream."

"The *same* drug? Molecularly identical? Or similar?"

"Yes, an important question, Signor Rhyme. But we don't know yet. The samples from his bedroom and in the victim's blood went to the main crime scene facility in Rome for full analysis."

"When will the results be back?"

"It might be weeks. Maybe longer."

Rhyme asked, "In Garry's bedroom? You said the police found trace. Was it pills?"

"No. The apartment was searched carefully. Just residue." The lawyer added, "And on the jacket from the party were traces of the victim's hair and DNA."

"They were making out," Charlotte McKenzie said. "Of course those were there. The date-rape drug, though, well, that's problematic."

Cinelli continued, "Then there was DNA found vaginally. Not Garry's DNA, though. Frieda had been with other men recently, she admitted. That might be the source. Her other partners will be tested too."

"DNA tests of the others at the party?"

"In progress." A pause, then she added, "I will say I have talked to a number of people—friends and fellow students of his. They report that Garry fancies himself quite the lover. He has apparently been with dozens of women—and he has been in Italy only a few months. He has no history of being, you might say, coercive. Or using date-rape drugs. But he has rather a large appetite sexually. And has bragged about his conquests. And there have been incidents where he was, let us say kindly, irritated when a woman rejected him."

"Irrelevant," Sachs said.

"No, I'm afraid it is not. Our trials, in Italy, are not as limited as in the U.S. Questions about character and prior behavior—whether or not criminal—are admissible and can, sometimes, be the pivotal factor in deciding innocence or guilt."

"Did they know each other before this?" Sachs asked. "Frieda and Garry."

"No. And she knew few others at the party. Only the host and hostess, Dev and Natalia."

"Would anyone have a motive to implicate him?"

"He said there was a woman who grew furious when he reneged on an offer to take her to America. A Valentina Morelli. She is from near Florence. She has not returned my calls. The police seem uninterested in her as a suspect."

"Where is the investigation now?" Rhyme asked.

"Just beginning. And it will take a long time. Trials in Italy can last for years."

It was the community liaison officer, Daryl Mulbry, who said, "The press are all over this. I'm getting requests for interviews every hour. And newspapers have already convicted him." A glance toward McKenzie. He said, "We want to push back with positive publicity, if you can find anything that even hints someone else was the attacker."

Rhyme had wondered what a PR officer was doing here. He supposed the court of public opinion was as universal as DNA and fingerprints. The first person to be hired by a rich criminal in the United States, after his lawyer, was a good spin doctor.

Sachs asked, "What's your opinion, Ms. Cinelli? You've talked to him. Is he innocent?"

"It is my opinion that he has exercised bad judgment in the past, living a life too lascivious and bragging about it. And he can have the arrogance of someone with charm and good looks. But I do believe he is innocent of this crime. Garry does not seem like a cruel boy. And someone who would knock out a woman and have relations with her is indisputably cruel."

"What do you want from us, specifically?" Rhyme asked.

McKenzie looked at Cinelli, who said, "A review of the evidence that has been gathered—the report, I mean. You cannot have access to the evidence itself. And, if possible, you might search the scenes again, to the extent you can. All we need is something to point to another suspect. Not a name necessarily, just the possibility that someone other than Garry committed the crime. To introduce reasonable doubt."

Mulbry said, "I'll get the buzz going in the media, and that might help get him released, pending trial."

McKenzie added, "The jail he is being held in is not a bad one. On the whole Italian prisons are rather decent. But he's charged with rape. Fellow prisoners despise those suspects nearly as much as child molesters. The Penitentiary Police are watching him but there have already been threats. A magistrate has the power to release him until trial, if he surrenders his passport, of course. Or to place him under house arrest. Or, frankly, if the evidence against him proves irrefutable, to allow him to plead guilty and work an arrangement for safe incarceration, so he may begin his sentence."

Sachs and Rhyme regarded each other.

Why now...?

He glanced into the lawyer's open briefcase and saw an Italian newspaper. He didn't need a translation of the headline to get the gist:

SOSPETTO DI VIOLENZA SESSUALE

Below that was a picture of an extremely handsome collegiate-looking blond man, flanked by police. A Midwestern frat boy. His face was an eerie mix of frightened and bewildered...and cocky.

Rhyme nodded. "All right. We'll do what we can. But our investigation for the serial kidnapper here takes priority."

"Yes, certainly," McKenzie said. Her face blossomed with gratitude.

"*Grazie*, thank you." From Cinelli.

Daryl Mulbry said, "About those interviews. Would you—?"

"No," Rhyme muttered.

Elena Cinelli nodded and offered, "I would recommend against publicly mentioning that Captain Rhyme and Detective Sachs are involved." To Rhyme, "You must be very discreet. For your own sake. The prosecutor handling the case against Garry is a brilliant man, that's not disputed, but he can be difficult and vindictive and he is cold as ice."

Sachs tossed a glance toward Rhyme, who asked the lawyer, "Is his name, by any chance, Dante Spiro?"

"*Santo Cielo!* How did you know?"

CHAPTER 27

W hen will it end? she thought.
And nearly smiled at the absurdity of that question.
It will *never* end.

This world, her world, was like that abstraction from mathematics class at boarding school so many years, so many lives ago: a Möbius strip, endless.

Rania Tasso, in a long gray skirt and high-necked long-sleeve blouse, strode to the front of the Capodichino Reception Center. At the moment buses, three of them, sat packed with men, women, children whose faces were dark—both of color and with uncertainty and fear.

Some of those visages were taut with sorrow, too. The weather in the Mediterranean had not been bad in the past week but the boats they had sailed on, from Tunisia and Libya, from Egypt and Morocco, much farther away, had been pathetically inadequate. Ancient inflatables, rickety wooden vessels, rafts meant for river transit. Often the "captain" was less competent than a cabdriver.

A number of these unfortunates had lost someone on the harrowing trip. Family, children, parents...and friends too, friends they had made on the journey. Someone in her employ at the camp (she couldn't recall who; people tended not to stay long in the business of asylum-seeking) had said the immigrants were like soldiers: people thrown together by impossible circumstance, struggling to complete their mission and often losing, in an instant, comrades to whom they'd become vitally attached.

Rania, the director of the Capodichino Reception Center, was giving orders, endlessly. Because the work to be done here was endless. She marshaled all her troops: the paid Ministero dell'Interno employees, the volunteers, the police, the soldiers, the UN folks and the infrastructure workers, being firm, though patient and polite (except perhaps with the insufferable celebrities who had a habit of jetting in from London or Cape Town for a photo opportunity, bragging to the press about their donation, then jetting off to Antibes or Dubai, for dinner).

Rania walked around a massive pile of life preservers, orange and faded-orange, piled like a huge, squat traffic cone, and ordered several volunteers to board the buses to dispense bottled water. The month of September had not proved to be a respite from the heat.

She surveyed the incoming stream of unfortunates.

A sigh.

The camp had been intended for twelve hundred. It was now home to nearly three thousand. Despite the attempts to slow immigration from North Africa—primarily Libya—the poor folks kept coming, fleeing rape and poverty and crime and the mad ideology of ISIS and other extremists. You could talk about turning them back, you could talk about setting up camps and protective zones in their origin countries. But those solutions were absurd. They would never happen.

No, these people had to escape from the Land of No Hope, as one refugee had referred to his home. Conditions were so dire that nothing would stop them fleeing to beleaguered settlements like hers. This year alone nearly seventy thousand asylum-seekers had landed on Italian soil.

A voice intruded on her troubled thoughts.

"There is something I would like to do. Please."

Rania turned to the woman, who had spoken in Arabic. The director scanned the pretty face, the deep-brown eyes, the faint hint of makeup on the light-mocha skin. The name...? Ah, yes, Fatima. Fatima Jabril. Behind her was her husband. His name, Rania recalled, was Khaled. The couple whose intake she herself had processed just the other day.

In the husband's arms lay their sleeping daughter, whose name she'd forgotten. Fatima apparently noted the director's frown.

"This is Muna."

"Yes, that's right—a lovely name." The child's round face was surrounded by a mass of glossy black curls.

Fatima continued, "Earlier, I was outspoken. The journey was very difficult. I apologize." She glanced back at her husband, who had apparently encouraged her to say this.

"No, it's not necessary."

Fatima continued, "We have asked and have been told that you are the director of the camp."

"That's right."

"I come to you with a question. In Tripoli I worked in health care. I was a midwife and served as a nurse during the Liberation."

She would be talking, of course, about the fall of Qaddafi and the months afterward, when the peace and stability, so long anticipated and so bravely fought for, had vanished like water in hot sand.

"Liberation"—what a mockery.

"I would like to help here in the camp. So many people, pregnant women, about to give birth. And sick too. The burns."

Sunburn, she meant. Yes, a week on the Mediterranean with no protection took a terrible toll—especially on young skin. And there were other diseases too. The camp's sanitation was as good as it could be, but many refugees were racked with illness.

"I would appreciate that. I will introduce you to the medical center director. What are your languages?"

"Other than Arabic, some English. My husband." She nodded to Khaled, who gave an amiable smile. "He is good with English. We are teaching Muna both languages. And I am learning Italian. An hour a day at the school here."

Rania nearly smiled—the girl was only two, and bilingual instruction seemed a bit premature. But Fatima's eyes were hard and her mouth taut. The director plainly saw that the woman's determination to help, and to be granted asylum and assimilate, was not a matter for humor.

"We have no way to pay you. No funds."

Fatima said quickly, "I don't wish to be paid. I wish to help."

"Thank you."

The refugees were mixed when it came to generosity. Some—like Fatima—volunteered selflessly. Others remained reclusive and a few were resentful that more was not being done for them or that the asylum-seeking process took so long.

Rania was telling Fatima about the medical center facilities when she happened to look through the fence and saw something that gave her pause.

Outside, amid the hundreds of those milling about—reporters, family members and friends of the refugees—a man stood by himself. He was in the shadows, so she had no clear image of him. But it was obvious he was staring in her direction. The thickset man wore a cap, the sort American sports figures wore, a cap you didn't see much in Italy, where heads went mostly uncovered. His eyes were obscured with aviator sunglasses. There was something troubling about his pose.

Rania knew she had incurred the anger of many people for her devotion to these poor people. Refugees were hugely unpopular among certain segments of the population in the host countries. But he was not standing with the protesters. No, his attention—which seemed focused on Rania herself—appeared to be about something else entirely.

Rania said goodbye to Fatima and Khaled and pointed to the medical facility. As the family walked away, Rania pulled her radio off her hip and summoned the head of security—a Police of State captain—to meet her fifty meters south of the main gate.

Tomas radioed back immediately saying he was coming.

He arrived just two or three minutes later. "A problem?"

"A man outside the fence. Something odd about him."

"Where?"

"He was by the magnolia."

She pointed but the view was blocked by yet another refugee bus crawling along the road.

When it passed, and the view was clear once again, she could see the man no more. Rania scanned the road and fields bordering the camp but found no trace.

"Do you want me to call a team together?"

She debated.

A voice from the office called, "Rania, Rania! The shipment of plasma. They can't find it. Jacques needs to talk to you. Jacques from the Red Cross."

Another scan of the roadway. Nothing.

"No, don't bother. Thank you, Tomas."

She swiveled about, to return to her office and cope with yet another cascade of crises.

Endless...

CHAPTER 28

D on't really want it to deflect us too much from the Composer, do we now, Sachs? But it's a curious case. An *intriguing* case."

Rhyme, referring to the Garry Soames matter.

She gave a wry laugh. "A landmine of a case."

"Ah, because of Dante Spiro? We'll be careful."

They were in their secondary situation room: the café across the street from the Questura. Sachs, Rhyme and Thom. Rhyme had tried to order a grappa but Thom, damn it, had preempted him with sparkling water and coffee for everyone. How was he going to acquire a taste for the liquor if he was denied access?

In fairness, however, the cappuccino was good.

"Ah, here we go."

Rhyme noted the lanky figure of Ercole Benelli stride from the police headquarters toward the café. He spotted the Americans, crossed the street, stepped past the Cinzano barrier and sat down on a rickety aluminum chair.

"Hello," he said formally, the tone revealing his curiosity. The young officer was, of course, wondering why Sachs had called and asked to meet out here.

Rhyme asked, "Has Beatrice found any prints on the plant leaves or any trace from the Composer's surveillance outside the restaurant near D'Abruzzo?"

Ercole grimaced. "The woman is quite *insopportabile*. You say, intoler-able?"

"Yes, or insufferable."

"*Sì*, insufferable is better! I asked her several times of her progress and she glared at me. And I wished to know if you can fingerprint the bark of a tree. An innocent question. Her expression, frightening. As if saying, 'Of course you can! What fool doesn't know that?' And can she not smile? How difficult is that?"

Lincoln Rhyme was not one to turn to for sympathy in matters like this. "And?" he asked impatiently.

"No, nothing, I'm afraid. Not yet. She and her assistants are working hard, however. I will give her that."

Ercole ordered something from the waitress and a moment later an or-ange juice appeared.

Rhyme said, "Well, we have another situation we need help with."

"You have more developments about our musical kidnapper?"

"No. This is a different case."

"Different?"

On the small table before them Sachs was spreading out documents: copies of the crime scene reports and interviews regarding the rape Garry Soames was accused of, provided by the lawyer he and his family had retained.

"We need translations of these reports, Ercole."

He looked them over, shuffled through them. "How does this connect to the Composer?"

"It doesn't. Like I said, it's another case."

"Another...?" The officer chewed his lip. He read more carefully. "Yes, yes, the American student. This is not one of Massimo Rossi's cases. It's being run by *Ispettore* Laura Martelli." He nodded at the Questura.

Rhyme said nothing more and Sachs added, "We've been asked by a State Department official to review the evidence. The defendant's lawyer's convinced the boy is innocent."

Ercole sipped his orange juice, which—like most non-coffee bever-ages in Italy, Rhyme had observed—had been served without ice. And Coca-Cola always came with lemon. The Forestry officer said, "Oh, but, no. I cannot do this. I am sorry." As if they'd missed something blatantly obvious. "You do not see. This would be *un conflitto d'interese*. A—"

Rhyme said, "Not really."

"No. How is that possible?"

"It *would* be, no, it *might* be a conflict of interest if you were working for the Police of State directly. But you are, technically, still a Forestry officer, isn't that right?"

"Signor Rhyme, *Capitano* Rhyme, that is not a defense that will be very persuasive at my trial. Or will stop Prosecutor Spiro from beating me half to death if he finds out. Wait...who is the *procuratore*?" He flipped through the pages. And closed his eyes. "*Mamma mia! Spiro* is the prosecutor. No, no, no. I cannot do this! If he finds out, he will beat me *fully* to death!"

"You're exaggerating," Rhyme reassured, though he admitted to himself that Dante Spiro seemed fully capable of a blow or two.

Difficult, vindictive, cold as ice ...

"Besides, we're simply asking you to translate. We could hire someone but it will take too long. We want to look over the evidence quickly, give our assessment and get back to the Composer. There's no reason for Dante to find out."

Sachs added, "This is very likely a case of an innocent American student in jail for a crime he didn't commit."

Ercole muttered, "Ah, we had a case like that a few years ago. In Perugia. It did not go well for anybody."

Rhyme nodded to the file. "And the evidence may very well prove Soames is guilty. In which case we will have done the prosecution and the government a service. At no charge."

Sachs: "Please. Just translation. What's the harm in that?"

With a resigned look on his face, Ercole pulled the papers forward and, with a glance around, as if Spiro were hiding in the shadows nearby, began to read.

Rhyme said, "Make a chart, a mini chart."

Sachs dug into her computer bag and pulled out a yellow legal pad. She uncapped a fine-point marker and looked toward Ercole. "You dictate and I'll write."

"I am still an accessory to a crime," he whispered.

Rhyme only smiled.

GARRY SOAMES INVESTIGATION—SEXUAL ASSAULT

— Location of attack.
- — Via Carlo Cattaneo, 18, top floor apartment (of Natalia Garelli) and roof (party Victim attended).
- — Via Carlo Cattaneo, 20, roof (site of attack).
— Examination of Victim. Frieda S.
- — She had experienced minor vaginal bleeding from forceful penetration.
- — Garry's DNA on her neck and cheek. Sweat or saliva, not semen.
- — Within Victim's vagina:
  - — Cyclomethicone, polydimethylsiloxane (PDMS), silicone, dimethicone copolyol, and tocopheryl acetate (vitamin E acetate). Silicone-based lubricant. Probably from Comfort-Sure condoms. No match with condoms in Garry's apartment or on person when arrested.
  - — Unidentified DNA from single source in vagina (sweat or saliva, not semen—from attacker applying condom to penis, most likely). No match in Europol, Interpol or CODIS (U.S.), Italian databases. Samples taken from 14 of 29 men present at party reveal no match. Presently scheduling additional tests. Samples will be taken from Victim's prior sexual partners.
  - — In Victim's blood, traces of gamma hydroxybutyric acid, similar to Rohypnol, a date-rape drug.
— No condom discovered.
  - — Thorough search of neighborhood, trash containers and sewers, five-block radius.
— Location of Implicating Evidence: Garry's apartment, bedroom.
- — Jacket worn to party.
  - — Contains small traces of gamma hydroxybutyric acid.
  - — Victim's hair. Head hair, not pubic.
  - — Victim's DNA, saliva.
- — Additional items of clothing: shirts, underwear, socks.
  - — Contain small traces of gamma hydroxybutyric acid.

— Two wineglasses on ledge, near the scene of the rape.
  — Garry's DNA on both glasses.
  — Frieda's DNA on one. Residue contained traces of gamma hydroxybutyric acid.
— Crime Scene: Roof of Via Carlo Cattaneo, 20 (Next door to Garelli's).
  — Pebbles on roof disturbed, where Victim was assaulted.
  — Hair of Victim.
  — Saliva of Victim.
  — No other evidence found.
— Roof deck of Natalia Garelli's flat (the smoking station).
  — Five wineglasses.
      — No trace of gamma hydroxybutyric acid.
      — Eight prints, no hits on any national or international databases.
      — No DNA hits in any national or international databases.
  — Two butts of marijuana cigarettes, burned down to 8mm stubs.
      — No DNA hits in any national or international databases.
  — Seven small plates, traces of food, sweets.
      — Thirteen prints; two match hostess of party; no hits on any national or international databases.
      — No DNA hits in any national or international databases.
  — Wine bottle on deck table near party.
      — Pinot Nero.
      — No trace of gamma hydroxybutyric acid in remaining wine.
      — Six fingerprints—hostess of party and two female guests, Natalia's boyfriend, Dev Nath.
      — No DNA hits in any national or international databases.
  — 27 cigarette butts in ashtray and on deck.
      — Four prints matched hostess of party and her boyfriend.
      — 16 other prints at smoking station. One positive, individual arrested on drug charge six months ago, Puglia. Said individual had left party before the assault.
          — No other hits in any national or international databases.
      — No DNA hits in any national or international databases.

When she had finished writing, they looked the pad over. Rhyme reflected: Solid work. He would have liked to have samples of the trace from the deck or roof area where the smoking station was located, and from the site of the attack itself. But this was good for starters.

Sachs glanced at the remaining pages of notes in Italian Ercole was staring at, the official report. "Go on," she insisted kindly. "Please. I want to hear the accounts."

Ercole apparently hoped he'd be let off the hook by simply translating the forensics. Reciting the witnesses' and suspect's statements seemed perhaps, in the young officer's mind, to move his crime into a different category, misdemeanor to felony.

Reading, he said, "Natalia Garelli, twenty-one, attends the University of Naples. She hosted a party in her flat for fellow students and friends. The victim, Frieda S., arrived at ten p.m. Alone. She remembered drinking and talking with some people—mostly Natalia or her boyfriend—but was a bit shy. She too is a student, just arrived from Holland. She vaguely recalls around eleven or midnight the defendant approaching her and talking. They both had glasses of wine at the table where they were sitting—this is downstairs—and Garry kept refilling her glass. Then they embraced and... *limonarono*... I do not know."

"Made out?" Sachs suggested.

"Sì. Made out." He read more. "It was crowded so they went to the roof. Then Frieda has no memory until four in the morning, waking on the roof of the adjacent building and realizing she'd been assaulted. She was still quite drugged but managed to get to the wall separating the two rooftops. She climbed over, fell and was calling for help. Natalia, the hostess, heard her cries and got her downstairs into the apartment. Natalia's boyfriend, Dev, called the police.

"Investigators checked the door to the roof of the adjoining building but it was locked and did not appear to have been opened recently. Natalia told police that she suspected Serbian roommates living downstairs in that building—they'd been crude and drank a lot—but the police verified they were out of town. And dismissed anyone else in that building as suspects.

"A few witnesses on the roof—at the table for smoking, the smoking station—saw Garry and Frieda together briefly, walking to an alcove on the roof, where there was a bench, but that is out of sight of the smoking station. Between about one a.m. and two, only they were up-stairs. At two a.m. Garry walked down the stairs to the apartment proper and left. Several witnesses reported that he seemed distressed. No one noticed that Frieda was missing. People assumed she'd left earlier. The next day there was an anonymous call—a woman, calling from a pay phone at a *tabaccaio* near Naples University. After she heard about the attack, she wanted to call the police and report that she believed she'd seen Garry mixing something into Frieda's drink."

"And no idea of her identity at all?" Rhyme asked.

"No." Ercole continued, "The call allowed the inspector to get a war-rant to search his flat. That led to the discovery of traces of the date-rape drug on the jacket he'd worn the night of the party and the other articles of clothing."

Sachs asked, "Garry's story?"

"He admits that he and Frieda were drinking wine downstairs. And, again, making out. They went upstairs for more privacy. There were peo-ple at the smoking station, so they went around the corner to a deserted area and sat down and did more making out. But she grew tired and bored and less interested. About one thirty, he was tired too and he went downstairs and left the party. She was on the bench on the roof, drows-ing, when he did."

"Tired too," Sachs suggested, "because he took a sip of her wine, which was spiked. His DNA was on her glass."

"Suggesting he didn't know about the roofie!" Ercole said, enthusiastic for just a moment, lost in the case. Then he went back to being guilty and nervous.

Rhyme said, "One problem with the government's case: The DNA found in Frieda's vagina. It wasn't Garry's." He looked at Ercole uncer-tainly. He wondered if the graphic aspects of the crime would trouble a young officer who'd never worked an assault before, much less a rape.

The Italian officer glanced at Rhyme and caught his concern. "*Cap-itano* Rhyme, last month I ran an undercover operation to arrest men passing off inferior bull semen as that from prize animals. I surrepti-tiously videoed the collection process. I am someone who has made bull porn, so such matters are not bothering to me, if that's your question."

Rhyme nodded in amused concession. He observed that one line in the report was crossed out—bold strokes and a written note beside it. "What's that?"

"The words translate: 'Inappropriate and irrelevant, reprimand the interviewer.'"

"What's crossed out?" Sachs asked.

It took a moment to discern the words beneath the thick marker. "It is a note from one of the Flying Squad officers interviewing party attendees. The officer wrote that the victim was considered by some at the party to be quite the flirt."

"Ah. That offended the inspector," Sachs said. "Or Spiro. As it should have."

Blaming women for their own sexual assault was unforgivable . . . and a lapse that seemed to transcend national barriers.

Sachs said, "So what's the scenario, if he's innocent?"

Rhyme said, "Some man, Mr. X, has his eye on Frieda. He gets close and spikes her drink but it's crowded and dark, so the witness thinks it's Garry. Before X can move in and get Frieda to a bedroom or a deserted part of the flat, she and Garry go upstairs. X follows and watches them. Frieda starts to go under and Garry gets bored and leaves. When the roof is deserted, Mr. X carries Frieda to the roof of the building next door and rapes her."

Ercole asked, "Ah, but the drug residue on Garry's jacket in his apartment? How is that explained?"

Rhyme responded, "One way: being close to the man who *did* drug her. But remember, read the chart, Ercole, there was drug residue on other clothing too."

"Yes, what are the implications of that?"

"We don't know yet. It could be that Garry is guilty and frequently carries around date-rape drugs. Or that he is innocent and someone broke in to implicate him, scattering drugs on other items of his clothing, not remembering or knowing what he wore to the party."

Rhyme stared at the translated document. "And something I don't like. 'No Other Evidence Found.' There is always evidence. Ercole, do you know the name 'Locard'?"

"I don't believe I do."

"A French criminalist. He lived a long time ago. He came up with a principle that is still valid. He felt that at every crime scene there is a transfer of evidence from the perpetrator to the victim or to the scene. And from that evidence it is possible, even if very difficult, to determine the perp's identity or location. He was speaking of trace evidence, of course."

Ercole, some sixth sense kicking in, it seemed, said quickly, "*Allora*, I am happy to have helped you. Now I must go. I will see if Beatrice has made some discoveries, as she probably has. Moving us closer to the Composer. Our important case." He looked to Sachs for help. None was forthcoming.

Rhyme said, "We need another search of Natalia's apartment, Ercole. Particularly the smoking station. I'll bet that's where Mr. X was waiting to keep an eye on Frieda. The roof next door too. And we need to examine Garry's apartment—to see if the drug residue was planted to incriminate Garry...Two simple searches. Shouldn't take more than a couple of hours. Oh, tops."

Both he and Sachs were staring intently at Ercole Benelli, who had taken to reassembling the file, as if by closing it he'd put this matter to rest forever. Finally, he could avoid them no longer and he looked up. "*Quello che chiedete è impossibile. Do you understand? Impossibile!*"

CHAPTER 29

The party where the rape had occurred had been held in an apartment in the Vomero neighborhood of Naples.

The area was atop a high hill that could be reached via funicular or a drive up steep, winding streets. From the crest, you had an Olympus-like view—of the bay, Vesuvius in the distance, and the infinite patchwork of colors and textures and shapes that was Naples.

This was, Sachs's chauffeur, Ercole Benelli, had told her, considered the nicest part of the city. The Vomero was dotted with Art Nouveau architecture and modern-style offices and residences, while mom-and-pop stores and vintage-clothing shops were found next to the chicest designer retail locations that Italy had to offer…and Italy, of course, had chic down cold.

As they'd begun the drive, after a persuasive argument by Rhyme, Ercole had been sullen. His *"impossibile"* eventually became *"forse"*—perhaps—and then what must have been the Italian equivalent of a grudging, "Oh, all right." Eventually his easy spirits had returned and as they careened through Neapolitan traffic, Ercole seemed resigned to the risk of being pummeled by Spiro, and he turned tour guide, pelting Sachs with sound bites of the history of the city, present and distant past.

GPS finally got them to Natalia's apartment, a classic Mediterranean-style structure on a small residential street, Via Carlo Cattaneo. They parked and Ercole led the way. Some children stared at them, enthralled, their attention seized by his uniform and the NYPD gold shield on her hip. Some boys tried to catch a glimpse under their jackets, hoping, she guessed, to spot a weapon. Others were more cautious.

Sachs was startled as a teenager sped past them at a run.

Ercole laughed. "*Bene, bene*...It's all right. In certain other neighborhoods in Naples, he would be going to warn his father or brother there is a cop present. Here, though, he is simply running. To a game or to a girl...or because he wants to be star runner someday. There is crime in Naples, yes. No doubt. Pickpocketing, purse snatching, auto theft. You must be careful in some places. The Camorra are in the suburbs of Secondigliano and Scampia and in the Spanish Quarters in the city. The African gangs closer to Pozzuoli. But here, no."

Natalia Garelli's building was in need of paint and plastering on the outside but through spotless glass it appeared the lobby was starkly elegant. Ercole hit the intercom button. A moment later a woman's voice clattered through the tinny speaker. The front door unlocked and they entered the lobby, dominated by an abstract painting, a swirl. A steel sculpture hung on another wall. An angel? Or a dove? Or purely fanciful? They took the elevator to the top floor, the fifth. There was a single apartment on this story.

Ercole lifted an eyebrow and kissed his fingertips, apparently meaning this was quite the posh place.

He rang the bell on a pale wooden frame and a moment later a very slim and very beautiful woman in her early twenties opened the door.

Ercole introduced himself and Sachs, and the woman nodded, smiling in a friendly way. "You are a policewoman from America, yes. Because Garry is American. Of course. Come in, please. *Sono* Natalia."

Hands were shaken.

From the girl's jewelry and clothes—leather pants, a silk blouse and enviable boots—Sachs deduced family money. The apartment too. Surely her parents had arranged for the place: student housing a lot better than most kids dwelled in. This place could have been the setting for a Prada fashion shoot. The walls were done in lavender stucco and hung with huge, boldly colored oil paintings, in two styles: abstract and nudes of both sexes. The couches and chairs were dark-green leather and brushed steel. A glass bar dominated one wall and a huge high-def TV the other. Silent music videos jerked across the screen.

"Lovely place."

"Thank you," she said. "My father works in design in Milan. Furniture and accessories. I am studying the subject here and will go into the profession too, when I graduate. Or fashion. Please, tell me, how is Garry?" Her English was perfect with a faint icing of accent.

She answered, "As well as can be expected."

Suitably ambiguous.

Ercole said, "We are looking into follow-up questions on the case. We will take little of your time."

Natalia said, "It was terrible, what happened! And, I will tell you, it had to be someone not with our group. They are all simply the nicest people. Someone from the next building—there are Serbians living there." Her nose creased in distaste. "Some men, three or four of them. I have often thought they might be up to trouble. I told your colleagues about them."

Ercole said, deferentially, "The residents of that building—everyone— were interviewed and dismissed as suspects. The police found the men you are speaking of were out of town that night."

"Still. Someone from the school? It is impossible."

"But someone might have tagged along with a student. You know what I mean."

"I do, yes. I should have been more careful, I suppose." Her beautiful lips, dark purple, tightened.

"Do you know Frieda well?"

"Not well. Only for a few weeks, when classes began. My boyfriend and I met her in European Political History."

"Did you see her with anyone at the party you didn't recognize?"

"It was crowded. I saw her with Garry and some girlfriends of ours. But I didn't pay much attention."

"If you don't mind, tell us again what you remember about that evening," Sachs asked.

"My boyfriend and I went to dinner around eight and came back here to set out wine and some snacks and *dolce*. The people started arriving about ten for the party." She shrugged, touched her hair, patting it into place. Sachs, as a former fashion model, knew beauty and Natalia was one of the most stunning women she'd ever seen. That would help immeasurably in a career in the industry, even if she chose simply to design, not model. The way of the world.

Beauty rules.

"Garry was in one of the first groups to arrive. I do not know him so good. I spoke to him. I like to hang out with the Americans and English and Canadians to improve my language. More and more people arrived and about midnight I saw Frieda and Garry together. They were very close. You know, the way people are when they meet and are flirting. Touching, kissing, whispering close. I saw them go up to the roof, carrying their drinks. They were both drunk." She shook her head. "Sometime later I saw Garry downstairs. He was, how do you say, groggy. Stumbling. I remember thinking I hope he doesn't drive home. He was not looking good. He left before I could say anything.

"The party went on and by about four, everyone had left. Dev, my boyfriend, and I were cleaning up. And we heard cries from the roof. I went up and found Frieda beside the wall separating the roofs. She had fallen. She was in a terrible state. Her skirt torn, scrapes on her legs. I helped her up. She was hysterical. She knew she'd been attacked but could remember nothing. Dev called the police and they were here soon."

"Can you show us where that was?"

"Yes."

Natalia took them to spring-loaded stairs that led to a trapdoor in the ceiling of the back hall. Even the stairs—a wire-and-steel contraption, which pulled down from overhead—were stylish. The climb would be a bit risqué in a skirt, Sachs thought. Like the hostess, though, she was in pants—jeans in her case, not thousand-dollar leather. On the roof was a wooden deck and several ten-foot-high sheds that may have been holding water tanks or tools. A sitting area, about twelve by twelve feet, contained metal chairs and tables, on which sat ashtrays.

The smoking station.

Sachs supposed that, unable to smoke indoors many places in Italy, nicotine addicts would migrate to places like this: decks and patios. The view was spectacular. You could see the entire expanse of Naples Bay, the misty form of the volcano to one side and, to the other, a massive castle, which was nearby.

Sachs walked from the smoking station around the corner of one of the sheds, secluded from view. There was a bench here, where Garry and Frieda would have settled in for their *limonarono*—or whatever the gerund of that verb might be.

Natalia said, in a weak voice, "The attack occurred over there." She pointed to the roof of the adjoining building, delineated by yellow police tape. "I will never look at this place again the same way. So pleasant once. And now, so terrible."

They walked to the tape. There was no gap between this building and the one next door; they were separated only by a brick wall, about three feet high. Looking left, Sachs and Ercole could see another cordoned-off area of police tape on the adjoining structure, where the actual crime had occurred. This was out of sight of the smoking station. A logical place for an attack.

"Let's go."

"But the tape!" Ercole whispered.

She smiled at him. Mindful of her joints, Sachs sat on the wall and eased onto the neighboring roof. Ercole sighed then leapt over. Natalia remained on the roof of her building. The pebbles covering the tar paper meant that they could find no footprints, so they didn't worry about booties or rubber bands. Pulling on latex gloves, Sachs took samples of the stones and flecks of tar from the place where the assault had occurred and the route leading to it.

When she was finished, she looked across the street and to the south at a tall building a half block away.

"What is that?"

Ercole noted the modern high-rise. "A hotel. The NV, I believe. A very nice place."

She squinted into the sun. "It looks like that's a parking garage."

"Yes, I think so."

"About level with the roof here. Let's find out if they have a CCTV, and if it's pointed this way."

"Yes, yes, good. Many parking structures have video security. I'll follow up on that."

She nodded and they returned to the smoking station and she performed a similar evidence collection there, as Natalia watched with curiosity. "It is like that show *CSI*. Isn't it?"

"Very much like that," Sachs said.

In ten minutes they were finished. Sachs and Ercole thanked the young woman. She shook their hands firmly and opened the door for them to leave. "Please, I am sure Garry could not have done this. In my heart I know." Her eyes darkened and she glanced in the direction of the building next door. "Those men, those Serbians, you should look once more at them. I read people very good. I do not trust them at all."

CHAPTER 30

S he is free."

"Free?"

Beatrice Renza continued speaking to Ercole Benelli. "She recently has broken up from a long relationship. But it had been ending for some time."

"Some time?"

"Why are you repeating my statements as questions?"

Honestly. This woman. Ercole's lips grew taut. "I don't understand. Who are you speaking about?"

Though he had an idea. No, he knew exactly.

"Surely you do. Daniela Canton, of course."

He began to repeat the name, as a question, but stopped fast, lest he give the brittle woman more ammunition to fire his way. (Besides, as a police officer, he well knew that repeating questions is virtually an admission of guilt: "Poaching? Me? How can you say that I'm poaching?")

Instead, a different inquiry: "Why are you telling me this?"

They stood in the laboratory on the ground floor of the Questura. The situation room for the Composer case was presently devoid of Ercole's colleagues. Only Amelia Sachs, Rhyme and his aide Thom were there—co-conspirators in the Garry Soames matter—so he felt confident in slipping into the lab to ask Beatrice to analyze the evidence they'd collected at the scene of the sexual assault, the roof of Natalia's apartment. Before he had been able to ask her to do this, however, she had regarded him with a tilted head and, perhaps seeing his lengthy glance toward Daniela, up the hall, had fired away.

She is free...

"It was a sad story." Apparently Beatrice had no interest in responding to his question about why she was sharing Daniela's story. She pushed her green-framed glasses higher on the bridge of her nose. "He was a pig," she snapped. "Her former lover."

Ercole was offended, for two reasons: One was this prickly woman's assumption that he had any interest whatsoever in Daniela. The other was his affection for pigs.

Still, interesting: Daniela. Unattached.

"I hadn't wondered about her status."

"No," the lab analyst said, clearly not believing him. Beatrice had a round face, framed by a mass of unruly black hair, presently tucked under a plastic bonnet. She was pretty in a baker's-daughter sort of way, Ercole reflected, though he knew no bakers, nor the offspring of any. Short of stature, she had a figure that could be described as, well, bustily squat. Her feet pointed outward and she tended to waddle when she walked, making a pronounced shuffling sound if she wore booties. Daniela moved through the halls with the grace of... what? Well, Beatrice had brought up the animal metaphor. Daniela moved with the grace of a lean cheetah. A lean and sexy cheetah.

Beatrice was more a sloth or koala bear.

Then, realizing the comparison was unkind and unfair, Ercole blushed in shame.

Pulling gloves on and taking the evidence bags, Beatrice said, "She was with Arci—Arcibaldo—for three years. He was somewhat younger. As you can see, Daniela is thirty-five."

That much? No, he could not see it, not at all. He was surprised. But he was intrigued that she liked younger men. Ercole being thirty.

"He wished to be a race car driver but that was a dream, of course; driving is not in his blood."

Unlike Amelia Sachs's, he thought ruefully, and reminded himself once more to take the Mégane in for a checkup. The gearbox did not sound healthy.

Beatrice said, "He merely dabbled at the sport, Arci did. But he was a handsome man."

"*Was*? Did he die in an accident?"

"No. By 'was' I mean that he is in the past tense to Daniela. As a handsome driver, however mediocre, he had plenty of opportunities for bunga-bunga."

The expression, popularized by a former Italian prime minister, defied exact definition but, then, a likely meaning could be easily ascribed.

Beatrice looked at the bags and set them on examination tables. She noted the chain-of-evidence cards (his name only, not Amelia's) and placed her signature below his. "He worked for a racing team in Modena. Doing basic things, assisting mechanics, shepherding cars here and there. What happened was that he and Daniela returned from Eurovision—"

"She went to Eurovision?"

"That's right." Beatrice gave a dismissing laugh, nearly a snort, and had to reseat her complicated glasses. "If you can believe that."

"You don't care for it?" Ercole asked her, after a thoughtful pause.

"Who on earth would? It's juvenile."

"*Some* feel that way, yes," he said quickly.

Based on an Italian festival that started six decades ago, Sanremo, Eurovision was a televised songwriting and -performing contest, countries competing against one another in a theatrical show that was lavishly and gaudily produced. The music was criticized as being bubblegum, with a patriotic topping and political bias. Still, Ercole loved it. He had been six times. He had tickets for the next Grand Final. Two tickets.

Ever hopeful, Ercole Benelli.

"They returned from the show and found police waiting at his flat. He had been selling fuel-system secrets to a competing team. The charges resulted in a fine only but in Italy, of course, people take driving very seriously. I myself was personally offended."

"You like car races?"

She said fervently, "I go to Formula One whenever I can. One day I will own a Maserati, the coupe. Used, of course. It will have to be. A

Ferrari... well, that is beyond my dreams, on a Police of State salary. Do you attend?"

"Not often. I can't find the time." In fact, auto racing held no interest for him whatsoever. "I enjoyed the movie *Rush*." He couldn't remember the drivers' names. And one was Italian.

"Ah, brilliant, wasn't it? Niki Lauda, an artist! He drove for Ferrari, of course. I own the DVD. I attend races quite a lot. But they aren't for everybody. You must wear sound protection, if you go. I take my earmuffs, the ones I use on the police pistol range. They also help me get good seats. People see *Police of State* printed on the cups and they make way for me."

For some reason he said, "I race pigeons."

"The birds?"

He said, "Of course the birds."

What other kind of pigeons were there?

"I have never heard of that. In any event, though Arci's offense was not serious, Daniela could hardly have a boyfriend who committed a crime."

"And one who was guilty, as well, of bunga-bunga when he was away at races."

"Exactly."

"Poor thing. She must have been devastated."

Beatrice clicked her tongue, the way a disapproving nun might do in class. "I wouldn't call her a *thing*. It's offensive. But, yes, of course she was upset." Beatrice looked into the other room, toward the woman who was a foot taller, seven kilos lighter and had the face of an angelic cheetah. She said kindly, "Even the beautiful can suffer from heartbreak. No one is immune. So, I say to you simply that she is available, if you wish to speak to her on the matter."

Utterly flustered, he blurted, "No, no, no. I have no interest in her in that way, none whatsoever. I'm merely curious. It's my nature. I am curious about everyone. I am curious about people from different regions. People of different ages. People of different races, different colors. I am curious about men, about women, black, white, brown..." He struggled to find something more to say.

Beatrice helped out: "Children, of any complexion?"

Ercole blinked, then realized she was making a joke. He laughed at her dry delivery, though uncomfortably. She gave no response, other than to study the bags.

"So. What do we have here?" She was holding the card. "'From the smoking station.' What is that?"

"The location of a possible witness to a crime. Or a perpetrator."

She read another card. "'The attack site.'"

He stepped forward, to tell her what it contained, but she waved him back, past a yellow line. "No, no, no. You are not gowned. Get back!"

He sighed and stepped away. "It's pebbles—"

"From a rooftop. Obviously."

He then asked, "And can you see if the NV Hotel in Vomero has a CCTV pointed northeast, from the top level of their parking garage?"

Beatrice frowned. "Me? It would be the Postal Police who could check that."

"I don't know anyone there." He tapped his Forestry Corps badge.

"I suppose I could. What case is this?"

He said, "An independent investigation."

"Well, Ercole Benelli, you come to the Police of State like a newborn hatchling from the Forestry Corps and leap into the role of investigator, fully formed. With a case of your own. You are the new Montalbano." The beloved Sicilian detective in the murder mystery series by Andrea Camilleri. "So understandably you do not know the procedures here. An evidence analysis request like this must reference a case number or at least the name of a suspect."

"We don't know his identity." This much was true. If the claim of Garry Soames's lawyer—and Garry himself—could be believed, someone else had raped the woman on the rooftop, a person unknown.

Ah. Perfect.

"Put down Unsub Number One."

"What does that refer to? 'Unsub'? I've never heard that."

"English. 'Unknown subject.' It's a term the American police use when referring to a suspect whose name they have not learned."

Beatrice looked him up and down. "If you are taken with American expressions I think you are maybe more Columbo than Montalbano."

Was this an insult? Columbo was that bumbling, disheveled detective, wasn't he? Still, he was the hero of the show.

"As for the forensic results, should I contact you or Inspector Rossi or Prosecutor Spiro? Or another prosecutor?"

"Me, please."

"Fine. Does this have priority over the Composer? I'm nearly finished with the analysis of the evidence you found outside D'Abruzzo."

"That should be first. The Composer may be set to strike again, though perhaps if you could call about the CCTV on the NV Hotel? I am interested in any tapes the night of the twentieth, midnight to four a.m."

"Midnight to four a.m. of the twentieth? Or the twenty-first of September?"

"Well, I suppose the twenty-first."

"So, what you really mean is the 'morning' of the twenty-first. You misspoke when you said 'night'?"

He sighed. "Yes."

"All right." She picked up a phone, and Ercole walked into the situation room, nodding to Captain Rhyme and Thom. Detective Sachs looked up at him, questioningly.

He whispered, "She will review it. And now she is calling the hotel. About the CCTV."

"Good," Rhyme said.

A moment later Beatrice stepped into the situation room. She nodded to those inside and said in Italian, "No, Ercole. The NV Hotel does have a camera but unfortunately it seemed not to be working at the time of the attack. There is nothing on the disk."

"Thank you for checking that."

She said, "Surely." Then seemed to look him over as she turned and left. He glanced down at his uniform. Was he as rumpled as Columbo? He brushed at some dust on his jacket sleeve.

"Ercole?" Captain Rhyme asked.

"Ah, yes. Sorry." And he told them about the CCTV.

"Always the way, isn't it?" Captain Rhyme asked in a voice that didn't seem surprised. "Put that on our portable chart."

"Our portable chart?"

Thom handed him the yellow pad on which Sachs, at the café, had transcribed his translation of the evidence of the Soames case from the report provided by Elena Cinelli, Garry's lawyer. He made a notation of the lack of video camera and slipped it under a stack of files on the table, out of sight. Well hidden. The last thing Ercole wanted was for Prosecutor Spiro to see it.

Captain Rhyme said, "We still need a search at Garry Soames's apartment. To see if there's any evidence of somebody planting the drugs."

Ercole's heart sank. But Captain Rhyme continued, "We'll wait on that, though. We should have the evidence analysis from your trip out to the country soon. Happy to do the consulate a favor, but, like I told them, the Composer has priority."

Relief coursing through him, Ercole nodded. "Yes, yes, *Capitano*. A good plan."

Then Ercole saw motion from the hallway and noted Daniela standing nearby, head down, playing with a braid absently with one hand as she read from a thick folder held in the other.

She's free . . .

For a solid sixty seconds Ercole Benelli wondered if there was some way he could credibly engage her in a conversation about police procedures and then smoothly—and cleverly—segue into the topic of his love for Eurovision.

He concluded that there was not.

But that didn't stop him from excusing himself and stepping into the hallway. He nodded hello to Daniela and said, with a shy smile, that he'd heard she liked the contest and, he was just curious, not that it was important, what did she think of the Moldavian entry last year, which he considered to be the best competition song to come along in years?

Ercole was surprised, to say the least, when she agreed.

CHAPTER 31

Now, move.
    Get going!
    Huddling in his musty bedroom in this musty house, Stefan forced himself to rise and, as always, first thing, don latex gloves. Shaky-hand, sweaty-skin... He wiped his brow and neck, slipped the tissue into his pocket for later disposal. Then he slipped a pill into his mouth. Olanzapine. Ten mg. After much trial and error, doctors had determined that the drug made him as normal as he could be. Or, as he'd heard it described, behind his back: rendering him less fucking schizoid than anything else could. (For Stefan, treatment and maintenance were pretty much limited to drugs; psychotherapy was useless for someone who was far more interested in the *sound* of words than the content. "So tell me your feelings when you walked into the cellar, Stefan, on that day in April and saw what you saw" was nothing more than a series of spoken tones that, depending on the doctor's voice, could be ecstatically beautiful, could downright thrill him or could induce a bout of anxiety thanks to the shrink's vocal fry.)

Olanzapine. The "atypical"—or second-generation—antipsychotic worked well enough. But today, he was struggling. The Black Screams were nipping at the edges of his mind. And the desperation swelled. He had to move, move, *move* along the stations of his own cross, en route to Harmony.

Shaky-hand, sweaty-skin.

Had he been a drinking man, he would have taken a shot of something.

A ladies' man, he would have bedded a woman.

But he wasn't either of those. So he hurried to do the one thing that would keep him from surrendering to the Black Screams: find the next "volunteer" for a new waltz.

So. Move!

Into his backpack he placed the black cloth hood, the thin sealed bag of chloroform, duct tape, extra gloves, the gag. And, of course, his calling card: the cello string wound into a small noose. He pulled off his blue latex gloves, showered, dressed in jeans and a gray T-shirt, socks and his Converse Cons. He pulled on new gloves and peered out the window. No threats. Then he stepped outside, locked the bulky door and collected his old Mercedes 4MATIC from the garage. In three minutes he was on the uneven country road that would eventually lead to the motorway and the city.

Another step to Harmony.

To Heaven.

Religion and music have been forever intertwined. Songs in praise of the Lord. The Levites carrying the Ark of the Covenant on their shoulders amid songs and the music of cymbals, lyres and harps. David appointing four thousand righteous to be the musical voice of the temple he had hoped to build. The Psalms, of course—150 of them.

Then that trumpet at Jericho.

Stefan had never attended church as an adult but had spent many, many hours of his early adolescence in Sunday school and vacation Bible study, deposited there by a mother who was savvy about finding convenient places to stash the boy for an afternoon here or a late morning there, sometimes a whole weekend. She probably recognized he was about to tumble into madness (bit of that herself) and she might have to keep him home, so Abigail rarely missed a chance to get him tucked away in finger-paint-scented basements or retreat tents before her male friends came a-calling.

The Sunday-school days were before the Black Screams had begun in earnest, and young Stefan was as content as a boy might be, sitting among the other oblivious youngsters soaking up a bit of the old theo, dining on cookies and juice, listening to tweedy teachers recite lesson plans with the devotion of, well, the devout.

The words were mostly crap, he knew that even then, but one story stuck: how, when God (for no reason that made sense) sent evil spirits to torment the first king of Israel, Saul, only music could comfort him. Music from David's harp.

Just like for Stefan, only music or sounds could soothe, and keep the Black Screams away.

Driving carefully, Stefan found his phone and went to his playlist. He now chose not pure sounds from his collection but a melody, "Greensleeves," not technically a waltz, though written in six-eight time, which was essentially the same. (And, rumor was, written by Henry VIII.)

"Greensleeves"...A sorrowful love ballad—a man abandoned by his muse—had a second life: It was borrowed by the church as the Christmas carol "What Child Is This?"

The world loved this song, absolutely loved it.

What, he wondered, was there about this particular melody that had persisted for so many years? Why did this configuration of notes, set to this tempo, continue to touch souls after a thousand years? The tune spoke to us like few others. Stefan had thought long about this question, and had come to no conclusion other than that sound was God, and God was sound.

Harmony.

The sad strains of the music looping through his mind, Stefan decided it set the stage for what was about to happen.

Alas, my love, you do me wrong, to cast me off discourteously...

He slowed now and made the turn onto the side road that would take him to the Capodichino Reception Center.

CHAPTER 32

In the situation room beside the Scientific Police's laboratory on the ground floor of the Questura, Beatrice Renza said in a matter-of-fact voice, "I am afraid I have created a fail." She was not particularly downcast about this glitch, whatever that might be, but it was hard to tell; she seemed to live in a perpetual state of overcast.

She was speaking to Rhyme, Massimo Rossi, Ercole Benelli and Amelia Sachs.

Rossi asked her a question in Italian.

The forensic analyst said in English, "I was able only to make reconstruction of a partial fingerprint from the leafs that you"—a nod to Ercole—"recovered. Yes, it was a print on the leaf, yes, I would assume it was left by our *furfante*, our villain, the Composer, for his footprint was below the place where you sawed the branch off. But it is merely a very minor portion of a friction ridge. It is not enough for the systems to match."

"And the trace?" Rhyme asked.

"I have had more successfulness there. From the soil in the tread marks of his Converse shoes I have discovered a several grains of soil...infused with carbon dioxide, unburned hydrocarbons, oxides of nitrogen, carbon monoxide, kerosene."

"Engine exhaust," Rhyme said.

"Yes, exactly as I had considered."

"What do the proportions suggest?"

"Jet aircraft. Because of the levels of kerosene. Not automobiles or trucks. And in addition, I found this: Fibers that are *coerente*..."

"Consistent," Ercole said.

"*Sì*, with those in napkins or paper towelettes. And in the trace and in the fibers were substances that are *consistent* with these foods: sour milk, wheat, potatoes, chili powder, turmeric, tomatoes. And fenugreek. You are familiar?"

"No."

Ercole said, "Ingredients in Northern African cuisine, most frequently."

Beatrice said, "Yes, yes. With those materials, *ingredients*, possibly it is being bazin, a bread from Liberia or Tunisia." She touched her belly and added, "I know food well. All types of food I know, I will say." No smile, no embarrassment.

She added, "*Allora*, I called restaurants in the area of his staking-out, fifteen kilometers around, a circle, from D'Abruzzo, and they are all traditional Italian. There are no establishments of Middle Eastern or North African eating nearby." She spoke to Ercole, who translated: "So, the Composer had recently been somewhere near cooking of this kind, a restaurant, a family."

Rhyme scowled.

"Is something wrong?" Massimo Rossi asked.

"The analysis is fine. The problem is I don't know how to put the evidence in context. You *have* to know the geography in this business. The landscape, the culture of your crime scenes."

"*Sì*, this is true," Beatrice said.

"*Allora*," Rossi said. "Perhaps, Captain Rhyme, I can be of help. We had an incident not long ago. Refugees from Africa refused to eat Italian pasta. True, it was simple, with only *pomodoro*—tomato—sauce." He wrinkled his nose. "I prefer *ragù* or pesto. But, my story is this: The refugees complained, can you believe that? And they insisted on native food. My feeling is, your expression in English, beggars cannot be choosers, but many people took their protests to heart and an effort was made to give the refugees traditional Libyan and North African food. But the refugee camps and facilities are not always able to do so. So, near the camps are many vendors selling Libyan and Tunisian ingredients and fully cooked food."

"That must cover much land."

Rossi suddenly smiled. "It does, except for—"

Rhyme interrupted: "The jet exhaust."

"Exactly! The biggest camp in Campania is the Capodichino Reception Center located near the airport. And there are North African food vendors there."

"Refugees," Ercole said. "Like Ali Maziq." To Rossi: "Could this be the pattern *Procuratore* Spiro was thinking of?"

"I would say we don't know enough yet. The Composer *might* have in mind as his next victim another refugee. But it might also be someone connected with the place. An employee."

Sachs said, "Send Michelangelo and the tac team to the camp. And tell the security people there. And I'm going too."

Rossi looked her way with a wary smile.

"I know, I know," she said. "Spiro won't be happy. But I'll deal with him later." She looked him over. "Are you going to stop me, Inspector?"

Rossi made a show of turning his back to her and staring at the evidence chart. He said, to no one in particular, "I wonder where Detective Sachs has gotten herself to. The last I saw of her, she was at the Questura. And now, gone. I would guess she is off to see the sights of Naples. The ruins of Pompeii, very likely."

"Thank you," she whispered to Rossi.

He said, "For what? I cannot imagine."

As she and the Forestry officer headed for the door, Rhyme noted that Ercole dug into his pocket, fishing for something. Then, for a reason Rhyme could not figure out, the young man's face tightened with dismay as he produced a set of car keys and dropped them into Sachs's outstretched palm.

CHAPTER 33

Their deduction was a solid one—that the Composer might be looking for victims at the refugee camp near the airport.

The forensics were good: Aviation fuel suggested an airport, and the ingredients in Libyan food suggested refugees' meals or vendors near a refugee camp like the Capodichino Reception Center.

And yet...

As sometimes happens with the most solidly and elegantly constructed theory, this was marred by a tragic flaw.

It had been made too late.

The Composer had done exactly what Rhyme and the others had guessed. Though with one variation: He had not bothered using a kidnapped person's gasping breath as the rhythm section for a waltz. He'd simply slashed the victim's throat and, after leaving his trademark noose, fled.

Amelia Sachs and Ercole Benelli had arrived about a half hour after the team at the Questura had deduced that the camp might be the site of the next kidnapping. Already present were a dozen Police of State and Carabinieri, along with some officers of the Financial Police, specializing in immigration laws. Sachs had spotted the flashing lights and the crowd just outside the camp, at the far end from the main gate. There, the chain link had been cut open, making an impromptu exit.

Perhaps a hundred people ganged outside—and from the vigilant way the officers were watching those present, Sachs assumed that many were refugees who'd slipped through the gate to view the incident. Others, workers from the vendor stands, protesters, journalists and passersby, milled about as well, hoping for a look at the carnage, Sachs supposed.

Sachs mounted an earphone and hit a call button, then slipped the live cell back into her hip pocket, sitting just above her switchblade knife.

"Sachs. The scene?"

"Beyond contaminated. Must be fifty people surrounding the body."

"Hell."

She turned to Ercole. "We have to get those people away. Clear the scene. Clear the whole area."

"Sì. I will do that. I will try. Look at all of them."

He stepped away from her and spoke to some of the Police of State officers, who at first paid little attention to him. She heard him mention the names "Rossi" and then "Spiro." And the men grew wary and attentive and began clearing the crowd in earnest. Some men and women, apparently soldiers with the army, assisted.

Sachs told Rhyme she'd call him back, she had to secure the scene, and disconnected.

"Find out who's in charge."

"Yes."

Pulling on gloves and donning rubber bands—even though it was pointless, given the trampled ground—she crouched, then lifted the corner of the sheet. She studied the victim.

He was a young, dark-complexioned man, eyes half-open. He lay in a thick pool of blood. A half-dozen cuts were prominent in his neck. He was in stocking feet. She laid the sheet back.

Ercole had a conversation with several officers and he and one of them walked up to Sachs. He was, she recognized, with the Police of State.

Ercole said, "This is Officer Bubbico. He was the first on the scene when the workers called about the death."

"Ask him who the victim is."

Bubbico offered his hand and Sachs shook it. He said, "I speak English. I studied in America. Many years ago. But I can speak all right."

But before he could say any more, a female voice sounded behind her. In Italian.

Sachs turned to see someone approaching quickly. A short woman with a pretty but severe face, a mass of thick auburn hair tied into a ponytail with a black ribbon. She was slim but seemed in fighting shape. She wore a dusty khaki blouse and a gray skirt, long, and had a lanyard around her neck, a clattering radio on her hip.

Her demeanor, more than the laminated credentials, spoke of authority.

The woman grimaced at the sight of the corpse.

Sachs asked, "You're connected to the camp?"

"Yes." Her eyes were still on the covered body. "I am Rania Tasso." Sachs noted that her badge said *Ministero dell'Interno*. "The director." Her English revealed a slight accent.

Sachs and Ercole introduced themselves.

"*Orribile*," she muttered. "This is our first murder. We've had robbery and fights but no rapes, no murders. This is horrible." The last word was solidly anglicized, with the "h" pronounced.

A moment later Massimo Rossi arrived and strode close, nodding to Ercole and Sachs. He identified himself to Rania and, after a few words in Italian, they both switched to English. The inspector asked the camp director and Bubbico what had occurred.

Rania said, "The guards are still looking for witnesses but one worker, a cook, saw the killer crouching over the body and setting the noose on the ground. Then he fled to those bushes and trees. He got into a dark car and sped away. I asked what kind of car, but the cook did not have any thought."

Bubbico said, "Several officers and I ran to the road as soon as we heard. But, as I told Director Tasso, he was gone by then. I ordered roadblocks but this is a congested area. We are near the airport and there are present many factories and some farms, of course—and there are many roads and streets by where he could escape." He opened a tissue and displayed the all-too-familiar noose, made of dark gut.

"Where was it?" Sachs asked. "The noose."

"There. Near the head," Bubbico explained.

"The victim? Do we know his identity?" Sachs asked.

Rania said, "Yes, yes. He had gone through the Eurodac procedure. The Dublin Regulation. You are familiar?"

"Yes," Sachs said.

"He was Malek Dadi, twenty-six. Tunisian by birth but he lived in Libya for the past twenty years, with his family—his parents and sister are still in Tripoli. He had no criminal record and was a classic economic refugee; he'd taken no public political stance in the conflict in Libya and was not a target of any of the factions there. He was not the sort the extremists, like ISIS, would target. He was here simply to make a better life and bring his family over."

Rania looked down and added, "So very sad. I could not say I know about everybody here. But Malek arrived recently so he is fresher in my memory. He was suffering from depression. Very anxious. He missed his family terribly and was very homesick. We have representatives in the camp of the Italian Council for Refugees—the CIR. They arranged for help for him. Psychological help. I think it might have done him good. But now this..." A look of disgust crossed her face.

Bubbico said, "And then, it was shameful. Some people ran out to the body and stripped things from him. They took his shoes and belt. Any money and his wallet."

Rania Tasso said, "I was devastated. Yes, people here are desperate but he was one of *them*. And to steal his clothing! They would have taken this shirt, it seems, but left it merely because of the blood. Terrible."

"Do you know who took them?" Ercole asked. "The articles might be important evidence."

Rania and the officer did not. She said, "They vanished." She waved a hand at the mass of refugees on the other side of the fence, within the camp proper.

She added something that Sachs found interesting: She'd seen a suspicious-looking man the other night, heavyset, looking at her. But he might have been studying the security, or just looking for victims. She had no information about him, other than a general description, and she could not say exactly where he'd been standing.

The Composer?

Daniela and Giovanni, Rossi's associates, appeared. They'd arrived earlier apparently and had been canvassing. Daniela walked up to her boss and spoke to him in Italian. Then the inspector asked Rania, "Can you make inquiries? Find out if anyone in the camp saw more? The refugees will not speak to us."

She answered in Italian, clearly in the affirmative.

Sachs added, "Tell them, reassure them that we don't suspect *them*. The killer is an American, a psychotic killer."

"This Composer I've read about."

"Yes."

Rania was looking through the fence at the wall of refugees. She said thoughtfully, "And Malek is the second immigrant he's killed."

"We saved the first one," Ercole pointed out. "But, yes, Malek is the second refugee victim."

"And it's clear why, of course," the camp director spat out.

Rossi and Sachs turned to her.

"The Burial Hour."

Sachs didn't know what this referred to and said as much, though Rossi was nodding in understanding.

Rania explained, "The title of a speech that a politician in Rome gave at some public forum. It has been widely reprinted. 'The Burial Hour' refers to the asylum-seeker problem. Many of the citizens in Italy, Greece, Turkey, Spain, France, feel that they are endangered—they are being buried by the hordes and hordes of migrants pouring into their countries. Like a landslide, crushing them.

"Accordingly, the citizens of the destination countries, like Italy, they are increasingly hostile to the poor souls." Now she was speaking to Rossi. "There are some who believe that the police, for instance, do not investigate crimes against the immigrants as energetically as they would crimes against citizens or tourists. This Composer may be psychotic but he is also clever. He knows about these attitudes of many people here— many officials—and he believes you won't work so hard to stop him. So he hunts refugees."

Rossi said slowly, "Yes, I have heard people say that. But you would be wrong in suggesting we don't care about the victims. I assure you we will investigate this crime just as carefully as we did the first one. Just as carefully as if the victim were a priest or the prime minister." He then could not help but smile, it seemed. "Perhaps *more* diligently than if he were a prime minister."

Rania clearly did not see the humor. "I do not observe many officers here." She looked around.

"This is Naples. We have street crime. We have Camorra. There are recent reports of terrorist cells planning operations throughout the EU, including Italy. We are too little butter spread on too much bread."

She was unmoved by his words. Her eyes again dipped to the sheet, now quite bloody, and she said nothing more.

The Scientific Police van arrived. From it climbed the officer Sachs remembered from the scene where they rescued Ali Maziq from the aqueduct reservoir room.

We're going to step the grid...

They got to work but after an hour of diligent searching, there seemed precious little to show. The footprints had been obliterated near the victim, though some were recovered near where the car had been parked, behind the line of trees. A few Libyan dinars and a Post-it were recovered from under the body. No phone or prepaid card or wallet. One witness came forward, an NGO worker from a charity based in London that helped in refugee camps around the Mediterranean. He had not seen the actual killing but he had glimpsed the Composer's face as he paused over the body, after leaving the noose.

The worker couldn't add any details, but Rossi summoned his uniformed associate Giovanni, with whom he spoke for a moment. The officer went to his Flying Squad car and returned a moment later with a laptop. He loaded a program and Sachs saw it was SketchCop FACETTE, a good facial reconstruction software program. Though the FBI prefers actual artists, even now in this high-tech age, most law enforcement agencies found that people with suitable talent are hard to find, and so they used this or a similar program.

In ten minutes an image of the Composer was complete—if pretty generic, in Sachs's opinion—and was uploaded to the Questura, where officers in turn sent it to police throughout Italy. Sachs would receive a copy too.

The evidence was packed into plastic bags and delivered into Ercole Benelli's waiting, and gloved, hands. He filled out a chain-of-custody card then looked around him, studying the scene. After a moment he said that he would place the evidence in the trunk of the Mégane. He wandered off in that direction.

Rossi received a call and, taking it, walked away from the scene, gesturing Bubbico after him.

Sachs was looking over the camp. What a sprawling, chaotic place it was. Many blue tents but also improvised shelters. Stacks of firewood, laundry lines from which flags of faded cloth dangled, hundreds of empty cardboard cartons, discarded water bottles and empty food tins. People sitting on rugs, on wooden cartons, on dirt. Mostly cross-legged. Some were squatting. Everyone seemed thin, and more than a few appeared to be ill. Many of the lighter-complexioned were badly sunburned.

So many people. Thousands of them. A flood.

No, a landslide.

The Burial Hour...

A voice startled her. "Ah, it appears that you too, Detective Sachs, suffer from a disability."

She turned and found herself face-to-face with Dante Spiro.

"*Your* disability is being hard of hearing."

She blinked at these words.

He slipped a cheroot into his mouth. Being outside, he lit it and inhaled deeply, then put the gold lighter away. "You were ordered to limit your work to crime laboratory assistance. And acting as an Arabic-language interpreter. You are not doing the former and you are not doing the latter. You are here in the thick of an investigation." He looked at her gloved hands and the rubber bands on her feet.

Dante Spiro will not be happy. But I will deal with him later.

Later is now, I'm afraid, Rhyme.

He approached. But, never one to shrink from a fight, Sachs walked up to him, stood just feet away. She was inches taller.

Another person approached. Ercole Benelli.

"And you! Forestry Officer!" The words were contemptuous. "*She* is not under my command but *you* are. Letting this woman onto the scene, out in public—exactly what I told you should not happen—is completely unacceptable!" As if the words didn't have enough edge in a foreign language, he switched to Italian. The young officer's face turned red and he lowered his eyes to the ground.

"*Procuratore*," he began.

"*Silenzio!*"

They were interrupted by a voice that called urgently from behind the yellow tape. "*Procuratore* Spiro!"

He turned, noted that the man addressing him was a reporter, one of several at the police tape line. Since the crime had occurred outside the chain-link fence, the reporters could get closer to the action than if it had happened inside. "*Niente domande!*" He gestured with his hand abruptly.

As if he hadn't spoken, the reporter, a young man in a dusty, rumpled suit coat and tight jeans, moved closer and lobbed questions to him.

At which Spiro stopped, completely still, and turned to the reporter. He asked something in Italian, apparently seeking clarification.

Ercole translated in a whisper. "The reporter is asking the prosecutor's response to a rumor that he is being praised in Rome for his foresight in asking two renowned American forensic detectives to come to Italy to help solve the crime."

Spiro replied, according to Ercole, that he was unaware of such rumors.

The young officer continued. It seemed that Spiro had put aside his ego and was considering what was best for the citizens of Italy, in protecting them from this psychotic killer. "Other, lesser, prosecutors would have been too territorial to bring such investigators here from overseas but not Spiro. He knew it was important to use Americans to get into the mind of a killer from their own country."

Spiro answered several more questions.

Ercole said, "They ask was it true that he himself deduced that the killer would strike here and nearly made it in time to catch the Composer. He answers that yes, that is true."

Spiro then made what seemed to be a brief statement, which the reporters scribbled down.

He strode to Amelia Sachs and, shocking her, put his arm around her shoulder and gazed at the cameras. "You will smile," he whispered harshly to her.

She did.

Ercole stepped forward too but Spiro whispered a harsh, "*Scappa!*"

The young officer backed away.

When the reporter had turned, to jockey through the crowd for pictures of the body, Spiro regarded Sachs and said, "You have a temporary—and limited—reprieve. And your appearing at scenes? I would not object to that. Though you will not talk to the press." He started away.

"Wait!" she snapped.

Spiro paused and turned, his face reflecting an expression that said he was not used to people addressing him in this tone.

Sachs said, "What you said? About disability? That was beneath you."

Their eyes locked, and neither moved a muscle for long seconds. Then it seemed he might, only might, have given her a minuscule nod of concession, before continuing on to Massimo Rossi.

He nearly crashed the Mercedes.

So upset was Stefan, about the disaster at the camp, that his eyes had filled with tears and he'd nearly missed a turn as he fled into the hills above Capodichino.

He parked, climbed from the car and sagged to the cool earth. In his mind, he was picturing the blood pouring out of the man's neck, making a shape like a bell in the sandy ground outside the camp. The man who would now never be the downbeat for his new composition.

The man who was now forever silent.

Alas, my love....

I'm sorry, Euterpe...I'm sorry...

Oh, don't ever turn your back on your muse. Never nevernevernever...

Never disappoint.

That Stefan hadn't *wanted* the man to die this way made no difference. Stefan's composition was ruined, his waltz—so perfect—was ruined.

He dried his eyes and glanced back at the camp.

Which was when the sight stunned him. If it had been a sound, it would have been a dynamite explosion.

No!

Impossible.

This couldn't be...

Stefan pushed his way down the hill—still remaining under cover of the pine and magnolias—and paused, his cheek against the bark of a gnarly tree.

Was it true?

Yes, yes, it was! His eyes closed again and he sagged to his knees. He was devastated.

For below him, at the very spot where the man had died, where his blood had spilled out so fast, so relentlessly, stood Artemis.

The red-haired policewoman from the factory in Brooklyn. Stefan knew that some people from New York had come to Italy to help in the investigation against *Il Compositore*. But he'd never thought it would be the same woman who had so cleverly tracked down the plant and burst through the fence, like the goddess from Olympus that she was, the huntress winging her way to her prey.

No, no, no...

All that mattered in Stefan's life was arriving at Harmony. He would not allow anything or anyone to deflect him from that state of grace, where the music of the spheres hummed in perfection. And yet here she was, Artemis, intent on stopping him and driving his life to discord.

He lay curled on the ground, knowing he should be moving, but shivering in despair. Nearby, an insect clicked, an owl hoo-ahed, a large animal broke a branch and swished some dry grass.

But the sounds brought him no comfort.

Artemis... In Italy.

Get back to your house, he told himself. Before she starts looking here. Because she will. She's lethal, she's keen and she's hungry for the hunt.

She's a goddess. She'll sense where I am!

He rose and stumbled back to the car. He started the engine, wiped the last of his tears and pulled back onto the road.

What would he do?

An idea occurred. What was the one thing that a huntress might not expect?

Obvious: that she would become another hunter's prey.

CHAPTER 34

L ater that evening, ten o'clock, the Composer team reconvened at
the Questura.

All except Dante Spiro, the man who kept his own hours...and
his own counsel.

Rhyme kept glancing impatiently into the lab, at Beatrice, who was
silently plodding away in her analysis of the evidence. Her fingers were
stubby, her hands small. Yet even from here Rhyme could see a deftness
about her movements.

Rhyme was also aware of Thom, who'd glanced pointedly at his watch
twice in the past few minutes. Yes, yes, I get it.

But Rhyme was in no mood to leave, certainly in no mood to sleep. He
was exhilarated, as always when on a thorny case. Tired from the travel,
yes, but sleep would remain evasive, he knew, even back in the luxurious
hotel.

Sachs said, "But the killing: Intentional? Or because the snatch—the
kidnapping—went bad? Somebody showed up. Or the victim saw him
and fought back. After he was dead he left the noose as a concession to
his plan."

"Or," Ercole offered, "his psychosis took over and he is becoming more
homicidal. He doesn't want to take the time to make more compositions."

Beatrice Renza walked into the room, carrying a yellow pad with her
notes. "Here, finally, is the things I have. For the board." She nodded to

an easel. "And I have included the report from the notes by one of the present officers."

Ercole handed her the marker, conceding the handwriting issue without a fight.

She said, *"Fammi la traduzione."*

He nodded and he both spoke and spelled some of entries for her in English, correcting her errors as she wrote.

CAPODICHINO RECEPTION CENTER

— Victim:
- — Malek Dadi, 26.
- — Tunisian national, lived in Libya, economic not political refugee.
- — Causa di morte: loss of blood due to lacerated jugular vein and carotid artery (see medical officer's report).
— No murder weapon recovered.
— Crime scene trampled, largely destroyed.
— Individual spotted observing the camp within past day or two, fitting the Composer's description. No further information.
— Traces of amobarbital (anti-panic drug) found in soil beside victim, in suspect's footprint.
— Miniature noose, made from musical instrument string, no manufacturer determined. Probably cello. 32cm in length.
— Tire tread: Michelin 205/55R16 91H, same as at other scenes.
— Footprints: Converse Cons, Size 45, same as at other scenes.
— Witnesses report suspect drove large black or navy-blue vehicle.
— Post-it note, yellow.
- — Unable to determine source.
- — Address written in blue ink (unable to determine source of ink): Filippo Argelati, 20-32, Milan.
- — No readable fingerprints.
- — Located under victim but unclear whether he or Composer or someone else was source.
— Camp officials presently searching for other witnesses.
— See FACETTE facial composite rendering.

The Composer's composite picture revealed a round, bald white man, depicted both with a hat and without. He resembled ten thousand other
round white men. Rhyme had worked very few cases in which an artist's
rendering provided leads that resulted in an arrest.

Looking at the chart, Rossi mused, "That Post-it note, Milan...What
could it be? Was it Malek Dadi's? Or does the Composer have a connection there? He might have flown in there, established a base, and then
drove to Naples for his mischief."

"Is it nearby?" Rhyme asked.

"No. Seven hundred kilometers."

Sachs said, "We have to follow up."

"Someone from the Milan police," Ercole suggested. "You must know
officers there, *Ispettore*."

"Of course I do. But one who can understand the nature of the case
quickly? What to look for? I think it would be better for someone here to
go. Daniela and Giacomo have other caseloads. Ercole, with respect, you
are new to this game. I wonder if—"

Sachs said, "I'll go."

"That is what I was going to suggest."

Rhyme said, "But what about Spiro?"

"Oh, I didn't tell you, Rhyme," Sachs offered. "I'm on the A list. Some
reporter was talking about him getting praised for the insight of flying us
here from America." She lowered her voice. "He came close to smiling."

"Dante Spiro smiling?" Rossi laughed. "As often as a pope's death."

Sachs said, "I'll find somebody in the consulate there to translate for
me." She looked at Ercole. "You can stay here and take care of other
matters."

Other matters...

He understood, as Rhyme did, that she was talking about the Garry
Soames case. There was still the student's apartment to search. Ercole
looked worried for a moment, concerned that she might mention this
mission in front of Rossi, but of course she did not.

She said, "The jet we flew here on is in England for the time being. Is
there an aircraft of yours I can use?"

Rossi laughed. "We have none, I'm afraid. We fly Alitalia, like everyone else, except in very rare cases." He looked at Ercole. "The Forestry Corps has aircraft."

"For forest fires. Bombardier Four-Fifteen Super Scoopers. We have a Piaggio P One-Eighty. But none of those are nearby."

He said this in a tone that, to Rhyme, really meant they were not available to shuttle American detectives anywhere, even if one had been nearby.

"I will check with Alitalia," Ercole said.

"No," Rhyme replied. Then to Sachs, "No commercial flights. I want you to have your weapon with you."

Rossi said, "Yes, it would add considerable time and paperwork." *Irregularness . . .*

Sachs asked, "Then what? An overnight drive?"

Rhyme said, "No. I have an idea. But I'll need to make a call." Then he looked Thom's way. "All right, all right. I'll do it from the hotel."

Besides, he was eager to continue his mission to acquire the acquired taste for grappa.

V

SKULLS AND BONES

CHAPTER 35

At 8 a.m. Rhyme, Sachs and Thom were once again displaying passports to the U.S. Marine guards at the well-fortified entrance to the U.S. consulate and were shown inside, to the lobby.

Rhyme was rested and had only a slight hangover—grappa seemed to be kinder in this regard than single-malt whisky.

Five minutes later they were in the office of the consulate general himself, a handsome, well-built man in his mid-fifties. He wore a gray suit, a white shirt and a tie as rich and blue as the water sparkling outside. Henry Musgrave had the studied manners and perceptive eyes of a lifer in the diplomatic corps. Unlike Charlotte McKenzie, he had no problem striding up to Rhyme and shaking hands.

"I've heard of you, of course, Mr. Rhyme. I get to New York and Washington. You make the news, even in the nation's capital. Some of your cases—that fellow, the Skin Collector, he was called. That was quite something."

"Yes. Well." Rhyme was never averse to praise but wasn't inclined to tell war stories at the moment; he was sure that the Composer was planning another attack—because the one at the reception center had failed or because he was indeed slipping further into madness.

Musgrave greeted Sachs and Thom with an enthusiastic grip. He sat down and his attention drifted to his computer screen. "Ah, it's confirmed." He read for a moment and looked up. "Just got a National Security briefing report. Not classified—it's going to the media now.

You'll be interested. The CIA and the Austrian counterterrorism depart-ment, the BVT, stopped a terrorist plot in Vienna. They scored a half kilo of C4, a cell phone detonator and a map of a mall in a suburb. No actors yet but they're on it."

Rhyme recalled that there'd been a flurry of reports of suspected ter-rorist activity—both in Europe and in the United States. That was why the Police of State had fewer officers to help investigate the Composer case than they otherwise might.

Okay, got it. Happy news for all. Let's move on.

Musgrave turned from the screen. "So, a serial killer from America."

Rhyme glanced toward Sachs, a reminder that they didn't have time to correct the diplomat about the Composer's technical criminal profile.

The consulate general mused, "The Italians have had a few—the Monster of Florence. Then, Donato Bilancia. He killed about seven-teen. There's a nurse currently suspected of killing nearly forty patients. And there were the Beasts of Satan. They were convicted of killing only three, though they're suspected of more. I imagine the Americans win the serial killer prize in terms of body count. At least if you believe cable TV."

Rhyme said in a clipped voice, "Colombia, China, Russia, Afghanistan and India beat the U.S. Now, as to our request? We're still good?"

"Yep. I just double-checked."

Last night, Rhyme had called Charlotte McKenzie, asking if she had access to a government jet to shepherd Sachs to Milan. She didn't but would check with the consulate general. Musgrave's assistant called Rhyme to report that an American businessman, in Naples for trade pro-motion meetings, had a private jet that was flying to Switzerland this morning. The plane could easily stop in Milan on the way. He'd meet them this morning to discuss the trip.

And now Musgrave's assistant appeared in the doorway, followed by a lanky man, topped with a shock of strawberry-blond hair. He grinned to all and stepped forward. "Mike Hill." He shook hands with everyone, Rhyme included, paying no attention to the wheelchair.

Rhyme was not surprised when the consulate general told him that Hill—nerdy and boyish, a younger Bill Gates—was here to hawk high-tech products to the Italians; his company exported broadband and fiber-optic equipment, built in his Midwest factory.

"Henry was telling me what you need, and I'm happy to help." He then frowned and now glanced at the wheelchair. "But have to say, the plane's not, you know, accessible."

Sachs said, "I'll be going alone."

"What's the timing?"

"If possible, I need to get up there this morning and back tonight."

"Definitely we can get you there in a few hours. The only issue is returning. The crew's got other flights after Milan. If they time out, they'll have to spend the night in Lausanne or Geneva."

"That's fine," Rhyme said. "The important thing is to get there as soon as possible."

Hill said, "Now, where do you want to go? There're two airports in Milan. Malpensa, the bigger one, is about twenty miles northwest of the city and depending on the time of day, the traffic can be pretty bad. Linate's the downtown airport. It's much more convenient if you've got to be in the city itself. Which would be better?"

Rossi had said the warehouse was in town, not in the suburbs. "Linate."

"Okay. Easy-peasy. I'll tell the crew. They'll need to file a flight plan. Coupla hours should do it. And I'll have my driver take you to the airport."

Sachs began, "Mr. Hill—"

"Mike, *per favore.*" Spoken with the worst Italian accent Rhyme had ever heard. "And if you're gonna bring up money, forget it. Won't cost much to make a stop in Milano. So consider this gratis."

"We appreciate it."

"Never had a chance to help catch a psycho and probably never will again. Glad to do my duty." Hill rose, pulled his phone from his pocket and stepped to the corner of the office, where, Rhyme could hear, he had conversations with the pilot and his chauffeur, coordinating the trip.

"Lincoln, Amelia." A woman's voice from the doorway. Rhyme looked up to see Charlotte McKenzie walk into the office, looking rumpled.

Her short blond hair was a bit spiky and her copper-colored blouse a bit wrinkled. Maybe her cold was taking its toll. "Henry." She nodded to Thom too.

"So, hitching a ride to Milan," she said to Rhyme. "That worked out?"

Musgrave nodded toward Mike Hill, still on the phone, and said to McKenzie, "Mike's plane'll get Detective Sachs up there this morning."

"Good. You think this guy, the Composer, he's left Naples? He's up there?"

Sachs said, "We don't know the connection. Just an address on a note from the crime scene at the refugee camp." She then said to Musgrave, "One thing I'm hoping. Is there someone at the consulate in Milan who could drive me, translate for me?"

Charlotte McKenzie said, "I have a colleague there. He does what I do, legal liaison. Pete Prescott. Good man. I can see if he's free."

"That'd be great."

She texted and a moment later her phone chimed with an incoming message. "Yes, he is. I'll text you his number, Amelia."

"Thanks."

Mike Hill joined them, slipping his phone away. Musgrave introduced him to McKenzie and then the businessman said to Sachs, "All set. You're good to go. My driver'll pick you up at eleven...where's good?"

She gave him the hotel address.

"Know it. Great old place. Makes me feel like I'm part of the Rat Pack when I stay there."

Another figure appeared in the doorway, the slim, very pale man of indeterminate age Rhyme remembered from the other day. Ah, yes, the public relations officer. What was the name again?

He nodded to those present and introduced himself to Hill. "Daryl Mulbry."

The slight man sat and said to Rhyme, "We're getting inundated with requests from the press—about both Garry and the Composer. Would you be willing to sit down for an interview?" Mulbry stopped short and blinked—undoubtedly at the awkward choice of a verb, considering Rhyme's condition.

As if he cared. "No," Rhyme said shortly. "I don't have anything to say at this point, other than that we've got a composite rendering of the Composer and that's gone to the press anyway."

"Yes, I've seen it. Intimidating-looking guy. Big. But what about Garry? Any statement?"

Rhyme could just imagine Dante Spiro's reaction when he read in the press that an unnamed "American consultant" was commenting on the case.

"Not now."

McKenzie added, "I should tell you: Garry's been getting threats. Like I mentioned, those accused of sexual assault are at particular risk. Add that he's an American . . . Well, it's a problem. The authorities keep an eye on him but there are no guarantees."

"No press," Rhyme said insistently. But he added, "While Amelia's away I'll be following up with his case, though."

McKenzie said, "Ah. Good." The uncertainty told Rhyme she'd be wondering how exactly he could follow up when his ass was parked in a wheelchair, in a country that did not seem to have the equivalent of the American With Disabilities Act in force.

He didn't tell her that he had a secret weapon.

Two, in fact.

CHAPTER 36

The Black Screams had begun.

But the failure at the camp and the sight of the redheaded policewoman had conspired to shake him awake early and fill his head with the screams, shrilling like a dentist's drill.

Yes, he had a plan for Artemis. Yes, Euterpe had whispered calming sentiments from on high. But, as he well knew, very little could stop determined Black Screams. He'd hoped to control them himself, but ultimately, he knew, he'd lose. It was the same as when you wake with that first twist in your gut, small, nothing really. Still, you understand without any doubt you'll be on your knees over the toilet in an hour with the flu or food poisoning.

Whispering screams, soon to become the Black Screams.

And soon they were.

Shaky-hand, sweaty-skin—these were *nothing* compared with a Black Scream.

Pacing the farmhouse, then outside in the wet dawn. Stop, stop, stop!

But they hadn't stopped. So he'd popped extra meds (that didn't work, never did) and, in the 4MATIC, sped to where he stood now: to chaotic downtown Naples where he prayed the ricocheting cacophony would drown out the screams. (That *sometimes* worked. Ironically, noise was his salvation against Black Screams—as much and as loud and as chaotic as possible.)

He plunged into the jostling crowds filling the sidewalks. He passed food vendors, bars, restaurants, laundries, souvenir stores. He paused outside a café. Imagined he could hear the forks on china, the teeth biting, the jaws grinding, the lips sipping...

The knives cutting.

Like knives slashing throats...

He was sucking up the noise, inhaling the noise, to cover the screams.

Make them stop, make them stop....

Thinking of his teenage years, the girls looking away, the boys never looking away but staring and, sometimes, laughing as Stefan walked into the classrooms. He was thin then, passable in sports, could tell a joke or two, talk about TV shows, talk about music.

But the normal didn't outshine the strange.

How often he would lose himself in the *sound* of a teacher's voice, the melody of her words, not the content, which he didn't even hear.

"Stefan, the sum is?"

Ah, such a beautiful modulation! A triplet in the last of the sentence. Syncopated. G, G, then B flat as her voice rose in tone because of the question. Beautiful.

"Stefan, you've ignored me for the last time. You're going to the principal. Now."

And "principal," an even better triplet!

Only then did he realize: Oh, messed up again.

And the other students either looking away or staring (equally cruel).

Strange. Stefan is strange.

Well, he was. He knew that as well as anybody. His reaction: Make me unstrange or shut the hell up.

Now, on this busy corner in a busy city, Stefan pressed his head against an old stone wall and let a thousand sounds pass over him, through him, bathing him in warm water, circling and soothing his rampaging heart.

Hearing, in his head, his fiery imagination, the tolling of the red bell on the dirt, spreading outward from the man's neck last night.

Hearing the sound of blood roaring in his ears, loud as a blood bell ringing, ringing, ringing.

Hearing the refugee's screams.

Hearing the Black Screams.

From the time of adolescence, when the Black Screams started, it had been a battle to keep them at bay. Sound was the lifeblood for Stefan, comforting, explaining, enlightening. The creak of boards, the stutter of branches, the clicking of tiny animal feet in the Pennsylvania garden and yard, the slither of a snake in the woods. But the same way that healthy germs can become sepsis, sounds could turn on him.

Voices became sounds and sounds voices.

Roadside construction equipment, driving piles was really a voice: "Cellar, cellar, cellar, cellar."

A bird's call was not a bird's call. "Look swinging, look swinging, look swinging."

The wind was not the wind. "Ahhhhhh gone, ahhhhhh gone, ahhhhhh gone."

The creak of a branch: "Drip, drip, drip, drip..."

And a voice from a closed throat that might have been whispering, "Goodbye, I loved you," became merely a rattle of pebbles on wood.

Now a Black Scream, a bad one, the whining drill. It was starting in his groin—yes, you could hear them down there—and zipping up through his spine, through his jaw, through his eyes, into his brain.

Noooooooooo...

He opened his eyes and blinked. People stared uneasily as they passed. In this part of town, fortunately, there were homeless men, also damaged, so he did not stand out sufficiently for them to call the police.

That would not be good at all.

Euterpe would not forgive him.

He managed to control himself enough to move along. A block away he stopped. Wiping sweat, pressing his face against a wall, he struggled to breathe. He looked around. Stefan was near the famed Santa Chiara church, on Via Benedetto Croce—the mile-long street that bisected the ancient Roman part of town and was known to everyone as Spaccanapoli, or the Naples Splitter.

It was a chaotic avenue, narrow, throbbing with tourists and pedestrians and bicycles and scooters and punchy cars. Here were vendors and shops offering souvenirs, religious icons, furniture, commedia dell'arte figurines, cured meats, buffalo mozzarella, limoncello bottles in the shape of the country, and the local dessert, sfogliatelle, crispy pastry that Stefan adored—not for the taste but for the sound of the crackly crust between teeth.

The morning was hot already and he took off his cap and wiped his shaved head with a paper towel he carried with him.

A Black Scream began but desperately he turned his attention back to the street sounds around him. The putter of scooters, shouts, a horn, the sound of something heavy being dragged along stones, a cheerful child's tune chugging from a boom box next to a street performer— a middle-aged man folded into a box that resembled a cradle. Only his head, covered with an infant's bonnet and positioned above a doll's body, was visible. The eerie sight and his bizarre singing captivated passersby.

The wind, snapping laundry overhead.

Mommy silent, Mommy silent.

He was then aware of another sound, growing louder.

Tap...tap...tap.

The rhythm caught him immediately. The resonant tone. He closed his eyes. He didn't turn toward the sound, which was behind him. He savored it.

"Scusati," the woman's voice said. "No, uhm, I mean: *Scusami.*"

He opened his eyes and turned. She was perhaps nineteen or twenty. Slim, braided hair framing a long, pretty face. She was in jeans and wore two tank tops, white under dark blue, and a pale-green bra, he could see from the third set of straps. A camera hung from one shoulder, a backpack from the other. On her feet were, of all things, cowboy boots with wooden heels. They were what had made the distinctive tap as she approached.

She hesitated, blinked. Then: *"Dov'è un taxi?"*

Stefan said, "You're American."

"Oh, you are too." She laughed.

It was obvious to him that she'd known this.

Obvious too that she was flirting. She'd liked what she'd seen and, college girl on her own, had moved in. The sort who had no problem making the first—or second or third—move. And if the boy, or maybe, for a lark, the girl, said no, she'd offer a good-natured smile, no worries, and move on, buoyed by the unbreakable union of youth and beauty.

He was round, he was sweaty. But handsome enough. And not a player. Safe, cuddly.

"I don't know where you'd get a taxi, sorry." He wiped his face again.

She said, "Hot, isn't it? Weird for September."

Yes, though the humid southwestern Italian air was not the source of his perspiration, of course.

A group of schoolchildren, in uniform, streamed past, guided by a protective Mother Hen of a teacher. Stefan and the girl stepped aside. They then shifted again the other way as a Piaggio motor scooter bore down on them. A grizzled deliveryman in a dusty fisherman's cap drove them yet another direction as he staggered under the weight of a carton-filled pushcart, glaring and muttering, as if the sidewalk were his own personal avenue.

"Crazy here! Don't you just love it?" Her freckled face was infinitely amused, and her voice was light but not high. If the sound had been flower petals, they would have been those from pink roses, plucked but still moist. He could feel the tones falling on his skin like those petals.

None of the crackly rasp of vocal fry that the music-hater refugee, Fatima, had.

As she spoke, the Black Screams grew quieter.

"Don't know anyplace back home like it, that I can think of," he said, because that was what somebody from back home would say. He thought New York City was like this actually but, given his recent adventures there, he didn't volunteer *that* observation.

She rambled, charmingly, about being in the south of France most recently, had he ever been? No? Too bad. Oh, Cap d'Antibes. Oh, Nice!

The screams abated some more as he listened. He looked too: such a beautiful young woman.

Such a lovely voice.

And those tapping boots! Like a rosewood drum.

Stefan had had lovers, of course. But in the old days. Before what the doctors would call—though never to his face—the Break, at around age twenty-two. It was then that he had simply given up fighting to be normal and stepped, comforted, into the world of sounds. Around the time Mommy went all quiet in the cellar, quiet and cold, in the quiet and hot cellar, the washing machine spinning the last load of towels ever washed in the house.

Around the time Father decided he wasn't going to be aproned to a troubled son anymore.

Before then, though, before the Break, sure, there'd been the occasional pretty girl, those who didn't mind the strange.

He rather enjoyed them—the occasional nights—though the sensation grew less interesting than the sounds of joining. Flesh made subtle noises, hair might, tongues did, moisture did.

Nails did.

Throats and lungs and hearts, of course.

Then, though, the strange got stranger and the girls started to look away more and more. They started to mind. Which was fine with him because he was losing interest himself. Sherry or Linda would whisper about taking her bra off and he'd be wondering about the sound of Thomas Jefferson's voice, or what the groans of the *Titanic* had been like as she went down.

Now the young woman in the cowboy boots said, "So, I'm here for a few days is all. My girlfriend, the one I was traveling with? She broke up with her boyfriend before she left, but then he called and they got back together so she just went home, pout, pout. And abandoned me! How about that? But here I am in Italy! I mean, like, I'm going back to Cleveland early? Don't think so. So here I am. Talking and talking and talking. Sorry. People say I do that. Talk too much."

Yes, she did.

But Stefan was smiling. He could affect a good smile. "No, it's all good."

She wasn't put off by his silence. She asked, "What're you doing here? You in school?"

"No, I'm working."

"Oh, what do you do?"

Presently slipping nooses around people's necks.

"Sound engineer."

"No way! Concerts, you mean?"

With the Black Screams now at bay he was able to act normal, as he knew he had to. He ran through his arsenal of blandly normal tones and words and launched a few. "I wish. Testing for noise pollution."

"Hm. Interesting. Noise pollution. Like traffic?"

He didn't know. He'd just made the career up. "Yep, exactly."

"I'm Lilly."

"Jonathan," he said. Because he'd always liked the name.

Triplet. Jon-a-than.

A name in waltz time.

"You must get lots of data, or whatever it is you do, here in Naples."

"It's noisy. Yes."

A pause. "So, no idea where to get a cab?"

He looked around because that was what a blandly normal person would do. He shrugged. "Where do you need to go?"

"Oh, a touristy thing. A guy at the hostel I'm staying at recommended this place. He said it's awesome."

Stefan was considering.

Not a good idea...He should be following up on his plan regarding Artemis (it was quite a good one). But, then, she wasn't here, and Lilly was.

"Well, I've got a car."

"No way! You drive? Here?"

"Yeah, it's crazy. The trick is you just forget there're traffic laws, and you do okay. And don't be polite and let people go ahead of you. You just go. Everybody does."

Blandly normal. Stefan was in good form.

Lilly said, "So you want to come with? I mean, if you're not doing anything."

A Black Scream began. He forced it to silence.

"What is this place?"

"The guy said it's totally spooky."

"Spooky?"

"Totally deserted."

So it would be quiet.

Quiet was never wise. Even the best intentions went away when there was quiet.

Still, Stefan looked Lilly over, head to toe, and said, "Sure. Let's go."

CHAPTER 37

S kulls.
　　　Ten thousand.
　　　Twenty thousand.
A hundred thousand skulls.

No. Even more than that.

Skulls arranged in orderly rows, eye sockets staring outward, triangles of darkness where noses had once been, rows of yellow teeth, many missing.

This was the place to which Lilly had directed Stefan. The Fontanelle Cemetery in Naples.

Spooky . . .

Oh, you bet.

It wasn't a burial ground in the traditional sense; it was a huge, forbidding cavern that, Lilly's guidebook explained, had been used as a mass grave site when half the population of Naples had died from plague in the 1600s.

"And there are rumors that underneath here're more, going back to Roman days. There could be a million skulls under our feet."

They stood at the entrance, a massive nature-made archway that led into the darkened expanse. This was no longer prime tourist season and the place had few visitors.

And those who were here seemed to be on missions of devotion, rather than sightseeing. They lit votives, they prayed.

Spooky...and quiet. Almost silent.

Well, he'd have to deal with it. Stefan wiped sweat, put the tissue away.

"You okay?"

"Fine."

They walked farther inside, her boots tapping and echoing. Lovely! Reading from her guidebook, she whispered—here was a place to inspire whispers—that Naples was savagely bombed during the Second World War, and this was one of the few places were the citizens could be safe from the Allied planes.

The lighting was subdued and flames from the candles cast eerie, unsteady shadows of bones and skulls—reanimations of victims dead hundreds, or thousands, of years.

"Creepy, hm?"

"Sure is." Though not because it looked creepy. Because of the quiet. The cavern was like a petri dish for Black Screams. A couple of them started to moan. Started to rise. Started to swell within.

Until he had a thought. A new mission. Good, good.

The Black Screams faded.

A new mission.

Which involved Lilly. And suddenly he was wildly grateful they had met. It was as if his muse had sensed his distress and sent her to him.

Thank you, Euterpe...

Of course, he realized, as he'd thought downtown, this was definitely not a good idea. But he also thought: As if I have any choice.

The failure last night...The swish, swish of the knife at the refugee camp. The spreading blood in the shape of a bell. The nightmares, the sound waves of approaching Black Screams.

Oh, he needed this.

He was looking Lilly over carefully. Probably hungrily. Before she caught him, he gazed off.

Lilly was acting girlish now. Smiling, despite the wall of skulls, the dark eye sockets turned their way. "Hello!" she called.

The echo danced back and forth.

Stefan heard it long after she'd turned her attention elsewhere.

They walked farther into the dim, cool space.

"Your face," she said.

Stefan turned, cocking his head.

"Your eyes were closed. What're you thinking about? Who all these people were?" She nodded to the skulls.

"No, just listening to things."

"Listening? I don't hear anything."

"Oh, there's a thousand sounds. You hear them too but you don't know you do."

"Really?"

"There's our blood, our heartbeat. There's our breath. The sound of our clothing against itself and our skin. I can't hear yours and you can't hear mine but the sounds are there. A scooter—that one's hard because it's an echo of an echo. A tapping. Water, I'd guess. There! That shutter. Somebody took a picture. An old iPhone Four."

"Wow. You can tell that? And it was so far away. I didn't hear a thing."

"You have to allow yourself to hear things. You can hear sounds everywhere."

"Everywhere?"

"Well, not exactly. Not in a vacuum. Not in outer space." Stefan recalled a movie, *Alien* (not a bad flick, by any means). And the advertising line was: *In space no one can hear you scream.*

He told Lilly about this now. And added, "You know in space movies, when you hear ray guns and spaceships colliding and exploding? Well, that's wrong. They'd be completely silent. All sounds—a gunshot, a scream, a baby's laugh—need molecules to bump against. That's what sound is. That's why the speed of sound varies. At sea level it's seven hundred sixty miles an hour. At sixty thousand feet, it's six hundred fifty miles an hour."

"Wow, that's way different! Because of the thinner molecules?"

"Right. In space there are no molecules. There's nothing. So if you opened your mouth and vibrated your vocal cords no one would hear you. But say you were with somebody else and he put his hand on your chest while you were screaming, he'd hear you."

"Because the molecule in his body would vibrate."

"Exactly."

"I like it when people're excited about their jobs. When you first said 'sound engineer,' I thought, hm, pretty dull. But you're, you know, totally into it. That's cool."

Funny when the one thing that makes you crazy keeps you sane.

He was looking over her now, as she turned and walked closer to an inscription in Latin, carved in stone.

Tap, tap, tap.

Her boots.

This isn't a good idea...

Stefan said to himself: Leave. Tell her goodbye. It's been fun. Have a nice trip back home.

But Stefan felt Euterpe hovering over him now, looking out, giving him permission to do what he had to do. Anything to keep the Black Screams away. She'd understand.

To the right the cave disappeared into a dim recess.

"Let's go in the back there." He pointed that way.

"There? It's pretty dark."

Yes, it was. Pretty dark but *completely* deserted.

Stefan wondered for a moment if he'd have to convince her but apparently Lilly believed she was in no danger. He was a little quirky maybe, he sweated a bit much, he was pudgy, but he was a sound engineer who didn't mind conversation and who said interesting things.

Women always fell for men who talked.

Oh, and he was an American. How much danger could he be?

"Okay, sure." A sparkle in her eyes.

They started in the direction he'd indicated.

On the pretense of looking around, he fell slightly behind her.

Hearing her boot soles and heels snapping:

Tap, tap, tap...

He looked around. They were completely alone.

Stefan reached into his pocket and closed his hand around the cool metal.

Tap, tap, taptaptaptaptap...

CHAPTER 38

Carl Sandburg.

"Carl...The poet, right?" Amelia Sachs asked the balding man driving a small, gray Renault.

The associate of Charlotte McKenzie's, he'd picked her up at Linate Airport, the smaller of the two aerodromes in Milan, closer to the city center. They were in thick traffic.

"That's right," Pete Prescott told her. "He wrote 'Chicago.'" The legal liaison dropped his voice a bit, to sound poetic, Sachs guessed, and recited the opening lines, about the Hog Butcher.

"You from there, Chicago?" Sachs didn't know where this was going.

"No, Portland. My point is the poem might've been about Milan. Milan is the Chicago of Italy."

Ah. Got it. She'd been wondering.

"Working, busy, not the prettiest city in the country, not by a long shot. But it has energy and a certain charm. Not to mention *The Last Supper*. The fashion world. And La Scala. Do you like opera?"

"Not really."

A pause. Its meaning: How could someone with a pulse not like opera?

"Too bad. I could get tickets to *La Traviata* tonight. Andrea Carelli is singing. It wouldn't be a date." He said this as if waiting for her to blurt, "No, no, a date would be wonderful."

"Sorry. I've got to get back tonight, if possible."

"Charlotte said you're working on the case. The kidnapper."

"Right."

"With the famous detective Lincoln Rhyme. I've read some of those books."

"He doesn't like them very much."

"At least people write about him. Nobody's going to write novels about a legal liaison, I don't think. Though I've had pretty interesting cases."

He didn't elaborate—she was pleased about that—but concentrated on his GPS. Traffic grew worse and Prescott swung down a side road. In contrast with this, the trip from Naples to Milan had been lightning-fast. Computer millionaire Mike Hill's driver, a larger-than-life Italian with thick hair and an infectious smile, had met her outside the hotel, where he'd been waiting with a shiny black Audi. He'd leapt forward to take her bag. In a half hour, after an extensive history lesson on southern Italy, delivered in pretty good English and with more than a little flirt, they had arrived at the private aircraft tarmac in Naples. She'd climbed onto the plane—even nicer than the one they'd flown to Italy on—and soon the sleek aircraft was streaking into the air. She'd had a pleasant conversation with one of Hill's executives, headed to Switzerland for meetings. Pleasant, yes, though the young man was a super geek and often lost her with his enthusiastic monologues about the state of high technology.

Prescott was now saying, "I prefer Milan, frankly, to other cities here. Not as many tourists. And I like the food better. Too much cheese in the south."

Having recently been served a piece of mozzarella that must've weighed close to a pound, she understood, though was tempted to defend Neapolitan cuisine. An urge she declined.

He added, "But here? Ugh, the traffic." He grimaced and swung the car onto a new route, past shops and small industrial operations and wholesalers and apartments, many of whose windows were covered with curious shades, metal or mesh, hinged from the top. She tried to figure out from the signage what the many commercial operations manufactured or sold, with limited success.

And, yes, it did resemble parts of Chicago, which she'd been to a few times. Milan was a stone-colored, dusty city, now accented with fading autumn foliage, although the dun tone was tempered by ubiquitous red roofs. Naples was far more colorful—though also more chaotic.

Like Hill's swarthy, enthusiastic driver, Prescott was happy to lecture about the nation.

"Just like the U.S., there's a north/south divide in Italy. The north's more industrial, the south agricultural. Sound familiar? There's never been a civil war, as such, though there was fighting to unify the different kingdoms. A famous battle was fought right here. *Cinque Giornate di Milano.* Five Days of Milan. Part of the first War of Independence, eighteen forties. It drove the Austrians out of the city."

He looked ahead, saw a traffic jam, and took a sharp right. He then said, "That case? The Composer. Why'd he come to Italy?"

"We're not sure. Since he's picked two immigrants, refugees, so far, he might be thinking it's harder for the police to solve the cases with undocumenteds as victims. And they're less motivated to run the investigation."

"You think he's that smart?"

"Every bit."

"Ah, look at this!"

The traffic had come to a halt. From the plane, she'd called Prescott and given him the address on the Post-it note found at the scene where the Composer had slashed Malek Dadi to death. Prescott assured her that it would take only a half hour to get there from the airport but already they'd been fighting through traffic for twice that.

"Welcome to Milano," he muttered, backing up, over the sidewalk, turning around and finding another route. She recalled that Mike Hill had warned about the traffic from the larger airport in Milan, thinking: Imagine how long it would take to fight twenty-some miles of congestion like this.

Nearly an hour and a half after she'd landed, Prescott turned along a wide, shallow canal. The area was a mix of the well-worn, the quirky chic and the tawdry. Residences, restaurants and shops.

"This is the Navigli," Prescott announced. He pointed to the soupy waterway. "This and a few others are all that're left of a hundred miles of canals that connected Milan to rivers for transport of goods and passengers. A lot of Italian cities have rivers nearby or running right through town. Milan doesn't. This was the attempt to create artificial waterways to solve that problem. Da Vinci himself helped design locks and sluices."

He turned and drove along a quiet street to an intersection of commercial buildings. Deserted here. He parked under what was clearly a no-parking sign, with the attitude of someone who knew beyond doubt he wouldn't be ticketed, much less towed.

"That's the place right there: Filippo Argelati, Twenty Thirty-Two."

A sign, pink paint—faded from red: *Fratelli Guida. Magazzino.*

Prescott said, "The Guida Brothers. Warehouse."

The sign was very old and she guessed that the siblings were long gone. Massimo Rossi had texted her that the building was owned by a commercial real estate company in Milan. It was leased to a company based in Rome but calls to the office had not been returned.

She climbed out of the car and walked to the sidewalk in front of the building. It was a two-story stucco structure, light brown, and covered with audacious graffiti. The windows were painted dark brown on the inside. She crouched down and touched some pieces of green broken glass in front of the large double doors.

She returned and Prescott got out of his vehicle too. She asked, "Could you stay here and keep an eye on the neighborhood. If anyone shows up text me."

"I…" He was flustered. "I will. But why would anyone show up? I mean, it looks like nobody's been there for months, years."

"No, somebody was here within the past hour. A vehicle. It ran over a bottle that was in front. See it? That glass?"

"Oh, there. Yes."

"There's still wet beer inside."

"If there's something illegal going on, we should call the Carabinieri or the Police of State." Prescott had grown uncomfortable.

"It'll be fine. Just text."

"I will. Sure. I'll definitely text. What should I text?"

"A smiley emoji's fine. I just need to feel the vibration."

"Feel...Oh, you'll have the ringer off. So nobody can hear? In case anybody's inside?"

No confirmation needed.

Sachs returned to the building. She stood to the side of the door, her hand near the Beretta grip in her side pocket. There was no reason to think the Composer had tooled up to Milan in his dark sedan, crunched the bottle pulling into the warehouse and was now waiting inside with his razor or knife or a handy noose.

But no compelling reason *not* to think that.

She pounded on the door with a fist, calling out a reasonable, "*Polizia!*"

Proud of herself, getting the Italian okay, she thought. And ignoring that she was undoubtedly guilty of a serious infraction.

No response, though.

Another pounding. Nothing.

Then she circled the building. In the back was a smaller door but that too was barred, with an impressive chain and padlock. She knocked again.

Still no response.

She returned to Prescott. "So?" he asked.

"Locked up nice and tight."

He was relieved. "We find the police? Get a warrant? You head back to Naples?"

"Could you pop the trunk?

"The...oh." He did.

She fished around and extracted the tire iron.

"You mind?" Sachs asked.

"Uhm, no." He seemed to be thinking fast and, perhaps, recalled that he'd never used the accessory, so it wouldn't be *his* prints on the burglar tool.

Sachs had decided that the front door—the one for humans, not the big vehicle doors—was more vulnerable than the chain on the back. She looked around—not a witness in sight—and worked the tire iron into the jamb. She pulled hard and the door shifted far enough so that the male portion of the lock slipped from the female and the door swung open.

She set the tire iron down, away from the door, where it couldn't be grabbed as a weapon. Then she drew the Beretta and stepped inside fast, squinting to acclimate her eyes to the darkness inside.

CHAPTER 39

How curious what life has in store for us.

Only a day or two ago he was a tree cop, a badger cop...a fungus cop.

Now he was a criminal investigator. Working on quite the case. Tracking down the Composer.

Officers—Police of State and Carabinieri—labored for years solving petty thefts, car hijackings, a mugging, a chain snatching...and never had the chance to be involved in an investigation like this.

Driving through the pleasant neighborhood near Federico II, the university, Ercole Benelli was reflecting, with amusement, that this actually was the *second* multiple killer case he had worked (yes, Amelia, I remember: The Composer is not a *serial* killer). The first crime, however, had involved as victims a dozen head of stolen cattle in the hills east of here. Kidnapping it was too, even if the unfortunates had wandered amiably and without protest into the back of the truck that spirited them away to become entrées and luncheon meat.

But now he was a true investigator, about to search a crime scene on his own.

Even more exciting: Ercole was Lincoln Rhyme's "secret weapon," as the famed officer had told him.

Well, one of the secret weapons. The other was sitting beside him. Thom Reston, the man's aide.

Unlike the first assignment on the furtive Soames investigation—to

Natalia Garelli's apartment—this mission didn't bother Ercole at all. He had, he supposed, caught the bug, so to speak. Thinking that there might in fact be another perpetrator who'd committed the heinous crime and was blaming innocent Garry Soames, he was inspired to do all he could to get the facts. Earlier, he'd cornered an expert. This specialist came in the luscious form of Daniela Canton. The beautiful—and musically savvy—officer was a basic Flying Squad cop but much of what she did, as the first person on the scene, was to isolate and preserve evidence for the Scientific Police, later to come. Naturally, she was the perfect person to ask. They'd sat in the cafeteria of the Questura, over cappuccinos, as the woman had lectured him matter-of-factly about what to look for, how to approach the scene and, most important, how not to contaminate or alter evidence in any way. Or allow others to do so.

Much of this, it turned out, he'd already learned from Amelia Sachs, but it was pleasant to sit across from Daniela and watch her heavenly blue eyes gazing toward the dusky ceiling as she lectured.

Watch her lengthy, elegant fingers encircle the cup.

A cheetah with azure-blue claws.

He had decided, though, that perhaps she was less creature of the wild than a movie star, albeit one from a different era: the sort appearing in the films of the great Italian directors—Fellini, De Sica, Rossellini, Visconti.

Accordingly, he resisted the sudden urge to show her a picture of Isabella. Proud though he was, there seemed no possible excuse to bring up the topic of a pregnant pigeon to this stellar woman. He simply took notes.

So, armed with her insights, and a fast review of the Scientific Police guidelines, Ercole Benelli had plunged into his mission. And now he eased the poor boxy car onto a sidewalk (parking Neapolitan-style) and climbed out—as did his co-conspirator.

Thom looked around the neighborhood. "What part of town is this?"

"Near the university, so there are many students. Writers. Artists. Yes, yes, it looks tough but it's rather pleasant."

The street was typical of this portion of Naples. Narrow apartment buildings painted yellow or gray or red—and most in need of more painting. Some walls were decorated with graffiti and the air was "fragrant"; it had been several days since the trash had been picked up—a condition not unusual, or entirely Naples's fault, as the Camorra largely controlled the trash collection and the dump sites. Waste removal could be fitful, depending on who was late in paying off whom.

Clothing hung from lines. Children played in the alleyways and the yards behind the stand-alone structures. At least four football games were in progress, the age of the players ranging from six or seven up to early twenties. The latter players, Ercole noted, were strapping and intense and skillful; some of them seemed of professional quality.

He himself had never played seriously—too tall, too gangly. Ercole's hobby as a boy had been bird-watching and board games.

"Did you play football? I mean soccer," he asked Thom.

"No. I fenced in college."

"Fencing! Very exciting. You were serious about it?" He regarded the man's thin, muscular frame.

"I won some awards." The words were modestly spoken.

Ercole managed to get the man to admit he'd nearly made it to the Olympics.

"That's the building there." Ercole strode toward the structure. It was a two-story affair and had apparently been modified for rental: A second door to the ground floor had been installed, clumsily. This, the lower-level living space, was the one that Garry Soames lived in. An easy deduction, since the cheap wooden panel was mounted with a bold placard warning that the space was closed by order of the police and one must not trespass. Was this typical? Closing a whole floor for merely a connection to a crime, rather than the site where an assault had occurred?

Perhaps for such a terrible wrongdoing as rape, yes.

Thom smiled. "That says we're not supposed to be here, right?"

"No trespassing, yes. Let us go to the back. We're easily seen here in front." They circled through a weed-filled alley to the back of the place.

As he did, his phone dinged with a text. It was the response to one he had sent not long before—while driving here.

Ercole. Yes, I am free for an aperitivo after work. May I suggest Castello's Lounge at 21:00.

A thump, low in his belly. Well, look at this. Convinced she wouldn't say yes to his proposal for a drink or dinner, he'd resigned himself to a rejection.

Badger cop. Fungus cop...

But she had agreed! He had a date!

He typed: *Good!*

Debated. Ercole removed the exclamation point and sent the text.

All right. Back to work, Inspector Benelli.

It was unlikely one could have broken into the front door to plant the date-rape trace without being seen. The back? There was one door here, on the first-floor deck. There were windows, but those large enough for someone to climb through were high—three meters up, not easily reachable. At the ground level were slits of windows on the sides of the structure, but only about twenty centimeters high, too small for entry. In any event, they were painted shut and clearly had not been opened in decades, if ever.

Thom pointed out two pudgy workmen painting the building next door. Ercole and he approached. The men regarded the officer's uniform and climbed from the scaffolding. Ercole asked if they'd seen anyone at the backyard in the past few days. They replied they'd noticed only some boys playing football yesterday or the day before.

Thom had Ercole ask if they kept ladders here overnight, one that an intruder might borrow. But they did not. They took all their equipment with them. A person wishing to break in might have brought his own ladder, of course. Ercole now borrowed one of the workmen's and used it to climb to each of the windows. They were locked or painted shut. He returned the ladder and stepped into the backyard.

Standing with hands on hips, he gazed at the rear of Garry's building. There was trash in the yard, and not much else. Under the deck were two large plastic flower pots, empty. There was no rear entrance on this level—only one tiny window to the right of the deck. Like the others, on the sides, it was painted shut.

He pulled on latex gloves and wrapped his feet with rubber bands. Thom did the same. They climbed to the deck, jutting from the first floor. On it was a lawn chair, faded and torn, and three more large flower pots, filled with dry, cracked dirt but empty of plants, living or dead. A windowed door led into the upper apartment. He tried it. Locked, as were these windows. Through the dust- and mud-spattered glass he could see a kitchen but no utensils or furniture. The counters were covered with undisturbed dust.

Thom squinted too. "Unoccupied. So, no witnesses in the form of Garry's upstairs neighbors."

"No. That is too bad."

Climbing down from the deck into the backyard once more, Ercole followed Daniela's advice and stepped away from the building, a good ten yards. He turned and surveyed the structure in its entirety. She'd explained that this gave you context.

Where were the doors, the windows, for entrance and exit? Where were alcoves and alleys—places where one could lie in wait and plan a break-in?

Where were the vantage points from which people inside could look out and where, from outside, could people peer in?

Were there trash bins that might contain evidence?

Were there hiding places for weapons?

The questions piled up. But there were no helpful answers. He shook his head.

Which was when Thom said in a soft voice, "You become him."

"Him?"

"The perp." The aide was looking his way and had apparently noted Ercole's stymied expression. "You know the word?"

"Yes, yes, certainly. 'Perp.' But become him?"

"It's why Lincoln was the king of crime scenes when he ran forensics at NYPD. And why he picked Amelia as his protégée years ago. I don't understand it myself." The aide added after a moment, "But the process is getting into the mind of the killer. You're not a cop anymore. You're the killer, the burglar, the rapist, the molester. You're like a Method actor: you know, getting into the minds of the characters they play. It can be pretty tough. You go to dark places. And it can take some time to climb back out. But the best crime scene investigators can do it. Lincoln says that it's a fine line between good and bad, that the best forensic cops could easily become the worst perps. So. Your goal isn't to find clues. It's to commit the crime all over again."

Ercole's eyes went back to the building. "So *I* am a criminal."

"That's right."

"*Allora,* my crime is putting the evidence in the apartment to make Garry Soames seem guilty."

"That's right," Thom said.

"But the front door is open to a busy street and many neighbors. I can't break in that way. Maybe I could pretend to be interested in letting the apartment upstairs and, when the real estate agent lets me in, I sneak down to Garry's flat and leave the evidence."

"But would you, as the criminal, do that?" Thom asked.

"No. Of course not. Because I would leave a record of my presence. So, I have to break in through the side or the back. But the doors and windows are locked or painted shut. And there are no signs of—"

"Ah, Ercole, you're thinking as an investigator. After the fact of the crime. You have to think like the *criminal*. You have to *be* the criminal. You're the real rapist who has to blame Garry. Or you're the girlfriend that he treated badly and who wants to get even. You're desperate. You need to make this work."

"Yes, yes," Ercole whispered.

So I am the perp.

I'm desperate or furious. I must get inside, and plant drugs in Garry's bedroom.

Ercole began to pace through the backyard. Thom followed. The officer stopped quickly. "I have to plant the drugs but that's only part of my crime. The other part is being certain that no one knows I've done it. Otherwise, the police will instantly conclude Garry is innocent and begin looking for me."

"Yes. Good. You said, 'me,' not 'him.'"

"How would I do this? I can't be a supervillain and abseil down the chimney. I can't tunnel up into the basement apartment..."

Ercole's eyes scanned the back of the building, actually feeling a twist of desperation in his belly. *I have little time because I can't be seen. I have no fancy tools because I'm not a professional thief. Yet I* have *to break in and make sure there are no signs of jimmied doors or windows.* He muttered, "No signs at all...How do I do that? How?"

Thom was silent.

Ercole, staring at the building he needed to breach. Staring, staring.

And then understood. He gave a laugh.

"What?" Thom asked.

"I think I have the answer," the officer said softly. "Flower pots. The answer is flower pots."

CHAPTER 40

Now was the time for blood.

Alberto Allegro Pronti moved silently from the shadows of an alleyway behind the Guida Brothers warehouse at Filippo Argelati, 20-32, in Milan.

While sitting at an unsteady table, sipping a Valpolicella, red of course, he had heard a noise from half a block away. A rapping. Perhaps a voice.

He'd stood immediately and hurried to where he believed that sound had come from: the warehouse.

He was now behind the old structure and could see what he believed was a flicker of shadow on one of the painted-over windows.

Someone was inside.

And that was good for Pronti, and quite bad for whoever that person might be.

The fifty-eight-year-old, wiry and strong, returned to where he'd been sipping and collected a weapon. An iron rod, about three feet long. At the threaded end was a square nut, rusted permanently onto the staff.

It was very efficient and very dangerous and very lethal.

He called to Mario that he would be handling this himself, to stay back. He then returned to the warehouse, easing quietly to the rear. He peered through a spot on the pane where he had scraped the paint away, when he'd been inside recently, so that he could do just this—spy on whoever might be there and deal with them as he wished.

Pronti glanced through the peephole fast, his pulse racing, half believing that he would see an eye looking directly back at him. But no. He noted, however, that there was a shadow in the entryway, where stairs led from here to the first floor. Yes, a target was inside.

He moved on the balls of his running shoes to the back door and withdrew a key from his pocket. He undid the lock and carefully threaded the chain out of the rings screwed into the frame and door, setting the links down—in a line on the dirt so they would not clink together.

The lock too he set down carefully, away from other metal. He spat quietly on the hinges to lubricate them.

Pronti had been well trained.

Then, gripping the deadly club in a firm hand, he pushed inside.

Silently.

It took a moment for his eyes to get used to the darkness, though Pronti knew the layout well: The warehouse was built like a huge horse stable, with six-foot-high dividers separating the ground floor into storage areas. All but one were filled with trash and piles of old, rotting building materials. The remaining one contained a tall stack of cartons and pallets, a recent delivery from a company letting out space here. The floor here was clean, dust-free, and he could walk to the cartons and hide behind them without fear of his target seeing footsteps. He now did so, and he waited, listening to the creaks from overhead, closing his eyes from time to time to concentrate more clearly.

Blood...

His target returned to the top of the stairs, and Pronti could hear him walking down them carefully. As soon as he stepped out of the stairway, he'd return to the front door or walk through the center aisle. Either way he would present his back to Pronti and the wicked club.

His tactically trained ears—like a bat's—would sense exactly where the son of a bitch was, and Pronti would step out, swinging his murderous weapon. He cocked his head and listened. Oh, yes, just like the old days...in the army. Fond memories, troubled ones too. He would bore Mario with his exploits in the service as they sat together over meals or wine.

He thought now of that time on the Po River...

Then Pronti grew stern with himself. Be serious here.

This is battle.

The footsteps descended the stairs and stopped. The victim was debating which direction to turn.

Left to the door, straight?

Either way, you're about to feel my fury...

Pronti took the club in both hands. He smelled the iron nut, close to his nose. Blood and rust smell similar and his weapon was about to reek of both.

But then... What's happening?

There was a thud—a footstep—followed by another, then another. In the back of the warehouse! The intruder had not taken the direct route—past him through the clear center aisle—but had picked one of the areas filled with construction trash, along the side wall. Pronti had assumed it impassable.

Well, no, my friend, you're not escaping me.

Pronti stepped from his hiding space and, holding the rod in two hands, stalked silently toward the rear of the structure, where his victim would be making for the back door, Pronti assumed. This would work just fine. The man would go to the door... and Pronti would crush his skull.

Quiet... quiet...

When he was nearly there, another footfall—close—made him jump.

Yet no foot was to be seen.

What is this?

Another thud.

And the bit of brick rolled to a stop in front of him.

No, no! His soldierly training had failed him.

The footsteps, the thuds, were not that at all. They were a distraction. Of course!

Behind him, the voice barked a command.

The order, delivered by, of all things, a woman, was in English, of which he spoke very little. But it was not much of challenge to deduce the meaning and so Pronti quickly dropped the rod and shot his hands into the air.

Amelia Sachs slipped her gun away.

She stood over the skinny, unshaven man, who sat defiantly on the floor of the warehouse. He wore filthy clothing. Pete Prescott was beside her, examining the metal bar he'd carried. "Quite a weapon."

She glanced at the rod. Yes, it was.

"*Il suo nome?*" Prescott asked.

The man was silent, eyes darting from one to the other.

Prescott repeated the question.

"Alberto Allegro Pronti," he said. He said something more to Prescott, who fished a card from the man's pocket.

This confirmed his identity.

A string of strident and defiant Italian followed. Sachs caught a few words. "He's a Communist?"

His eyes shone. "*Partito Comunista Italiano!*"

Prescott said, "It was dissolved in 'ninety-one."

"*No!*" Pronti barked. More Italian followed. A lengthy, fervent monologue. Sachs guessed he was a holdout from the old movement, which had lost relevance to all but a few.

The man rambled on for a moment, now grimacing.

Prescott seemed amused. "He said you are very good to have fooled him. He's a trained soldier."

"He is?"

"Well, I don't know about the training but he probably served. In Italy all men used to have to serve a year." Prescott asked him a question.

Looking down, Pronti answered.

"It seems he was a cook. But he points out that he did take basic training."

"What's his story? And tell him no politics please."

It seemed that he was homeless and lived in an alley about a half block away.

"Why was he going to attack me?"

Prescott listened to the man's response with a cocked head. Then explained: "Until a few weeks ago he was living in this warehouse, which had been abandoned for at least a year. He'd even put a chain and lock on the back door, so he could have access whenever he wanted and feel safe from street thugs. He had it fixed up nicely. Then the owner or somebody leasing it came back to store things and a man threatened him and threw him out. Beat him up. And he kicked Mario."

"Who's Mario?"

"*Il mio gatto.*"

"His—

"Cat."

Pronti: "*Era scontroso.*"

Prescott said, "The man who threw him out was...unpleasant."

As most cat-kickers would be.

"Today he heard someone and assumed that the man had come back. Pronti wanted to get revenge."

"Was someone here earlier?" She mentioned the broken bottle.

Pronti's response, Prescott said, was that, yes, some workers either dropped off a shipment for storage or picked something up. "About two hours ago. He was asleep and missed them. But then he heard you."

Sachs dug into her pocket and handed the homeless man a twenty-euro note. His eyes grew wide as he calculated, she was sure, how much cheap wine it might buy. She displayed the composite picture of the Composer and the passport photo of Malek Dadi.

"Have you seen them?"

Pronti understood but shook his head in the negative.

So, the most logical explanation for the Post-it was that it had been given to Dadi by someone in the camp, maybe as a possible lead for a job when he was granted asylum.

On the slim chance, though, that there was a connection to the Composer, she said, "You see him." Pointing to her phone. "You call me?" Mimicking making a phone call like a stand-up comic and pointing to herself.

"*Nessun cellulare.*" He offered her a disappointed pout. As if he'd have to give back the euros.

"Is there a place near here where I could get him a prepaid?"

"There's a *tabaccaio* a block or so away."

The three of them walked to the tiny quick-mart and Prescott used Sachs's cash to purchase a phone and some minutes for text and voice.

She entered her number into the phone. "Text me if you see him." She handed him the Nokia and another twenty.

"Grazie tante, Signorina!"

"Prego. Ask him how his cat, Mario, is? After getting kicked."

Prescott posed the question.

With a dark face, Pronti answered.

"He says Mario wasn't badly hurt. The greatest injury was to his pride." Prescott shrugged. "But, then, isn't that often the case?"

CHAPTER 41

Capitano Rhyme glanced up as he was finishing a call to Amelia Sachs.

Ercole fell silent, noticing the phone.

Sachs, still in Milan, was reporting no success; it was almost certain that the clue they'd found—the Post-it note—was from Malek Dadi, not the Composer. For completeness's sake, she was taking soil samples in the warehouse, and photographing footprints. As for fingerprints, she'd found nearly three hundred latents, too many for a practical analysis. But the effort was surely futile; it was unlikely the Composer had any connection to the place.

Rhyme was disappointed, though not surprised. He was disappointed too that Sachs wouldn't be able to return to Naples until tomorrow. The crew of Mike Hill's private plane would stay in Switzerland that night and would collect Sachs in the morning, early.

She reported, though, that she'd found a great hotel, the Manin, across the street from what had been the famed Milan zoo. It was also within walking distance of La Scala, the opera house, and the Duomo, the Milan cathedral. She was lukewarm about tourist sites but would probably hit them, since there wasn't time to do what she really wanted: head out to Maranello—the home of Ferrari—and take an F1 out on the track for a joyride.

Rhyme now looked up at the Forestry officer. "Yes, yes, Ercole. Tell me." He nodded too to Thom, indicia of his thanks.

"Beatrice Renza has finished her analysis of the evidence." Ercole lowered his voice, unnecessarily, for they were alone. "In the Soames case. I will report to you now. First, about the apartment where the attack occurred."

Ercole walked to the desk and found the yellow pad that the unauthorized investigative team was using for the renegade assignment—the mini chart. He wrote carefully, apparently recalling his bad marks for penmanship:

THE SMOKING STATION, NATALIA GARELLI'S APARTMENT, VIA CARLO CATTANEO

- Trace:
  - Acetic acid.
  - Acetone.
  - Ammonia.
  - Ammonium oxalate.
  - Ash.
  - Benzene.
  - Butane.
  - Cadmium.
  - Calcium.
  - Carbon monoxide.
  - Cumin.
  - Enzymes:
    - Protease.
    - Lipases.
    - Amylases.
  - Hexamine.
  - Methanol.
  - Nicotine.
  - Phosphates.
  - Potassium.
  - Red wine.
  - Saffron.

— Sodium carbonate.

— Sodium perborate.

— Curry.

— Tobacco and tobacco ash.

— Cardamom.

— Urate.

THE ATTACK SITE, ADJOINING ROOF, VIA CARLO CATTANEO

— Trace:
  — Cumin.
  — Enzymes:
    — Protease.
    — Lipases.
    — Amylases.
  — Phosphates.
  — Saffron.
  — Sodium carbonate.
  — Sodium perborate.
  — Cardamom.
  — Curry.
  — Urates.

"As you can see," Ercole said excitedly, "there are similarities, common elements of the two. So it's likely that the same person at the smoking station, who left that trace, also was the attacker."

Not necessarily likely but certainly possible, Rhyme thought. Scanning the listings, considering possibilities, plugging in theories, unplugging others.

"Beatrice is working to tell us what the chemicals might mean."

"Fine, fine, fine, though I think we might not need her to."

The Forestry officer paused. Then he said, "But alone, they're just substances. How can we tell what they might be from? We need to see what they combine to become."

Rhyme muttered, "Which is what I've done. The chemicals at the smoking station—for instance, the acetic acid, acetone, ammonia, benzene, butane and cadmium—are, no shock here, from cigarettes."

"But they're poisons, aren't they?"

Thom laughed. "Don't smoke, Ercole."

"No, I don't. I won't."

Rhyme frowned at the interruption. "So, I was saying. At the smoking station, cigarette smoke residue. But, the other ingredients: I see laundry detergent. The spices, of course, are obvious. Curry. Indian food. Now, at the site of the assault? Laundry detergent and spices only. Now, think back, Ercole. On the roof, was there laundry hanging anywhere nearby? I've seen that everywhere in Naples."

"No, I'm sure there was not. Because I, as a matter of fact, looked for that very thing myself. I was thinking that someone reeling in laundry might have seen the attack."

"Hm," Rhyme offered, and refrained from yet another lecture about the unreliability of witnesses. "The couple whose apartment this was, do you have their number?"

"The woman of the pair, yes. Natalia. She's a fellow student. And most beautiful."

"Do I care?"

"You would if you saw her."

"Call her. Now. Find out if she did laundry before the party. And if the food served at the party was Indian. Curry."

Ercole searched his phone then placed a call and, Rhyme was pleased to hear, got through immediately. A conversation in Italian ensued; like most, it sounded passionate, more expressive than a similar English exchange.

When Ercole disconnected, he said, "Yes, to the laundry question, I am sorry to report. She had just washed the clothing for the beds that afternoon, thinking some guests might wish to stay over, rather than drive back home late. The clue did not come from the rapist.

"And, unfortunately, as to food, the same. There was, at the party, nothing other than chips—you know, potato chips and the like—and nuts and *dolce*, sweets. But at dinner before the party she and her boyfriend ate curry. I remember a picture of him. He's Indian. So, that too is bad news for us."

"Yes, it is."

The spices and detergent at the smoking station would have come from Natalia when she was either mixing with guests or cleaning up afterward. And she would have left those bits of trace at the site of the attack when she went to the woman's aid.

Ercole asked, "You had mentioned, I believe, that Garry thought perhaps a former lover of his was blaming him to get revenge."

Rhyme said, "His lawyer told us that. Someone, Valentina Morelli. She is apparently in Florence or nearby there. She's still not returning calls."

At that moment Ercole's phone chimed and he glanced at the screen. He seemed to be blushing. And smiling. He typed a response.

Rhyme and Thom looked at each other. Rhyme suspected they were thinking the same: a woman.

Probably that attractive blonde, Daniela, whom he'd been fawning over.

Well, the young man could do worse than date a beautiful, intense policewoman.

Lincoln Rhyme knew this for a fact.

Ercole put his phone away. "I have saved the best for the last."

"Which means what?" Rhyme groused. Sachs was not present to temper his delivery.

"Now, at Garry's flat, Signor Reston was very helpful in instructing me. He counseled that I should *become* the perp. And I did that and we found something quite interesting."

Impatient eyebrows.

"The building was typical construction, symmetrical. For every window on the right, there was one on the left. For every gable in the front, there was one in the back. For every—"

"Ercole?"

"Ah, yes. But in the back, there was only one low window—about twenty centimeters high—for allowing light into the cellar apartment. To the right as you faced the rear of the building. Only the one. Why was there no window to the left? Symmetry everywhere but there. The yard itself was not higher on the left than to the right, except in the very place where the window would have been. There was a small hill. Now, beneath the porch were empty flower pots. They matched flower pots on the deck above—but those were full of earth."

Rhyme was intrigued. "So the perp broke into the window on the left. It was Garry's bedroom?"

"Yes. And he, or she, scattered the drugs inside and used the dirt in a couple of the pots to cover up the window."

"But the crime scene people didn't find glass or dirt on the floor?"

"Ah," Ercole said. "He—or she—was clever. They used a glass cutter. Here, look." He extracted from a folder some eight-by-ten glossy shots and displayed them. "Beatrice has printed these out."

Rhyme could see the even fracture marks, in the shape of a rough rectangle.

Ercole continued, "And after he was finished he put a piece of cardboard he'd found in the yard against the open window before piling the dirt up to conceal the break-in. I am sorry to tell you there were no fingerprints on the flower pots or cardboard. But I did see marks that were left by..." He paused. "That were *consistent* with marks left by latex gloves."

Good.

"And I found footprints that were probably left by the breakerer-and-enterer. Is that a word?"

"It will do." Rhyme reflected that the young man had quite the career ahead of him.

Ercole added to the mini evidence chart.

GARRY SOAMES'S APARTMENT, CORSO UMBERTO I, NAPLES

— Low window cut open.
  — No fingerprints, but marks consistent with latex gloves.
  — Blocked by cardboard before dirt piled up to conceal break-in.
— Footprints outside broken window and on floor just inside.
  — Size 7½ (m)/9 (f)/40 (European), leather sole.
— Gamma hydroxybutyric acid, date-rape drug.

— Tire print, in mud in backyard.
  — Continental 195/65R15.
— Soil collected from footprint.
  — Awaiting analysis.

"And the date-rape drug? Where was that?"

"On the windowsill."

Staring at the chart, Rhyme mused, "Who the hell's the intruder?"

The breakerer-and-enterer…

He continued, "Is it the same as the person who called the police and gave them Garry's name? That was a woman's voice. And the shoe size could be a woman's."

Ercole said, "I looked up the tire tread information. The Continental tire. We don't know if it was the intruder's but it was only a day or two old. And it makes sense to park there so as not to be seen from the street."

"Yes, it does."

"Unfortunately, many, many types of cars can use that tire. But we can—"

A voice interrupted, cutting through the room like a whip. "Forestry Officer. You'll leave the room. At once."

Rhyme wheeled about to face Dante Spiro. The lean man was wearing a black suit with a tie-less white shirt. With his goatee, bald head and enraged expression he looked particularly demonic.

"Sir…" Ercole's face was white.

"Leave. Now." A vicious string of Italian.

The young officer shot a glance toward Rhyme.

"He is not your superior—I am," Spiro growled.

The young man walked forward, carefully navigating around Spiro.

His eyes still boring into Rhyme's, the prosecutor muttered to Ercole, "Close the door as you leave."

"*Sì, Procuratore.*"

CHAPTER 42

How could you do this? You are working *against* a case that I am
prosecuting?"

Spiro stepped toward Rhyme.

Thom moved forward.

The prosecutor said, "You, too. You will leave."

The aide said calmly, "No."

Spiro turned to face Thom but, looking into the American's eyes, apparently decided not to fight this battle and demand that he leave. Which
the aide would not have done, in any event.

Back to Rhyme: "I have never wanted you here. Never wanted your
presence. Massimo Rossi felt it might be advantageous and since he is
the lead investigator I—in my foolish weakness—said yes. But, as it turns
out, you are just another one of them."

A frown of curiosity from Rhyme.

"Another meddling American. You have no sense of propriety, loyalty,
of boundaries. You are part of a big, crass machine of a nation that
stumbles forward wherever it wishes to go, crushing those in your path.
Always without apology."

Rhyme wasn't inclined to point out the superficiality of the words; he
hadn't flown four thousand miles to defend U.S. foreign policy.

"Yes, admittedly, you have come up with helpful thoughts in the case
but, if you think about the matter, it is a problem of your own making!

The Composer is an American. You failed to find and stop him. Accordingly your assistance is the *least* you can do.

"But to do the opposite—to *undermine* a case, *my* case, the case against a man charged of a horrific sexual assault, against an unconscious woman? Well, that is beyond the pale, Mr. Rhyme. Garry Soames is not the subject of a witch trial. He has been arrested according to the laws of this nation, a democracy, on the basis of reasonable evidence and accounts, and is being afforded all of the rights due him. Inspector Laura Martelli and I are continuing to pursue the leads. If he proves to be innocent, he will be freed. But for now he appears to be guilty and he will be incarcerated until a magistrate decides he may be released pending trial."

Rhyme began to speak.

"No, let me finish. If you had come to me and said you wished to offer suggestions to the defense, suggest forensic advice, I would have understood. But you didn't do that. To add insult to this travesty, you enlisted into your service our *own* officer, that young man, who until a few days ago investigated the condition of goat barns and issued citations for trying to sell unwashed broccolini. You used police facilities for unauthorized defense investigations. That is a serious breach of the laws here, Mr. Rhyme. And, frankly, worse, in my opinion, it is an affront to the country that is acting as your host. I will be drawing up charges against you and Ercole Benelli. These charges will be lodged formally if you do not leave the country immediately. And I assure you, sir, you will not enjoy the amenities of the prison that I will recommend for your incarceration. That is all I have to say on this matter."

He turned and walked to the door, pulling it open.

Rhyme said, "Truth."

Spiro stopped. He looked back.

Rhyme said, "There's only one thing that matters to me. The truth."

A cold smile. "Do I suspect an excuse is about to wing my way? That's something else Americans love: *excuses.* They can do anything, then excuse away their behavior. We kill thousands wrongly, but it was because we were blinded by a higher cause. How your country must feel shame. Day and night."

"Not an excuse, Prosecutor. A fact. There is absolutely nothing I will not do to arrive at the truth. And that includes going behind your back and anyone else's if I need to. What we did here, I knew it was against procedure, if not against the law."

"Which it is," Spiro reminded.

"Garry Soames could very likely be guilty of raping Frieda S. I don't care. I honestly don't. If my line of inquiry proves him guilty, I'll give those details to you as happily as if I found exculpatory evidence. I told Garry's lawyer as much. But what I can't do is allow any uncertainty to remain. Has this piece of evidence told us everything it possibly can? Is it being coy? Is it being duplicitous? Is it pretending to be something else entirely?"

"Very clever, Mr. Rhyme. Do you use that personification in your courses, to charm your students?"

He did, as a matter of fact.

"I found your investigation into the rape case well done—"

"Condescension! Yet another quality you Americans so excel in."

"No. I mean it. You and Inspector Martelli have done a fine job. But it's also true that your case is lacking. I identified threads of investigation that I thought it was a good idea to pursue."

"*Ach*, these are just words. You have my ultimatum. Leave the country at once or face the consequences."

Again he turned.

"Did you know about the break-in at Garry's apartment?"

He paused.

"Someone wearing latex gloves broke the window of his bedroom and hid the break-in, covering the cut-out window with dirt. And it was the room where the date-rape drug traces were found on his clothing. And the window frame and sill—*outside* the building—contain traces of the drug too."

Rhyme nodded to Thom, who found the yellow pad, the mini chart. He handed it toward Spiro, who waved his hand dismissively.

He continued to the door.

"Please. Just take one look."

Sighing loudly, the prosecutor returned and snatched the pad. He read for a moment. "And you found evidence linking someone at the, as you say, smoking station with the scene where the victim was attacked. The trace, the *detersivo per il bucato*—the soap—and the spices."

So he recognized the ingredients in the detergent. Impressive.

In a firm voice, he said, "But that proves nothing. The source for that trace would be the hostess, Natalia. She went to the victim's aid. And her boyfriend, Dev, is Indian. Explaining the curry." The prosecutor's face softened. He cocked his head as he said to Rhyme, "I myself was suspicious of him at first. I took his statement at the school and while doing so I observed that he frequently would look over women students as they passed. His eyes seemed hungry. And he was seen talking to the victim, Frieda, earlier that evening. But every minute of the party he was accounted for. And his DNA did not match that which was inside the victim."

Rhyme added, "And a CCTV at a nearby hotel had malfunctioned."

"As they will do."

"Yes, you're right: The evidence at Natalia's isn't helpful. But what we discovered at Garry's is. The footprint at the scene."

Spiro's eyes now revealed curiosity. He read. "Small man size, or *woman's*. And it was a woman who called to report that Garry was seen adulterating Frieda's wine."

"Ercole collected soil from where the perp walked. It's being analyzed now. By Beatrice. That might be helpful." Rhyme added, "It might have been the actual rapist. But it might have been someone just wishing to get him into trouble—the woman who called. Garry's lawyer told us that he was quite the ladies' man. A player, you know?"

"I know."

"And maybe didn't treat them the way they would like to have been treated. There's a woman in Florence who might—"

Spiro said, "Valentina Morelli. Yes. I am trying to locate her myself."

Silence for a moment. Then Spiro's face took on an expression that said: Against my better judgment. "*Allora, Capitano* Rhyme. I will pursue this aspect of the investigation. And will temporarily put on hold my complaint against you and Forestry Officer Benelli for misuse of police facilities and interference with procedures. Temporarily."

He took a cheroot from his breast pocket and lifted it to his nose, smelled the dark tube, then replaced it.

"My reaction to your presence, you might have perceived, was perhaps out of proportion to your, if I may, crime. You came here at great risk to your personal safety—one in your condition cannot have an easy time traveling. There are dangers."

"That's true for everyone."

He continued without comment, "And there is no guarantee that even if the Composer is captured you would be successful in your attempt to extradite him back to America. Remember—"

"The Wolf Tits Rule."

"Indeed. But here you came anyway in pursuit of your quarry." He tilted his head. "In pursuit of the *truth*. And I resisted at every turn."

A pause as Spiro regarded the Composer evidence pads. Slowly he said, "There was a reason for my resistance. A personal reason, which is, by its very definition, unacceptable in our endeavors."

Rhyme said nothing. He was pleased for any chance to continue to pursue the two cases—not to mention pleased to remain out of an Italian prison—so he let the man talk.

The prosecutor said, "The answer goes back a long time—to the days of the Second World War, when your country and mine were sworn enemies..." Spiro's voice softened. "...and yet were not."

CHAPTER 43

Y ou will not have heard of the *Esercito Cobelligerante Italiano*."

"No," Rhyme told Spiro.

"The Italian Co-Belligerent Army. A complex name for a simple concept. Another fact most Americans do not know: Italy and the Allies were antagonists only at the start of the war. Both sides signed an armistice in nineteen forty-three, ending their hostilities long before Germany fell. True, some fascist soldiers fought on, in league with the Nazis, but our king and prime minister joined with the Americans and British and fought *against* the Germans. The Co-Belligerent Army was the Italian wing of the Allies.

"But, as you might guess, war is complicated. War is *sciatta*. Messy. After September 'forty-three, although the armistice was in full force and we were supposed to be fighting together, many of the American soldiers did not trust the Italians. My grandfather was a brave and decorated infantry commander who was in charge of, you would say, a company of men to assist the U.S. Fifth Army and break through the Bernhardt Line, halfway between Rome and Naples. A very stubborn defense on the part of the Nazis.

"My grandfather led his men behind the line, near San Pietro. They attacked from the rear and achieved a gorgeous victory, though suffered heavy losses. But when the U.S. troops moved forward, they found my grandfather's unit *behind* the lines. They hadn't heard about his operation. They disarmed the thirty or so survivors of my grandfather's company and rounded them up. But they did not bother to talk to their headquarters. They didn't listen to my grandfather's pleas. And threw them all together in a PoW camp, populated with three hundred Nazis." He gave a chill laugh. "Do you want to imagine how long the Italians lived, at the hands of their 'colleagues'? About ten hours, the story goes. And the report was that most died very unpleasant deaths, my grandfather among them. The Americans merely listened to the screams. When the truth came out, a major with the Fifth Army issued an apology to the six survivors. A *major* issued the apology. Not a general, not a colonel. A major. He was twenty-eight years old.

"I will add this: War is not only messy but it has consequences we cannot foresee. Now, my mother was a little girl when her father died in that camp. She barely knew him. But something about his loss affected her mind. This, my grandmother believed, in any case. She was never quite right. She married and gave birth to me and to my brother but began to have episodes just after I was born. They grew worse. Depression then mania, depression then mania. Disrobing in public, sometimes when she had arrived to collect my brother and me from school. Sometimes in church. Screaming. She received treatments, extreme treatments."

It's rare that someone knows the raw ingredients of electroconductive gel . . .

"Those did nothing more than destroy her short-term memory. The sadness remained."

"And her condition now?"

"She is in a home. My brother and I visit. She sometimes knows us. New medications, they have stabilized her. It is, they say, about the best we can hope for."

"I'm sorry to hear it."

"Can I blame your country for this, too, in addition to her father's death? But I have chosen to, and for some very unfair reason that relieves the burden. *Allora*, that is what I have to say. All I have to say."

Rhyme nodded, acknowledging the oblique apology, which, he knew, was heartfelt nonetheless.

Spiro slapped his thigh, signaling that the discussion on this topic was at an end. "Now, we are agreed that our goal is the truth behind the Garry Soames case. What approach do we take now?"

"The results of the date-rape drug analysis in Rome should be expedited. We must find out if the samples in his apartment are the same as what was in Frieda's system."

"Yes, I will look into that."

"And Beatrice is completing an analysis of the soil outside Garry's window."

"*Bene.*"

"But I have another idea. I'd like to run one more analysis. Ercole can talk to Beatrice about that."

"Ah, the Forestry officer. I had forgotten about him." Spiro walked to the door. Stuck his head out and barked a command.

Ercole stepped inside, looking consummately awkward.

"You are not being dismissed, not *yet*, Ercole." Spiro glowered. "Captain Rhyme here has saved your bacon. An American expression, well suited for a Forestry officer."

Ercole was smiling, albeit without a splinter of humor.

Spiro's face turned even colder. "But if you ever try to run an end—"

End run, Rhyme nearly corrected, though he decided not to.

"—your career will be over."

"But what are you speaking of?"

"Isn't it obvious? And I don't mean that nonsense of enlisting Detective Sachs to translate Arabic, though the transparency of that ploy was laughable. What I am speaking of is the reporter at the Capodichino Reception Center: Nunzio Parada. The man pelting me with questions the night Dadi was killed. He is a friend of yours, is he not?"

"I...well, I am somewhat familiar with him, yes."

"And did you not, after you saw me arrive, slip away and coach him to ask me about my brilliance in inviting the Americans here?"

The officer's cheeks glowed bright red. "I am so very sorry, *Procuratore,* but I thought we could benefit if Detective Sachs assisted, and you, with all respect, did not seem willing to allow her to do so."

"*La truffa,* your scam, served a purpose, Ercole, and so I played along, even though I saw it as such. It was a chance for the investigation to save face, while allowing the talented Detective Sachs to work on the case directly. But your plan was, in English, cheap. And most embarrassing for you, it was pathetically inept."

"Why do you say that, *Procuratore*?"

"Did it not occur to you that rather than being lauded for my choice, I might be ridiculed for inviting to Italy detectives whom the serial killer managed to elude in New York?"

Rhyme and Thom smiled.

"Thank the Lord that the press are sufficient idiots that they missed that contradiction too. But in the future you will be straightforward with me. Do I not have the persona of a purring kitten?"

"*Allora, Procuratore*, the fact is . . ."

"You behave as if you are afraid of me!"

"I think many people are afraid of you, sir. With all respect."

"Why is that?"

"You are stern. You are known to bark, even scream at people."

"As do generals and artists and explorers. Of necessity."

"Your book . . ."

"My book?"

Ercole looked down at the man's pocket; the gilt-edged, leather-bound volume was just visible.

"What of it?"

"*Allora*, you understand."

He snapped, "How can you assert I understand something if I have just asked you to explain?"

"Sir. You write down in it the names of people who offend you. Who you wish to get even with."

"Do I now?"

"I have heard people say that. Yes, I have."

"Well, Forestry Officer, tell me how many names you see, names destined for the pillory." Spiro handed the book to Ercole, who took it timidly.

"I—"

"Read, Forestry Officer. Read."

He cracked open the pages and Rhyme could catch a glimpse of dense and very precise Italian script. The lettering was minuscule.

Ercole frowned.

Spiro said, "The title. Read what is at the top of the first page. Aloud."

Ercole read: "*La Ragazza da Cheyenne.*" He looked toward Rhyme and Thom. "It means *The Girl from Cheyenne.*"

"And below?"

"*Capitolo Uno.* First Chapter."

"And below that, please continue. Translate for *Capitano* Rhyme."

Ercole puzzled for a moment. He cocked his head and read in a halting voice, as he translated, "'If the four twenty-five train to Tucson had not been attacked, Belle Walker would have married her fiancé and her life would have settled into the same dull, predictable routine as that of her sisters, and their mother before them.'"

Ercole looked up.

Spiro said, "It is a hobby of mine. I like very much American cowboy stories and I read many of them. I have from the time I was a boy. You know Italy and American Westerns are inextricably linked. Sergio Leone. The Clint Eastwood movies. *A Fistful of Dollars. The Good, the Bad and the Ugly.* Then there is the masterpiece *Once Upon a Time in the West.* Sergio Corbucci's *Django*, which starred Franco Nero. And of course there are the scores for so many of those films by Ennio Morricone. He even scored a most recent movie by Quentin Tarantino.

"I particularly enjoy Western novels written by women in the nineteenth century. Did you know some of the best were written by them?"

Didn't have a clue, Rhyme reflected. And don't much care. But he nodded agreeably.

Ercole, perhaps relieved not to be inscribed in the prosecutor's book of doom, said, "Fascinating, *Procuratore.*"

"I believe so too. Mary Foote wrote a clever novel about mining in 1883. Helen Hunt Jackson wrote *Ramona*, quite famous, the next year. And one of the most interesting is by Marah Ellis Ryan, *Told in the Hills.* It is as much about race relations as it is an adventure story. I find that remarkable. Well more than one hundred years ago."

Spiro nodded at the book, which Ercole continued to read. The prosecuter said, "I too try my hand at Westerns and have created that character, Belle Walker. A society woman from the East who becomes a hunter of outlaws. And, ultimately, in future books, a prosecutor. So, as you can see, Forestry Officer, you do not need to worry about ending up in the pages of my book. Though, this is not to say that the least failing on your part will not result in catastrophic consequences."

"Yes, yes." The young officer's eyes then dropped once more to the pages.

Spiro lifted the book out of his hands.

"But, please, who were the train attackers, *Procuratore*? Savages? Bandits?"

Spiro waved his hand with a grimace, and Ercole instantly fell silent.

"Now, we have two cases to work on. And at the moment Captain Rhyme wants you to arrange for Beatrice to run a further analysis regarding the Garry Soames case...What would this be?"

Rhyme answered, "I was reading the charts and the accounts of the crime. And I would like a full analysis of the wine bottle found at the smoking station."

"The contents were checked for the date-rape drug and the outside for fingerprints and DNA."

"I understand but I would like an examination of trace on the surface of the bottle and the label."

Spiro said to Ercole, "Do that now."

"Yes, I will see Beatrice about this. Where would the bottle be?"

"The evidence facility is up the hall. She will know. Is there anything else, Captain Rhyme?"

"Lincoln, please. No, I think that will be enough for now."

Spiro looked him over. "You have a question about the wine served at the party. I myself find another question equally intriguing."

"And what is that?"

"This third person, who broke into Garry Soames' apartment, might have planted the evidence to shift guilt to an innocent man either to protect the actual rapist or to visit revenge on Soames."

"Yes. That's one theory."

"There is another, you know: The intruder might also be a friend of Soames who committed the break-in in hopes that we would come to the very conclusion we just have: that he is being framed...when in fact he's guilty as—what do you Americans say?—guilty as sin."

THE HOUSE OF RATS

CHAPTER 44

The G6 jet settled low on the approach to Naples airport, smooth as a Cadillac in soft-suspension mode.

Amelia Sachs was the only passenger today and the flight attendant had doted.

"More coffee? You really should try the croissants. The ones filled with prosciutto and mozzarella are the best."

I could really get used to this...

Now, breakfasted and caffeinated, Sachs sat back and looked below the plane, on final. She got a clear view of the Capodichino Reception Center. From here it was a messy sprawl, much bigger than it appeared from the ground. Where, she wondered, would all those people end up? In ten years, would they have homes here? In other countries? Or would they have been sent back where they had come from—to meet a fate merely postponed by their voyage here.

Would they be alive or dead?

Her phone hummed—the crew didn't require mobiles to be powered off—and she answered.

"Yes?"

"Detective Sachs...I am sorry, *Amelia*. It is Massimo Rossi. Are you in Milan still?"

"No, just landing, Inspector."

"In Naples?"

"Yes."

"Good, good. For we have received an email on the Questura website. The writer says that he—or she, there's no name—saw a man on a hilltop near the camp the night of the murder of Dadi, just afterward. He was beside a dark car. The Italian is bad so we are certain he used a translation program. I would guess he is one of the vendors and Arabic is his first language."

"Does he say where?"

"Yes." Rossi gave her the name of a road. He'd gone to Google Earth and found a footpath to a hilltop that overlooked the camp. He described it to her.

"I probably just flew over it. I'll stop on the way."

"I will have Ercole Benelli meet you there. In case translation is necessary." He chuckled. "Or a real badge must be shown to loosen tongues."

She disconnected. Well, a concerned citizen had come forward.

A *somewhat* concerned citizen.

Would there be any evidence?

Maybe, maybe not. But you never missed any opportunities for the collection of even a microgram of trace.

Amelia Sachs sat in the back of Mike Hill's limo, the cheerful driver flirting once more and regaling her with additional details of Naples. The eruption of Vesuvius was today's topic, and she learned to her surprise that it was not ash or earthquake or lava that killed. It was poisonous fumes.

"In only, it was, a few minutes. *Poof.* You would say poof?"

"Yes."

"Poof and then: dead! Thousands dead. That certainly makes you think, does it not? Never waste a moment of life." He winked, and she wondered if he regularly used references to natural disasters to seduce women.

She'd given him the destination and the Audi limo wound through hills north of the camp. In a tree-line gully, she found Ercole Benelli, and asked the chauffeur to stop.

They greeted each other and she introduced him to the driver. The men shared a brief conversation in Italian.

"Can you wait here? I won't be long," Sachs said to the driver.

"Yes, yes! Of course." The big man smiled, as if anything a beautiful lady asked would be granted.

"That's the path?" she asked Ercole.

"Yes."

She looked around. It was impossible to see the camp from here, but she assumed that the walkway would take her to a good vantage point.

They slipped rubber bands over their shoes and started. The way was steep, mostly dirt and grass, but some stepping-stones were smooth and seemed intentionally planted. Was this an ancient Roman route?

Climbing, breathing hard. And sweating. The day was hot, even at this early hour.

A breath of wind surrounded them with a sweet smell.

"Telinum," Ercole said. He'd apparently noted her head turn toward the scent.

"A plant?"

"A perfume. But made of some of what you're smelling: cypress, calamus and sweet marjoram. Telinum was the most popular perfume in Caesar's day."

"Julius?"

"The only and one," Ercole said.

"One and only."

"Ah."

They crested the top of the hill. It was free of trees and, looking down, she saw that, yes, she did have a good view of the camp. She was discouraged to see no obvious signs that the Composer had been here. They walked farther, to the center of the clearing.

Ercole asked, "Milano? Captain Rhyme reported that you found nothing."

"No. But we eliminated a clue. That's as important as finding one that pans out."

"As important?" he asked wryly.

"Okay. No. But you have to pursue it anyway. Besides, I just had croissants on a private jet. So, I'm hardly complaining. You know, I don't see any footprints or...well, anything. Where would he have stood?"

They both looked about, and Ercole walked in a careful perimeter around the clearing. He returned to Sachs. "No, I see nothing."

"Why would the Composer come here? It was after the murder, the witness said."

"To see who was after him?" The young officer shrugged. "Or to communicate with the gods or Satan or whoever might be directing him."

"That makes as much sense as anything."

Ercole shook his head. "He would have some cover behind those trees. I will look."

"I'll check out down there." Sachs stepped off the crest of the hill and walked to a small clearing closer to the camp.

Wondering again: What was his point in coming here?

It would have been out of his way—would have taken ten minutes of precious time needed for his escape—to climb the path.

Then she stopped. Fast.

The path!

The only way to see the camp—and to be seen from it—was here, on the crest, after climbing from the road. Yet the emailer had said the suspect had been spotted standing "beside" a dark car as he looked over the camp.

Impossible.

There was no way to get a car up here; the vehicle would have had to remain in the valley, out of sight.

It's a trap!

The Composer himself had sent the email—in bad Italian, a program translating it from English—to lure her or other officers here.

She turned and was just starting back to the crest, calling Ercole's name, when she heard the shot. A powerful rifle shot, booming off the hills.

At the crest, Sachs dropped to a crouch in the brush that formed the perimeter of the clearing, drawing her Beretta. She glanced into the valley and saw Hill's driver, panicked and crouching behind the fender of the Audi. He was on his mobile, apparently shouting as he summoned the police.

And then she looked over the fringe of dry, rustling weeds and saw Ercole Benelli sprawled facedown in the dust beside a regal magnolia. She started to rise and run toward him when a second bullet slammed into the ground right in front of her and, a moment later, the boom of the powerful gun's report filled the air.

"One interview?"

The man on the other end of the line was speaking in his soft Southern (U.S. not Italian) drawl. This always seemed to make a request more persuasive.

Still Rhyme told Daryl Mulbry, "No."

The pale fellow was nothing if not persistent.

Rhyme and Thom sat in the breakfast room of their hotel. Rhyme rarely had much interest in an early meal but in Europe the room rate included a full breakfast and, perhaps because of the travel, or the intensity of the cases, his appetite was stronger than normal.

Oh, and there *was* the fact that the food here was damn good.

"Garry was beat up. Anything we can say about the case might help get him moved from general population." Mulbry was on speakerphone in the office Charlotte McKenzie was using at the consulate. She was with him and now said, "The Penitentiary Police are decent folks and they're looking out for him. But they can't be there all the time. I just need one fact that suggests he's innocent, to get him to a different facility."

Mulbry came on the line. "At least could you give *us*," he asked, "an idea of what you've found?"

Rhyme sighed. He said, trying to be patient, "We have some indication he might be innocent, yes." He didn't want to be more specific, for fear Mulbry would leak it.

"Really?" This was McKenzie. Enthusiasm in her voice.

"But that's only half the story. We need to be able to point to the real perp. We're not there yet." Spiro had blessed their involvement but no way was Rhyme going to make a press statement without the prosecutor's okay.

Mulbry asked, "Could you give us any clue?"

Rhyme looked up, across the breakfast table. "Oh, I'm sorry. I have an important meeting now. A man is here I have to see. I'll get back to you as soon as I can."

"Well, if—"

Click.

Rhyme turned his attention to the man he'd referred to, who was approaching the breakfast table: their server, a slim fellow in a white jacket with a flamboyant mustache. He asked Rhyme, "*Un altro caffè?*"

Thom began, "It means—"

"I can figure it out and yes."

The man left and returned a moment later with the Americano.

Thom looked around the room. "Nobody's fat in Italy. Have you noticed?"

"What was that?" Rhyme asked Thom. His tone suggested he was not fully present mentally. He was considering both the Garry Soames and the Composer cases.

The aide continued, "Look at this food." He nodded to a large buffet of different kinds of ham, salami, cheese, fish, fruit, cereal, pastries, a half-dozen varieties of fresh bread, and mysterious delicacies wrapped in shiny paper. And there were eggs and other dishes cooked to order. Everyone was eating a full meal, and, yes, nobody was fat. Plump, maybe. Like Beatrice. But not fat.

"No," Rhyme said in a snappy tone, summarily ending what would probably have been a conversation about American obesity—a topic that he had absolutely no interest in. "Where the hell is she? We need to get going."

Mike Hill's private jet had collected Amelia Sachs in Milan and had transported her back to Naples. She'd landed a half hour ago. She was going to meet Ercole to check out a possible clue in the hills above the refugee camp, but Rhyme hadn't thought that would take this long.

The waiter was hovering once again.

Thom said, "*No, grazie.*"

"*Prego.*" Then, after a dawdle: "It is possible for *un autografo?*"

"Is he serious?" Rhyme muttered.

"Lincoln," Thom said in his most admonishing tone.

"I'm a cop. A *former* cop. Who cares about my autograph? He doesn't know me from Adam."

Thom said, "But you're on the trail of the Composer."

"*Sì! Il Compositore!*" The waiter's eyes were bright.

"He'd be happy to." Thom took the waiter's proffered order pad and set it in front of Rhyme, who gave a labored smile and took the offered pen. In a stilted maneuver, he signed his name.

"*Grazie mille!*"

Thom admonished, "Say—"

"Don't be a schoolmarm," Rhyme whispered to Thom and then said to the server: "*Prego.*"

"The eggs are excellent," Thom said. "*Le uova sono molto buone.* Is that right?"

"*Sì, sì! Perfetto! Caffe?*"

"*E una grappa.*" Rhyme gave it a shot.

"*Sì.*"

"No." From Thom.

The man noted the aide's steely eyes and headed off, with a conspiratorial glance toward Rhyme. He took this to mean perhaps not now, but grappa would figure in the near future. Rhyme smiled.

He glanced through the large plate-glass window and noted Mike Hill's limousine pulling to a stop in front of the hotel. Sachs climbed out and stretched.

Something was odd. Her clothes were dusty. And, what was this? She had a fleck of blood on her blouse. She wasn't smiling.

He looked Thom's way. The aide too was frowning.

The driver, a big, dark-complexioned, hirsute man—so very Italian—leapt out and grabbed her small bag from the trunk. She shook her head—at the unnecessary gallantry; the bag weighed ten pounds, tops. They exchanged a few words and he tipped his head, then joined a cluster of other drivers for a smoke and—as Rhyme had observed about the Italians—conversation.

She joined Rhyme and Thom.

"Amelia!" Thom said, rising, as she walked into the lobby.

"What happened?" Rhyme asked firmly. "You're hurt?"

"Fine. I'm fine." She sat down, drank a whole glass of water. "But..."

"Oh, hell. A trap?"

"Yep. The Composer. He's got a rifle, Rhyme. High caliber."

Rhyme cocked his head. "Ercole? He was with you."

"He's all right too. I thought he'd been hit, but the Composer was probably shooting iron sights, no scope. He missed and Ercole went to cover. He just dropped. Played dead. I got a slug parked near me but then I laid down covering fire and we got off the hill."

"You're all right?"

She touched some scrapes on her neck. Then glanced down at her tan blouse, grimacing. "Got some spray, gravel or something, but Hill's driver, he'd called the police and they were there real fast. The Scientific Police're running the scene now. But I had no clue where he was shooting from and he only fired twice, so he probably took the brass with him. They'll find the slugs, I hope. They were using metal detectors when I left. Ercole's there helping."

The Composer, armed. Noose. Then a knife. Now a rifle.

Well, that changed everything. Every scene, from now on, they'd have to assume he was nearby and eager to stop them.

Whatever his mission was, saving the world from demons or reincarnated Hitlers, it was important enough for him to do anything—even killing police—to make sure he finished it.

Sachs sipped from Rhyme's coffee. Calm, as always after a run-in like this. It was only boredom and quiet that flustered her. She took a call, listened and hung up.

"That was Ercole. They can't find the site of the shooter and he's bypassed or gotten through all the roadblocks they set up. They found one slug. Looks like a Winchester two-seventy round."

A popular hunting rifle cartridge.

Rhyme explained about Spiro's catching the unauthorized operation, to try to exculpate Garry Soames. But then softening.

"Did Beatrice blow the whistle?"

"No, she didn't know it wasn't officially sanctioned. I think Dante's just a very, very good investigator. But we kissed and made up. That is, up to a certain point. But from now on, we clear things with him."

Rhyme then added details about the analysis of evidence from the roof of Natalia Garelli's flat, where the attack took place, and at Garry's flat.

"Well. Interesting development."

"Still waiting for the Rome date-rape drug analysis. And some soil samples Ercole picked up at Garry's. But let's get to the Questura. See if our friend was careless enough to load his hunting rifle without those damn latex gloves."

"Fatima!"

Hearing the friendly voice, Fatima Jabril turned and saw Rania Tasso approaching through the crowded walkways between the tents. The woman, normally severe—as much as Fatima herself—was smiling.

"Director Tasso."

"Rania, please. Call me Rania."

"Yes, you said that. I am sorry." Fatima set down her backpack, filled with medical supplies—it must have weighed ten kilos—and the paper package she held. She straightened and a bone in her back popped.

"I heard about the baby!" Rania said.

"Yes, both are well. The mother and the child."

Fatima had been the midwife for a delivery just a half hour ago. Births were not uncommon, in this "village" of thousands, but the baby girl had been a milestone—the hundredth infant born in Capodichino this year.

And, surprising everyone, the Tunisian parents had named her

Margherita, after the queen consort of the king of Italy in the late nine-teenth century.

"It is going well for you?" Rania asked. "In the clinic."

"Yes. The facilities are not bad." She nodded at the backpack of med-ical supplies. "Though I feel like a doctor in a battle zone sometimes. Going here and there, fixing scraped knees, bandaging burns. The people are careless. A man bought some goat—from the vendors." Fatima glanced outside the fence, where the booths and kiosks were set up. "And he started a fire in his tent!"

"No!"

"They would have asphyxiated if their son hadn't run up to me and said, 'Why are Mommy and Daddy sleeping?'"

"Not Bedouins, of course," Rania said.

"No. Tribal peoples would know how to live in tents. What is safe and what is not. These were from the suburbs of Tobruk. They will be fine, though their clothing will smell thick with smoke forever."

"I will send out a flyer that people are not supposed to do that."

Fatima picked up the package, which Rania glanced at. The refugee smiled—perhaps the first such expression she'd shared with anyone here, other than her husband or Muna. She indicated the wrapped paper par-cel. "A miracle! My mother sent some tea from Tripoli. It was addressed to me at the 'Cappuccino' Reception Center in Naples."

"Cappuccino?" Rania laughed.

"Yes. Yet it arrived."

"That is quite amazing. The Italian post has been known to misdeliver mail with even the accurate addresses."

The women exchanged parting nods and went their separate ways, Fa-tima laboring under the backpack. She returned to the tent and, setting down the burdens, greeted her husband, then scooped up her daughter and hugged the girl. Khaled had a pleased look on his face. Also, one of conspiracy.

"What, my husband?"

"I have just learned of some chance for work, after our asylum is approved. There's a Tunisian who's lived here for years, who owns an Arab-language bookshop, and he might want to hire me."

Khaled had been happiest as a teacher—he loved words, loved stories. After the Liberation, when that was no longer possible, he had become a merchant. That was both unfulfilling and unsuccessful (largely because the men in the streets would rather loot than build a democracy). Fatima smiled at her husband but then looked away...and did not share with him that in her heart she knew it wouldn't work out. All that had happened over the past month told her it would be impossible to simply restart a content, pleasant family life here in Italy, as if nothing had happened.

Impossible. She felt a mantle of doom ease down upon her shoulders and she clutched her daughter more tightly.

Yet her husband was so naive, she couldn't destroy his hope, and when Khaled said that the bookseller would meet him for tea, outside the camp, would she join them, she said yes. And struggled to put aside memories of drinking tea with him on their first evening together, near the massive plaza in Tripoli that was, ironically, built by the Italians in the colonial days, originally called Piazza Italia. Now, Martyrs' Square.

Liberation...

She shivered with rage.

Fools! Madmen! Who are ruining our world, who...

"What, Fatima? Your face, it seems troubled?"

"Ah, nothing, my husband. Let us go."

They stepped outside and delivered Muna to a neighbor, who had four children of her own. Her tent was an informal child-care center.

Together, husband and wife walked to the back of the camp. Here was one of the impromptu gates—really just a cut in the chain link. The guards knew about these exits but no one made much of an effort to keep people from slipping out to make purchases or to visit with friends and relatives who had been granted asylum and moved out of the camp. They now ducked through the cut portion of the fence and walked along a row of trees and low brush.

"Ah, look," Fatima said. Khaled continued a few steps on while Fatima was pausing at a low, flowering plant. The blossoms were like tiny purple stars, set among deep green leaves. She would pick some for Muna. She started to bend down. And froze, gasping.

A large man was pushing suddenly through the brush. He was light-complexioned and wore dark clothing, a dark cap and had sunglasses on. His hands were encased in blue rubber gloves.

The sort that she'd just worn to deliver beautiful little Margherita.

One hand held what seemed to be a hood, made of black cloth.

She began to scream and turn toward her husband.

But the intruder's fist, coming from nowhere, connected solidly with her jaw and she fell backward, as silent as if God, praise be to Him, had struck her mute.

Within the hour, the Composer task force had assembled in the window-less situation room, just off the forensic lab. In addition to Rhyme, Sachs and Thom were Spiro and Rossi, and Giacomo Schiller, the sandy-haired Flying Squad officer.

"You are injured?" Spiro asked, his eyes dipping to Sachs's cut.

Sachs replied that she was fine.

Rhyme asked about any more news of the Composer's getaway after the sniper attack on Sachs and Benelli.

"No," Rossi said. "But the Scientific Police found his sniper's nest. Prints of his Converse shoes. They are scanning all the ridges with metal detectors but it is likely he took with him the shell casings." A shake of his head. "And I am sorry to report that there are no fingerprints on the recovered bullet, nor does it match any in our national criminal firearms database. I assume it would be a weapon he acquired or stole here."

Rhyme agreed. The Composer wouldn't dare bring a gun in from the United States. Even if he could do so legally, there would be too many questions at Customs.

Ercole Benelli now arrived, offering, "*Scusatemi, scusatemi!* I am late."

Spiro eyed the young man with concern. "Not a worry, Ercole. Un-touched?"

"Yes, yes, fine. It is not the first time I have been shot at."

"Shot at before, Forestry Officer?"

"Yes, a blind farmer believed I was a thief, on his property to steal his prize sow. He missed by a long way." A shrug.

Spiro said, "Still, a bullet is a bullet."

"Exactly."

Sachs: "Any witnesses?"

"No, we searched the whole area. None." The officer frowned. "It makes little sense. It doesn't seem to fit his profile. A weapon like that."

Sachs disagreed. "I think he's getting desperate. The amobarb drug tells us he has panic attacks and suffers from anxiety. His condition could be getting worse."

Rhyme asked, "Where would he get the weapon?"

Rossi said, "It would not be so difficult. Handguns and automatic weapons, yes. You would need an underworld connection; the Camorra has access to whole arsenals. But I would think he stole it. There are many hunters in the countryside."

Rhyme added, "We all need to be particularly careful now. Assume scenes are hot. You know what I mean? That the Composer is nearby with his rifle or another weapon."

Rossi said he would put the information out on the law enforcement wire, alerting all the officers to the risk.

"So," Spiro said to Sachs, "I understand from Lincoln that there seemed to be no connection between the Composer and the warehouse?"

"Very unlikely. No one saw anybody matching his description. There were footprints but no Converse Cons. No fingerprints. I've left soil samples with Beatrice. She might find there's trace that connects him with the place but I really doubt it."

Ercole said, "I will say too that after we had dinner I spent the evening reviewing airport security footage looking for someone who might resemble the Composer, flying to Milan. Unfortunately, most flights are connections through Rome. I had hundreds to look at. And it was several days' worth of video. But I saw no sign of him."

Rhyme noted the pronoun. *We* had dinner. And recalled Ercole's texts and his glances toward Daniela Canton.

Beatrice walked into the office. She addressed them, struggling through English. "I am having the results of the tests that have been run. *Primo*, the soil samples you have gave to me, Ercole, from Garry Soames's apartment, near the break-in. There is not some distinctive profile. If we are locationing some other spot, other shoes, we can link them but now, there is not a thing helpful."

A nod toward Sachs. Now, rather than trying English, Beatrice spoke to Ercole. He translated, "She is mentioning the trace in the Milan warehouse. Yes, there was soil that could be associated with the soil here in Campania. Because of Vesuvius, of course, we have a great deal of unique volcanic residue. But there is much commerce between Milan and Naples—trucks drive there daily. So the presence of Neapolitan dirt in Milan does not necessarily mean much.

"But the other trace didn't have any particular connection with Campania or Naples, and is typical of what you would find in a warehouse: diesel fuel, regular petrol..." He asked her to repeat something, which she did. Then he asked her once more. She frowned and repeated slowly, "Molybdenum disulfide and Teflon fluoropolymer."

He glared her way and said something in Italian. A brief exchange ensued and she said something heatedly. Ercole replied, "How would I know what those are?" Then to the others: "She says it is a grease intended for heavy outdoor equipment, lifters, conveyor belts. And there was jet fuel again. Typical too for warehouses—where the trucks drive to and from airport cargo areas."

Massimo Rossi took a call. Rhyme could see immediately his dismay.

"*Cristo!*" the inspector muttered. "The Composer has struck again. And at Capodichino, the camp, once more."

"Another murder?"

"No, a kidnapping. He's left another noose."

Rhyme said, "Have the Postal Police start monitoring the streaming sites. It's just a matter of time until he uploads a new composition."

Then a look toward Sachs. She nodded. "Ercole?"

Sighing, the Forestry officer dug his keys from his pocket, dropped them into her palm, and they jogged out the door.

CHAPTER 45

A melia Sachs braked the Mégane to a hard stop toward the back of the Capodichino Reception Center, guided to the crime scene by the phalanx of Flying Squad cars, lights flashing. The Composer had snatched this victim from the west side of the camp, opposite from where he had slashed to death Malek Dadi.

She and Ercole Benelli climbed from the small car and strode to a uniformed officer who was directing an underling to string yellow police tape around the perimeter. He seemed not the least surprised to see an American detective with a useless NYPD badge on her hip and a Beretta in her waistband, accompanied by a tall young officer in Forestry Corps grays. Apparently Rossi or Spiro had explained who they were and by what authority they were present.

After a brief conversation with the officer, in Italian, Ercole said to her, "He is saying that the victim was outside the fence, about there."

Sachs followed his finger and saw another improvised gate.

"The kidnapper approached from those bushes and there was a scuffle. In this case, though, he was able to get the hood over the victim's head and vanished. But more interesting and more helpful to us, I think: Someone came to the aid of the victim and fought with the Composer."

Ah, Sachs thought. Transfer of evidence.

"Was it a guard? Police? The person who fought?"

"No. It was the victim's wife."

"Wife?"

"Sì. They were walking along those trees, the two of them. The Composer hit her, knocked her down. But she rose again and began fighting him. Her name is Fatima Jabril. The man taken was Khaled. They were recent arrivals."

The Scientific Police van arrived and the two officers exited the vehicle and began to robe. She recognized them from the prior scenes. They exchanged greetings.

Sachs too pulled on a Tyvek jumpsuit, booties and cap and gloves. Though there was no formal division of labor, the woman SP officer asked, through Ercole, if Sachs would work the main scene—where the struggle had occurred—while they took the secondary scene: the far side of a stand of magnolia and vegetation, where the Composer had parked his car and, presumably, lain in wait for the victim.

"Sì," Sachs said. "Perfetto."

The woman smiled.

For a half hour, Sachs walked the grid, using the Italian number cards to mark spots for photography and collection of trace, including the trademark noose. She made one particularly good find in a bush beside a spot where people had clearly grappled: a Converse Con shoe—a low-top model.

When she was finished, the SP officers entered the scene and collected the trace, the noose and the shoe and then photographed and videoed around the numbers.

Outside the perimeter, Sachs stripped off the Tyvek and took the bottled water Ercole offered. "Thanks."

"Prego."

"I want to talk to the victim's wife," she said and downed the water, then wiped her face with her sleeve. Did it ever cool off here?

They went to the front of the camp, where—as she'd seen before—buses waited in line to discharge more refugees. They walked through the gate, and an armed soldier led them to a large trailer on which was a sign that read: Direttore.

Inside the cluttered office, which was—thank you—air-conditioned, a tired-looking brunette sat behind a desk, piled high with papers. She directed them to a door in the back. Sachs knocked and identified herself. She heard, "Come in."

She and Ercole entered and nodded to Rania Tasso. She was sitting with a dark-complexioned woman and an adorable child, a girl of about two years old. As the woman glanced at Ercole, her eyes widened and she quickly grabbed a cloth that rested on a chair beside her and covered her head.

Rania said, "This is Fatima Jabril." She added, "She's comfortable being uncovered before *kaafir* women, like me and you, but not before men."

"Should I leave?" Ercole asked.

"No," Rania said. "You can stay."

Sachs's impression from this exchange was that Rania was respectful of others' customs and beliefs but also insistent that they accept the protocols of their new home.

"Sit, please."

Fatima was attractive, with a long, narrow face—swollen and marred by a small bandage—and close-set dark eyes. She wore a long-sleeve, high-necked tunic and jeans, though her nails were polished bright red and she wore modest makeup. Her attention kept returning to her daughter and her eyes, otherwise piercing, softened when she looked at the girl. She asked something urgently in Arabic. Rania said to Sachs and Ercole, "She speaks some English but Arabic is better. She is, of course, worried about her husband. Have you learned anything?"

"No," Sachs said. "But since the kidnapping was successful, we don't think the man has hurt him, yet. Khaled is his name, right?"

"Yes." From Fatima herself.

Rania asked, "You say not killed him *yet*?"

"Correct."

Rania considered this, then translated for Fatima

Fatima's reaction was both dismay...and anger. Fury. The woman was slim but not small and Sachs imagined that she'd given the Composer a good fright.

The director turned to Sachs and said, "I know you will want to ask Fatima some questions. But one thing I must tell you first. I have just learned something about Malek Dadi's killing, the refugee who was knifed to death? From what they tell me, this Composer was *not* responsible for his murder."

"No?"

"Several men reported—separately—that they saw the Composer in the bushes. What do you say? Staking out?"

"Yes."

"The Composer was staking out the informal gate in the east fence. As soon as Dadi slipped outside, he ran forward. He was holding what might have been a black mask in his hand—the sort he used today on Khaled. But suddenly several other men from the camp hurried after Dadi and jumped on him, to rob him, it seems. He fought back and one of the men slashed him in the throat and took his money. The American, the Composer, actually tried to save him."

"Tried to *save* him?" Ercole asked. "This is certain?"

"Yes. He ran toward the men, shouting, but he was too late. They fled back into the camp. When the Composer saw Dadi lying on the ground, he simply stood over him, looking shocked. Shaking his head. Then he set the noose on the ground and he too fled."

"All right. That's interesting news, Rania. Thank you. Did they say anything else about him? The identification of the car?"

"No. It happened very quickly."

Sachs turned to Fatima. "Please say I'm sorry for her trouble."

But the woman answered in English. "I am thanks for that."

"What happened, exactly, please?"

Fatima gave a fast response, in Arabic, the words edgy and staccato.

Rania explained, "She and Khaled left Muna, this is her daughter, there, with a neighbor and went outside to meet a man about a job for Khaled after they were granted asylum. The Composer approached them there. He struck Fatima and pushed her down—it's very bad for a non-Muslim to touch, much less strike, a Muslim woman. This shocked and stunned her. Then he slipped a hood over Khaled's head, and immediately Khaled grew groggy. Fatima jumped up and fought. But he hit her again hard and she fell back, dazed. When she climbed to her feet, they were gone and a car was speeding away. She couldn't see what kind it was either. Dark. That was all she said."

"I kick-ed him and scratch-ed," Fatima said in cumbersome English, speaking slowly as she sought the words. "He was..." She said a word in Arabic to Rania.

"Surprised," Rania translated. "Unprepared."

"His shoe came off in the struggle?" Ercole asked.

"Yes. I pull-ed it. Holding to his leg."

"Did you see anything unusual about him? Tattoos, scars. His eye color? Clothing?"

After translation, Rania said, "His sunglasses fell off and his eyes were brown. A round face. She might recognize him again but she is not sure. All Westerners look alike to her. There were scars on his face, from where he had shaved, it seemed. He wore a hat. But she can't recall his other clothing. Except it was dark."

"She'll be all right?"

"Yes, our doctors say it was a superficial injury. Nothing broken. A bruise."

Fatima cast her eyes onto Ercole's gray uniform. Then she turned to Sachs and gazed at her desperately. "Please. Fine-ed Khaled. Fine-ed my husband. It so much is important!"

"We'll do everything we can."

Fatima gave a hint of a smile, then grabbed Sachs's hand and pressed it to her cheek. She muttered in Arabic, and Rania translated. "She says, 'Bless you.'"

CHAPTER 46

The injury wasn't bad.

Stefan had been more shocked than hurt when the woman rose from the ground outside the Capodichino Reception Center and, screaming and flailing, attacked him.

He walked into his farmhouse now, carting the Browning .270 hunting rifle in his gloved hands. He hung it on hooks above the fireplace and set the box of shells beneath it. Ironic, he thought: using a hunting rifle against Artemis, the goddess of the hunt.

Well, she would be much less likely to pursue her prey now. Oh, he didn't think she'd give up the search for him. But she'd be scared. She'd be distracted. They all would.

And that meant they'd make mistakes . . . and be far less likely to introduce discord into the music of the spheres.

Sitting now in his hideaway, he examined his stinging arm and leg. Just bruises. No broken skin. Still, he was shaky-hand, sweaty-skin . . . and a Black Scream was just waiting to burst out.

He'd lost his shoe. This was more than a little inconvenient, since he only had one pair and was reluctant to buy another, for fear the police would have put out word to retailers to alert them to a rotund white American in stocking feet buying shoes. With his prey safely unconscious in the trunk of his Mercedes, he'd driven past one of the beaches outside Naples and, when he was sure no one was looking, and there were no CCTVs, he'd snatched a pair of old running shoes a swimmer had left near the road. They fit well enough.

Then he'd hurried back here.

Stefan now walked into the darkened den off the living room. The rhythm section of his next composition lay here, on a cot. He gazed down at Khaled Jabril. The man was so scrawny. His wife had been more substantial. A man of narrow face, bushy hair, full beard. His fingernails were long and Stefan wondered what they would sound like if he clicked them together. He recalled a woman patient, in the hospital, *one* of the hospitals, New Jersey, he believed. She had worn a sweatshirt, pink, stained with a portion of her lunch. She was gazing out the window and clicking her nails. Thumbnail against index finger.

Click, click, click.

Again and again and again.

Another patient was obviously irritated by the noise and kept glaring at the woman angrily but staring at a mental patient to achieve a desired effect is the same as asking a tree for directions. Stefan had not been the least troubled by the sound. He disliked very few sounds—vocal fry was a rare exception.

Babies crying? So many textures of need, want, sorrow and confusion. Beautiful!

Pile drivers? The heartbeat of lonely machines.

Human screams? A tapestry of emotions.

Fingernails on a blackboard? Now, *that* was interesting. He had a dozen recordings in his archive. It comes third in the ranking of cringe-worthy sounds, after a fork on a plate and a knife on glass. The revulsion isn't psychological: Some researchers thought people responded as if the sound were a primitive warning cry—it isn't. No, it's purely physical: a reaction to a particular megahertz range, amplified by the peculiar shape of the ear and painfully stabbing the amygdala region of the brain.

No, very few sounds troubled Stefan, though he would be fast to point out there's a distinction between tone and volume.

Whatever the sound, crank up the decibels and it can move from unpleasant to painful...even to destructive.

Stefan knew this firsthand.

Now, *that* was a memory he cherished.

Shaky-hand.

He wiped sweat and put the tissue away.

Oh, Euterpe...Calm me down, please!

Then he saw Khaled's fingers twitch several times. This was not, however, a sign of waking. He would be snoozing for some period of time. Stefan knew his drugs well. Crazy people are savvy pharmacists.

Stefan relaxed. He now had a task. He sat beside Khaled. He reached down and, on a whim, took the man's hand. He clicked his own fingernails against Khaled's.

Click, click...

Delicious.

From his pocket he took his recorder and undid the man's shirt.

Now he turned the device on and pressed it against Khaled's chest. The heartbeat was, of course, slow and soft, as with anyone in sleep, but because the room was so quiet the sound was captured clearly and distinctly.

He had the beat. Now he needed the melody. Scrolling through his library, he found one that practically begged to be the soundtrack of his next video.

Stefan could think of no other waltz that so perfectly blended music and death.

CHAPTER 47

A bout time," Rhyme muttered.

The evidence from the most recent kidnapping had arrived and Ercole was assisting Beatrice in setting it out on the examination tables in the lab. Rhyme, Sachs and Thom were observing from the situation room.

"His shoe?" Rhyme asked. This discovery surprised, and pleased, him. Shoes are wonderful forensically; not only do they often offer distinctive tread marks to help link a perp to a scene, but the shoe itself can contain a treasure of DNA, fingerprints and, in running shoes like this, trace tucked into the cavities of the sole. Rhyme had once nailed a perp because of the precious way he tied his oxfords.

Sachs explained how the Composer had lost it in the struggle with the victim's, Khaled's, wife.

In a gloved hand, Ercole carried the shoe to Rhyme. "A Converse Con, in the proper size."

Beatrice barked, "Why you have picked it up?"

He turned and glared at her. "I simply am showing it to Captain Rhyme. He had commented on it. It's in an evidence bag. And I am wearing gloves."

"But now we are needing to include another chain-of-custody entry! And everywhere a piece of evidence travels, there can be risk of contaminated."

310 / JEFFERY DEAVER

True. Rhyme lifted an eyebrow to Ercole, who sighed, set the shoe down on a table and signed the card Beatrice offered.

Dante Spiro and Massimo Rossi joined them.

Spiro cast a look Ercole's way. "*Now*, Forestry Officer, it is safe to say we have the start of a pattern. Will you concede that?"

"Refugees."

"*Sì*. That is his preferred target—in Italy, at least. We have three such victims."

Rossi said, "The director of the camp is convinced that he is targeting asylum-seekers because he believes we will not be so diligent in pursuing the case. Although that is hardly true." He waved at the charts.

"But," Ercole said, "I am wondering…"

Spiro said, "How this is in harmony with the businessman in New York?"

"Correct, *Procuratore*."

"There will be a way to incorporate that, I believe. Patterns are not always symmetrical. We are not sure yet. We are, however, advancing."

Sachs then said, "You mentioned the director, Rania Tasso. One thing she told me that was interesting. I'm not sure what to make of it. She said the Composer didn't kill Malek Dadi. He tried to *save* him."

"Is this true?" Rossi asked.

Spiro was frowning but said nothing.

"She was sure," Sachs continued.

"Who then was the killer?"

"Muggers, thieves. Some refugees in the camp. They got to him before the Composer did and when Dadi fought back, the Composer ran toward them to stop them. But it was too late."

Ercole said, "Odd. A curious element to his profile."

Rhyme, however, wasn't interested in profiles. "Two lions going after a gazelle. Neither wants to give up his prey, which is going to end up as a main course one way or the other. Nothing remarkable about that. Let's see what the evidence tells us."

Rossi placed a call and, after a conversation in Italian, disconnected. "No video yet has been posted online."

A half hour later Beatrice Renza walked from the sterile portion of the lab and joined them, clipboard in her grip. She handed it to Ercole without comment and picked up a marker. He translated and she wrote.

CAPODICHINO RECEPTION CENTER KIDNAPPING

- Victim:
    - Khaled Jabril, Libyan citizen, 36. Asylum-seeker. Tripoli.
    - Eurodac: No criminal/terrorist connection.
- Tire print Michelin 205/55R16 91H, same as at other scenes.
- Perpetrator's shoe recovered in struggle.
    - Converse Con, Size 10½ (m)/13 (f)/45 (European)
        - Minimum wear.
        - No fingerprints, but evidence of latex glove prints present.
        - DNA evidence collected.
            - Matches Composer's.
        - Gamma hydroxybutyric acid.
        - Triacylglycerols, free fatty acids, glycerol, sterols, phosphatides, dark-green pigment. Microscopic fragments of what appears to be organic material.
- Miniature noose, from musical instrument string, as at other scenes.
    - Cello.
    - No fingerprints.
    - No DNA.
- Trace collected from clothing of Fatima Jabril.
    - Soil from Capodichino area.
    - Nothing else distinctive.

"No fingerprints on his shoe?" Rhyme muttered. "What the hell does he do? Wear gloves in his sleep?" Then, frowning. "That entry: the gamma hydroxybutyric. The hell is that doing there?"

Spiro said, "Yes, how can that be?"

Ercole had a conversation with Beatrice. He said, "It was recovered from soil in the tread of the Composer's shoe."

"Impossible. It's not from *this* case. It's from the Garry Soames case. That's the date-rape drug. There's been cross-contamination. Hell."

Rossi now explained this to Beatrice, who replied in an even tone, not in the least defensive. The inspector said, "She says she too was surprised to find the drug on the shoe. She was very careful with the evidence. There was no contamination in the lab. Garry Soames's clothing was processed in a different part of the lab and by a different examiner."

All eyes were now on Ercole. Spiro said, "You picked it up, Forestry Officer. And you collected the drug trace at Garry Soames' apartment."

"Yes. And I wore gloves. Then and now. And the shoes were in a sealed evidence bag."

"Still, there is obvious contamination."

"If I am responsible for this, then I'm sorry. But I do not believe I am."

Beatrice turned her round, stony face his way.

Rhyme saw the dismay in the young man's eyes. Lesson delivered. "It's not the end of the world, Ercole. The problem will be at trial. A defense lawyer could get the evidence from the shoe thrown out on those grounds. But we can ignore it for the moment. Our goal is to find him. The contamination'll be the U.S. attorney's problem at trial in the Southern District."

Spiro chuckled. "You mean, Lincoln, it will be *my* problem in the *Tribunale di Napoli*."

Rhyme shot him a wry look.

The Wolf Tits Rule . . .

Reading again, Rhyme said, "Now, those triacylglycerols, free fatty acids, pigment."

Ercole said, "Beatrice has provided a chemical chart here. Should we write that down?"

Rhyme glanced at the molecular diagram. "No, not necessary. We've got what we need. Triacylglycerols—or triglycerides."

"What are they?" Spiro asked.

"Fat basically. They're energy reserves for living things. Molecules that contain glycol and three fatty acid chains. Hence, *tri*-glyceride. They're found in both plants and animals. But animal fats tend to be saturated."

"What does that mean?" Rossi made this inquiry.

"In a nutshell, saturated fats—the bad ones, if you listen to the health-minded—are so named because their carbon chains are *saturated* with hydrogen. This makes them more solid than unsaturated fats, which have *less* hydrogen." He nodded at the diagram. "These are missing some hydrogen and therefore it is a plant fat."

"But what kind?" Ercole asked.

"The sixty-four-thousand-dollar question."

"The...what? I am not understanding," Beatrice said.

"American cultural reference from a long time ago, fifty, sixty years or so."

The officer translated for Beatrice, who gave a rare smile and said something, which Ercole translated: "She said that is not so 'long ago,' compared with cultural references in Italy."

Sachs laughed.

Rhyme said, "We need to find out what plant. Is there a database of plants in the Scientific Police?"

Beatrice's response was that there was one in Rome. She would go online and search it. She typed and spoke to herself as she did so. "*Allora.* A triglyceride molecule, unsaturated, *una* hydrocarbon chain, twenty-two carbon atoms in way of length. Dark green, the pigment. What plant, what plant...?" Finally she nodded. "*Bene.* I have gotten it. But helpful, I am not thinking so much. It is olive oil."

Rhyme sighed, then glanced at Rossi. "How much olive oil would you say is produced in Italy?"

The inspector, in turn, handed off to Ercole. This would be, of course, his area of expertise. The young officer answered, "About four hundred and fifty thousand tons every year. We're the world's second-largest producer." He grimaced and added defensively, "But we are closing in on Spain."

How helpful is *this*? Rhyme thought, irritated. It could have come from anywhere in the country. "Hell."

This was the most frustrating occurrence in forensic work, struggling to discover a clue, only to learn that while it probably did have some connection with the perpetrator, the substance was so common that it was useless forensically.

Then Ercole said something to Beatrice and she stepped away, returning a moment later with some photographs.

He studied them carefully.

"What, Ercole, you see something?" Rhyme asked.

"I believe I do, *Capitano*."

"And?"

"The reference on the chart—to the organic material. Bits of solids. Look at the photo."

Rhyme glanced at the images. He could see hundreds of tiny dark fragments.

Ercole added, "Since we now know about the olive oil, I would say that this trace is not olive oil alone. It is pomace. That is the paste left over after the pressing of the olives."

Spiro said, "So this might have come not from a restaurant or someone's home but from a producer?"

"Yes."

Narrowing things down some. But how much? He asked, "Do you have a lot of producers here?"

"In Campania, our region, we don't have as many as in Calabria, farther south. But still many, many, yes."

Rhyme: "Then why is this helpful? And why do I see a goddamn smile on your face?"

Ercole asked, "Are you so often in an unpleasant mood, Captain Rhyme?"

"I'll be considerably more cheerful if you answer my question."

"I am smiling because of the one thing I do *not* see in this picture?"

Rhyme lifted an impatient eyebrow.

"I do not see any residue of olive stones—the pits, you know."

Sachs asked, "Why is *that* important?"

"There are two ways to make olive oil. To crush the fruit with the pits intact or to destone them first. Cato, the Roman writer, felt that *denocciolato* oils—destoned before pressing—were superior. Some swear by this, others say no. I am familiar with the subject because I have, in fact, fined producers for claiming their oil is *denocciolato* when it is not."

"And," Rhyme said, not exactly smiling himself, but close, "it is a much more time-consuming and expensive process and therefore fewer producers use that technique."

"Exactly," Ercole said. "I would think there are only a few in the area that do so."

"No," Beatrice said, head down as she viewed her computer. "Not 'few.' *Solo uno.*" She stabbed a blunt finger onto the map of Naples, indicating a spot no more than ten miles away. "*Ecco!*"

CHAPTER 48

Through the dirty windshield, Amelia Sachs looked over the hilly fields outside Naples.

The afternoon air was dusty, filled with the scent of early autumn. Hot too, of course. Always hot here.

She and Ercole were driving past hundreds of acres of olive trees, about eight to ten feet high. They were untidy, branches tangled. On the nearest, she could see the tiny green olives—fruit, Ercole said they were called.

They were not having much luck in the hunt for the Composer.

The Police of State and the Carabinieri had divided up the fields around the Barbera olive oil factory—the only one making oil from destoned olives—in their search for Khaled Jabril and the Composer. This was the sector Sachs and Ercole had drawn. As they had approached down a long road, she was discouraged to see...well, very little. This area, northeast of Naples, was largely deserted. Farmhouses, small companies—generally construction and warehousing—and fields.

They stopped at the few residences scattered around the Barbera factory. And they learned that, no, a man resembling the Composer was not inside. No, a man resembling Khaled Jabril was not inside, either. And neither of them had been seen recently. Or ever.

Ci dispiace...

Sorry.

Back into the car.

Soon Sachs and Ercole were bounding along a badly kept road. Now there were no businesses or residences at all, just the acres and acres of Barbera company olives.

"Dead end," Ercole said.

"Call the other teams," Sachs said, distracted. She swatted lazily at a bee that had zipped into the Mégane. "See if they've had any success."

But after three conversations, Ercole reported unsurprisingly that none of the other search parties had found anything helpful. And he confirmed that the Postal Police were carefully monitoring social media and streaming sites. But: "He has not uploaded the video yet."

So Jabril was still alive. Probably.

They returned to the road.

"Hm." Sachs was frowning as she looked over the fields.

"Yes, Detective? Amelia?"

"The paste in the Composer's shoe? The olive oil residue. You call it what again?"

"The word is 'pomace.'" He spelled it.

"Is it thrown out after the oil is extracted?"

"No, no, it's valuable. It can be used for fuel in producing electricity. But around here it is mostly used to make organic fertilizer."

"Then he might not have picked it up at the Barbera oil operation."

He gazed at her with a look of concern. "In fact, he would *not* pick it up here. This factory would be careful not to spill or waste any. They would package it and sell it. Now that I am thinking: Most likely the Composer would have picked it up on his shoes at an organic fertilizer farm. Not here."

"And do you know where one of those farms might be?"

"Ah, the sixty-four-thousand-dollar question. And the answer is, yes, I do."

In twenty minutes they were deep in the countryside, near a town called Caiazzo, surrounded by pale wheat crops glimmering in the hazy sun.

Sachs was racing along the highway that would take them to Venturi Fertilizzanti Organici, SpA. She pushed the tiny car up to 120 kph, thinking: Oh, what I could do on this road with a Ferrari or Maserati... She downshifted and took a turn at close to forty. The skid was not remarkable; the volume of Ercole Benelli's "*Mio Dio*" was.

A glance at the GPS map told her they were approaching the turnoff road and she slowed and veered onto it.

Five minutes later: "Look there." Ercole pointed.

The operation was small: what appeared to be an office structure and several warehouses or processing plants, then fields containing ridges of dark material, about fifty yards long and three feet high. "There. Those are the composting piles?"

"Yes."

She braked to a stop.

"Look, that one at the end is on top of a slope. With any rain the pomace could run down to the property in the valley. Is there a house there, can you see?"

Ercole could not.

Sachs drove to the end of the fertilizer company's property. They discovered a small road that skirted the place. It was dirt. She started down it slowly.

"There!" Ercole called.

Ahead of them, set back a hundred feet from the road, was a structure just barely visible through the weeds, shrubs and oak, myrtles, pine and juniper trees

Sachs kept the car in third gear to make sure the transmission was quiet. She tricked the clutch constantly to keep from stalling.

Finally, near the driveway that led to the house, she pulled off the road into a stand of bushes and killed the engine.

"I don't think I can get out." Ercole was trying the door—the blockade of vegetation prevented its opening.

"Need to stay as much out of sight as we can. Climb out my side."

Sachs got out and he joined her, awkwardly surmounting the gearshift.

Ercole pointed down at their feet. "That's pomace." Indicating a dark grainy substance. She could definitely smell the pungent scent of fertilizer in the making.

He asked, "Should we call Inspector Rossi?"

"Yes, but just have him send a half-dozen officers. There's still a chance he's somewhere else."

As he called she looked toward the house. It appeared quite old, a farmhouse, of wood and uneven brick construction. The place wasn't small. She motioned to him and they started down the long driveway, sticking to the shadows of the trees along the side.

When Ercole had disconnected, she said, "Let's move fast. He hasn't uploaded his video yet but I don't think Signor Khaled has much time."

Through brush, over fallen trees, they moved steadily toward the building. Insects streaked toward them, mosquitoes and gnats. Not far away a dove exhaled its breathy call, mournful, comforting and eerie. The smells were of smoke and something pungent, perhaps the decaying olive oil fertilizer.

They followed the driveway to the left, where the unattached garage was located. The home was even bigger than it had appeared from the road, a rambling structure of several buildings, connected by windowless hallways.

"Gothic," she whispered.

"Like *Gotico*? Spooky? Stephen King."

She nodded.

The garage was locked and there were no windows. It was impossible to tell if anyone was inside.

"What do we do now?"

"Do you know Peeping Toms, in Italy?"

"Yes, yes. We know the term. From a movie, many years ago, that was popular here." He gave a harsh laugh. "And curious. The movie is about a serial killer who films his victims. The English title is *Peeping Tom*."

"Well, we're going to peep." She drew her weapon. She turned to Ercole to tell him to do the same but saw that he already had. They circled the house and began looking, quickly, through the few curtainless windows. At first it didn't seem like anyone lived here but then she caught a glimpse of clothing in a pile. Some empty soda cans.

Was there a light on? In a distant room? Or was the illumination from the sun falling through a slit in a curtain?

Sachs saw inside a large wooden door that, she believed, led down to a cellar. It was closed. Could Khaled be down there now?

Stephen King...

They had nearly completed the circuit of the house. One window remained. It was to the left of the front door. The curtain was partially askew so she lifted her head quickly and glanced inside.

Well.

The room was unoccupied but there was plenty to seize her attention. Above the fireplace was a hunting rifle. She couldn't be sure, but it might very well have been a .270-caliber.

And sitting prominently in the middle of a table were a half-dozen musical-instrument strings. One had been tied into a noose.

CHAPTER 49

Khaled Jabril woke to fear, pure fear.

He found himself in a dim room that was damp and fetid with mold and rotting food smells. Perhaps sewage too.

Where, where?

God, praise be to Him, where am I?

Nothing made sense. He had no memory of the past...well, how long? An hour, a week? No memory at all. A vague recollection of being in a tent. It was—yes, it was under the sun. Hot sun. A tent, his home. Why was he in a tent? Had something happened to his home in Tripoli?

No, *their* home.

He and others. Someone...Yes! His wife! He could now picture her. Ah: Fatima! He remembered the name, praise be to God! And their child.

And she—he believed the child was a girl—was named...He could not recall, and this made him want to cry.

So cry he did.

Yes, yes, she *was* a girl. A beautiful curly-haired daughter.

Although was she, the girl he pictured, in fact, *their* daughter? She might have been his brother's. Then another thought came to him. Italy. He was in...in Italy.

Wasn't that right?

But where was he now? *Here?* He'd been in a tent. *That* he was pretty sure about, though for what reason, he had no idea. A tent, then nothing, then he was in this place. That was all he could recall. His memory was so bad—the result of some drug? Or had he been suffocating, his brain cells dead? Maybe. His throat hurt. And his head too. Dizzy.

A dark room. Cold.

A basement, he believed.

Who had done this? Why?

And why was his mouth gagged, sealed with tape?

Something brushed his bare feet and he screamed, loud to him, soft to the world, because of the gag.

A rat! Yes, there were several of them. Skittering, twitchy.

Were they going to devour him alive?

Oh, my God, praise be to You!

Save me!

But the half-dozen—no, dozen, no, more!—creatures passed him by on their way toward the wall to his right. They weren't interested in him.

Not yet.

All right. What is happening here? Hands bound, feet bound. Kidnapped. Gagged. But why on earth? Why would God—praise be to Him—allow this? Now more pieces of memory returned—though none recent. Recalling being a teacher in Tripoli until education in Libya became so fraught that his secular school was closed. Then he managed an electronics store, until the economy in Libya became so fragile that the shop was looted.

Only his wife's salary as a nurse was left to support them.

And life grew even worse. No dinars, no food, the spread of the fundamentalists, ISIS and Daesh, taking over Derna, Sirte and other cities and towns, like an infection. Were *they* behind his kidnapping? Those men would certainly abduct and torture. Khaled and his family were moderate Sunnis, and believed in secular government. Yet he'd never vocally opposed the extremists. How could the mullahs and generals of ISIS even know he existed?

And the Libyan government?

Well, *governments*, plural. There was the House of Representatives, in Tobruk, along with the Libyan National Army. And then there was the rival General National Congress, based in Tripoli, whose questionable claim was enforced by the Libya Dawn militia. Yes, Khaled favored the House of Representatives but did so discreetly.

No, this kidnapping could not be political.

Then a bit of memory returned, like a kick. A boat...rocking on a boat. Vomiting frequently, burning in the sun...

The image returned of the tent...

And his daughter. Yes, *his* daughter. What *is* her name?

He carefully scanned the place where he was being kept. An old structure. Brick walls, beams overhead. He was in a cellar. The floor was stone and well worn, scarred and uneven. He looked down to see what kind of chair he was seated in and felt a pressure at his neck. A cord of some sort. He looked up.

No!

It was a noose!

The thin cord rose to a beam over his head. It continued to the far wall, over another beam then down to a weight, one of those big round ones that are attached to the ends of barbells. It was upright and resting on a ledge about five feet off the ground. The ledge was at an angle, and had the weight been free it would have rolled off and tugged the noose taut, strangling him. But thank God—praise be to Him—it was wedged in place.

He tried to make sense of this. Then he noted movement again, from the corner of his eye.

On the floor. More rats. And, like the others, they paid him no mind. They were much more interested in something else.

And then, to Khaled's horror, he saw what drew the squirmy creatures, with their tiny red eyes and sharp yellow teeth: a block of something that was preventing the deadly weight from rolling off the ledge and tugging the noose up to strangle him. Pink, streaked with white. A piece of meat. That was what kept the weight from rolling and pulling the noose taut.

The first of the rats, moving cautiously, untrusting, approached it now. They sniffed with their pointed noses, they leapt back, then moved closer. Some were pushed aside by others—the more aggressive—and it was collectively decided that this addition to their lair was not only harmless...it was tasty.

The four rats soon became seven and then became a dozen, swarming the meat like huge, gray bacteria.

Some fights broke out, screeching and biting. But on the whole, they shared.

And began the serious effort of dining.

Khaled shouted and screamed through the gag and shook in the chair.

Which drew the attention of one or two of the rodents and their response was merely to glance at him with curiosity as they happily chewed and swallowed.

In five or ten or twenty minutes, they would devour the meat entirely. And the weight would begin its fall.

Despair.

But then came a flash of joy.

Yes, yes, thank you, God, praise be to Him. He had remembered his daughter's name.

Muna...

At least he would have her name—and the memory of her happy face, her thick curly hair—to accompany him to his death.

CHAPTER 50

They tried. Both of them tried, slamming into the front door of the farmhouse.

But houses built in an era before alarms, when solid oak and maple had to provide the front line of defense, were not easily breached. Then or now.

Ercole had called Rossi again, who in turn had located the closest police station. It was the rival Carabinieri, but for a case like this every officer in Italy was on the same side. A car would be there in ten to fifteen minutes. The Police of State dispatched earlier would be about the same.

"Shoot the lock out," Ercole said to Sachs.

"That doesn't work. Not with handguns."

They circled the farmhouse quickly, still staying vigilant. They had no evidence that the Composer wasn't inside or nearby. And by now he could know he had visitors. And would have seen or at least guessed it was police.

Ercole stumbled over an old garden hose and jumped back to his feet, wincing. He'd cut his palm on some broken crockery. Not badly. She was keeping her eyes—and concentration—on the windows, looking for both threats and for a means of entry.

She found one. A window in the back, one they'd looked through earlier, was unlocked.

Out came her small but blinding tactical flashlight. "Stay back, away from the window," she called to Ercole.

He dropped into a crouch. She clicked the light on and, holding it in her left hand, high above her head, stepped quickly to the window and played the beam inside while aiming her Beretta with her right. If the Composer were inside, armed and ready to shoot, he would instinctively aim for the light or near it. She might take a round in the arm but would have a second or two to fire before she collapsed in pain.

Or died from a brachial artery shot.

But the room yawned back, its only occupants dusty boxes and furniture covered with mismatched sheets as drop cloths.

"Boost me up."

He helped her inside, then he vaulted the sill and joined her.

They walked to the closed door that led to the hallway.

He tapped her arm. She smiled. He was holding out rubber bands.

They put them on their feet. He whispered, "But no gloves. Tactical."

Nodding, she whispered, "We clear every room. That means we assume that he's on the other side of any closed door or he's hiding behind anything big enough to hide behind. I'll hit the room once, fast, with the light, high, like I did at the window. Then back to cover. Then we go in low, crouching. He'll be expecting us standing. And I mean low."

"And if we find him and he doesn't surrender, we shoot for his arms or legs?"

She frowned. "No, if he's armed, we kill him."

"Oh."

"Shoot here." She touched her upper lip, just below the nose. "To hit the brain stem. Three shots. Are you okay with that?"

"I—"

"You have to be okay with it, Ercole."

"I am." A firm nod. "Sì. D'accordo."

A few deep breaths, and so began the hunt. This was a game you never got used to, a game you hated and yet was the most exquisite drug ever concocted.

First, she directed him to the den, where she'd seen the rifle. They cleared the room and she lifted the gun down and removed and pocketed the bolt, so it couldn't fire. Then they began a room-by-room search, from the back of the house to the front. Most rooms were empty. There was a small bedroom that had to be the Composer's. A single Converse Con sat beside the bed.

The kitchen, too, had been used with some frequency.

They continued on.

And hit every room on the ground floor of the place, then upstairs. The Composer was not here.

Finally, they returned to the door that Sachs believed led to the cellar.

She tested the wrought-iron latch slowly. It was unlocked.

Amelia Sachs loathed basements. With a full tactical operation, you could pitch down a flash bang grenade, stun a barricaded suspect and leap down fast. But now? Just the two of them? She'd have to descend the stairs, her legs then hips then torso in full view of whatever weapon the Composer had. When he'd stolen the rifle, had he gotten away with a pistol as well?

Two shots to the knees and she'd fall, helpless and screaming in pain, ready for the final kill.

She glanced up and noted that Ercole, while he would not have had any such experience, was determined and calm. She was confident he'd do fine, if anything happened to her.

She whispered, "If Khaled is anywhere, it's down there. Or the garage. More likely here, I'm thinking. So let's go. You pull the door. And I go down, fast."

"No, I will be the one."

She smiled. "This is my thing, Ercole. I'll go."

"Let me. If he fires or attacks you will be able to shoot him better than I can. It is not a subject I excelled in at training. Truffle smugglers rarely carry AK-Four-Sevens." A smile.

She gripped his arm. "All right. Go fast. Here's the light."

He took a deep breath. And muttered something. A name. Isabella, she believed. Maybe a saint.

"Ready?"

He nodded.

She yanked the door open. It crashed into the wall with a cloud of dust.

Neither moved for a moment.

It wasn't a cellar. It was a closet. Empty.

Breathing fast.

"Okay. Garage. We need something to break the padlock."

They rummaged for tools and, in the kitchen, Ercole found a large hatchet. They left the house and made their way, crouching, to the out-building.

They prepared for entry again—different this time, since they could both establish a field of fire. He would break the lock and pull the sliding door open, while Sachs crouched and aimed into the small building with her flashlight and Beretta. He would do the same.

She nodded.

One swing of the tool and the padlock flew off. He yanked the door open . . . and just like with the closet, empty space greeted them.

A sigh. They put their weapons away and walked back to the house.

"Let's see what we can find."

How much time did they have until Khaled died? Not much, she knew.

They walked into the living room and, donning blue gloves now, looked over the desk, the papers, files, notes, instrument strings. Searching for anything that might give a clue where the Composer and Khaled might be.

Her phone hummed—she'd put it on silent before the entry.

"Rhyme," she said into the microphone attached to her earbud cords. "It's his hidey-hole. But they're not here. The Composer or the vic."

"Massimo says the Carabinieri should be there any minute."

She could hear the sirens.

Rhyme said, "There's not much time. He's uploaded his video. Massimo sent the link to Ercole's phone. The Postal Police are trying to track his proxies through the Far East. He doesn't have Edward Snowden's chops but it'll still be a few hours before they get a specific site."

"We'll keep at it here, Rhyme."

She disconnected and continued the search, telling the Forestry officer, "Check your phone."

Ercole showed her the screen. "Here."

The video showed the unconscious form of Khaled Jabril, sitting in a chair, a noose around his neck, mouth gagged. Even through the small speakers of the mobile, it was easy to hear the bass beat, keeping time to the waltz that played underneath the visuals. The tune was eerie.

Ercole said, "Ah, he's not using gasping breath for the rhythm, like before. It's the victim's heartbeat."

Sachs said, "It's familiar, that music. Do you know what it is?"

"Ah, yes. It is the 'Danse Macabre.'"

Sachs actually shivered, hearing the pulsing, ominous piece. She then squinted as she gazed at some papers in front of her.

No. Impossible.

She hit redial.

"Sachs. You've found something?"

"It's far-fetched, Rhyme, but it's the only chance we've got. Where's Massimo?"

"Hold on. You're on speaker."

"I'm here, Detective Sachs," Rossi said.

"Here's an address. In Naples." She recited it.

"Yes, it's in the Spanish Quarters, not too far away from us. What's there?"

"Khaled Jabril, I'm pretty sure. The only question is, is he still alive?"

CHAPTER 51

S achs saw Massimo Rossi, standing before what seemed to be an old factory, long abandoned, boarded up. The word *"Produzione"* was legible, appearing below another word—a person's name or a product or a service—that was not.

The inspector saw them and called, *"Qui.* This way."

She and Ercole were on foot. They had to be on foot, for the address they sought was in what Rossi had described as *Quartieri Spagnoli,* a congested, chaotic warren of narrow streets and alleyways in Naples. "Named for the Spanish garrison that was stationed nearby in the sixteenth century," Ercole told her. "If you see a boy running *here,* unlike the Vomero, he very likely *is* alerting his father or brother to the presence of police. Camorra are here. *Tanti* Camorra."

Above her, laundry on white lines fluttered in the soft breeze, and scores of residents watched the flashing lights and the manhunt under way by dozens of uniformed officers. The spectators' vantage points were balconies and open windows—which were probably where they spent much of their time; there were no yards, front or back, or even door stoops to sit on and rock babies or talk about politics and the day's adventures at work, in the evening with a beer or wine.

Sachs was startled as a large basket descended to the ground just ahead of her. A boy ran to it and dropped in a plastic grocery bag. The basket ascended; three stories above his father or older brother began to haul the heavy load upward.

Life in the Spanish Quarters seemed to be largely overhead.

They entered the factory now. The air was dank, nose-pinching with mold. The bases of some type of equipment were still bolted into the floor, though what had been mounted to them was impossible to tell. The place was not large and was now made smaller by the many police officers inside. Little sunlight reached in; bright lamps had been set up and, while the rooms were naturally spooky, something about the stark white illumination made them seem even more troubling, like a bright light shining into an open wound. She saw Daniela and Giacomo and nodded. They greeted her in return.

Rossi pointed to the back of the facility and she and Ercole continued to the doorway he indicated. "Down there. The Composer has outdone himself this time," he muttered.

The inspector was already wearing booties and now Sachs and Ercole paused to slip them on too. Blue latex gloves, as well. They entered a small room and descended to the basement of the factory.

The area did not cover the entire footprint of the building but only the back half. The sting of mold and mildew was greater here. Decay too. Overhead were beams, and the floor was pocked stone, giving the place a medieval appearance.

A torture chamber.

Which was exactly what it had been. Khaled Jabril had been stationed—in a chair again, as with Ali Maziq—against a damp wall, the backdrop for the Composer's latest video.

"He was taped down and the noose went over the beams. It was tied to that." He pointed out a body-builder's circular weight, sitting on the floor, in a large evidence bag. Another bag held the noose.

"*Qual è il peso?*" Ercole asked.

Rossi replied, "Ten kilos."

About twenty-five pounds. Maziq was going to be strangled by a water bucket that would have weighed roughly the same, Sachs guessed.

Rossi clicked his tongue. "But what is so devious. Look there."

On the ledge where a number card sat was a piece of meat.

Sachs understood.

Ercole asked, "*Ratti?*"

"*Sì*. Exactly. *Il Compositore* set the meat up as a block to prevent the weight from rolling, and then rats sensed it and began to eat. So the victim had time, perhaps much time, to contemplate his impending death."

"Did anyone see the Composer arrive or leave?" Ercole asked.

"No. There is a pushcart outside. We think he covered the unconscious victim in blankets and wheeled him here from the square nearby. He would look like any other merchant. We are conducting a canvass but even though the *Quartieri Spagnoli* is a small area, there are so many people, so many businesses and shops that nobody would pay him any mind." Rossi's shrug translated into the hopelessness of the efforts.

Then he brightened. "But now, let us go upstairs. You might wish to meet the man whose life you saved. For his part, I know he wishes a word or two with you."

Khaled Jabril sat in an ambulance. He appeared groggy and had a bandage on his neck but otherwise he seemed unharmed.

The medics spoke to Rossi and Ercole in Italian, and Ercole paraphrased to Sachs. "Mostly he is disoriented. From the chloroform or other drugs used to keep him submissive."

Khaled gazed at Sachs. "You are the one who saved me?" His Libyan accent was pronounced but she understood him.

"And Officer Benelli here," Sachs said. "Your English is good."

"I have some, yes," the man said. "I studied in Tripoli. University. My Italian is not good. I believe I was told my wife is all right. They told me she was struck by the man who did this. I have no memory of that."

"She's fine. I've spoken to her since the attack."

"And my daughter? Muna?"

"She's good. They're together."

The medic spoke to Ercole and he translated. "They will meet you at the hospital. A car is bringing them from the camp."

"Thank you." Then Khaled was crying. "I would have died if not for you. May God bless you forever, praise be to Him. You are the most brilliant police ever on earth!"

Sachs and Ercole shared a brief glance. She didn't tell Khaled that the deduction as to his location was not so profound. The paper she had stumbled upon on the Composer's desk in the farmhouse near the fertilizer farm was a list of names of his victims—Maziq, Dadi and Khaled Jabril—and the places where they were to be stashed for the video. Sachs didn't quite believe it could be so obvious.

It's far-fetched, Rhyme, but it's the only chance we've got...

After she'd given Rossi the address, the inspector had sent Michelangelo and his tactical force here.

And, in the basement, they'd found Khaled.

Sachs was relieved that she could conduct an interview in English... though the results were far from satisfying. The unsteady Khaled Jabril had no memory of the kidnapping itself. In fact, he could remember very little of their days in the refugee camp. He'd woken and found the noose around his neck. He'd screamed himself hoarse through his gag, trying to scare the rats away as much as plead for help (neither worked).

Ten minutes of questioning led to nothing. No description of the kidnapper, no words he'd uttered, no memories of any car Khaled had been transported in. He supposed he'd been blindfolded for much of the time but couldn't say that for certain.

A medic spoke and Sachs understood that they wanted to get him to the hospital for a more thorough examination. "*Sì,*" she said.

As the vehicle nosed through the crowd, she, Ercole and Rossi stood in a clutch, watching it leave.

"*Dov'è il nostro amico?*" Rossi muttered, his eyes sweeping over this chaotic part of the city.

Where is our friend? Sachs believed was the translation.

"Maybe the evidence will tell us," she said. She and Ercole turned back to the torture chamber.

CHAPTER 52

Rhyme watched Dante Spiro as he disconnected the phone. Yes, as Ercole Benelli had suggested, his face's waiting state was a scowl, his eyes probing, as if they could stun like a Taser. But following the conversation, it seemed to Rhyme that his mood was particularly searing.

"Ach. There is no sign that the Composer is returning to the farmhouse in the country."

Rhyme and Spiro were alone in the situation room in the Questura. Rhyme, with no need to be anywhere but here, and bodily functions taken care of, had given Thom time off again to see the sights. The aide—irritatingly—kept checking in. Rhyme had finally said, "Hang up! Have some fun! I'll call if there's a problem. Phone reception's better here than in parts of Manhattan." Which it was.

He now digested Spiro's news. Unlike at the aqueduct scene, with Ali Maziq, the Composer had no warning system at the farmhouse to alert him that his hidey-hole had been breached. Rossi had set up surveillance at the house and around the organic fertilizer company, hoping he might return. They'd held off running the crime scene. But two hours had passed and Rossi now yielded to Rhyme's—and Beatrice Renza's—pressure to walk the grid.

Rhyme called Sachs and told her to go ahead with the farmhouse search. She, Ercole and the Scientific Police had finished with the factory in the Spanish Quarters, where Khaled Jabril had nearly been strangled.

Beatrice, in the doorway of the situation room, nodded approvingly when she heard the scene would be searched. *"Bene."* She cocked her head, crowned with a Tyvek bonnet. "'Even seconds can mean the difference between the successful preservation of evidence and its destruction. Scenes must be searched, evidence collected and protected, as quickly as possible.'"

The grammar and syntax were perfect, even if the delivery was mired in her thick accent.

Spiro shot her one of his glances. "And you are lecturing me for what reason, Officer Renza?"

Rhyme had to chuckle. "She's *quoting*, Dante. Not lecturing. And she is quoting *me*. My textbook. And I believe that's verbatim."

She said, "It is used here but only in English. It should be translated."

"That may very well happen." He explained that just this morning Thom had received a call from one of the best literary agents in Italy, a man named Roberto Santachiara, who had read the press account that Rhyme was in Naples and wanted to talk to him about an Italian translation of his book.

"It will be on the bestseller list. Among us, the Scientific Polices, at the least." Beatrice then lifted a file folder. "Now. I have made a discovery that is pertains to something else. This is relating to the Garry Soames case. The wine bottle Ercole wished me to run an analysis."

The bottle at the smoking station on the deck the night of the attack.

She handed the lengthy report to Dante Spiro, who scanned the text and said to Rhyme, "I will translate. There were the same results as in the first analysis, the friction ridges, the DNA, the Pinot Nero wine, which showed no traces of the date-rape drug. But there was new trace found on the surface of the bottle."

"And?"

"Beatrice found present cyclomethicone, polydimethylsiloxane, silicone, and dimethicone copolyol."

"Ah," Rhyme said.

Spiro looked his way. "Is this significant?"

"Oh, yes, it is, Dante. Significant indeed."

She was stunningly beautiful.

Though in a different way from Amelia Sachs, Rhyme reflected. Sachs radiated a hometown, neighborhood-girl attractiveness. The sort you could approach and talk to, without intimidation.

Natalia Garelli was a different species of beauty—an appropriate word, for there was something animal-like about her. High, hard cheekbones, eyes close together, the color an otherworldly green. She wore tight black leather pants, boots with heels that boosted her height three inches over Spiro's, and a thin, close-fitting brown leather jacket. As supple as water.

Natalia looked over Rhyme and Spiro, the only people in the situation room at the moment, though Rhyme saw Beatrice cast a curious look at her from the lab. The Scientific Police officer turned back to a microscope.

The woman had no interest in Rhyme's disabled condition. Her thoughts were elsewhere. "Have you brought me here for, *come si dice?* For a lineup. To identify a suspect?"

"Sit down, please, Signorina Garelli. You are comfortable with English? My associate here does not speak Italian."

"Yes, yes." She sat, flipping her luxurious hair. "*Allora.* A lineup?"

"No."

"Why am I here then? May I ask?"

Spiro said, "We have more questions about the sexual assault of Frieda Schorel."

"Yes, of course. But I spoke to you, *Procuratore,* and to *Ispettore* . . . What was her name?"

"Laura Martelli. Yes. Of the Police of State."

"That's right. And then I spoke to that American woman and, curiously, a Forestry Corps officer the other day."

Spiro tossed a wry look Rhyme's way. He turned back to Natalia. "One detail I am curious about. You say you and your boyfriend had a meal of Indian food the day of the party."

A pause. "Yes, that is correct. Dinner."

"What did you have?"

"I cannot recall for certain. Possibly korma and saag. Tikka masala. Why?"

"And you did laundry in the afternoon?"

"Yes. As I told you. Or told someone who asked. So I might have clean linens in the event a guest wished to stay the night."

Spiro leaned forward slightly and asked in an abrupt tone: "The night of the party, for how long was Frieda Schorel, the victim, flirting with your boyfriend, Dev?"

"I . . ." He had caught her completely off guard. "They weren't flirting. Who told you that?"

"I cannot talk about witnesses who give statements in cases."

Even nonexistent ones, Rhyme reflected.

The green eyes widened momentarily. A potent color. Shamrock green. Rhyme suspected contact lenses. She sputtered: "They were joking, Dev and Frieda. That is all. Your witness is mistaken. It was a party of university students in Naples. A beautiful autumn night. Everybody was having fun."

"Joking."

"Sì."

"Do you know if Dev has ever bought Comfort-Sure condoms?"

She blinked. "How dare you ask me a personal question like that?"

Spiro's tone was persistent. "Please respond."

After a hesitation she said, "I do not know what he buys."

"You are his girlfriend and this you don't know?"

"No. I don't pay any attention to such things."

"If I were to look in your medicine cabinet would I find Comfort-Sure condoms?"

"I resent that question and I resent your attitude."

Spiro gave a Gallic sneer, his lower jaw extended. "It is of no matter. After you left to come here, an officer went through your apartment. She found no Comfort-Sure."

"What? How can you do that?"

"Your apartment is a crime scene, Signorina. That is how. Now, as I was saying: None were found. However, credit card records show that your boyfriend did buy a box of Comfort-Sure three days ago. A box of twenty-four condoms. And yet there were none in the house. Where did they go? Who threw them out? For disposing of them is—let us be frank—the only way two dozen condoms might disappear within three days. Some youths have voracious appetites in that regard. But, honestly, two dozen?"

"Are you accusing my boyfriend of the rape? He would never do such a thing."

"No, I am accusing you of the sexual assault of Frieda Schorel."

"*Me?* You are mad!"

"Ah, Signorina Garelli. Let us explain what we have found."

He glanced at Rhyme, who wheeled to face her. He said evenly, "The lip and neck of the wine bottle on the smoking deck contained traces of condom lubricant, which profiled to be Comfort-Sure brand. It could be associated with—forgive me. I am parsing too fine here. It *matched* the lubricant on Frieda's thigh and within her vagina.

"In my associate's search of the scene at your apartment, she found laundry detergent and Indian food spices—you, the source of both—at the smoking station *and* at the scene of the assault." Rhyme's lips tight-ened with displeasure. "Well, of course you were at the smoking station, because it's your apartment and you hosted the party. But at the scene of the assault itself? How did that happen? I should have thought of it earlier—it was my mistake to miss it. You and the victim both reported that she was climbing back onto your roof over the wall that separated the two buildings when you heard her cries for help and ran to her aid. That was many yards from the attack site. So how did curry and laundry detergent trace get to the place where she was actually assaulted?"

"You're mad too!"

Spiro took up the narrative: "We believe your boyfriend was flirting with Frieda at the party—and that they had been seeing each other off and on from the start of school—after you all met on the first day of class. *You* slipped the drug into Frieda's wine. *You* followed her and Garry up-stairs, hoping she would pass out and Garry would rape her while she was unconscious. That would be humiliating enough for her, you believed. But he didn't; he went downstairs, leaving her alone. And you took up the matter yourself. You got one of your boyfriend's condoms and, when the deck was empty, dragged the unconscious Frieda over the wall to the neighboring roof and violated her with the bottle. Then you hid the condom, to be disposed of later, with the others, the next day, and went about your duties as hostess."

Rhyme knew that Natalia was the person who placed the anonymous call claiming to have seen Garry spiking the wine, and she herself would have broken into his apartment to plant the date-rape drug on his clothing; the footprints Ercole and Thom found could easily be a woman's size.

"Lies!" Natalia raged, eyes flashing with pure hatred.

Spiro now continued, "Our inquiries as to guests at the party focused on men. We will be interviewing witnesses about your whereabouts, at the time of the rape. We have been comparing DNA with that of the *men* at the party. And Frieda's other boyfriends. We will now get a warrant to compel a test of *yours*."

She scoffed. "This is ridiculous." Her indignation was profound. "I cannot be treated like this."

Rhyme's impression was that she truly believed normal rules did not apply...because she was so beautiful.

Natalia rose. "I will not put up with this any longer. I am leaving."

"No, you are not." Spiro stood to block her way and gestured into the hall. Daniela Canton approached, pulling cuffs from her belt, then ratcheting them on Natalia's wrists.

"No, no! You can't do that. It is...not right!"

Natalia stared down at her wrists, and it seemed to Rhyme that the horror registering in her eyes was not from the fact she was cuffed but that the silver of the shackles clashed with the gold of her bracelets.

Though this surely had to be his imagination.

CHAPTER 53

Hopeless.

His life was over.

Garry Soames was close to crying when he left the interview room and was let out into the prison's common area, about two acres of anemic grass and sidewalks, largely deserted at this time of day. He walked slowly back to the wing in which his cell was located.

His lawyer, Elena Cinelli, had told him that although the police were considering the possibility that he had been set up as a fall guy for the rape of Frieda Schorel, the magistrate had turned down her request that he be released, even with the surrender of his passport.

This was so unfair!

Elena had told him that two of the best forensic scientists in America, who happened to be in Naples on another case, were assisting with the evidence. But assisting wasn't the same as proving he was innocent. Valentina Morelli, the girl who'd turned on him so viciously, had been located and had given a statement—subsequently verified—that she had been in Mantua the night of Frieda's assault. Suspicion had returned once again to him.

What a nightmare this had become...

He was in a strange land, with "friends" who were suddenly wary of visiting him. His parents were still in the midst of making arrangements to fly to Italy (Garry's younger brothers and sisters had to be sorted out). The food was terrible, the hours of solitude—and despair—stretching on and on.

The uncertainty.

And the looks the other prisoners gave him. Some offered sly, conspiratorial glances, as if they shared a rapist's inclination. Those were just plain creepy. And then there were the glares—of those who seemed to want to short-circuit the judicial system and dish out fast, uncompromising justice. Several times he'd heard, in stilted English, the word "honor." Offered like a whip, lashing him for his crime of debasing a woman.

And the goddamn pisser of it all? The reason the night with Frieda on the roof, under the stars of Naples, could not have turned out to be sexual assault?

He hadn't been able to get it up. Me, Garry Soames. Mr. Ever-ready. Kissing, touching...and he'd stayed limp as a rag.

Sorry, sorry, sorry...It's out of my hands. I can't control it.

A fact he hadn't dared to share with anyone. The most shameful thing he could think of had to be kept a secret. He couldn't tell the police, couldn't tell his lawyer. No one. "No, I couldn't have raped Frieda, even if I'd drugged her—which I didn't. No, Old Dependable hadn't worked that night."

And now? What would happen—?

His thoughts were interrupted as two men appeared nearby in the prison yard, stepping from the doorway of a wing nearby. He didn't know the short, muscled prisoners very well, other than that they weren't Italian. Albanian, he thought. Swarthy and forever unsmiling. They kept to themselves or hung out with a few others that looked somewhat like them. The two, brothers, had never said anything to Garry and had largely ignored him.

Now it was the same. They looked toward him once and returned to their conversation, continuing on a path roughly parallel to his, about twenty steps behind.

He nodded. They returned the gesture and kept walking, heads down.

Garry thinking: Why the hell did I go to that party in the first place?

I should have been studying.

He didn't regret coming to Italy. He loved the country. He loved the people and the culture and the food. But now he was looking at the whole adventure as a mistake. I could have gone anywhere. But, no, I had to be the big famous world traveler, show everyone from a punk-ass suburb in middle America that I was different. I was special.

Garry observed the two Albanian prisoners moving slightly faster. They would catch up with him in the shadow of the children's climbing wall—in a small area where prisoners could play with their children and visit with their wives on Sunday.

But he ignored them and thought again of the party at Natalia's. He never should have left Frieda on the roof. But seeing her drowsy eyes and feeling her head on his shoulder . . . and feeling nothing down below, he'd had to flee. It never occurred to him that she'd been drugged and would be at risk.

What a mess . . .

The Albanians were now closer. Ilir and Artin, he believed, were their names. They claimed to have been wrongly arrested simply for helping refugees flee oppression. The prosecutor's charges were a bit different: that they spirited young girls away from their homes and set them up working in brothels in Scampia, a grim suburb of Naples. The altruistic argument they made—that they were saviors of the oppressed—fell on deaf ears, as most of the girls they "rescued" came not from North Africa but from the Baltic states and small towns in Italy itself, lured by their promise of modeling careers.

Garry didn't like that the men had sped up and were just a few steps behind. He diverted, hoping to avoid them.

But it was too late.

The squat, swarthy men lunged and flung him to the grass.

"No!" Gasping, his breath knocked from his lungs.

"Shhh. Quiet!" Ilir—the smaller—raged in Garry's ear.

His brother looked around to see there were no guards or other prisoners present and drew a long, thick piece of glass from his pocket, a shiv. The base was wrapped in cloth, but six inches of razor edge glistened.

"No! Please! Come on, I haven't done anything!" Maybe they thought he'd been with the prison police, just now, informing on them. "I haven't said anything!"

Artin smiled and eased back, letting Ilir hold him down. In thickly accented English, he said, "Now, here. Here it is. Yes? Here is what is going to happen. You are knowing Alberto Bregia?"

"Please! I haven't done anything to you. I just—"

"Now, now. You are answering me. Yes, there you go. Answer me. Do not baby-cry. Answer me."

"Yes, I know Bregia."

Who wouldn't? A huge, psychotic prisoner—six foot four—who terrified everyone who crossed him, even if their betrayals were pure figments of his bizarre imagination.

"So, it is this. Bregia has problem with my brother and me. And he is wishing to murder us. Now, now. What we are doing is this."

Garry struggled to push Ilir off. But the wiry man held him down firmly. "Stop," he muttered. Garry complied.

"We are having to hurt you some. Stabbing you, yes." He held up the glass knife. "But we not kill you. Cut you some much. But you will not be dying. And then you will be saying that Alberto Bregia did this."

Ilir said, "So he will go to other prison. For dangerous prisoners. We have seen into this. It is how this works. All good."

"No, don't! Please!"

Artin was nodding. "Ah, it won't be much. Six, seven times. Which is nothing. I am being stabbed. Look at these scars. People here in prison, they talk. They say you should have balls cut, you rapist." He brushed the point over Garry's crotch. "No, no. We are not be doing that." They both laughed. "Just some girl you fuck? Who care? So, you good. Just face, chest, maybe cut ear bad."

"Cut off," his brother said.

"Has to look like Bregia, something he would do."

"Look, baby-cry, stop that. Okay, Artin. Cut him and we go. Hurry!"

Artin muttered something in Albanian and Ilir clamped his filthy hand over Garry's mouth and gripped him with fierce strength.

Garry tried to scream.

The glass point moved toward his ear.

And then a distant voice: "Signor Soames! *Dove sei?*"

From the doorway he'd just exited through, the hallway that led to the interview rooms, a man was calling him.

"Are you still in the yard?"

The Albanian brothers looked toward each other.

"*Mut,*" Ilir spat out.

The knife vanished and they rose quickly.

Garry struggled to his feet.

"You are saying nothing!" Artin whispered. "Silence, baby-cry." They turned and walked away quickly.

Garry stepped from the wall.

He saw who'd just called to him. It was the assistant director of the prison, a narrow, balding man who wore the uniform of the Penitentiary Police. It was perfectly pressed.

Garry joined the man in front of the doorway.

"You are well? What has happened?" He was regarding Garry's gray, grass-stained jumpsuit.

"I fell."

"Ah, fell. I see." He didn't believe him, but in prison—even in this short period of time, Garry had learned—the authorities don't question what they choose not to question.

"*Sì?*" Garry asked.

"Signor Soames, I have for you good news. The prosecutor in your case has just called and informed me that the true attacker has been identified. He has applied to a magistrate that you be released."

Breathlessly, Garry asked, "For sure?"

"Yes, yes, he is certain. The documents for release have not been signed yet but that will happen soon."

Garry looked back at the doorway to his cell wing, thinking of the two Albanians. "Do you want me to wait in my cell?"

The assistant director debated a moment looking over Garry's torn sleeve. "No, I think that's not necessary. Come into the administrative wing. You can wait in my office. I will bring for you *caffè.*"

Now the tears came. And came in earnest.

CHAPTER 54

The team had assembled in the situation room near the lab on the ground floor of the Questura.

Sachs and Flying Squad officer Daniela Canton had brought the evidence collected at the farmhouse near the organic fertilizer farm, and Beatrice Renza was completing her analysis. The evidence was here too from the factory in Naples, which had been dubbed by Daniela's partner, Giovanni Schiller, *Il Casa dei Ratti*.

Spiro stood in the corner of the room, arms crossed. "Where is Ercole?"

Sachs explained that she'd sent him on another assignment; he would be back soon.

Rossi was on the telephone and when he disconnected, he explained that he had located the owner of the farmhouse, who'd rented the place to the Composer. He lived in Rome and had driven to Naples to meet an American, who had given his name as Tim Smith, from Florida. The owner confirmed he resembled the composite picture of the kidnapper. He'd paid cash for two months plus a bonus.

"A bonus," Rossi said with a wink in his voice, "for *riservatezza*. Discretion, you would say. That's not what the landlord said but it was what I understood. He supposed the man wanted a place for his mistress. He didn't suspect a crime, he insisted. Of course he *did* but he hardly cared."

The landlord had told Rossi he had none of the cash left—hence, no fingerprint possibility—but he did have a thought about the make of the man's car. Though the renter had parked out of sight, the landlord had coincidentally driven off the main road to get to a restaurant outside town and gotten a look at an old dark-blue Mercedes. A quick search confirmed that the Michelin tire size was compatible with older Mercedes. Rossi put the notice out to all law enforcement agencies to look for such a sedan.

FARMHOUSE OUTSIDE OF CAIAZZO

— Dell Inspiron computer.
  — Passcode-protected, sent to Postal Police.
— Western Digital, 1 TB drive.
  — Passcode-protected, sent to Postal Police.
— Browning AB3 rifle, caliber: Winchester .270.
  — Serial number indicates stolen three years ago, private residence in Bari, probably sold on the underground market.
  — Box of 23 Winchester .270 cartridges, two empty brass shells.
  — Ballistics indicate same weapons used to fire at American detective Amelia Sachs and Officer Ercole Benelli at Capodichino refugee camp.
— Six E-note bass strings, one tied in a noose.
— Drives an older-model, dark-blue Mercedes.
— Four tire treads in driveway.
  — Michelin 205/55R16 91H (same as earlier scene), probably from the Mercedes.
  — Pirelli model 6000 185/70R15.
  — Pirelli P4 P215/60R15.
  — Continental 195/65R15.
— Various items of clothing, some suspect's, some from victims (see inventory).
  — Unable to trace purchase.
— Various items of toiletries (see inventory).
  — Unable to trace purchase.
— Food (see inventory).
  — Unable to trace purchase.
— Fodor's guide to Italy.

- — Unable to trace purchase.
- — Berlitz Italian phrase book.
  - — Unable to trace purchase.
- — List of victims, personal details, locations where they were to be held for videoing. (printout).
  - — Ali Maziq.
  - — Malek Dadi.
  - — Khaled Jabril.
- — Additional traces of olanzapine and amobarbital.
- — Friction ridges:
  - — Only the victims'.
    - — Ali Maziq.
    - — Khaled Jabril.
  - — Areas in house seem to have been swept, alcohol used.
  - — Latex glove marks revealed throughout.
- — Two dozen footprints, not matching any earlier.
  - — Size 7½ (m)/9 (f)/40 (European), leather sole.
  - — Size 10½ (m)/13 (f)/45 (European), unknown running shoe, well worn.
  - — Size 9 (m)/10½ (f)/43 (European), unknown style, probably hiking boot or running shoe.
  - — Converse Cons, as before—The Composer's.
  - — Three others of indistinct size, two plain leather soles, one Rocky Lakeland hiking boot.

"Why all the footprints?" Spiro wondered aloud.

Rossi: "Some possible tenants looking at the rental, I would assume. And the victims. The Composer kept them there until he was ready to make his video. They might have walked to and from the car—even if they can't remember it now."

Rhyme sighed. "I hope one of those prints isn't *another* vic. Just because a name wasn't on the list doesn't mean he hasn't taken somebody else."

Beatrice said, "It is so extremely curious, no fingerprints. None at all, excepting for the victims'. It is as if, as you say, Captain Rhyme, he wears the gloves in his sleep."

Spiro scowled. "He makes it difficult at every turn."

"Oh, no," Rhyme said, "the absence of fingerprints is very good for us. Isn't it, Sachs?"

She was staring at the chart. "Uh-hum."

"How do you mean?" Rossi asked.

There was a voice in the doorway, "*Ciao*." From Ercole Benelli, carting a trash bag with him.

Noting the Forestry officer was smiling at her, Sachs said, "Here's the answer to your question, Inspector."

Rhyme explained, "We had a case a few years ago. A professional hit man. We found his hidey-hole and there wasn't a single print. He wore gloves all the time. But that meant he had to dispose of those gloves frequently—since, of course, they retain prints *inside* the fingers perfectly. He was unlucky enough to throw them out in a refuse bin two blocks from his place. We found them. We identified him. We caught him. I suspect that's where Officer Benelli has been, searching trash bins."

"Yes, yes, *Capitano* Rhyme." He lifted the green plastic bag. "I found this in a bin behind an IP station—a petrol station—on the road between Caiazzo and Naples. I'm afraid I wasn't successful as regards the gloves."

He lifted three metal paint cans out of the bag and carefully set them on the table. Rhyme took one sniff and, smelling the astringent scent, scowled. "Methyl isobutyl ketone."

"What is that?" Rossi asked.

In slow English, Beatrice answered. "It is being a solvent. Particular effective in melting latex."

"Yes," Rhyme said.

Ercole said, "There is simply a blue mess, sludge, you say? In the bottom. The gloves have dissolved."

Spiro regarded the Forestry officer. "But you don't look as upset as you might, given the news you have delivered. Are you being oblique intentionally? Do not be coy. Explain."

"Yes, *Procuratore*. The trash bin that these cans were in had a lid on it, and I found no glove prints on the lid but some fingerprints. From, I hope, where he opened the bin to deposit the cans, never thinking we would find them." He produced an SD card and handed it to Beatrice. She sat at the computer and called up the images. Ercole had used fingerprint powder—an old standby—to raise the images. They were all partials, some better than others.

Rhyme could see, however, they were not enough for an identification. But he turned to Beatrice, who nodded knowingly. She had anticipated him. She typed at the keyboard and a moment later another print appeared, in a separate screen, beside the partials from the trash bin. They were the Composer's other prints, pulled from the leaves on the branch where he'd spied on Ali Maziq at dinner the night he was kidnapped at the bus stop.

"This might be a moment or several." She began playing Rubik's Cube with the two sets of prints, trying to place them together, enlarging and shrinking, rotating them, moving them from side to side. The room was silent, every eye on the screen.

She adjusted her elaborate, green-framed glasses, studying it carefully. She spoke in Italian.

Ercole said, "She believes this is the Composer's print, three partials combined into one nearly whole."

Beatrice began to type fast as a machine gun. She said something in Italian. Ercole turned to Rhyme and Sachs. "She has sent it already to Eurodac, Interpol, Scotland Yard, and IAFIS, in the United States." Beatrice sat back but kept her eyes focused like gun muzzles on the print.

Spiro was about to ask a question but Ercole said, "And I asked the owner of the station but he saw no one at the trash bin. And his employees did not either."

The prosecutor nodded with an expression that explained that this was to have been his question. He opened his mouth once more.

Ercole said, "And no CCTV."

"Ah."

After two excruciating minutes, a noise interrupted. A beep from Beatrice's computer. She bent to the screen and nodded.

"Ecco. Il Compositore."

She turned the monitor toward them.

The face of a bearded, shaggy-haired man was on the screen. It was a Bucks County, Pennsylvania, Sheriff's Office mug shot. He was pudgy and stared at the camera with piercing brown eyes.

Below was the text that accompanied the Integrated Automated Fingerprint Identification System report. "His name is Stefan Merck, thirty years old. He's a mental patient, committed indefinitely for assault and attempted murder. He escaped from the hospital three weeks ago."

CHAPTER 55

Amelia Sachs, on her phone, turned back to the room and announced, "I've got the director of the mental hospital in Pennsylvania. She's Dr. Sandra Coyne. Doctor, you're on speaker."

"Yes, hello. Let me understand. You're in Italy? And this is about Stefan Merck?"

"That's right," Sachs said. And explained what her patient had been up to.

The woman reacted with silence, presumably stunned. Finally she spoke. "Oh, my," she said in a husky voice after a moment. "Those kidnappings in Naples. Yes, they made the news here. The stories said the crimes were modeled after one in New York, I think. But it never occurred to us that Stefan might be the one behind them."

Rhyme asked, "What's his diagnosis?"

"Schizophrenic personality, bipolar, severe anxiety disorder."

"How did he escape?"

"We're a medium-security facility. And Stefan had been on perfect behavior since he'd been here. He had grounds privileges and apparently some very careless landscapers left a shovel outside. He found it and dug under the chain link."

"He was committed for attempted murder?"

"At another facility, yes. He permanently injured him. He was found incompetent to stand trial."

Rossi said, "I am an investigator here, in Naples. Please, Doctor. How could he have paid for this, the trip? He has resources?"

"His mother died years ago, his father disappeared. There was some trust money and he's had some relatives visit recently, an aunt and uncle. They might have given him something."

"Can we get their names?" Sachs asked.

"Yes, I'll find them in the files." She took down Sachs's contact information and said she'd send the information as soon as they hung up.

"Is there anything you can think of," Sachs asked, "that might help us understand why he's doing this?"

After a pause, the woman said, "Stefan has his own reality. His world is a world of sounds and music. Nothing else matters to him. I'm sorry to say we don't have the money or authority to give patients like him access to what would help. In Stefan's case, instruments or the Internet. He's told me for years he's starved for sounds. He was never dangerous, never threatening, but something must have pushed him even further from reality." A pause, then she said, "You want to know the kind of person you're dealing with here? In one session he told his therapist he was very depressed. And why? Because he didn't have a recording of Jesus's crucifixion."

Those words resonated with Rhyme. He sometimes imagined walking the grid at famous historical crime scenes, using modern forensic techniques to analyze the crimes. Calvary was perhaps number one on his list.

Sachs asked, "Why Italy? Any connection here?"

"Nothing from his past. But I do know that just before he escaped, in one session, he kept referring to a special woman in his life."

"Someone with an Italian connection? Can we talk to her?"

A laugh. "That would be pretty difficult. It turned out he was referring to a three-thousand-year-old mythological being. Euterpe, one of the nine muses in Greek and Roman lore."

"The muse of music," Ercole said.

"Yes, that's right."

Sachs asked if there were any special foods he might eat, any special interests he had—anything that might help them find stores or places he would tend to go.

She could think of nothing, except to add the curious comment that Stefan didn't care about the taste of food. Only the *sound* of eating. He preferred crunchy foods to soft.

Hardly helpful, from an investigative perspective.

Rhyme asked if she had pictures of Stefan other than the mug shot.

"Yes, let me find them. Give me an email."

Rossi recited the address.

A moment later they appeared, a half-dozen images depicting a stout, intelligent-looking young man with perceptive eyes.

Spiro thanked her.

The woman added, "Please, obviously, he's suffered a break, a bad one. But until now, he's always been eminently reasonable. With these kidnappings, he's become dangerous. That's clear. But if you find him please, before you hurt him, just try to talk."

"We'll do our best," Sachs said.

Disconnecting the call, Rossi muttered, "Try to talk? To a man who didn't think twice about sniping at two officers?"

Spiro gazed at the pictures of the kidnapper. In a soft voice he said, "What are you up to, *amico mio*? How does your assault on these poor souls in New York and in Naples help you find comfort?"

Rhyme, with no interest in that question, was wheeling forward, examining the evidence chart.

Rossi spoke to Daniela Canton in Italian and she pounded the keys. He announced to the room, "I'm sending the pictures to our public information office. They will get them on our website and to the press. The images will go to the other law enforcement agencies too. Soon there will be a thousand officers looking for him."

Rhyme wheeled closer yet to the evidence charts, scanning them. Again and again. The process was like reading a classic novel—every time you pick up the book again, you find something new.

Hoping for some insight, the slightest nudge toward understanding.

But he was hardly prepared for the particular revelation that burst into his thoughts.

At first, he scowled. No, it couldn't be. There had to be a mistake. But then his eyes came to one entry and stopped abruptly. Eyes still on the easel, Rhyme asked in an edgy voice, "Does something up there strike anyone as odd?"

When those in the room looked toward him blankly, he added, "The tread marks and shoe prints."

Sachs barked a surprised laugh. "It doesn't make sense."

"No, it doesn't. But there you have it."

Spiro understood next: "One of the shoe prints at the farmhouse is the same size as the shoe print at Garry Soames' apartment."

Ercole Benelli added, "And one of the auto treads, the Continental tire that I found at Garry's, is the same as one of those at the farmhouse. How can this be?"

Rhyme said, "Suggesting that the same person who broke into Garry's apartment was at the Composer's farmhouse."

"But Natalia Garelli broke into Garry's," Ercole said.

Rhyme turned to Spiro. "We *assumed* that. But we never asked her about it."

"You are right. We did not."

Sachs added, "And Natalia didn't blame Garry when we talked to her. She said he was innocent. She wanted the Serbs next door to take the fall."

Rossi touched his mustache and said, "It looks like you didn't cross-contaminate anything, Ercole, with the date-rape drug trace. The two scenes—Garry's apartment and the Composer's lair—are legitimately linked."

Spiro: "But how?"

Lincoln Rhyme said nothing. His attention was wholly on two evidence charts—not ones from Italy, but the first two, describing the scenes in New York.

213 EAST 86TH STREET, MANHATTAN

— Incident: Battery/kidnapping.
   — MO: Perp threw hood over head (dark, possibly cotton), drugs inside to in-
      duce unconsciousness.
— Victim: Robert Ellis.

- Single, possibly lives with Sabrina Dillon, awaiting return call from her (on business in Japan).
- Residence in San Jose.
- Owner of small start-up, media buying firm.
- No criminal or national security file.
- Perpetrator:
  - Calls himself the Composer.
  - White male.
  - Age: 30 or so.
  - Approximately six feet, plus or minus.
  - Dark beard and hair, long.
  - Weight: stocky.
  - Wearing long-billed cap, dark.
  - Dark clothing, casual.
  - Shoes:
    - Likely Converse Cons, color unknown, size 10½.
  - Driving dark sedan, no tag, no make, no year.
- Profile:
  - Motive unknown.
- Evidence:
  - Victim's phone.
    - No unusual calls/calling patterns.
    - Short hair, dyed blond. No DNA.
    - No prints.
  - Noose.
    - Traditional hangman's knot.
    - Catgut, cello length.
    - Too common to source.
  - Dark cotton fiber.
    - From hood, used to subdue victim?
    - Chloroform.
    - Olanzapine, antipsychotic drug.
  - YouVid video:
    - White male (probably vic), noose around neck.
    - "Blue Danube" playing, in time to gasps (vic's?).

— "© The Composer" appeared at end.

— Faded to black and silence; indication of impending death?

— Checking location where it was uploaded.

WYCKOFF AVENUE, BUSHWICK, BROOKLYN. KIDNAPPING SITE

— Gasoline accelerant to destroy evidence. No source determined.

— Swept floor, but Converse Con impressions remain.

— Substance trace:

   — Tobacco.

   — Cocaine.

   — Heroin.

   — Pseudoephedrine (methamphetamine).

— Two additional short, blond hairs, similar to those at scene of kidnapping on 86th Street.

   — Robert Ellis reports—his girlfriend's most likely.

— Four pieces of paper.

   — Passport photo picture.

— Hat and T-shirt, largely burned.

   — DNA collected, not in database.

   — Unable to source.

— Hood, largely burned.

   — Unable to source.

   — Traces of olanzapine (antipsychotic drug).

   — Traces of chloroform.

— Musical-instrument keyboard, destroyed. Serial number recovered. Bought with cash from Anderson Music, West 46th Street. No CCTV.

— NetPro Wi-Fi router.

   — Purchased with cash from Avery Electronics, Manhattan. No video transaction of sale.

— Technology Illumination Industries halogen battery-powered lamp.

   — Unable to source.

— Broom handle used as gallows.

   — No friction ridges.

   — Unable to source.

— EyeSpy webcam.
  — Unable to source.
— Upright bass strings (E note), tied together (carrick bend knot), and one in hangman's noose.
  — Unable to source.
— Currency exchange receipt.

After reading the charts twice Rhyme sighed, shaking his head.

Ercole asked, "What, Captain Rhyme?"

"It was right there in front of us. The whole time."

"But what?"

"It's obvious, isn't it? Now I've got to make a call to America. But in the meantime, Massimo, put together a tactical team. We'll have to move fast if the answer is what I think it is."

Forty minutes later, the team was assembled on a quiet street in a residential neighborhood of Naples.

A dozen SCO officers were divided into two groups, each on either side of a door to a modest single-family home, painted mustard yellow. Rhyme could see the glint of the low sun off the equipment of a third team, heading through an alley to cover the back door.

He himself was on the street, his wheelchair parked beside the Sprinter van. Dante Spiro stood beside him, his cheroot, unlit, clamped between his teeth.

Amelia Sachs, he could see, was behind the front entry team, the one on the right, though she'd been told, to her irritation, that she wouldn't be allowed to join in, if a dynamic entry—that is, six-guns blazin'—was necessary. The leader of the unit, the massive officer named Michelangelo, let her remain in a forward position, though. And he'd given her a bulletproof vest, *Polizia* printed on the front and back. She wanted to keep it as a souvenir, after the case was over.

When they'd arrived on the scene, Michelangelo had looked Sachs over and, with a sparkle in his eyes, said, "*Allora!* Dirty Harriet."

She'd laughed. "Make my day!"

Now Massimo Rossi climbed from the front seat of a Flying Squad car. He pressed an earbud deeper into his ear as he listened to a transmission. He straightened. Apparently the team in the rear was ready. He walked to the house and nodded to Michelangelo. The big officer knocked with a fist—Rhyme could hear the blows from this distance—and called, "*Polizia. Aprite!* Open this door!" And stepped back.

What followed was anticlimactic in the extreme.

No gunshots, no barricades, no battering rams.

The door simply opened and although he was too far away to hear, it was clear to Rhyme that Charlotte McKenzie, from the U.S. Consulate, uttered nothing by way of protest. Nor did she express any surprise. She nodded and held up her arms in surrender. The man standing behind her, Stefan Merck, did exactly the same.

CHAPTER 56

Michelangelo's tactical team had cleared the house.

Hadn't taken long; like most single-family homes in this part of Naples, it was small. The well-worn place had mismatched furniture, most of it a decade old. The feel of a rental.

With the help of two SCO officers, Rhyme's clever wheelchair surmounted the single step and wheeled into the living room, where Charlotte McKenzie was sitting on a divan with her hands together, as if she'd just put aside her knitting. Rossi and Spiro stood nearby, each on his own mobile, speaking quietly and quickly, the inspector's face animated, the prosecutor's stony. Sachs, pulling on booties and latex gloves, headed into the back of the house.

McKenzie glanced at her with the confidence of someone who has hidden all the incriminating evidence off-premises.

We'll see about that...

The room was warm with yellow light and the air smelled of cinnamon. Stefan stood behind the woman's chair, looking more bewildered than anything. While McKenzie was not in irons, the serial killer—the *faux* serial killer—had been cuffed. The tactical policemen who'd helped Rhyme into the apartment kept eyes on the prisoners. They were both dark of flesh, not big—much smaller than their boss, named after the famed artist—but were in sinewy, taut shape and looked prepared to strike fast if they needed to.

Since the police arrived, the kidnapper had said nothing other than one word to Amelia Sachs.

"Artemis."

A Greek goddess, Rhyme believed, recalling both Ercole's speculation and the mental hospital director's comments that Stefan's crimes had a mythological connection.

He now looked over Stefan carefully. There was nothing unusual about his appearance or expression. He was just another handsome young man, pudgy but more or less fit, stubble just returning to his shaved head, which glistened with sweat. He was dressed in jeans and a Mark Zuckerberg gray T-shirt (this was the term that had been used by Rossi; Rhyme didn't know, but believed he was some computer guy).

Rhyme noted one curious habit of Stefan. From time to time he would close his eyes and ease his head to the side. Occasionally he would smile. Once, he frowned. At first, Rhyme didn't understand these gestures and expressions. Then he realized that Stefan was *listening*. To sounds, it seemed. Not to words or to conversations—only Italian was being spoken and he probably wasn't fluent, certainly not at the rat-tat speed of the officials in the room.

Just sounds.

But what noises might engage him wasn't clear. Initially there didn't seem to be many in the still apartment but, aware that Stefan was so engaged, Rhyme too closed his eyes and filtered out the voices and became aware of one or two sounds, then a dozen, then many more. The clink of Stefan's handcuff chains. Footfalls of Sachs in the nether regions of the house. A distant siren. A creak of door. A tap of metal upon metal from outside. A tiny whine of floorboard under Spiro's weight. A buzz of insect. A crick of metal. A skittle of vermin. A hum of refrigerator.

What had been quiet, almost silent, was in fact a smorgasbord of noise.

Spiro disconnected first and spoke to the uniformed officers in Italian. When Rossi was off the phone, he and the prosecutor agreed that Stefan would be taken to a prisoner transport van outside and kept there while Charlotte McKenzie remained here for an interview. Stefan's part as a serial kidnapper was not disputed, while the woman's role was not completely known. And there was one very important question that had yet to be answered.

"This way, sir," an officer said to Stefan, his English languid.

Stefan looked toward McKenzie, who nodded. She then said, firmly, to Spiro and Rossi, "Give him his phone, so he can listen to music. Take the SIM card out if you want, so he can't make calls. But it's better if he has music."

The SCO officer looked quizzically at Spiro, who debated and lifted the young man's phone from the table, slipped the card out and gave it to Stefan, along with a set of earbuds taken from him earlier.

As they walked away McKenzie said to him, "Don't say anything to anyone, Stefan."

He nodded.

Now Sachs returned. She held up four plastic bags. Two contained over-the-counter medicine bottles. Rhyme regarded them. "Yes," he said. The other bags held shoes. Sachs displayed the tread.

So not *all* the evidence was elsewhere.

Rhyme could not help but notice, though, that Charlotte McKenzie remained untroubled.

He tipped his head to Spiro, who consulted notes and said, "You will be charged with some very serious crimes, Signorina McKenzie, and we are hoping for your cooperation. We know that you and Stefan Merck were not alone in the farmhouse where you held Ali Maziq and Khaled Jabril. At least two or three of your associates were there. And there is at least one associate inside the Capodichino Reception Center working for you. So, there are several other people whose identities we wish to know, and your cooperation in helping us find them will go a long way. I'm a prosecutor and it is I who make recommendations to the magistrates for charges and for punishments. Now, to let you know where you stand, I will turn to *Capitano* Rhyme, who has largely built the case against you and Signor Merck."

Rossi nodded his agreement.

Rhyme wheeled slightly closer. She easily held his gaze. "I'll lay it out very succinctly, Charlotte. We have evidence placing you at the scene of Stefan's first kidnapping, in Brooklyn. The cold medicine. Pseu-doephedrine."

Her eyes narrowed but only slightly.

This was the main insight Rhyme had had, the one that prompted his exasperated comment in the situation room not long before.

It's obvious, isn't it?

"We thought it was pseudo from meth cooking at the abandoned fac-tory but, no, it was from the medicine you'd been taking for your cold. And, I'm sure, the composition will be the same as that." He nodded to the bottles in one of Sachs's plastic bags. "We can get a warrant and take hair samples to verify the presence of the drug in your system."

An inquiring glance at Spiro, who said, "Most easily."

How calm she was. Like a soldier who'd been expecting to be captured by the enemy.

"On the subject of hair, you have a short cut, dyed blond. Forgive me, but Ms. Clairol *is* involved, isn't she? We found similar strands at the Brooklyn kidnap site and on Robert Ellis's phone. I'm sure they'll be con-sistent with yours."

If she displayed any expression, she seemed curious how Rhyme and the others had unraveled the story. But only *mildly* curious.

Rhyme wasn't there yet, however. "Now, we have evidence placing you at Stefan's farmhouse here. Your shoes." Gazing at another of Sachs's evidence bags. "Looks like those tread marks're the same as prints at Ste-fan's. There'll be trace in the treads associated with the soil there."

He held up a hand, to nip quiet an impending question. "Please? I'll finish. Let's talk about the other charge against you: wrongfully impli-cating Garry Soames for sexual assault. And interference with judicial process." Another look at the law enforcers, a questioning furrow of brow.

Rossi said, "It would be interference with a police investigation—on the same pitch. And accusing someone of a crime wrongfully is a sepa-rate offense in Italy. Quite serious. As Amanda Knox learned."

Rhyme resumed. "Shoes again: These'll match the prints left outside Garry's window. And Ercole has collected soil from the site, which . . . well, again we'll check against trace in the shoes.

"Now, tire treads. A car mounted with Continental 195/65R15s tires had been parked behind Garry's apartment. And a car mounted with Continental 195/65R15s had been parked at the farmhouse. And there's a car mounted with Continental 195/65R15s parked a block away. A Nissan Maxima, with U.S. diplo plates on it, checked out to you from the embassy in Rome. The Nissan, by the way is parked next to Stefan's car, a two thousand seven Mercedes 4MATIC, mounted with the Michelins we've found at all the scenes.

"So. The Composer case and the Garry Soames case are linked. You are involved in both. Why? Because when you heard we had come from New York to help the police here, you knew you had to stop us, or at least slow us down. I'm not sure how you learned about the rape and that Garry was one of the people being questioned but it was easy enough: monitoring, or hacking, the Italian police reports, I'd imagine. You broke his bedroom window and sprinkled date-rape drug residue inside. You made the anonymous call implicating him. Then you called us in with a sob story about an innocent young American student wrongly arrested. To keep us distracted from searching for Stefan.

"And when that wasn't enough, you got your boy the hunting rifle. Stefan used that to 'discourage' us. Slow us down. I'm sure he wasn't shooting to hit anyone, just to make us think that he was willing to kill police, make us wary."

He grimaced and felt true regret. "I might've tipped to it a bit earlier: The shoe that Stefan lost struggling with Khaled Jabril's wife also had the date-rape drug on it. We—rather unfairly, I admit—gave one young officer hell for cross-contamination. But when I realized how diligent he'd been, I wondered if the Composer *had* been near a source of the date-rape drug. And obviously he had: you.

"And why did I start thinking about all of this in the first place?" Rhyme paused. Perhaps it was overdramatic, but this seemed appropriate. "It was the *names*, Charlotte. The names on the list." He turned to Dante Spiro.

"Yes, yes, Signorina McKenzie. At the farmhouse Detective Sachs found a list of the names of the victims Stefan was targeting. Ali Maziq, Malek Dadi and Khaled Jabril. Their names, their mobile numbers and the locations of the sites he was going to place them for his hanging videos. That is not how serial killers behave. No, you recruited Stefan to kidnap those men specifically. And why?"

Rhyme filled in the pause with: "Because, of course, you're a spy." He frowned. "I assume you people still call yourselves that, don't you?"

CHAPTER 57

Charlotte McKenzie's face continued to reveal nothing.

Rhyme originally thought that she was feigning innocence but that wasn't accurate, he realized. Hers was the expression of someone who, though guilty as sin, didn't care if she'd been nabbed or not. That image from before, a captured solider, came to mind again. With this qualification: a soldier who had already accomplished her mission.

Rhyme said, "I spoke to an FBI agent in New York an hour ago. I asked him to make some calls. I was particularly interested to know about a legal liaison officer with the State Department named Charlotte McKenzie. Yes, there was. But a little more digging and he hit a dead end. No specifics, no C.V. other than a generic resume. Which is exactly what happens, he told me, in a quote 'official cover' situation. Somebody apparently working for State is actually working for the CIA or another security agency. Legal liaison is a frequent official cover.

"I asked him to see about any U.S. security operations in Italy. A blank there too but he *did* find out at least that there'd been a lot of encrypted communications into and out of Naples. To and from some new government agency called the AIS. Alternative Intelligence Service, based in northern Virginia.

"Well, my theory: You're a field agent for this AIS and were assigned to interrogate three suspected terrorists in Italy, who'd come here from Libya, pretending to be asylum-seekers. It's happened before—an ISIS terrorist was arrested by Italian police in a refugee camp in Bari, the Puglia region—just last year."

Her eyes said, Yes, I know. Her mouth was silent.

"Now, I'm guessing the Alternative part of your organization means you use unusual methods to detain and interrogate your suspects. You came up with the idea of using a serial killer as a cover for extraordinary rendition and interrogation. Somehow you learned about Stefan and thought he'd be a good pick for your project. You and another officer met with him in the hospital—pretending to be his aunt and uncle—and cut some kind of deal with him.

"The first snatch—in New York, the one the little girl witnessed—was fake all around. The victim was a fellow agent. You needed to make it seem like Stefan was really psychotic, with no particular interest in refugees. I thought that that kidnapping seemed odd. The vic's girlfriend never getting back to us. Robert Ellis never seemed particularly upset about nearly being hanged by a crazy man." Rhyme tilted his head to the side. "You had to be concerned that we were getting close to Stefan, when he was in the factory. Did you pull Fred Dellray and the FBI off the case? Make any phone calls to Washington?"

She said nothing, her eyes revealed nothing.

Rhyme continued: "After that prelude, you set up Stefan over here, you and others in your team. And you went to work tracking the terror suspects, then kidnapping them and interrogating them in the farmhouse."

Rhyme turned to Spiro: "Your pattern is now clear, Dante."

"It is, yes. Finally. Now, that is our case. And it will all go before the court. *Allora*, Signorina McKenzie, we need the names of your associates. And we need you to admit that this is what has happened. Since no one died at your hand, and the kidnap victims were apparent terrorists, the punishments for you and your co-workers will not be extreme. But, of course, punishments there must be. So, what have you to say?"

At last, after a considered moment, she spoke. "I need to talk to you. All of you." Her voice calm, confident. As if she were the person who'd convened this meeting. As if she were the one in charge. "Everything I am about to tell you is hypothetical. And in the future I'll deny every sentence."

Spiro, Rossi and Rhyme looked at each other. Spiro said, "I'm not agreeing to any conditions of any kind."

"Agreement is not an issue. What I just said is a statement of fact. This is hypothetical and I'll deny everything if asked." Without waiting for any response she said, "Abu Omar."

Rhyme didn't get the reference but noted that Dante Spiro and Massimo Rossi both reacted. They shared a glance and a frown.

Spiro said to Rhyme, "Sì. An incident in Italy a few years ago. Abu Omar was the imam of Milan. He was abducted in an extraordinary rendition conducted by your CIA and our own security agency. He was taken to Egypt, where, he claims, he was tortured and interrogated. Prosecutors here brought charges against the CIA and our officers who conducted the operation. The incident, I've read, virtually closed down the CIA's Italian operation for a long time, and resulted in prison sentences, in absentia, against some of your senior agents."

McKenzie said, "The Abu Omar case is typical of the two problems that intelligence services face overseas. First, sovereignty. They have no legal right to arrest or detain anyone on foreign soil, unless that government agrees. If foreign governments find out, there are serious repercussions—like the CIA station chief being indicted. The second problem is finding a suitable means of interrogation. Waterboarding, torture, enhanced interrogation, imprisonment without due process—that's not our policy anymore. And, frankly, that's not what America is. We need a humane way to extract information. And a more efficient way. Torture doesn't work. I've studied it."

Begging the questions: How and where and against whom?

Sachs now spoke. "So your AIS sets up fictions, like theater, to kidnap and interrogate subjects?"

"You could say that." Hypothetically.

Rhyme had a thought. "Ah, the amobarbital. I thought it was a sedative Stefan took for panic attacks. But you used it for its original purpose. Truth serum."

"That's right, though in conjunction with other synthetic psychotropics we developed ourselves. Combining the drugs and specialized interviewing techniques, we can hit an eighty-five to ninety percent cooperation rate. The subject has virtually no will to deceive or withhold information." There was pride in her voice.

But Dante Spiro said, "You say humane but these men were at risk!"

"No. They were never in any danger."

Sachs gave a faint laugh. "You know, the gallows *were* very shoddy."

"Exactly. We designed them to fall apart before they'd do any damage. And in any event, an anonymous call would be made to the police reporting a crime and a victim held captive."

"And Malek Dadi, the man killed outside Capodichino?" Rossi asked.

"Ah, but he was killed coincidentally by robbers."

"Stefan tried to save him. He was very upset that the man had died. He took it personally."

Lifting his hands, palms up, Spiro said, "But one matter confuses me. The victims—"

"The suspects, the *terrorists*," she corrected in a firm voice.

"—the victims would know about the interrogation. They could tell someone and word would get out about your operation."

Sachs said slowly, "Except they didn't. Maziq and Jabril didn't remember anything that happened. And that seemed genuine."

"It was."

"Of course," Rhyme said. Those in the room turned to him. "We assumed the electroconductive gel found at the first kidnapping site in Naples was from Stefan's treatments. But, no, you gave the *victims* shock treatment. To destroy their short-term memory."

McKenzie nodded. "That's right. They might have fragments of memories, but those'd be like memories of a dream."

Rhyme said, "But what happens to them afterward? They're still terrorists."

"We monitor them. Hope they change their ways. If not, we have a preemptive talk with them. At worst, relocate them where they won't do any damage." She lifted her shoulders. "What in life is one hundred percent effective all the time? We're stopping terror attacks humanely. There'll be speed bumps along the way, but on the whole our project is working."

Spiro regarded her with his narrow eyes. "Your operation...The fake kidnapping in New York, the real kidnappings here, the release of a psychotic patient, exotic drugs... So very much work. So very complicated."

McKenzie didn't hesitate. She said evenly, "You could try to fly from here to Tuscany by balloon and, if the winds cooperated and with some luck, end up in the vicinity of Florence, after a day or so. Or you could get into a jet and be in the city, efficiently and quickly, whatever the conditions, in one hour. A balloon is a very simple way to travel. A jet much more complicated. But what's the most effective?"

Rhyme was sure she had made this argument before—probably before a Senate or House finance committee.

McKenzie continued, "I'll tell you my background... and the background of the director of our organization."

Rossi said, "Intelligence officers usually come from the military or other branches of government. Academia sometimes."

"Well, I was government service and he was army intelligence, but before that: I was a producer in Hollywood, working on indie films. He was an actor in college and worked on Broadway some. We have experience turning the implausible into the believable. And do you know what people buy into the most? The biggest fantasies. So outrageous that nobody thinks to question them. Hence, Stefan Merck, the psychotic kidnapper, composing waltzes to die by. How could he possibly be involved in espionage? And even if he told anyone, why, he'd be dismissed as crazy."

Sachs said, "Still, even if nobody questioned your cover story, picking Stefan was risky—he was committed for kidnapping, assault and attempted murder."

"Those are the bald facts," McKenzie said. "But it's more complicated than that. A few years ago, while Stefan was an outpatient at a facility in Philadelphia, he saw a male nurse abusing patients, some very disabled. The nurse was reported but the executives at the hospital did nothing about it, and he went on abusing women, but was just more careful.

"Stefan found out where the man lived and broke in. He taped the man to a chair—that was the kidnapping charge—and put homemade earphones on the man. He hooked them to a sound generator and turned up the volume so high that it ruptured the man's eardrums. He's permanently deaf."

"The attempted murder?"

"Apparently if you play sound loud enough for a long-enough period of time, it can be fatal. Stefan's lawyers claimed that wasn't his intention. I'm sure it wasn't. To Stefan, being deaf is worse than dying. His psych evaluation led the judge to rule he wasn't fit for trial, and he was committed indefinitely."

"How did you find him?" Spiro asked.

"We wanted a functioning mental patient, with a history of schizophrenic behavior. We searched, okay, hacked medical records. Stefan seemed like a good possibility. The deal you were talking about, Lincoln? I told him if he helped us, I guaranteed he'd be moved to a nicer facility. He'd have access to music, the Internet. He'd get an electronic keyboard. He was starved for his music, for his collection of sounds. He'd be in Harmony if I'd do that, he said."

Rhyme recalled that Stefan's doctor, the director of the mental facility, had said much the same.

McKenzie said, "No, Stefan is unsettling but he's not dangerous. He's actually quite timid. Shy. He met a girl the other day. He was having an episode, so he went to downtown Naples. The noise, the chaos in the streets helps him. Calms him down. It's silence that's bad for him. Anyway, he met this girl. Her name was Lilly. He went with her to the Fontanelle Cemetery—an underground cavern here."

Rossi and Spiro nodded, obviously familiar with it.

She said, "An unstable person might have hurt her, assaulted her. But you know what he did? He secretly recorded her footsteps. Apparently he loved the sound her boots made in the cavern. After, he drove her home. That's the kind of 'danger' Stefan Merck represents. And, yes, the rifle shots? Only to scare you off."

Sachs said, "But Garry Soames? He could have been convicted."

"No. That wouldn't've happened. We have absolute proof that Natalia Garelli assaulted Frieda. As soon as the operation was completed here—"

Sachs shook her head with dawning awareness. "*You* have the god-damn CCTV video from the hotel across the street."

McKenzie was nodding. "We hacked the security system and downloaded it, then overwrote their drive. It clearly showed Natalia committed the crime. I'll send it to the police tomorrow."

The comment about the security tape reminded Rhyme of something. "And the videos Stefan made? You had him do that?"

"No, no. His own idea, actually. We thought he might leave a noose and maybe a note to the press. But he thought the video would make the world think he was truly psychotic."

"Why the waltz?" Spiro asked.

"He loves them, for some reason. He's never told me why. Something about his parents, I think. This might be too tidy, but they weren't married when he was born. He was ten when they got married. I saw a picture of them dancing together. Stefan was there, watching them. She had problems too, drinking and prescription drugs—and serial affairs. She eventually killed herself. His father just vanished. disappeared. Maybe he associates waltzes with a happier time. Or a sad time. I don't know. He told me he found his mother's body in the family cellar."

"She hanged herself?"

"That's right." McKenzie shook her head. "What a terrible thing for a child to see."

Explains a few things, Rhyme reflected. In this line of work you reject the obvious, and dig for unnecessary subtlety, at your peril.

"He wouldn't say anything more. No reason for him to. We're close in some ways. Close enough so that he does whatever I ask him to. Well, whatever Euterpe tells him."

Sachs said, "*You're* Euterpe. His muse."

"That's what he calls me. When I said I could get him access to music and computers, he hugged me and said I was his muse. I'm his inspiration to get to Heaven—well, he calls it Harmony. Stefan has a very complex worldview. It's based on the medieval concept of the music of the spheres. And I'm helping him on his way to enlightenment—Harmony." McKenzie's face broke into a smile. "And you, Detective, are Artemis. The goddess of the hunt. We're half sisters, by the way."

Ah, *that* was Stefan's meaning not long ago.

Rhyme said, "Okay. The big question: How successful was AIS here?"

"Very. We found out through our techniques that Ali Maziq's terrorist assignment was to travel to Vienna, collect explosives from a garage outside of town and detonate them in a shopping mall."

Rhyme recalled that Henry Musgrave, the consulate general, had told them about a foiled attack.

"The calls to Bolzano," Spiro said. "The Trenitalia trip, six hours to get him there."

"Yes. He'd meet a German-speaking contact who would drive him into Austria. We didn't have a chance to interrogate Malek Dadi before he was killed. *His* target was in Milan. But *you* helped us there—finding the Post-it note with the address of the warehouse in Milan."

Sachs shook her head. "Ah. Your quote 'legal liaison,' Prescott? He's with AIS too. Of course. Before Mike Hill's private plane landed at Linate, I gave Prescott the address of the warehouse. But he didn't drive me right there. He took me all over Milan, complaining about the traffic— but that was to give your team time to raid the place. I found a broken beer bottle on the driveway apron. Your people must've finished removing the explosives just before we got there."

McKenzie said, "That's right. We recovered another half kilo of C4. We don't know what the target was, somewhere in Milan. But that's one attack that's not going to happen."

Rossi asked, "And Khaled Jabril? The third terrorist you interrogated?"

Her face tightened. "That was bad intel. Our asset in Libya gave us his name but he turned out to be innocent. We interrogated him thoroughly but he didn't know about any plots. Our techniques are very, very good. If there'd been anything, we would have found it." McKenzie looked from one to the other. "So, I've told you everything. Hypothetically, of course. Now I need your help. There's a problem."

Rossi said, "I must say, Signorina, I have met many criminals in my day but no one who is as immune to *contrizione*...contrition, as you."

She turned cool eyes toward him. "This is for everyone's own good. Your country, as well as ours."

Spiro said, "Continue, *per favore*."

"The terrorists here, Malik and Dadi, were recruited in Tripoli by a man named Ibrahim. We don't know much about him or his affiliation, maybe ISIS or al-Qaeda. Or other radicalized groups. Or he might be freelancing, working for anyone who pays him. Ibrahim's accomplice is in Naples, or nearby. He was the terrorists' contact here. He supplied the explosives and was the on-the-ground person planning the attacks in Vienna and Milan."

Sachs said, "He's the man Ali Maziq had dinner with before he was kidnapped near D'Abruzzo."

"Exactly. Under interrogation Maziq said that his name was Gianni. A code name, of course. But he didn't have any more information."

Rhyme recalled that Beatrice had found samples of Neapolitan soil—rich with volcanic trace—in the warehouse. It would have come from this man. He mentioned this now.

"Yes, Gianni would be the one who left the explosives in Vienna and in Milan then returned here. Now, the point of our operation wasn't just to stop the attacks; it was also to learn Ibrahim's real identity and address in Tripoli. Finding Gianni is our only hope. But we have no more leads. Will you help me?"

And in her eyes, true, there was not a wisp of contrition. It seemed that she had hardly heard of—and certainly didn't care about—the case against her that had just been laid out.

Spiro and Rossi shared a glance. Then the prosecutor turned. "And what, *Capitano* Rhyme, is your thinking on this matter?"

THE SOUND OF SENSE

CHAPTER 58

A t 9 a.m., much of the team was assembled once more in the situation room, the basement of the Questura.

Rhyme, Sachs and Dante Spiro, along with Thom, of course, ever-present Thom. Ercole Benelli was in the building, but elsewhere at the moment. Massimo Rossi had ordered him to bundle up all of the physical evidence in the Composer case, now that it was more or less closed, and log it into the Questura's evidence room.

Rossi himself would join them soon. He was in his office upstairs with fellow inspector Laura Martelli, preparing the documentation to have Garry Soames officially released, verifying the evidence and interviewing Natalia, her boyfriend and others who'd been at the party. Garry had been released from prison but was still being held in a minimum-security facility in downtown Naples, pending the magistrate's signature.

Stefan was in a holding cell, too, but Charlotte McKenzie was present. No longer saddled with her fake role as a diplo, she was wearing black slacks, a dark blouse and a supple leather jacket. She was still grandmotherly—but she was a grandmother who might practice tae kwon do and enjoy white-water rafting, if not big-game hunting.

A uniformed officer wearing a shiny white belt and holster stood, nearly at attention, outside the door with orders not to let her leave the room.

Before he'd left, Rossi had said to him sternly: *"Qualcuno la deve accompagnare alla toilette,"* which was pretty clear, even in Italian.

Though Ercole had taken the evidence to storage, the charts were still in place, on the easels surrounding them, and Sachs had created a new one—about their prey, Gianni, the terrorist Ibrahim's accomplice.

GIANNI (COVER NAME)

— Believed to be in Naples area.

— Associate of Ibrahim, who is presently believed to be in Libya, mastermind of terror plots in Vienna and Milan.

— White, though dark-complexioned.

— Italian.

— Described as "surly."

— Large build.

— No known distinguishings.

— Curly dark hair.

— Smoker.

— Knowledge of and access to explosives.

With such a sparse description and no helpful physical evidence—and with Ali Maziq unable to provide details, after the drugging and electroconvulsive treatment—Rhyme, Spiro and Sachs decided that the best way to track him was through phone calls made to and from the mobile of the refugee he'd run: Ali Maziq.

Both the Postal Police and the domestic Italian spy agency had spent the night establishing calling patterns to and from the phones. They could identify Gianni's phone, from which he'd sent and received calls to and from Maziq, and learned that Gianni had also frequently called and received calls from a landline—a café in Tripoli. It was undoubtedly the phone Ibrahim was using, not a mobile, for security's sake.

Gianni's phone, however, was now dead; he'd have a new one. And it was this new mobile they needed to find, so they could triangulate and track it—or at least tap the line and see if he gave away his location or more about his identity in conversation.

Massimo Rossi returned to the office and regarded the occupants, debating a strategy to discover Gianni's new number. Spiro explained the situation.

Rossi said, "A landline, hm. Clever of him. In no small part because there has always been antagonism between Italy and Libya—we occupied them, you know, as a colony. And now our government is angered by their approach to the immigrant crisis—which is no approach at all. No one in Tripoli or Tobruk will cooperate with us."

Dante Spiro said, "I must say I can think of a solution."

Everyone in the room turned his way.

He added, "The only difficulty is that it is in a small way illegal. A prosecutor could hardly suggest it."

"Well, why don't you tell us," Rhyme suggested, "*hypothetically?*"

New York has been called the City That Never Sleeps, though in fact that motto applies only to a few isolated establishments in Manhattan, where expensive liquor licenses and early work schedules keep the place pretty well shut down in the wee hours.

Contrast that with a very different burg, a small town outside Washington, DC, where thousands labor constantly in a massive complex of buildings, day and night, no holidays, no weekends off.

It was to one of those workers, a young man named Daniel Garrison, that Charlotte McKenzie had placed a call a half hour before, at Dante Spiro's coy suggestion.

Garrison had some fancy title within the National Security Agency, which was located in that never-sleeping town: Fort Meade, Maryland. But his informal job description was simple: hacker.

McKenzie had sent Garrison the information about the coffeehouse whose pay phone Ibrahim had probably used to communicate with Gianni about the terrorist plans. Now, with the okay from bigwigs in Washington, Garrison was overseeing the effort of a very earnest, hardworking bot, as "she" (the NSA officer's pronoun) prowled at lightning speed through the records of Libya Hatif w Alaittisalat, or "Telephone and Telecom." Theirs was not, Garrison had reported, a difficult "switch to run an exploit on. Stone easy. I'm embarrassed for them. Well, not really."

Soon Garrison's bot was plucking records of calls between the pay phone in the Yawm Saeid—Happy Day—coffeehouse in Tripoli, where Ibrahim hung out, and mobiles in the Naples area: scores in the past day, many hundreds over the past week. Apparently—and unfortunately—the landline was a popular means of communicating with those in southern Italy.

Ercole Benelli was printing out the lists and taping them to the wall. If there were not too many numbers the Postal Police could trace them. With some luck, one might turn out to be Gianni's new phone.

As he looked over the number, Rhyme was startled to hear a pronounced gasp from beside him.

He looked at Charlotte, actually thinking she was ill, the sound from her throat was so choked.

"No," she said. "My God."

"What is it?" Rossi asked, seeing her alarmed face.

"Look." She was pointing to the chart. "That outgoing call there—from the coffeehouse in Tripoli to Gianni's old phone. A few days ago."

"Yes. We can see." Spiro was staring at McKenzie, clearly as confused as Rhyme.

"The number *above* it? The call made from the coffeehouse just before he called Gianni?"

Rhyme noted it was to a U.S. line. "What about it?"

"It's *my* phone," she whispered. "My encrypted mobile. And I remember the call. It was from our asset on the ground in Libya. We were talking about Maziq's abduction."

"*Cristo*," Spiro whispered.

Sachs said, "So your asset, the one who gave you the intel about the attacks in Austria and Milan, *is* Ibrahim, the man who recruited the terrorists in the first place."

CHAPTER 59

Mi dispiace," Dante Spiro snapped. "Forgive me for being blunt. But do you not vet these people?"

"Our asset—" McKenzie began.

Rhyme, his voice as testy as the Italian's, said, "Not your *asset*. The man who *pretended* to be your asset, the man who sold you out. Not to put too fine a point on it."

"We know him as Hassan." She muttered this defensively. "And he came highly recommended. He was accredited at the highest levels—the U.S. Senate Intelligence Committee, the CIA. He was a veteran of the Arab Spring. A vocal supporter of the West and of democracy. Anti-Qaddafi. He was nearly killed in Tripoli."

"You mean, he *said* he was," Sachs replied laconically.

"His history was that he was a small businessman, not a radicalized fundamentalist." She added to Spiro, "In answer to your question, yes, we vetted him."

Ercole Benelli had returned from the evidence room and Rossi had briefed him on the latest developments. The young officer now said, "*Mamma mia!* This is true?"

Spiro was speaking. "*Allora.* A U.S. government asset—Ibrahim/Hassan—in Libya recruits two terrorists, Ali Maziq and Malek Dadi, and sends them to Italy masquerading as asylum-seekers, to orchestrate bombings in Vienna and Milan. He's got an operative on the ground here—this Gianni—who is providing explosives and helping them. The two men are in place and the weapons are ready. But then this Ibrahim/Hassan gives *you* information about the attacks, so you can put together an operation with your madman kidnapper to foil them. Why? I see no avenue in which this makes sense."

McKenzie could only, it seemed, stare at the floor. Who knew what she was thinking?

Spiro extracted and sniffed his cheroot then replaced it in his pocket, as if the accessory distracted him.

Rhyme said to Spiro, "Something you mentioned. A moment ago."

"What was that?"

"'Masquerading as asylum-seekers.'"

"*Sì.*"

Rhyme to McKenzie: "You reported to Washington who the terrorists were, how they'd gotten into Italy—pretending to be refugees."

"Of course."

"And the CIA would contact the Italian security services about it?"

She hesitated. "After our operation was over, yes."

Rossi said, "But I don't see the implication that seems significant to you, Captain Rhyme."

Spiro was nodding. "Ah, but I do, Massimo." He looked toward Rhyme and added, "The conference that's going on in Rome now. About the im-migrants."

"Exactly."

Rossi was nodding. "Yes. A number of countries are attending."

Rhyme said, "I read about it on the flight over. The *New York Times.* Can we find the article?"

Ercole sat down at a computer and called up the online version of the paper. He found the story. Those in the room clustered around the screen.

CONFERENCE SEEKS TO ADDRESS REFUGEE CRISIS

ROME—An emergency conference on the flood of refugees from the Middle East and northern Africa is under way here, with represen-tatives of more than 20 countries present.

Humanitarian issues top the agenda, with sessions detailing the plight of the asylum-seekers, who risk death on the high seas and mistreatment at the hands of human smugglers who abandon, rob and rape those desperate to escape from war zones, poverty, drought, religious extremism and political oppression.

The crisis has reached such proportions that countries that up until now have resisted taking any significant number of asylum-seekers are considering doing so. Japan and Canada, for instance, are entertaining measures to increase the quota for refugees considerably, and the United States—traditionally resistant to the idea—has a controversial bill before Congress that will authorize the immediate intake of 100 times the number of refugees now allowed into the country. Italy's parliament too is considering measures relaxing deportation laws and making it easier for refugees to attain asylum. Right-wing movements in Italy, and elsewhere, have vocally—and sometimes violently—opposed such measures.

"Ah, *Capitano* Rhyme," Rossi said, his face twisted into a troubled smile, "this makes sense: Ibrahim and Gianni are not terrorists at all but soldiers of fortune."

Rhyme said, "They were hired by someone on the political right, here in Italy, to recruit asylum-seekers to carry out terrorist attacks. Not for any ideological reasons but just to make the case that refugees pose a threat. It'd be used as ammunition by opponents of the new measure that your parliament's considering, about relaxing deportation." A chill laugh. "Seems you got played, Charlotte."

She said nothing but gazed at the article with a stunned expression.

"*Cristo*," whispered Ercole.

"We thought it was curious," Charlotte McKenzie said, "Ali Maziq and Malek Dadi were the actors. Neither of them was radicalized. They had moderate, secular histories."

Rossi offered, "They were coerced, forced to go on their missions."

Amelia Sachs was grimacing. "You know, I was thinking when we heard the story about the planned attack in Vienna—the consulate general mentioned a half kilo of C4. Dangerous, yes. It could cause fatalities, but not a massive explosion."

Rhyme added, looking at McKenzie, "In Milan too. Didn't you say, in the warehouse, it was just a half kilo?"

Dismay on her face, McKenzie said, "Yes, yes. Of course! Whoever hired Ibrahim and Gianni didn't need to kill a lot of people. It was just to show that terrorists *could* be hidden among the refugees. And that would scare parliament in Rome into rejecting the proposal."

"So who is the mastermind? Behind the plan?"

Spiro looked at Rossi and shrugged briefly. Rossi said, "There are many who would oppose making immigration easier or deportation harder. The Lega Nord Party, of course, which opposes our being in the EU and accepting refugees. There are others as well. But for the most part those movements are regular political parties not given to violence or illegal activity like this."

Spiro's eyes gleamed coldly. "Ah, but there is also Nuovo Nazionalismo. The New Nationalism."

Rossi nodded. He seemed troubled at the mention of the name.

The prosecutor continued, "The NN *does* advocate violence against immigrants. And the movement has boasted they have infiltrated governmental institutions. I wouldn't be surprised if a senior NN official hired Ibrahim and Gianni to carry out this plan."

Rhyme's attention then slipped to Ercole Benelli, who was gazing at a blank wall, troubled.

"Ercole?"

He turned back to the others. "There's something that occurs to me. It might be nothing…" He paused. "No, I think it is something. Most *definitely* it is something."

"Go on," Spiro said.

Ercole cleared his throat: "Your spy," he said to McKenzie. "Hassan, or Ibrahim, told you there were *three* plots, not two. Vienna, Milan and another one. Correct?"

"Yes, here in Naples. But Khaled Jabril was thoroughly interrogated and he knew nothing of any attacks. That was the failure of intelligence I mentioned. It was a mistake."

"No, no," Rhyme whispered, understanding Ercole's point.

The Forestry officer continued, speaking in an agitated voice, "But mistake is impossible. If Ibrahim reported three attacks, there had to *be* three attacks because he'd arranged all three of them *himself!*"

Wide-eyed, McKenzie said, "Yes, I see what you're saying. But Khaled, he knew nothing. I'm *sure*. Our techniques work."

Rhyme asked, "Did your asset actually give you the name 'Khaled'?"

"Yes, and that he was being held in the Capodichino Reception Center." She fell silent. "But, wait, no. Actually he didn't. All he gave me was the family name. Jabril."

Rhyme glanced toward Spiro, who said, "You kidnapped the wrong person, Signorina McKenzie. The terrorist is Khaled's wife, Fatima."

CHAPTER 60

S achs and Ercole sped to the refugee camp, about ten kilometers from downtown.

Sachs parked outside the camp, at the main gate, where they were greeted by Rania Tasso, who gestured them inside and hurried them through the congested spaces between the tents.

Breathing hard from the fast pace, Rania said, "As soon as you called, I sent our security people to seal all the exits. All around the perimeter. It's secure. We have guards and police watching Fatima's tent—they are being discreet, hiding nearby—and she has not come out...if she was inside. That we don't know."

"Could she have left the camp?"

"It's possible, before we sealed it. As you asked, we haven't been inside the tent or contacted her husband. He has not been seen either."

After a fast walk to the center of the camp, Rania pointed. "This is the tent." Light blue, mud-spattered, several rips in the Tyvek. Laundry hung outside like semaphore flags on old-time ships. Only bedding and men's outer clothing and children's garments fluttered in the wind. Was that all that could be properly displayed to the world?

The tent door was closed. There were no windows.

A uniformed officer, very dark skin, dark eyes, sweat dripping from beneath his beret, joined them. He'd been watching from behind a stand offering water bottles.

"Antonio? Have you seen inside?"

"No, Signorina Rania. I don't know if Fatima's there or not. Or anyone else. No one has come in or out."

Sachs opened her jacket, exposing the Beretta. Ercole unsnapped his holster.

Sachs said, "Ercole. I know what you're thinking. She's a woman and a mother. And may not be a hard-core terrorist. We don't know what Ibrahim and Gianni are using as leverage to force her to do this. But we have to assume she'll detonate the device in an instant if she thinks we'll stop her. Remember: Shoot for her—"

"Upper lip." He nodded. "Three times."

Rania was looking about her, her quick gray eyes reflecting both bright sun and her heart's dismay. "Please be careful. Look."

Sachs saw what the woman indicated: In a vacant area next to the tent a half-dozen women sat on impromptu seats like tires and railway ties and water cartons, holding babies. Other children—from ages two to ten, or so—ran and laughed, lost in their improvised games.

"Clear the area as best you can. Quietly."

Rania nodded to Antonio and he reached for his radio.

"No," Sachs said fast. "And turn the volume off."

Both he and Rania silenced their units and gestured to other security people. The officers did their best to shepherd people away from the tent. As soon as the officers moved on, though, the empty space filled with the curious.

Sachs glanced at them. Well within stray bullet range.

Nothing to do about it.

She asked Rania about the layout of the interior of the tent. The woman replied from memory: clothes neatly folded in cardboard boxes against the right wall, a dining area to the left. Prayer rugs rolled and put away. Three beds—one for the adults, one for their daughter, and a spare. Separated by sheet-like dividers.

Hell, good cover.

And the daughter, Muna, had a number of toys given to the family by volunteers. Rania remembered them scattered on the floor. "Be careful not to trip."

"Suitcases or trunks that someone might hide behind?"

Rania gave a sad laugh. "Plastic bags and backpacks are the only luggage these people bring with them."

Sachs touched Ercole's arm and he looked down into her eyes. She was pleased to see his own were confident, balanced. He was ready. She whispered, "You go right."

"*Destra*, yes."

Drawing her pistol, Sachs held her left index finger up in the air then pointed it forward. He too drew his Beretta and then she gestured to the door and, with a nod, pushed inside, moving very quickly.

Khaled Jabril gasped and dropped his glass of tea, which bounced on the Tyvek floor, scattering the steaming contents everywhere. Sachs stepped over the toys—and the boxes they had come in—and quickly swept aside the divider. He was the only occupant.

Khaled recognized Sachs, of course, but he was still groggy and disoriented from the drugs. "*Aiiii*. What is this?"

Sachs motioned Rania inside, then said to Khaled, "Your wife. Where is she?"

"I don't know. What is going on here? Is she all right?"

"Where did she go? And when?"

"Please tell me! I'm frightened."

It was clear he hadn't known about his wife's mission when he'd been interrogated, though Fatima might have explained later. But, after Sachs gave him a synopsis of Ibrahim and Gianni's plan of using her as an apparent terrorist, it was clear he was taken completely aback.

His initial response was a gasp of horror. But then he was nodding. "Yes, yes, she has not been herself. She has not been acting in a normal manner. Someone forced her to do this!"

"Yes, probably." Sachs crouched across from him and said in a firm tone, "Still she's going to hurt people, Khaled. Help us. We need to find her. Is she in the camp?"

"No. She left an hour ago. She was going to be buying some things for Muna. At the shop here in the camp or maybe at one of the vendors outside. I don't know if she said more. She might have. After my incident, after what happened to me, my mind is very, you would say, uncertain. Confused."

"Does she have her phone?"

"I suppose she does."

"Give me the number."

He did and Charlotte McKenzie, listening over speaker, said, "Got it. I'll send it to Fort Meade, see if they can track it."

Sachs asked the refugee, "Do you remember if she'd met with anyone recently? Did anyone give her anything?"

He frowned. "Perhaps...Let me think." He actually tapped his forehead. "Yes. She got a package. It was tea from her family."

Rania's stern but pretty face tightened in a grimace. "Yes, I remember." He pointed to a locker. "I think she put it in there."

Ercole opened the lid and handed Sachs a brown cardboard carton.

Sachs held the box to her nose.

A sigh.

"This too," Ercole said. He'd found plastic wrapping for a cheap mobile phone, but not the label that gave the phone's number or details of the SIM card; Fatima had taken that with her.

Pulling on her headset, she speed-dialed a number.

"What?" came the abrupt response. "We've been waiting."

"She's not here, Rhyme. And she got a delivery: C4, maybe Semtex. Like the others, looks like a half kilo. And another phone. For the detonator."

Mobile phones had supplanted timers and radios as the most popular way to set off explosive devices.

"A bomb? Are we the target here?" Rania asked Sachs in a grim voice.

Those in the Questura had heard and, after a brief discussion, Rhyme answered, "No, very unlikely. The whole point of the plot is to sabotage the immigration legislation in Parliament. That means Italian citizens have to be hurt, not refugees."

Khaled found his own mobile and asked, "Should I call her? Try to talk her out of this madness?"

Rhyme and Spiro, she could hear, were debating this.

But McKenzie came on the line. "Never mind. Meade says it's dead. They'll keep monitoring but I'll bet she tossed it." Then the woman said, "Wait. They've got something." There was a pause and Sachs could hear computer keyboard clatter. "This could be good. The NSA bot just logged a call to the coffeehouse in Tripoli from a burner mobile in Naples that was just activated this morning. It's still live."

"Gianni?" Sachs asked.

Rossi said, "If we are lucky. Where is it?"

McKenzie called out longitude and latitude, and a moment later, after some keyboarding, the police inspector said, "At the Royal Palace. Downtown Naples. I'm sending a team there now."

CHAPTER 61

L uigi Procopio, for this job known also as "Gianni," was presently leaning against his car parked on the edge of the plaza in front of the Royal Palace of Naples, the massive and impressive structure that had once been home to the Bourbon kings, when they were rulers of the Two Kingdoms of Sicily, in the eighteenth and nineteenth centuries. Procopio loved his Italian history.

Procopio came from the Catanzaro district of Calabria, a region south of Campania.

Calabria is the very tip of the boot of Italy. This region is known for its fiery pork paste, stoccafisso dried cod and many types of preserved foods, owing to the hot climate, which traditionally meant that meats and seafood should be cured to avoid spoiling.

Calabria is known too for the 'Ndràngheta, the famed organized crime outfit. The name "'Ndràngheta" means "loyalty," and it was a well-known fact that the six thousand members of the organization were true to their comrades, who made up the 150 or so small cells within Italy. But that didn't mean that members might not strike out on their own—they could, and did, as long as no conflicts of interest existed.

This was especially the case when the member was affiliated not with a crew in Calabria itself but with one of the satellite operations, such as those in the UK or the United States. The 'Ndràngheta had, in fact, been active in East Coast criminal activity for more than a hundred years. A gang in Pennsylvania mining country had extortion and protection rackets in the early 1900s, and the organization had been involved for years in U.S. drug and money-laundering operations, often working with transplanted members of the Mafia and Camorra, as well as local Anglo and Caribbean gangs. (Senior 'Ndràngheta officials in America were reportedly angered by *The Godfather*, as they felt the Mafia was far less glamorous and clever and ruthless than they were.)

Big, dark, hairy and intimidating, Luigi Procopio was one such freelance operator. His good language skills, military and trade union contacts, and willingness to do whatever he needed to had let him carve out a specialty as a middleman, putting together deals among interests in southern Italy, North Africa, Europe and the United States.

His instinct let him walk the delicate high-wire between self-interest and the 'Ndràngheta's, and he'd become successful.

Anywhere there was money to be made, Procopio had a presence: the old standbys, of course, arms, drugs and human trafficking, as well as newer twenty-first-century markets.

Say, terrorism, for instance.

He had just called Ibrahim at the Happy Day coffeehouse in Tripoli to update him on the developments here in Naples, and was now smoking and looking over the massive square.

Glancing up the street he happened to see black vans and marked police cars speeding his way. Lights were flashing but the vehicles' sirens were silent.

Close, closer...

Then the entourage zipped past him, not a single driver or passenger looking his way.

Instead, the law enforcers sped across the square and skidded to a stop in a semicircle around a trash container. They jumped out, highly armed men and women, and scanned about them for their target.

Which was, of course, him.

Or, to be more accurate, the mobile phone on which he'd just called Ibrahim. Procopio had left the phone live in a paper bag at the foot of the trash bin. A young Police of State officer carefully examined the container—a bomb was a possibility under the circumstances—and then found the phone. He held it up. One officer, apparently the commander, shook his head, undoubtedly in disappointment, if not disgust. Other officers looked at nearby buildings, surely for CCTV cameras. But there were none. Procopio had made sure of that before leaving the bait phone.

He now stubbed out his cigarette. He had learned all he needed to. This, in fact, was the entire point of the call to Tripoli. He needed to see just how far along the police had come in their investigation.

So. They knew about Ibrahim's existence, if not his name, and that there was an operative here. And they were scanning the landline and mobiles.

It would be total phone silence for the time being.

He settled into the car's comfortable seat and started the engine. He wanted to find a café and enjoy another cigarette, along with an *aperitivo* of a nice Cirò red wine, and some hard, dried Calabrian salami and bread.

But that would have to wait.

Until after the bloodshed.

CHAPTER 62

The street was colorful.

Some tourists, but also many people who seemed to be true Neapolitans—families, women with strollers, children on bicycles...and preteens and teen, boys and girls. They strutted and shied and revealed themselves, wearing proud boots and bold running shoes and high heels and patterned tights and languid shirts, and they displayed, with understated pride, their latest: necklaces and clever purses and anklets and eyeglasses and rings and ironic mobile phone covers.

The flirts seemed harmless and charming, the youngsters innocent as preening kittens.

Oh, and the view: beautiful. Vesuvius ahead in the distance, the docks and massive ships. The bay, rich blue.

But Fatima Jabril paid little attention to any of this.

Her focus was on her mission.

And pushing the baby carriage with care.

"Ah, *che bellezza!*" the woman of a couple, herself pregnant, cried. And, smiling, she said something more. Seeing that the Italian language wasn't working, she tried English. "Your daughter!" The woman looked down into the carriage. "She is having the hair of an angel! Look, those beautiful black curls!" Then, noting the hijab her mother wore, she paused, perhaps wondering if Muslims believed in angels.

Fatima Jabril understood the gist. She smiled and said an awkward, "*Grazie tante.*"

The woman cast another look down. "And she sleeps so well, even here, the noise."

Fatima continued on, hiking the backpack higher on her shoulder. Moving slowly.

Because of the crowds.

Because of her reluctance to kill.

Because of the bomb in the carriage.

How has my life come to this?

Well, she could recall quite clearly the answer to that question. She'd replayed it every night falling asleep, every morning rising to wakefulness.

That day some weeks ago...

She remembered being pulled off the street in Tripoli by two surly men—who had no trouble touching a Muslim woman not a relation. Terrified and sobbing, she had been bundled off to the back room of a coffeehouse off Martyrs' Square. She was pushed into a chair and told to wait. The shop was called Happy Day. An irony that brought tears to her eyes.

An hour later, a horrific hour later, the curtain was flung aside and in walked a sullen, bearded man of about forty. He identified himself as Ibrahim. He looked her over stonily and handed her a tissue. She dried her eyes and flung it back at his face. He smiled at that.

In Libyan-inflected Arabic, a high voice, he had said, "Let me explain why you are here and what is about to happen to you. I am going to recruit you for a mission. Ah, ah, let me finish." He called for tea and almost instantly it arrived, carried by the shopkeeper, whose hands trembled as he'd set out the cups. Ibrahim waited until the man left, then continued, "We have selected you for several reasons. First, because you are not on any watch lists. Indeed, you are what we call an Invisible Believer. That is, you are to our faith what a Unitarian might be to Christianity. Do you know what Unitarian is?"

Fatima, though familiar with much Western culture, was not aware of the sect. "No."

Ibrahim said, "Suffice to say *moderate*. Hence, to the armies and the security services of the West you are *invisible*. You can cross borders and get to targets and not be regarded as a threat."

Targets, she thought in horror. Her hands quivered.

"You will be assigned a target in Italy and you will carry out an attack."

She gasped, and refused the tea Ibrahim offered. He sipped, clearly relishing the beverage.

"Now we come to the second reason you have been selected. You have family in Tunisia and Libya. Three sisters, two brothers, all of whom, praise be to God, have been blessed with children. Your mother too is still upon this earth. We know where they live. You will fulfill your obligation to us, complete these attacks, or they will be killed—every family member of yours from six-month-old Mohammed to your mother, as she returns from the market on the arm of her friend Sonja, who will die too, I should say."

"No, no, no..."

Ignoring the emotion completely, Ibrahim whispered, "And now we come to the third reason you will help us in this mission. Upon completion of the assignment, you—and your husband and daughter—will be given new identities and a large sum of money. You will get British or Dutch passports and can move where you wish. What do you say?"

The only word she could.

"Yes." Sobbing.

Ibrahim smiled and finished the tea. "You and your family will travel to Italy as refugees. A smuggler I work with will give you details tonight. Once you arrive, you will be taken to a refugee camp for processing. A man named Gianni will contact you."

He'd risen and left, with not another word.

They'd no sooner landed in the Capodichino Reception Center than Gianni in fact called her. He explained in a guttural voice, clear and still as ice, that there would be no excuses. If she fell ill and could not detonate the bomb, her family would die. If she were arrested for stealing a loaf of bread and could not detonate the bomb, her family would die. If the bomb did not go off because of mechanical failure, her family would die. If she froze at the last moment...well, she understood.

And what should happen but, of all horrific coincidences, her husband had been snatched by that psychotic American! That in itself had been terrible—she loved him dearly—but the incident had also brought the police. Would they find the explosives and phone and detonator that Gianni had left for her? Would they relocate her and her daughter while they searched for Khaled?

Yet he had been saved.

That was, of course, wonderful. Yet it tore Fatima's heart in two. Because everyone, from Rania to the American police to the Italian officers, had worked so very hard—some even risking their lives—to save Khaled, a man they didn't know, a man who had come to this country uninvited.

Certainly there were those who resented immigrants but, apart from some protestors outside the camp, Fatima had yet to meet them. Why, look at the woman a moment ago.

Your daughter, she has the hair of an angel!

Most Italians were heartbreakingly sympathetic to the asylum-seeker's plight.

Which made what she was about to do, two hours from now, all the more shameful.

But do it she would.

If you fail in any way, your family will die . . .

But she wouldn't fail. She saw the target ahead of her. Less than two hours remained until the attack.

Fatima found a cluster of unoccupied benches not far from the water. She sat in one that faced the bay. So that no one could see her tears.

CHAPTER 63

The lead to the Royal Palace had been a bust. Rhyme was sure Gianni had made the call to the Tripoli coffeehouse solely to see how much the police knew and if they were tracking phones. He'd learned that they were and so he'd gone off the grid.

Without any chance of finding him via phones, and no physical leads to Fatima, the team turned to the question of what might the intended target of the bombing be. Speculation, sure, but it was all they had.

Because the refugee camp was near Naples airport, Rhyme and Spiro thought immediately that Fatima was going after an airplane or the terminal.

The prosecutor said, "She can't get a bomb on board an aircraft. But she might cut a hole in the fence, run to a full aircraft about to take off and detonate the device on the runway."

McKenzie said, "These aren't suicide attackers. They're remote detonation devices, using cell phones. I don't see airports. Train station maybe. Less security."

Rossi called security at Trenitalia. After disconnecting he said, "They're sending officers into the stations. We have our history of domestic terrorism too, like you in America. In nineteen eighty a terrorist group left a bomb in the central train station in Bologna—nearly twenty-five kilos. It was placed in the waiting room and because the day was hot—it was August—many people were inside the air-conditioned room. Very few buildings were air-conditioned in Italy then. Over eighty people were killed and more than two hundred wounded."

Spiro said, "And shopping malls, city centers, amusement areas, museums..."

Rhyme's eyes were on the map of Naples.

A thousand possible targets.

Charlotte McKenzie's phone hummed. She glanced at the screen and took the call.

"What?" Her eyes narrowed. "Good, good...'Crypt it and get it to me ASAP. Thanks."

She responded to the querying glances from the men in the room. "We've caught a break. That was Fort Meade again. When I sent them Fatima's phone, the number was automatically checked against the NOI list. That's Number of Interest. The supercomputers snagged a conversation on that phone a few days ago. The bot heard the word 'target' in a conversation between Libya and Naples, where there've been recent terrorist alerts. The algorithm recorded the conversation. As soon as I sent the request with her number, the bot flagged the recording and it went to First Priority status. They're sending it now, the recording." She tapped a few keys, read a screen. She hit a button and placed her phone on a table near them all.

From the speaker: the sound of ringing.

"Yes?" A woman's voice, speaking English with an Arabic accent. Fatima.

The gruff Italian male voice—it would be Gianni—said, "It is me. You are in Capodichino?"

"Yes, I am."

"You'll be getting the package soon. Everything will be inside. Ready to go. A new phone too. Don't take this one with you. Throw it away."

"I will doing that." Fatima's voice was shaky.

"Your husband, when he was kidnapped? He told no one anything that would make them suspicious?"

"What could he say? He knows nothing."

"I..." He paused. There was a great deal of ambient noise—which seemed to be coming from Gianni's end of the line. He continued, "I'm in Naples now. I can see the target. It's good. At the moment, there are not so many people."

More noise. Motor scooter engines, shouts. Voices calling.

Gianni said something else, but the words were drowned out. Birds screeching and more shouts.

"...not so busy now, I was saying. But on Monday, there will be many people. A good crowd and reporters. You must do it at fourteen hundred hours. Not before."

Beside Rhyme, Spiro whispered, "Ninety minutes from now. *Cristo*."

"Tell me the plan," Gianni instructed.

"I remember."

"If you remember then you can tell me."

"I go to location you have told me. I will go into a bathroom. I will have Western clothes with me and I wear them. I turn on the mobile taped to the package. I leave it where the most people will be. Then I walk to a big doorway."

"The arch."

"Yes, the arch. The stone will protect me. I dial the number and it will go off."

"You remember the number?"

"Yes."

Rhyme, Spiro and Rossi looked at each other. Please, Rhyme thought. Say it out loud! If either of them did, the team could send it to the NSA to hack and disable the phone in seconds of its being turned on.

But Gianni said only, "Good."

Fuck, thought Rhyme. Spiro mouthed, "*Mannaggia*."

"After the explosion, you will fall down, cut your face on the stone and stumble out of the wreckage. You know stumble?"

"Yes."

"The more injured you are, the more everyone will think you are innocent. Bleed, you should bleed. They will think it was a suicide bomb at first and you are merely another victim."

"Yes."

"I am going now."

"My family..."

"They are relying on you to make sure this happens."

There was the click of disconnection.

Rhyme muttered, "Any location for his phone?"

McKenzie said, "No. The NSA bot wasn't tracking GPS. Just recording."

Again the map of Naples took his attention.

Spiro said, "Can we tell anything more about the site of the attack from their conversation? It seemed like an event of sorts today. Fourteen hundred hours. And something that will draw media. What could it be?"

"In the afternoon. A sports event? A store opening? A concert?"

"On Monday, though?" Ercole asked.

Rhyme said, "There's a stone arch, a doorway she'll hide in. For protection from the blast."

Ercole scoffed. "That is about three-quarters of Naples."

Silence for a moment.

Then Rhyme said, "Dante, you asked if we can we tell anything more from the recording. You meant the conversation. What about what isn't *in* the conversation?"

"The background sounds, you mean?"

"Exactly."

"It's a good thought." Spiro said to McKenzie, "Can you send the recording to the email here? We will put it through good speakers, so we can hear better." The inspector gave her the address.

A moment later the computer chimed. Rossi nodded to Ercole, who looked over the in-box and downloaded what Rhyme could see was an MP3 file.

The young man typed keys and the conversation played again. Through these speakers the words were much more distinct. But try though he might to hear past Gianni's and Fatima's words, Rhyme could draw no conclusions about the source of the sounds.

"Hopeless," Rossi said.

"Maybe not," Rhyme offered.

CHAPTER 64

S tefan Merck was a curious man.

Shy, and with eyes that were dark yet glowed in a child's glimmer. An innocence about his round face.

Still, he was large and strong as an engine, Rhyme could see. Just his genes, probably. He didn't have the physique of someone who worked out.

His hands were shackled when he was brought to the situation room. Rhyme said, "Take them off."

Spiro considered this, nodded to the officer with Stefan and spoke in Italian.

The chains were removed, and Stefan had a very odd reaction. Rather than rub his wrists, as anyone else might have done, he cocked his head, closed his eyes and listened, it seemed, to the tinkling of the tiny steel rings of the shackles as they were pocketed by the officer.

Similar to what he'd done in Charlotte McKenzie's house the night they were arrested.

It was as if he was memorizing the sound, storing it away.

He opened his eyes and asked for a tissue. Rossi handed him a box and he plucked one from the top and wiped his face and the crown of his head. When McKenzie said, "Sit down, Stefan," he did, immediately. Not from fear, but as if she were a portion of his conscious mind and he himself had made the decision.

She was, of course, more than an associate. She was Euterpe, his muse, the woman guiding him on the path to Harmony.

"These men will explain what we need to do, Stefan. I'll tell you later everything that's happened. But for now, please do what they say."

His head rose and fell slowly.

She looked at Rhyme, who said, "We have a recording, Stefan. Would you listen to it and tell us all the information you can figure out? We need to find somebody and we think the background sounds might be able to lead us to them."

"A kidnapping phone call?"

Rhyme said, "No, a call between two people who're planning a terror attack."

He looked at McKenzie, who said, "Yes. One of the people we were after. I made a mistake and we got the wrong one. There's someone else. We need to stop her."

"*Her*. Ah. I kidnapped her husband, and it was really the wife." A smile. "Who stole my shoe."

"Yes."

Intelligent. Good.

Spiro asked, "Would it help to shut the lights out?"

"No, I don't need that."

Ercole played the audio. Now that he was aware of its potential value, Rhyme listened carefully. He made out a few noises that he hadn't noticed in the first or second hearing but not much.

"Again." Stefan's voice was firm. He wasn't the least deferential. Odd how even the most insecure grow assertive when practicing their special art.

Ercole played it once more.

"And again."

He did so.

"Can I have a pen and paper, please?" Stefan asked.

Spiro produced them instantly.

"It is hard, I am sure, to hear past the voices," Rossi said.

Stefan responded with a bemused frown. Apparently he could hear past the voices just fine.

"Sound is better than words. Sounds have meanings that are more trustworthy. Robert Frost, the poet, talked about the sound of sense. I love that, don't you? He said you could experience a poem recited on the other side of a door without hearing the words. The sounds alone would convey the intended emotion and meaning to you."

Not exactly the ramblings of a madman.

He began to jot notes in perfect script. Beatrice Renza would approve of it.

As he wrote, he said, "The caller was not far from the harbor. I hear Klaxons and warning and announcement horns. Passenger and commercial vessels. Tugboat diesels."

"Not from trucks?" Rossi asked.

"Of course not, no. They are clearly echoing off undulating water. You can hear the horns and liner diesels too, right?"

Rhyme could not. They were hidden in a morass of noise.

Stefan scribbled quickly, then stared at the sheet. Closed his eyes. They sprang open and he crossed out what he'd just inscribed and then started again.

"I need to control the playback." He scooted close to the computer, nudging Ercole out of the way.

"These keys can—"

"I know," Stefan said brusquely and typed. He rewound the audio and replayed certain parts, jotting notes. After ten minutes, he looked up.

"I can hear transmissions downshifting and increasing in volume, as the cars get closer to the phone. That means the caller's on top of the hill. The hill's steep. They are mostly cars, mostly small ones, both diesel and gas. One has a muffler about to go. Some vans, I think. But no large trucks."

Another playback. Staring at a blank wall. "Birds. Two different types. First, pigeons. There are many of them. I can hear their wings flutter from time to time: once, when a roller board—those things boys ride on—went by. Once, when children, about four or five years old, ran after the birds. I can tell the age from their footfalls and the laughs. The pigeons returned at once. They didn't fly off when cars went by. That tells us that they're in a square or plaza. Not a street."

Their eyes went to the map of Naples, where Spiro had circled the docks with a red marker. He now put X's near a number of public squares and piazzas in the general area of the waterfront and on what he must have known were hills.

"The second birds are seagulls. They'd be everywhere in and around Naples, of course, but here there are only four, I think. One is giving a copulation call. He's some distance. The three closer to the phone are giving assault calls and alarm calls. They're fighting aggressively, probably over food, since they wouldn't be nesting there. And because there are only three, I think they're fighting over trash in a small bin, behind a restaurant or house. They are farther away from the waterfront; closer, there would be more and there would be a lot of sources for food—fishermen and trash—so the fighting would not be as vicious."

Stefan played the tape back once more and paused it. "There is a school nearby, grade school, we'd say in America. I would guess it's a parochial or a private school—many of the children have leather soles. I can hear no running shoes. Leather soles would mean uniforms. So private or religious. It's a school because they're laughing and running and playing and then, almost as once, it stops, and the sound of their feet changes as they all walk at the same pace back to class." He looked at the others, all staring at him. "They're grade school—I can tell this because of the sound of the voices and the interval of their footfalls. I said that before. There is construction going on not far away. Metal work. Cutting metal and riveting."

"The ironwork of a building," Rossi said.

"I don't know if it's a building," Stefan corrected. "It might be anything metal. A ship."

"Of course."

"Now, we can't ignore words. Do you hear that American voice? A man's asking, 'How much?' Speaking slowly and loud, as if that will improve understanding. Anyway, he'd be speaking to an outdoor vendor. Or, possibly, a shop with an open window.

"There's a man vomiting. Then he receives angry comments. So, I would think he's a drunk, not somebody who's sick. Somebody ill would get sympathy, and we'd hear a siren. This means there might be a bar not far away. I hear scooter engines starting, then running for a few minutes, then stopping. They seem, *some* of them seem, to be misfiring. The sound of tools."

"A repair shop," Ercole said.

"Yes." He listened to more of the tape. "Church bells." Stefan replayed it. "The notes are D, G, G, B, G, G."

Spiro asked, "You are able to tell?"

"I have absolute pitch. Yes, I know those notes. I don't know what they are playing. We have to find out."

Rossi asked, "Perhaps, can you sing it?"

Without referring to the tape again Stefan sang the notes in a clear baritone. "I'm an octave lower," he said, as if that were important information.

Ercole was nodding. "Yes, yes, it's the Angelus, *l'Ave Maria del mezzo-giorno*, I would guess. The midday tolling."

"A Catholic church," Rhyme said.

"Not very close but no more than a hundred yards, I'd think. Perhaps connected to the school."

Dante Spiro marked churches in the area they'd been focused on.

Stefan listened to the tape once more. Then he shook his head. "I'm afraid that's about it."

Spiro asked, "That's all you can hear?"

Stefan laughed. "Oh, no, I hear much more. Airplanes, the trickle of gravel, a gunshot very far away, a glass breaking—a drinking glass, not a window...but they are too general. They won't help you."

"You've done fine, Stefan," Rhyme said.

"Thank you," McKenzie said to the young man.

Spiro exhaled. "*Sei un'artista.* That is to say, you are a true artist."

Stefan smiled, shy once more.

Spiro was then leaning forward, his dark, focused eyes staring at the map. His finger stabbed a spot. "*Ecco.* I think Gianni had to be here. Monte Echia. It is not far from here. A large hill downtown overlooking the bay. That would explain the gear shifting. It's largely residential but below are shops like the one that could be the scooter repair place and the bar where the man was sick. With the vistas, it is a tourist spot, so there could be vendors there, selling food and souvenirs. The docks are not that close but within hearing range. And there is a church just below it, the Chiesa di Santa Maria della Catena."

"Tourists?" Rhyme asked. "It might be a good target."

Rossi said, "It's not a major tourist attraction but, as Dante says, there are many residents and some restaurants. The gulls might have been fighting at one of their trash bins."

Ercole then said, "Ah, there *is* a possible target for Fatima: the military archive, Caserma Nino Bixio."

"I don't know that it's still open," Spiro said. "But, even if not, there would be residents and tourists nearby and bombing a state building would get the attention of the world."

Rossi was already calling the SCO team.

Rhyme looked at the digital clock: 12:50.

An hour and ten minutes until the attack.

Amelia Sachs was pushing Ercole's poor Mégane to the limit once more, though this time not speeding; the unfortunate lower gears were struggling to ascend the steep slope of Monte Echia.

They breached the top and saw ahead of them two dozen tactical officers from the SCO, as well as a number of regulars from the Police of State and the Carabinieri. The Naples Commune Police was present too, along with soldiers from the Italian army.

Towering Michelangelo, the tactical force commander, gestured angrily for two police cars to back up and let Sachs pull closer. He smiled as Sachs jumped from the car and they played the Dirty Harriet/Make My Day game again.

She rigged her headset, and she and Ercole walked into a square beside the large red stone building that was the archive. At the western edge, where a sheer cliff descended to the street below, there were tourist stations—a sketch artist who'd do a portrait of customers with Vesuvius in the background, vendors of gelato and flavored shaved ice, a man behind a pushcart, selling Italian flags, limoncello liqueur in bottles the shape of Italy, Pinocchio dolls, pizza refrigerator magnets, maps, and cold drinks.

Though the day was sunny, the temperature moderate, the area was largely deserted.

Now that Rhyme had told her of Stefan's analysis of the phone call between Fatima and Gianni, she too was aware of the sounds that he'd identified—the pigeons, the gulls ganging over a garbage bin nearby, cars downshifting to make the summit, as she'd just done. Much dimmer were the other sounds—the ships at the docks in the far distance, south toward the volcano, the scooter repair shop, other vendors, tourists, children in a parochial school yard.

She and Ercole joined in the search, and the Forestry officer told Michelangelo that they would survey the vendors and the customers, since the police soldiers had the archives covered.

"*Sì, sì!*" the massive man said and plunged toward the archives with his men, his face registering disappointment, as if peeved that there was no one yet to shoot. The big, dun-colored building was not, in fact, open at the moment, but there were many alcoves and shadows and doorways where a bomb might be hidden—and that would kill or injure dozens, as Dante Spiro had pointed out.

Ercole and Sachs canvassed up and down the streets, she displaying the picture of Fatima, he asking if anyone had seen her, adding that she would be dressed in Western clothing and without the head covering, most likely. Since the photo, though, depicted the woman in hijab, the tourists and vendors surely thought that terrorism might be involved and they gazed at the picture with the eager intent to remember seeing her.

But none had.

The two walked up and down the winding street, stopping at residences and questioning people they passed, while uniformed police officers and Carabinieri swept the cars lining the curbs, some using mirrors on poles to look beneath them for the explosive.

And how much time?

Sachs's phone showed: 1:14.

Forty-six minutes till the attack.

They returned to the top of the plateau, where Michelangelo was talk-ing to a Carabiniere, obviously a commander, to judge from the medals and insignias on his breast and shoulder. His hat was quite tall.

The tactical commander saw Sachs and shook his head, ringed with fuzzy, red hair, with a grimace. He returned to the search.

She called Rhyme.

"Found anything, Sachs?"

"Nothing. And, you know what? This doesn't feel right."

"As in, it doesn't seem like a target?"

"Exactly." She was looking around her as wind stirred up shrapnel of crisp food wrappers and plastic bags and newspapers and dust. "The ar-chive's closed and there just aren't that many people around."

Rhyme was silent a moment, and then: "Odd. Gianni said the target would be crowded today."

"It ain't going to get more crowded in forty minutes, Rhyme. And no press. No *reason* for any press."

Then: "Ah, no. Goddamn it."

Sachs's pulse quickened. This was his tone of anger.

She gripped Ercole's arm and he stopped quickly.

Rhyme was saying, "I made a mistake." He was then speaking to the others in the Questura—Charlotte McKenzie, Spiro and Rossi—but she couldn't hear the words.

He came back on the line. "Monte Echia isn't the target, Sachs. I should have known that!"

"Didn't Stefan identify it right?"

"He did fine. But *I* didn't pay attention to what Gianni told Fatima. He didn't say he was at the target. He said he could *see* the target. He was standing there and looking it over."

She explained this to Ercole, who grimaced. They caught Michelan-gelo's attention and Sachs gestured him over. The man stalked closer and Ercole told him about the mistake.

He nodded and spoke into his microphone.

Sachs was staring over the vistas. "I can see the docks, Rhyme."

He was on speaker and Spiro had heard. He said, "But, Detective, they are filled with security. I do not think she could get close."

Ercole said, "We see the Partenope walkway and street. It is somewhat crowded."

Then Sachs's eyes slipped to the stony island in front of Via Partenope. "What's that?"

"Castel dell'Ovo," he answered. "A popular tourist attraction. And there are, as you can see, many restaurants and cafés."

Spiro said abruptly, "That could be it. Gianni told Fatima to get behind a stone wall before the explosion. Yes, the castle has dozens of alcoves where she can hide."

"And look!"

Two large buses were just then pulling up in front of the bridge that led to the island the castle was on. People in suits and elaborate dresses began to climb out. On the side were banners.

"What do they say?" Sachs asked Ercole.

"It's publicity for a fashion event here. Some designer or clothing company."

"And there would have been a press announcement, so Gianni would have learned it started at two o'clock."

She told those in the Questura what they were looking at.

"Yes, yes, that has to be it!" Rossi said.

Sachs tugged Ercole's arm. "Let's go." Into the headset she said, "We're headed there now, Rhyme."

She disconnected and they jogged to the Mégane, which she fired up and put into gear. Michelangelo and the tactical officers were jogging back to their vehicles.

Sachs skidded in a U-turn and sped down the switchbacks to the street beneath the mountain. She swerved onto the concrete, steered into the skid and floored the accelerator. Sachs was blustering her way through an intersection when she glanced in her rearview mirror, wondering how close Michelangelo was, when she saw a flash of yellow and orange flame.

"Ercole, look. Behind us. What happened?"

He turned as best he could and squinted. "*Mamma mia!* A fire. At the bottom of the road we just came down, there's a car on fire. Sitting in the middle of the street."

"Gianni."

"He's been watching us! He's running guard for Fatima. Of course. He broke into a car, I'd guess, and rolled it into the road, then set it on fire."

"To block the police. They're trapped on the mountain now."

Ercole was calling in this latest development.

On speaker she heard Rossi say he would get more officers and a fire brigade to the base of the mountain to the castle.

"Looks like it's just us, Ercole."

No longer an uneasy passenger, he stabbed his finger toward the road and cried, "*Per favore*, Amelia. Can you not go any faster?"

CHAPTER 65

Like a hockey player swerving around the goal, the Mégane veered onto Via Partenope and screeched to a stop, deftly—and narrowly—avoiding a gelato vendor, two fashion models in neon-green dresses and, by inches, a Bugatti coupe, which Sachs believed was worth just north of a million dollars.

Then she and Ercole were out and sprinting to the promontory that tied Castel dell'Ovo to the mainland.

Sachs called, "Fatima's in street clothes, remember."

"Sì."

"And remember your target. You've got to stop her instantly."

"Upper lip. Sì. Three bullets."

Sirens cut through the air—the fire trucks headed to clear the way from Mont Echia, and the urgent wail from reinforcements, Police of State and Carabinieri heading to the castle now, to join Sachs and Ercole in the search for Fatima Jabril.

It was 1:30.

What a fat target this was: To the left of the massive castle, on the island, there were shops and restaurants and docks, today filled with tourists and locals enjoying the sun and the promise of Neapolitan food and wine and a lazy voyage in a sailing or motorboat upon cerulean Naples Bay. The site was plumped up all the more by the hundred or so fashion industry glitterati. A tent had been set up in the shadows of the towering castle.

Add the many tourists, and there had to be a thousand people here.

Sachs jumped as her phone rang, thinking of the bomb, which would have a cell-phone-activated detonator; that her sensitivity to ringtones was unreasonable didn't calm her heart.

"Rhyme."

"Where are you?" he asked.

"On the promontory to the castle."

Spiro's voice. "Yes, yes, Detective. We see you. CCTV."

Two uniformed officers—guards at the castle—approached. They had apparently been briefed by Rossi or Spiro and the pair, a blond woman and dark-haired man, hurried to Ercole, who confirmed their identities, as if the badges and weapons left any doubt.

Sachs said into the phone, "Evacuate the place, Rhyme?"

Rossi spoke. He explained that they had decided against that approach, at least for now; the castle and the island on which it sat were accessed only by the narrow strip of land, like a bridge, they were moving over now. Panic would create a deadly crush, and more would die from a leap into the water or onto the rocky shore. "At five minutes until two, perhaps we will have no choice. But that will be certain death for a number of people. We will be closing off the entrance now."

Sachs, Ercole and the two castle guards walked quickly over the promontory and into the throngs on the island. The officers were scanning the grounds and docks where hundreds of pleasure craft bobbed lazily at their slips. Looking for a slim, dark-haired woman, probably by herself, dressed in Western clothing and carrying a package or purse or backpack. Of course, Sachs reflected, here they were in a region brimming with slim, dark-haired women, dressed Western.

Scanning, scanning the crowds.

Impossible...

Rossi came on the line. "The fire's out and the car is being moved aside. Michelangelo's men will be ten or fifteen minutes."

Just in time for the detonation.

Rossi now said, "Ah, I've heard from some undercover officers. They were investigating a smuggling case on the dock, coincidentally. They are nearby and moving in. They're aware of you and Ercole. They should be there now. They have Fatima's picture."

Sachs told Ercole about the undercover officers—and just at that moment one young man in a leather jacket and tight jeans caught their eye. He moved aside his jacket and displayed a badge. He was with a woman in her thirties. She, too, nodded. They, the two castle guards and Sachs and Ercole met near the entrance to a seafood restaurant. They agreed to split up and go in three different directions.

It was 1:40.

She and the lanky Forestry officer were moving quickly west, toward the side of the castle that jutted farthest into Naples Bay. The tourists here were listening to a street musician, playing guitar and singing what sounded like an Italian ballad from the last century. She saw couples embracing, teenagers flirting and joking, a young blonde pushing a baby carriage, families strolling, men walking side by side, their wives arm in arm behind, children in giddy orbit, boys with soccer balls unable to resist showing off their crafty footwork.

No one who looked like Fatima, even in Western clothing.

And as for the bomb?

It could be anywhere. In one of the trash receptacles, under a table in one of the restaurants or bars, behind a kiosk, near the raised stage for the fashion show.

Perhaps in the potted plant she was walking past just now.

C4 explosive, known officially as RDX, Research Department Explosive, travels outward at nineteen thousand miles per hour, nearly sixty times the speed of sound. The vapors and blast wave annihilate anything in their path. Skin, viscera and bone simply disappear into a crimson mist.

She sent Ercole to the left, toward the stage were the fashion show was about to start. Reporters were taking random shots of some of the more beautiful woman—and a beautiful man or two. In a soft voice, as if not wishing to startle her, Rossi spoke into her earbud, "Detective Sachs,

Michelangelo and the other officers are almost there. We have to evacuate now. It's thirteen fifty."

Ten minutes to two.

Ten minutes till the bomb.

"I do not want to, Detective. I know there will be a panic. But there is no choice. I'll send the officers in—"

"Wait," she said. A thought: The woman with the baby carriage . . . it was out of place. There was a park nearby, at the western end of the Via Partenope. The pretty place, nicely landscaped, had pathways and gelato stands and gardens and benches. Ideal for a mother with a carriage. But the Castel dell'Ovo, with the crowds and warren of docks? No.

And she'd had a backpack over her shoulder. Where better to hide a bomb?

Blond, though? Well, if you were going shopping for a baby carriage for a prop, why not buy a wig too?

Turning abruptly back to where she'd seen the woman: "Give me just a minute more," she whispered into the headset. "I have a lead."

"Detective, there's no time!"

Rhyme's voice said, firmly, "No. Let her run with it."

"But—"

Spiro said, "Sì, Massimo. Let her."

Sirens were sounding now, growing closer. Heads were turning toward the mainland. Smiles cooling to frowns of curiosity . . . and then concern.

Sachs continued south, in the direction she'd last seen the woman and the baby carriage. Hurrying over the stone paths, hundreds, perhaps a thousand years old. Her head swiveled, eyes squinted.

Her hand? Inches from the grip of the Beretta.

1:55.

Where are you, Fatima? *Where?*

And then the answer: At the southernmost wall of the castle, the blonde with the carriage emerged from the building's shadows near the docks. She stopped beside a pier, at which were tied a half-dozen gorgeous yachts, white as cold moonlight, ropes coiled perfectly on the decks and silver fixtures glinting. On the boat: older beautiful people, tanned and coiffed—"jet-setters" in an earlier era.

There was no target here—it wasn't that crowded—but there was a solid archway that would protect her from the blast.

Fatima—Sachs could see her face clearly now as she looked back nervously—was wheeling toward this archway now. The dull-toned blond wig clashed with her olive skin. The backpack was over her shoulder still. It wouldn't contain the bomb any longer. No, she would have planted it in a more populated part of the island.

Sachs drew her weapon but kept it hidden under her arm and jogged forward. She was thirty feet away when the woman saw her and froze.

Speaking softly, Sachs said slowly and in a low, clear voice, "You have been tricked, Fatima! Ibrahim is not who you think. He is using you. He's lied to you."

Fatima frowned, shook her head. "No. No trick!" Her eyes were wide—and damp with tears.

Sachs walked a few feet closer. Fatima moved back, turning the carriage and keeping it between her and Sachs.

"I don't want to hurt you. You'll be safe. Just put your hands up. Let me come talk to you. You don't want to do this. You'll be hurting people without any reason. Please!"

Fatima stiffened.

Sachs said, "I saved your husband. I saved his life. Remember?"

Then Fatima lowered her head. A moment later she looked up with a smile. "Yes. Yes, miss. Yes. Thank you for that. *Shukran!*" The smile twisted into a look of profound sorrow and Sachs saw tears. Then Fatima shoved the baby carriage toward the water. There was no barrier, or even a low lip, on the pier and it tumbled, as if in slow motion, twenty feet into the water.

Sachs caught a glimpse of blankets and black hair rising inside as it landed with a loud splash. The carriage settled and sank fast.

Sachs, however, didn't do what Fatima hoped. She ignored the buggy and went into a combat shooting stance as the woman dug for her phone to call the mobile wired to the detonator.

"No, Fatima, no!"

Above them, screams pealed from the top of the castle, fifty feet above her, where tourists had seen the carriage go into the water.

Fatima yanked the phone free. It was a flip phone. She opened it, looking down at the keypad, reaching a finger out.

Amelia Sachs inhaled, held her breath and squeezed the trigger. Three times.

CHAPTER 66

*N*on siamo riusciti a trovare nulla," the scuba diver said.

Ercole Benelli translated. The man was sorry but he and his colleagues in the Italian navy had found nothing in the water below the looming castle.

"Keep searching," Lincoln Rhyme said. He, Ercole, Sachs, Spiro and Rossi were near the spot where Fatima had shoved the carriage into the water, in the shadow of the blunt, ruddy castle. Curiously, much of the entrance route to the edifice, centuries old, was disabled-accessible.

The diver nodded and walked backward along the pier—he wore flippers—then turned and, stiff-legged, strode into the water. Rhyme glanced at the half-dozen eruptions of bubbles on the surface of Naples Bay from the aquatic search party below.

A wail sounded to their left, a woman's keen of despair. The sixtyish-year-old matron pointed at Sachs and fired off a vicious fusillade of words.

Ercole started to translate but Rhyme interrupted. "She's upset that my Sachs here was so devoted to stopping a terror attack that she ignored a drowning baby. Am I in the ballpark?"

"Ballpark?" A questioning frown.

"Am. I. Correct?"

"You are close, Captain Rhyme. But she didn't raise any question of devotion to stopping the villain. In essence she accuses your partner of being a child killer."

Rhyme chuckled. "Tell her what really happened. If it'll shut her up."

Ercole gave the woman the story—a very abbreviated version of the full tale, which was that it wasn't a baby in the carriage, but a doll.

Sachs had known all along that Fatima's and Khaled's little girl, Muna, was not in the carriage. When she'd been to the Capodichino Reception Center earlier that day, after Fatima had vanished, Sachs had seen Muna in the care of a neighbor, in the vacant lot beside their tent. And among the boxes inside their tent was an empty carton that had once held— from the picture on the side—a dark-haired doll, the size of a large baby. Sachs had caught a glimpse of the toy in the carriage.

A clever diversion. Rhyme had to give Fatima credit.

He glared at the agitated tourist until she fell silent, turned and left.

Prosecutor Spiro approached. "Have they found the phone yet?"

"No," Rossi told him. "Five divers in the bay. But nothing."

This was the object of the navy divers' search. They hoped to recover the SIM card from Fatima's new phone and track Gianni's or other numbers that might lead to him, to Ibrahim, or to whoever within the Italian anti-immigrant movement had hired them to derail the pro-immigrant legislative proposal in Rome.

But the currents in the bay were not, it seemed, cooperating.

The Carabinieri's bomb team, directed by Fatima Jabril, had found and removed the explosive device, which had been placed deep in a stone recess of the castle, not far from the fashion show reception. It was a bad placement, from a terrorist's point of view. The solid walls would have protected almost everyone from the blast. Dogs had searched and found no other explosives and a team had cleared Fatima's backpack, too, which contained no weapons, but only medical supplies—bandages and antiseptics and the like. An ID badge from the refugee camp indicated that Fatima was a nurse/aide.

The woman herself was nearby—in the castle, being treated by a medical team. The injuries were minor—two broken carpals, finger bones, and one hell of a bruise. But the 9mm slugs, which had destroyed the phone, had not broken any skin.

Sachs had not shot to kill.

After the phone had been so dramatically removed from her hand,

Fatima had grown hysterical. She said that—because she'd failed—Ibrahim would now kill her family in Libya.

But Sachs explained that that was unlikely, given that the plot was not what it seemed. Ibrahim and Gianni weren't terrorists; they were mercenaries being paid to stage phony attacks. Still, to reassure Fatima—and snag her cooperation—Spiro told her that Italian agents in Libya would keep an eye on her family.

She readily agreed and gave a statement about everything she knew about him: It wasn't much, true, but she confirmed he was a tanned, unsmiling man who smoked foul-smelling cigarettes, was clean-shaven and had thick curly hair, an athletic build. She described him as a man who traveled much, whose hours were not his own. When they spoke he was often out of town and usually on the road.

Rossi's phone hummed and he answered. "Sì, pronto?"

Rhyme couldn't deduce from the conversation whether the inspector was receiving good news or bad. At one point he lifted a pen from his breast pocket, pulled the cap off with his teeth and jotted something in a notebook.

After he disconnected he turned to the others and said, "Beatrice. She found one print on the detonator phone. It came back positive. An Albanian—in the country legally."

"Legally?" Rhyme asked. "Then why was he in the system?"

"He was required to have a security check because he works at Malpensa airport. In Milan. He is a mechanic for fuel trucks and those big vehicles that tow and push airplanes. All airport workers are fingerprinted. He would have, I think, some connection with the Albanian gangs. He could smuggle drugs without having to pass through Customs. Explosives too, it seems."

Sachs was looking out to sea, squinting. It was her intense look. Her huntress look. Rhyme enjoyed watching her at moments like that.

Rhyme asked, "Sachs? Enjoying the view?"

She mused, "Malpensa's the other airport in Milan."

"Yes," Spiro said.

She said, "Didn't Beatrice say she'd found samples of industrial grease at the warehouse in Milan? And jet fuel too?"

"She did, yes. But we didn't pursue it because it didn't seem there was any connection between the warehouse and the Composer."

She turned to Spiro. "Everyone in Italy, citizens, has an ID card, right?"

"Yes. It is the law."

"With a picture?"

"That's right."

"If I give you a name can you get me an image?"

"If the name is not too common, yes. Or you have an address or at least a commune, a town."

"It's not that common a name. I'll need the picture sent to my phone and I'll forward it to someone."

"I will arrange it. Who is this person you wish to send it to?"

"Do you know the phrase 'confidential informant'?"

"Ah, so you have a snitch, do you?" Spiro asked, pulling out his mobile.

CHAPTER 67

Amelia Sachs sat beside Lincoln Rhyme in the back of the disabled-accessible van, parked on one of the better streets in Naples, the Via di Chiaia, overlooking the beautiful park that had, in part, tipped her to Fatima's presence. It would be here, not the Castel dell'Ovo, where a single mother would stroll with her child.

Dante Spiro was with them, listening through an earbud to the operation, which was being run by Michelangelo.

Dirty Harriet.

The view out one window was a magnificent panorama of the bay, the Castel dell'Ovo to the right and the deceptively placid Vesuvius to the left.

Like everyone else, however, Sachs was uninterested in the bay; she was concentrating on the considerably more modest sight through the other window: a pleasant, if old, residential abode, stone construction, yellow paint. A pensione—a bed-and-breakfast-style inn. It was gem-like and would have cost plenty per night.

"We're sure he's inside?" she asked. Referring to the man who had put together the entire plan. Who had hired Ibrahim and Gianni. Who had tried to kill dozens of innocents, solely to turn public opinion further against the refugees, and defeat the pending legislation that might improve their plight.

All under the perverse banner of nationalism.

Spiro was listening to police transmissions through a wired earpiece.

His head was cocked. He said, "*Sì, sì.*" Then to Sachs and Rhyme: "Yes, he's in there." A grim smile. "And the assessment is that he's unarmed."

"How do they know that? Do they have eyes on him?" Rhyme asked insistently.

He would be thinking, Sachs knew, that if she was walking into the room where the mastermind of the scheme was—as Spiro would say—holed up, they should damn well know for sure whether he was armed or not.

She was less concerned; she had her Beretta. And a fine piece of work it was, she'd announced. The Italians were good at food, cars, fashion and weapons. None better.

Spiro replied, "Michelangelo reports that their surveillance has determined he will certainly be unarmed. But that will not last for long. We should move now."

Sachs glanced at Rhyme, who said, "Don't let anyone shoot anything up if they can avoid it, Sachs. This's important evidence. This's the main bad boy."

Then she and Dante Spiro were out the van's door.

They moved quickly to the front of the structure, where four SCO officers met them, led by Michelangelo. Unlike their commander, these men were not large, though they were made bulky because of their gear: body armor, breaching equipment, boots, helmets. The H&K submachine guns favored by the tac teams were unslung and ready to fire.

Spiro gestured and the men moved through the front door of the pensione and, as quietly as they could, up the stairs to the first floor.

The hallway was dim and hot, the air oppressive. The rooms might have air-conditioning but the hallways did not. Paintings of old Italy dotted the walls, most of them of Naples; a smoking volcano looming in the background. In one, though, Vesuvius was busily erupting as toga-clad citizens stared in horror, though a small dog seemed to be smiling. Every piece of artwork hung crookedly.

After a pause and a listen to the surveillance control van outside, Michelangelo gave hand signals and the SCO officers divided into two teams. One, crouching below the peephole, moved past the door of the suspect's room and turned. The second team remained on the near side.

Sachs and Spiro stopped ten feet short. What was that noise? Sachs wondered.

Screech, screech, screech...

Stefan could have told them in an instant.

Then Sachs heard a moan.

Of course. A couple was making love.

That was why the assault team, with the auditory surveillance system, had concluded that the occupants of the room were not armed. A gun might be nearby but it was highly unlikely either one was concealing a weapon on their person.

Michelangelo heard something through his headset—Sachs could tell from his cocked head. He stepped back to Spiro and spoke in Italian. The prosecutor said to Sachs, "The second team is behind our other target. He is up the street, in his car. They'll move in when we do, coordinated."

From the room the sounds of lovemaking had grown louder, the grunts more frequent. Michelangelo whispered something to Spiro, who translated his comment to Sachs. "He's wondering if we should wait a moment. Just because..."

Sachs whispered, "No."

Michelangelo grinned and returned to his men. He gestured toward the door, his hand making a slicing movement, like a priest blessing a communicant.

Instantly they went into action. One hefted a battering ram and swung it hard into the door near the knob. The flimsy wood gave way instantly. He stepped back, dropped the ram and unslung his machine gun as the others sped in, their weapons up, muzzles sweeping back and forth. Sachs hurried forward, Spiro behind her.

In the bed, in the center of the quaint room, a dark-haired Italian woman, no older than eighteen or nineteen, was squealing and frantically grabbing at bedclothes to cover herself. But it was a tug-of-war for the sheet and blanket with the man in bed with her. She was winning.

Pretty funny actually.

"*Allora!*" Spiro called. "Enough! Leave the sheets! Stand and keep your hands raised. Yes, yes, turn around." In Italian he spoke to the woman, apparently repeating the command.

His boyish face blazing, hair askew, Mike Hill, the American business-man whose private jet had shepherded Sachs to Milan the other day, did as ordered. He glanced once at Michelangelo's pistol, then at Sachs and apparently decided to keep his hands raised and not cover his conspicu-ous groin. The woman with him did the same.

One officer had gone through their clothes. He said, "*Nessun arma.*"

Spiro nodded and the officer handed the garments to the couple.

As he dressed, Hill snapped, "I want an attorney. Now. And make sure it's one who speaks English."

CHAPTER 68

The suspects were in jail.

Il Carcere di Napoli.

Michael Hill was in a holding cell, awaiting the arrival of his "ball-breaking" attorney, who would show them a thing or two about criminal law.

Rhyme and Sachs were in the Questura situation room, receiving updates from a number of sources.

Hill's wife had arrived at the jail at the same time as the prostitute in the pensione was being released. The teenager had received a legal warning. Spiro had reported that "the businessman's spouse's expression, I will say, was a bit like that of fans witnessing a car crash at an auto race. Horrified, yes, but modulated with a certain hint of glee. I suspect the divorce settlement will be *impressionante.*"

Mike Hill's arrest had come about quickly, after Sachs's speculation that the infamous Gianni might, in fact, be the American businessman's chauffeur, name of Luigi Procopio.

What had brought the man to the forefront of suspects was a series of recollections by Sachs as she had stared over Naples Bay not long ago, following Fatima's arrest.

Beatrice had found volcanic soil trace in the warehouse. Which meant someone from Naples had likely been in the warehouse recently. The forensic scientist had also discovered the grease there, the sort used in heavy, outdoor equipment. The Albanian who provided the explosives was a mechanic at Malpensa airport, working on such equipment. He had probably met the person who'd traveled from Naples at the warehouse to deliver the explosives.

Who had a connection with both Malpensa and Naples? Mike Hill. Since he knew about the traffic from the airport to downtown Milan, he had obviously been there before—and on the private plane tarmac, where explosives could have been transferred out of sight of Customs and security.

Hill himself probably wouldn't deal with bombs or paying Albanian smugglers. But his driver might. Luigi—a smoker, clean-shaven, long dark hair, swarthy complexion. And he was a man who traveled a great deal, as Fatima had told them, often driving.

Had it been coincidence that Hill just happened to call Consulate General Musgrave, mentioning that his private plane was headed north, so Sachs could hitch a ride to Milan? Of course not. Hill, Gianni and Ibrahim would have known all about Rhyme's and Sachs's presence here and would have bugged either their phones or hotel room, learning that they had a lead to Milan. Concerned about the progress of the investigation, Hill had immediately contacted the consulate general and let it be known that he had a plane ready to go . . . so he could keep an eye on the investigators.

Hardly certain, it was, nonetheless, a reasonable theory worth exploring.

To find out, Sachs sent Luigi's picture to her snitch, Alberto Allegro Pronti, the homeless Don Quixote of a Communist in Milan. Ercole translating, Pronti verified that Luigi Procopio was the man who had thrown him out of the warehouse.

Ercole had smiled as he'd listened to the man's words. He said to Sachs, "Alberto asks if the cat-kicker will go to jail." He turned back to the phone. "*Sì certamente.*"

Luigi had surrendered to Michelangelo's second tactical team in the parking lot behind the pensione, where he'd been smoking and texting, as he waited for his boss to finish his liaison with the local call girl.

Dante Spiro had been particularly pleased to nab Procopio. Not only was he instrumental in Hill's plot to implicate refugees in the fake terror attacks, but he was an international member of the 'Ndràngheta. Spiro explained that Flying Squad officer Daniela Canton, who specialized in gang work, had learned days ago of some 'Ndràngheta operative active in the area. She'd learned nothing more about it. Now the source of the intelligence was clear.

Mike Hill's involvement changed the entire focus of the plot. It was not an Italian official or member of a right-wing party, like the Nuovo Nazionalismo, who was the mastermind of the fake terrorist plot; it was an American.

Mike Hill's plan had the purpose they'd originally speculated—though not to derail Italian immigration reform. It was to sway public opinion in the *United States* and turn lawmakers against the pro-refugee bill in Congress, offering "proof" that terrorists were hiding among immigrants like tainted pieces in a bag of candy.

Hill was not in Naples by coincidence. He'd come here to oversee his operation and make sure that it succeeded. There remained the question as to whether Hill himself was the sole mastermind. His phone records revealed texts to and from a Texas senator, Herbert Station, a staunch opponent of the immigration bill and a nationalist in his own right. The texts were innocent—but too innocent, Sachs thought. "The senator's guilty as sin," she said. "It's code. You don't text overseas to tell somebody about the best potato salad in Austin and ask at three in the morning when's UT going to play Arkansas next."

Time—and the evidence—would tell.

Spiro now walked into the room, cheroot in one hand, his own Louis L'Amour Western-in-progress in the other.

"About our friends," he said. Referring to Charlotte McKenzie and Stefan Merck.

Now that they'd snagged Gianni and Hill, the case against the Composer was back on keel. That Hill had manipulated her—and her AIS—was irrelevant: Kidnapping is a crime.

And so is wrongful accusation.

Just ask Amanda Knox . . .

Both McKenzie and Stefan were presently in the lockup, too, in separate cells.

Massimo Rossi walked into the room. "Ah, ah, here you are. Don't you say 'y'all' in America?"

"I don't," replied Rhyme.

The inspector continued, "We have interviewed Fatima. She is being held downstairs. It is a complicated case, regarding her. She is accused—and clearly guilty—of terrorism and attempted murder. We cannot ignore that. There are mitigating factors, though. She planted the bomb in a way that it would have been very unlikely that someone would be hurt. And she had taken a job at the refugee camp hospital in part to obtain bandages and medical supplies to help anyone who *was* wounded in the explosion. They were in her backpack. She has cooperated in finding Signor Hill and Luigi Procopio, and offering information on Ibrahim, or Hassan, or whatever his name might really be. It's clear that she—like Ali Maziq and Malik Dadi—was forced to do what Ibrahim wished, fearing for her family's life back in Libya. Those will be important factors in the case against her and Maziq."

He turned to Rhyme. "In Italy, if you haven't already gathered, we have a more—*come si dice?*—a more holistic approach to justice. The magistrates and the juries take many things into account—not just in setting the punishment but in establishing guilt in the first place." He added, "One last remaining matter has been resolved. Garry Soames has been released, and Natalia Garelli formally charged for Frieda S.'s assault." He rubbed a finger across his mustache. "Natalia was quite astonishing. Her first question, upon hearing the formal charges, was what brand cosmetics were sold in prison and if she could get a cell with a makeup table and mirror."

Ercole Benelli appeared in the doorway. Rhyme saw immediately that his face was troubled.

"Sir?"

Both Rossi and Spiro looked his way, though it was clear he meant the inspector.

"*Sì*, Ercole?"

"I just... something is curious. Troublesome, that is to say."

"*Che cosa?*"

"You recall, as you wanted, I took the evidence to the locker room, everything the Scientific Police and Detective Sachs and I collected regarding Fatima and Mike Hill and the incident at the Castel dell'Ovo—everything, of course, except the C4 explosive itself, which is at the army bomb facility. I asked that this evidence be filed with the Stefan Merck and Charlotte McKenzie evidence."

"That was right," Rossi said. "The cases are related, of course."

"But the administrator of the evidence room looked at the records and said there was no file for Stefan or Charlotte. No evidence had been logged in."

"Not logged in?" Rossi asked. "But didn't you do so?"

"Yes, sir. Yes. Just as you asked. Everything from the bus stop, the camp, the aqueduct and underground, the farmhouse near the composting facility, the factory in Naples...all the scenes! *Everything!* I went directly there from here. But the administrator looked twice—and then, at my request, again." His miserable eyes zipped from Rossi's to Spiro's and settled on Rhyme's. "Every bit of evidence in the Composer case. It has vanished."

CHAPTER 69

Massimo Rossi strode to the landline telephone unit on a fiberboard table and placed a call, dialing three numbers. After a moment, he cocked his head and said, "*Sono* Rossi. *Il caso del Compositore? Stefan Merck e* Charlotte McKenzie. *Qual è il problema?*"

He listened and his face grew troubled. After a moment, he looked toward Ercole. "*Hai la ricevuta?*"

Ercole fell into English. "The receipt? For the evidence, you mean?"

"*Sì.* When you logged it in."

The young officer was blushing furiously. "I received one just now—for the recent evidence. But earlier? No. I left everything at the Evidence Room intake desk. There was a man in the back—I didn't see who. I called to him that I was dropping off evidence, along with the proper paperwork, and I left."

Rossi stared at him, whispering, "*Nessuna ricevuta?*"

"I . . . no. I'm sorry. I didn't know."

Rossi closed his eyes.

As a forensic scientist, Rhyme could think of no greater sin among law enforcers than being careless with—much less losing—the evidence in a case.

Another string of words into the phone, Rossi's face growing more grim yet. He listened. "*Grazie. Ciao, ciao.*" He disconnected, eyes on the floor, his expression one of incredulity. "It's gone," he said. "Vanished."

Rhyme snapped, "How?"

"I do not understand. It's never happened before."

Sachs said, "CCTV?"

"Not in the evidence room itself. It is not a public area. There's no need."

Spiro looked suspicious. "Charlotte McKenzie?"

Rossi considered. "Officer, you took the evidence there when I told you to."

"Immediately, sir."

"Charlotte was in custody by then. Stefan too. They could not have done it. Her associates—whoever they might be—might have been behind this. A theft from the Questura...that is something not even the Camorra would dare attempt. But American intelligence?" He shrugged.

Rhyme said, "We need the evidence. We have to find it." Without that, the cases against McKenzie and Stefan could proceed only with witness statements and confessions...and he knew that everything McKenzie had told them about the Alternative Intelligence Service and the operation here she would deny. And Stefan, of course, would not dare to contradict his muse.

In a stumbling voice, Ercole said, "Inspector, sir...I am sorry. I..." The voice faded to thick silence.

Rossi was looking out the window. He turned back. "Ercole, I must tell you that this is a problem. A serious one. It is of my making. I should have known that you were inexperienced, yet I asked you onto our operation."

His long face crimson, Ercole was chewing his lip. He probably would have preferred a tongue-lashing to this quiet regret.

"I think it is best you report back to Forestry Corps now. I'll send this matter to Rome. There will be an inquiry. You will be interviewed and make a statement."

Ercole seemed far younger than his thirty-some-odd years at the moment. He nodded and then his gaze dipped to the floor. He wasn't completely to blame, Rhyme supposed, though he recalled Rossi saying that the officer should "log in" the evidence, which suggested there would be a paper trail for the transfer.

Rhyme knew Ercole had hoped this assignment might be a springboard to a career with the Police of State.

And with this one incident, that chance was probably over.

Spiro asked him, "Ercole? The evidence against Mike Hill and Gianni? That receipt?"

He handed it to the prosecutor, who took it.

Ercole's eyes were sweeping everyone in the room. "I have been honored to work with you. I have learned a great deal."

His expression seemed to add the qualifier: But, it seems, I didn't learn enough.

Sachs hugged him. He and Rhyme shook hands, then with a last glance at the evidence board, he nodded and left.

Rossi's gaze followed the man's receding figure. "A shame. He was smart. He took initiative. And, yes, I should have been more attentive. But, well, not everyone is made out to be a criminal officer. He is better off in Forestry. More to his nature, I would think, anyway."

Tree cop...

Rossi said, "*Mamma mia. La prova.* The evidence..." He asked Spiro, "Where do we go from here, Dante?"

Regarding the inspector for a moment, Spiro finally said, "I don't see how we can proceed against Signorina McKenzie and Stefan. They will have to be released."

Rossi said to Rhyme, "The case against Mike Hill and Procopio, however, will proceed. I know you wish to extradite Hill, at least, back to the United States for trial. But we cannot let you do that. Rome— and I—intend to try him and his associate here. I'm sorry, Lincoln. But there is no other way. Are you going to look for a lawyer from Wolf Tits now?"

The new friends were now opponents once again.

"We have no choice, Dante."

With a sad face, Spiro ran his cheroot beneath his nose. "Did you know that the emperor Tiberius, one of our more infamous forebears, had a luxurious villa not far from where we are just now? Perhaps more than most emperors, he loved gladiatorial contests."

"Is that right?"

"I will paraphrase what he said at the beginning of each, when the warriors and spectators faced him: 'Let the extradition games begin.'"

CHAPTER 70

"Y ou don't trust us?"

Charlotte McKenzie was speaking to Lincoln Rhyme and Amelia Sachs outside police headquarters. Stefan stood beside her.

Two agents from the FBI's Rome office were standing beside a black SUV, a man and woman, both in dark suits that must have been nearly unbearable; a heat wave had settled over Naples, as if Vesuvius had woken and spewed searing air over all of Campania.

Rhyme himself was sweating fiercely but, as with most other sensations, good and bad, he was largely immune. His temples tickled occasionally but Thom was always there to mop.

And remind. "Out of the sun soon," the aide said sternly. Extreme temperatures were not good for his system.

"Yes, yes, yes."

Sachs repeated to Charlotte McKenzie, "Trust you?"

"No," Rhyme answered bluntly. They'd found no proof but he thought it likely that the AIS unit had somehow staged an op to steal the evidence against her and Stefan from the Questura evidence room and ditch it. He added, "But it wasn't really our call. Your travel arrangements were made by Washington. You'll be on a government jet to Rome, then onward to Washington, and agents'll meet the fight. They'll make sure that Stefan gets to his hospital. And you get to...wherever your mysterious headquarters is."

"A parking garage at Dulles will be fine."

"After that it'll be up to the U.S. attorney and the DA in New York to see where your new address'll be."

Though he knew there would be no charges brought for the Robert Ellis kidnapping, which was not, of course, a kidnapping at all.

Stefan was looking over the city, which here was filled with a cacophony of sounds. His attention was entirely elsewhere and his head bobbed from time to time and his lips moved once or twice. Rhyme wondered what Stefan was hearing. Was this, for him, like an art lover gazing at a painting? And, if so, was the experience a Jackson Pollock spatter or a carefully composed Monet landscape?

One man's lullaby is another man's scream.

A Flying Squad car pulled up and an officer climbed out, collecting two suitcases and a backpack from the trunk: McKenzie's and Stefan's belongings—from her place and from the farmhouse near the fertilizer operation, Rhyme supposed.

"My computer?" Stefan asked.

The officer said, in fair English, "It was with the items stolen from the file room. It is gone."

Rhyme was watching McKenzie's eyes. No reaction whatsoever at this reference to the theft of the evidence against them.

Stefan grimaced. "My files, the sounds I've collected here. All gone?"

McKenzie touched his arm. "Everything's backed up, Stefan. Remember."

"Not Lilly. In the cemetery. Tap, tap, tap…"

"I'm sorry," she said.

The officer said, "Arrivederci." His tone was not unfriendly. He returned to his car and sped off.

Stefan focused on those around him now and walked up to Rhyme. "I was thinking about you, sir. Last night."

"Yes?"

He smiled, genuine curiosity on his face. "With your disability, your condition, do you think you hear things better? Sort of like compensation, I mean."

Rhyme said, "I've thought about that. I'm not aware of any experiments but, anecdotally, yes, I think I do. When someone walks into my town house I know them instantly from the sound, if I've heard them before. And, if not, I can tell height from the length of time between steps."

"The interval, yes. Very important. And sole of shoe and weight too."

"That might be beyond me," Rhyme said.

"You could learn." Stefan offered a shy smile, stepped into the SUV and moved over to the far seat.

McKenzie began to climb in too, then turned to Rhyme. "We're doing good things. We're saving lives. And we're doing that in a humane way."

To Rhyme, this was as pointless a comment as could be.

He said nothing in reply. The SUV door closed and the vehicle eased away: Charlotte McKenzie to return to her world of theatrical espionage, Stefan to his new hospital, where—Rhyme hoped—he would find harmony in the music of the spheres.

Rhyme turned to Thom and Sachs. "Ah, look, across the street. It's our *coffee* shop. And what does that mean? It's time for a grappa."

CHAPTER 71

A t six that evening Lincoln Rhyme was in their suite at the Grand
Hotel di Napoli.

His phone hummed. He debated and took the call.

Dante Spiro. He suggested they meet in an hour to discuss their gladiatorial contest, the extradition motion.

Rhyme agreed and the prosecutor gave them an address.

Thom fetched the van, plugged in the GPS and soon they were cruising through the countryside outside Naples—a route that took them,
coincidentally, past the airport and the sprawling Capodichino refugee
camp. At this time of night, twilight, the place exuded the ambience of a
vast, medieval village, as it might have existed when Naples was its own
kingdom in the fourteenth century (Ercole Benelli, Forestry officer and
tour guide, had explained this, with bright eyes of an amateur historian).
Perhaps the only differences were that now the flickers of light came not
from smoky, sputtering fires but the many handheld screens, small and
smaller, as the refugees texted or talked to friends, to family, to their over-
burdened lawyers, to the world. Or perhaps they were simply watching
Tunisian or Libyan...or Italian soccer.

The place Spiro had chosen for the meeting was not a hotel conference room or even the prosecutor's own villa. Their destination was a
rustic restaurant, ancient but easily accessible for Rhyme's chair. The
owner and his wife, both stocky forty-somethings, both immensely cheerful, were honored to have esteemed American guests of this sort. That

the fame was B list—not movie stars, not sports figures—did little to dim their excitement.

The husband shyly brought out an Italian-language edition of a book about Rhyme—detailing his hunt for a killer known as the Bone Collector.

That overblown thing?

"Rhyme," Sachs admonished in his ear, noting his expression.

"I'd be delighted," he said enthusiastically and did the autograph thing; his surgically enabled hand actually produced a better signature than his natural fingers had, before his accident.

Spiro, Sachs and Rhyme sat at a table before a massive stone fireplace—unlit at the moment—while the owners took Thom, the only cook among them, on a tour of the kitchen, which was not accessible.

A server, a lively young woman with flowing jet-black hair, greeted them. Spiro ordered wine: a full-bodied red, Taurasi, which he and Rhyme had. Sachs asked for a white and was given a Greco di Tufo.

When the glasses came, Spiro offered a toast, saying in a rather ominous tone, "To truth. And rooting it out."

They sipped the wine. Rhyme was impressed and would tell Thom to remember the name of the red.

Spiro lit his cheroot—a violation of the law but then again he *was* Dante Spiro. "Now, let me explain what I have planned for our meeting this evening. We will conduct our business regarding the extradition and, if we are still speaking to one another, then dine. My wife will be joining us soon. And another guest too. The menu I think you will enjoy. This restaurant is unique. They raise or grow everything here, except for the fish—though the owner's sons do catch it themselves. The place is completely self-sufficient. Even these wines come from their own vineyards. We will start with some salami and prosciutto. Our next course will be paccheri pasta. Made from durum flour. Hard flour. It is the best."

"Like the Campania mozzarella is the best," Sachs said, with a smile that was both wry and sincere.

"*Exactly* like the cheese, Detective. The best in Italy. Now, accenting the pasta, the sauce will be *ragù*, of course. And then branzino fish, grilled with oil and rosemary and lemon only, and to accompany: zucchini, fried, and served with vinegar and mint. Finally, *una insalata* of incappucciata, a local lettuce that you will find heavenly. *Dolce* will be, as it must, sfogliatelle, the shell-shaped pastry that Naples gave to the world."

"Not for me," Rhyme said. "But perhaps grappa."

"Not perhaps. *Definitely.* And they have a fine selection here. We can try distillato too. Distilled wine. They have here my favorite, Capovilla. It is from Veneto, in the north. It is superb. But that will be for after the meal."

The server refilled the wineglasses, as Spiro directed.

Sachs eyed the prosecutor warily.

He laughed. "No, I'm not trying to 'liquor you down.'"

"'Up,'" she corrected.

Spiro said, "I must change that in my Western novel." He actually made a note, using his phone. He set it down and placed his hands flat on the table. "Now, obviously, we are opponents once again."

Rhyme said, "When it comes to negotiation about legal issues, I have no say in the matter. I'm a civilian. A consultant. My Sachs here is an officer of the law. She's the one who pitches the case to the powers that be in New York. And of course, there will be FBI agents involved, from the field office in Rome. U.S. attorneys too, in the United States."

"Ah, a truly formidable army of legal minds I am up against, it seems. But let me state to you my position." His narrow, dark eyes aimed their way.

Rhyme glanced at Sachs, who nodded, and he said, "You win."

Spiro blinked. One of the few times since they'd met that he seemed surprised.

"*Our* position is we're going to recommend against extraditing Mike Hill back to the United States."

Sachs shrugged. "He's all yours."

Spiro drew on his cheroot, blew smoke ceilingward. He said nothing, his face revealed nothing.

Rhyme said, "Hill is technically in violation of U.S. laws, sure. But the kidnap victims weren't U.S. citizens. And, yes, he scammed a U.S.

intelligence agency but the AIS doesn't exist, remember? Everything Charlotte McKenzie said was hypothetical. We wouldn't get very far with *that* case."

Sachs then said, "We can't guarantee that someone in our Justice Department, back in the States, won't want to pursue extradition. But my recommendation's going to be against that."

Spiro said, "And I suspect you carry some weight back there, Detective Sachs."

Yep, she did.

"*Allora.* Thank you, Captain, Detective. This man, Hill, I despise what he did. I want justice served." He smiled. "Such a cliché, no?"

"Perhaps. But some clichés are like comfortable, well-worn shoes or sweaters. They serve a needed purpose." Rhyme lifted his wineglass toward the man. Then his face grew somber. "But, Dante, you'll have a difficult time with the case. If you charge Hill and Gianni—Procopio—with the whole scheme, you'll have no witnesses: The refugees' memories are shot. And Charlotte and Stefan are out of the country. I'd recommend you simplify the case. You could—"

"Charge them only with illegal importation of explosives," Spiro interrupted.

"Exactly."

"Yes, I have been thinking this is what we must do. The Albanian airport worker will give evidence. We have the C4. Fatima Jabril can testify to that aspect of the plot. Hill and his accomplice will get a suitable sentence." A tip of his wineglass. "A sufficient justice. Sometimes that is the best we can do. And sometimes it is enough."

This plan would also align with the Composer's fate. News stories, based on accounts by a "reliable but anonymous" source (surely Charlotte McKenzie or one of her associates at AIS) were leaked that the serial killer had fled Italy for parts unknown. The kidnapper, this individual stated, had been stymied by the Italian police and knew he was days away from being captured. Among the possible destinations were London, Spain, Brazil or, heading home, America.

Thom returned to the dining room, bearing a bag. "Pasta, cheese, spices. The chef insisted." He took his place at the table and asked for, and received, a glass of the white wine. At Rhyme's request he took pictures of the labels.

A figure appeared in the doorway of the restaurant. And Rhyme was surprised to see Ercole Benelli approach.

The young officer, in his gray Forestry Corps uniform, had a matching expression.

Greetings all around.

"Ah, Hercules," Spiro said, offering the English pronunciation. "The man of the twelve labors."

"Sir."

The prosecutor gestured toward the table and caught the waitress's eyes.

Ercole sat and took a glass of red wine. "Once again, Prosecutor Spiro, I must apologize for my error the other day. I know there were... *conseguenze.*"

"Consequences. Oh, yes. Without the evidence there can be no case against the American spy and her psychotic musician. But I did not ask you here to berate you. I would not hesitate to do that, as you know, but not under these circumstances. Now, let me explain why you are here. I will say this up front, bluntly, for if you are going to make your way in the world of law enforcement, you cannot shy, like a colt, from the truth— unpainted?" He looked at Rhyme and Sachs.

She said, "Unvarnished."

"*Sì.* You cannot shy from the unvarnished truth. And that truth is this: You have done nothing wrong. Even if the evidence against Stefan Merck and Charlotte McKenzie had been properly logged in, it would still have gone missing."

"*No! Procuratore, è vero?*"

"Yes, sadly it is quite true."

"But how?"

"I am sorry to have to tell you, and our guests here, that it was Inspector Massimo Rossi who arranged for the disappearance and destruction of the evidence."

The young officer's face was the epitome of shock. "*Che cosa?* No. That cannot be."

Rhyme and Sachs shared a surprised look.

"Yes, it is the case. He—"

"But he was managing the case, he is a senior member—"

"Forestry Officer." Spiro lowered his head toward the young officer. "*Mi perdoni!* Forgive me." He fell silent.

"You have learned quite a bit about the nature of police investigation in the past few days." Spiro leaned back. "Forensics, tactical operations, body language, interrogation..."

A wry expression on his face, Ercole glanced toward Sachs and whispered, "High-speed pursuit." Then back to Spiro, who fixed him with a glare for interrupting again. He repeated, "*Mi perdoni*. Please continue, sir."

"But I think you have yet to master one other important, no, vital aspect of our profession. And that is the politics within law enforcement. Is this not true, Captain Rhyme?"

"As certain as fingerprints are unique."

Spiro said, "We have more police officers per capita than any other country in the European Union. More police *forces* too. So, logically, we have more law enforcement individuals to...what is the word in English, 'game' the system."

Rhyme said, "'Game' is a noun. I don't accept it as a verb. But I will concede that many people use it. The Jargonites, I call them."

Spiro chuckled. "*Allora*, but you understand my meaning. And do you, as well, Ercole?"

"I believe I do, sir."

"Our colleague Signor Rossi has gamed the system. Though he is admittedly a most talented investigator and civil servant, he is somewhat more. He is active politically."

"How do you mean, sir?"

"It is not known to the public but he's a member of the NN."

Rhyme recalled: the Nuovo Nazionalismo. The right-wing anti-immigrant party. The one guilty of violence against refugees...and originally suspected by the team of setting up the fake terror attacks.

"He is allied with a senior government official in Campania, Andrea Marcos, who also is a member of NN. Rossi uses his role as a police inspector to give himself credibility but in fact when the possibility arises he tries to further the goals of his brethren. Goals that I myself find unfortunate. No, *reprehensible*. Yes, the refugees are a burden. And some are risks, and we must be vigilant. But Italy is a country of so many different peoples: Etruscans and Germans and Albanians and Silesians and Greeks and Ottomans and North Africans and Slavs and Tyroleans. Why, we even have French here! There are northern Italians and southern and Sicilians and Sardinians. The United States is perhaps the greatest melting pan on earth but we are a mixed country, as well. We are also a nation with a heart, moved by the plight of families risking death to escape the madness of failed states.

"Inspector Rossi believes—indeed believed from the moment he realized that this serial kidnapper might be targeting refugees—that the perpetrator was doing the right thing. Oh, Massimo did his job but in his heart he wished asylum-seekers to be punished. If the killer succeeded, word might get back that Italy was as dangerous as Libya and they might think twice about coming to our shores."

"The Burial Hour." Sachs said these words.

They looked her way, and she explained to them about a speech in Parliament, one that Rania Tasso, of the Capodichino refugee camp, had mentioned. An Italian politician had coined the phrase to refer to the belief that citizens were being suffocated by the waves of immigrants.

Spiro said, "Yes, I have heard that. The Burial Hour. Massimo Rossi felt that way, apparently."

Ercole said to Spiro, "Inspector Rossi fought to take over the Ali Maziq case. At the bus stop, he tricked the Carabinieri so that he could retain control of the investigation and interfere with it. And he might have, sir, had you not been the prosecutor."

Spiro tilted his head, acknowledging the comment. Then added, "And had our American friends not come here to assist." The prosecutor took a sip of wine and savored it. "Now, Ercole, I must deliver news more difficult than this. And that news is that Massimo Rossi invited you onto the case for the sole purpose of you being a scapegoat."

"*L'ha fatto?*"

"Yes. He did. He wanted ways to limit or even dismiss the case, but he couldn't do it himself. Nor did he want his protégé, that young officer . . . What is his name?"

"Silvio De Carlo."

"Yes. He couldn't have his protégé do so either. Silvio is destined for high places in the Police of State. Massimo wanted you, a Forestry officer, to take the blame for the case's failure. So he assigned you to log the evidence in, arranged to have it stolen and pointed his finger at you."

Ercole took a large sip of wine. "And now my name is on record as having ruined a major investigation. My chances of moving into regular policing are gone. Maybe even my career at the Forestry Corps is endangered."

"Ah, Ercole. Let us pause a minute here, may we? Think. Rossi has blamed you for a mistake, not a crime. Yet he himself has committed a crime by arranging for the disappearance of physical evidence. The last thing he wants is any further examination of the matter."

"Yes, that makes sense."

"So, true, within the Police of State, there will be no career opportunities for you."

Ercole finished his wine and set the glass down. "Thank you, sir. It's kind of you to tell me that I'm not, in fact, responsible for the destruction of the case. And to have the courage to break the news to me about the consequences to my career." He sighed. "So, *buona notte*. I will get home to my pigeons now." He extended his hand.

Spiro ignored it. He muttered, "Pigeons? Are you making a joke?"

"No, sir. I am sorry. I—"

"And did I say that our conversation is over?"

"I . . . No. I'm . . ." The stammering young man dropped to his seat again.

"Now perhaps you will be silent and let me finish telling you why I have summoned you here. In addition to dining with our American friends, of course."

"Oh, I didn't realize I was invited to dine."

Spiro snapped, "Why would I ask you to a restaurant, one of the best in Campania, by the way, if not to have you join us?"

"Of course. Very kind of you, sir."

"*Allora*. My comment is this: I have made some inquiries. It is largely unprecedented for a Forestry Corps officer, especially one as old as you, to transfer directly into the Carabinieri training program. But, of course, interoffice politics can have a positive side as well as a negative. I have called in favors and arranged for you to be accepted into the service and will begin military and police training in one month."

"Carabinieri?" Ercole whispered.

"As I have just said. And as you have just heard. I was told that it has been a goal of yours for some time to join them."

The young man was breathless. "*Mamma mia! Procuratore* Spiro, I don't know what to say. *Grazie tante!*" He took the prosecutor's hand in both of his and Rhyme thought for a moment he was going to kiss the man's fingers.

"Enough!" Then Spiro added, "One month should give you time to finish up any assignments that are pending at Forestry. I understand from speaking to your superior officer that your arrest of a particularly troublesome truffle counterfeiter was interrupted by the arrival of *Il Compositore*. I assume you wish to close that case."

"I do indeed." Ercole's eyes narrowed.

"One thing more I should add. The regulations of the Carabinieri have changed. You may know that in the past, officers were required to be assigned posts far from home. This was so that they might remain undistracted and do their job most efficiently. That is no longer the case. Accordingly, Beatrice Renza, of the Scientific Police, will not have to worry that her new boyfriend will be assigned some distance from Campania. You can be posted here."

"*Beatrice?* Oh, *Procuratore*, no, I...That is to say, yes, we had an *aperitivo* the other night at Castello's Lounge. I walked her to her flat." A huge blush. "Yes, perhaps I stayed the night. And she will be attending my pigeon race tomorrow. But I do not know that there can be any future between us. She is an exceedingly difficult woman, even if she exhibits quite some intelligence and has a peculiar charm."

His rambling—and red face—amused them all.

"Not Daniela?" Sachs asked. "I thought you were attracted to her."

"Daniela? Well, her beauty is quite clear. And she is very keen in her police skills. But, how can I say?" He looked to Sachs. "You, as a lover of automobiles, will understand: The gears do not engage between us. Am I making sense?"

"Perfectly," Sachs replied.

So, Rhyme had been wrong. It had been Beatrice who'd lit the fire in Ercole's heart, challenging though she was. Well, Lincoln Rhyme himself would take challenge over slipped gears any day, however beautiful the automobile.

The restaurant door opened and a tall woman—with a fashion model's figure and poise—stepped into the room, smiling to the table. She wore a dark-blue suit and carried an attaché case. Her dark hair was pulled back into a buoyant ponytail. Spiro rose. "Ah! *Ecco mia moglie*—my wife, Cecilia."

The woman sat and Spiro signaled to the waitress for the meal to begin.

VIII

THE DRAGONFLY AND THE GARGOYLE

CHAPTER 72

M ay have a problem."

Thom was speaking over his shoulder to Rhyme and Sachs. He was peering through the front window of the accessible van as it approached the security entrance to the private aircraft portion of Naples airport.

Rhyme cricked his neck to the left—the wheelchair was fixed perpendicular to the direction of traffic—and noted the black SUV, pulling forward and blocking their way.

Behind it were uniformed guards—Italian officers—standing at lackadaisical attention at the gate but they had little interest in either vehicle. This was not their business.

Sachs sighed. "Who? Massimo Rossi?"

"On what theory?"

Thom offered a potential answer. "He and Mike Hill share a certain bigoted philosophy? Brothers in arms?"

Hm. A reasonable theory.

Sachs nodded. "Possible, sure. Though I think Dante's right and Rossi wants as little publicity as possible about the whole thing now. Besides, I wonder if vans like that are in the Police of State budget."

They certainly weren't in the NYPD's.

But as the ominous vehicle bounced forward over the uneven asphalt, like a boat in chop, closing the distance, Rhyme could see the U.S. diplo license tag.

So the odds of ending up in an Italian jail were minimized.

A U.S. penitentiary?

Ahead of them, on the other side of the chain link, was their borrowed jet, waiting to hustle the three of them away. The aircraft, with stairs extended, was nearby, in terms of distance, and the phrase "making a run for it" tipped into Rhyme's mind. Though the wheelchair made that cliché technically impossible, and in any case it was an unlikely solution to the problem of avoiding arrest by the U.S. authorities.

No, there was nothing to do but stop. And Rhyme told Thom to do so.

The aide eased to a halt, the brakes giving a triplet squeak.

After thirty seconds the SUV passenger door opened and Rhyme was surprised to see who climbed out. The diminutive man, face so very pale, sweat stains visible on his shirt under the gray suit, smiled amiably and held up a wait-a-minute finger; he was on his mobile. Rhyme looked to Sachs. She too was frowning. Then she recalled, "Daryl Mulbry. From the consulate."

"Ah. Right." The community and public relations liaison.

"The door," Rhyme said.

Thom hit a button. With another squeak, not unlike that of the brakes, the door beside which Rhyme sat slid open.

"The ramp?" Thom asked.

"No. I'm staying put. *He* can come to us."

Mulbry disconnected the call and put his phone away. He walked to the van. Without waiting for an invitation he pulled himself up inside and sat directly in front of Rhyme.

"Hey there," he said to them all, an amiable voice, the dusting of Southern accent upon both words, the second of which was pulled into two syllables.

Sachs asked, "Busy day for public relations?"

Mulbry smiled. "After that news story that the Composer vanished from the country, journalists have been pelting us with requests. Positively *pelting*."

Rhyme said, "You wrote that story. You're one of Charlotte McKenzie's associates."

"Her boss, actually. I'm director of Alternative Intelligence Service."

Ah, the New York actor. Yes, Rhyme could see him getting great notices for a character part. Probably stealing the show.

Rhyme asked, "Is anybody in your business who they seem to be?"

Mulbry laughed once more and wiped sweat.

"One question?" Rhyme asked.

"Only one?"

"For the moment. Ibrahim."

Mulbry grimaced. "Ah, yes. Ibrahim. Aka Hassan, our 'trusted' asset in Tripoli. Ibrahim's real name is Abdel Rahman Sakizli. Freelancer. Mercenary. He'll run ops for ISIS, he'll run ops for the Lord's Resistance Army, he'll run ops for the Mossad. He's loyal to whoever pays him the most. Sadly, Hill had more money than we did, so Ibrahim chose to cheat on us." Mulbry clicked his tongue.

"Where is he?"

A frown, but an exaggerated frown. "Good question. He seems to have disappeared."

Rhyme chided, "And you, the kinder, gentler face of national security."

"'T'wasn't us. Last we heard he was in the company of a couple of women who were charming and beautiful and, coincidentally, rumored to be members of the Italian external security agency. Now, Captain Rhyme—"

"Lincoln really is fine. If you're going to detain us at least use my first name."

"Detain?" He seemed genuinely confused. "Why would we detain you?"

"Because we handed Mike Hill over to Dante Spiro for trial here without a fight."

"Oh, *that*. We'll let him float in the soup here for five to ten years. You knew we couldn't bring a case on the terrorism charges. Since we don't exist. Dante'll get justice enough for both countries. Damn smart, charging Hill for the explosives only. You have a hand in that?"

Rhyme's expression: Don't know what you mean.

Mulbry continued, "As for his buddy, the senator from Texas?"

Sachs asked, "You're aware of him?"

Mulbry settled for a sardonic smile. "Some folks in Washington'll take *him* out to the woodshed on the QT. Y'all might appreciate this: I had a thought last night: Compared with Mike Hill, Stefan Merck was the saner of the two. More interesting too. I'll tell you, I'd have a beer with *that* fellow. Now, I'm sure you're wondering, what exactly am I doing here?"

The interior of the van *was* hot and getting hotter, with the full-on sun taxing the lethargic AC. Mulbry dried his brow yet again. "Want to hear a story? You know that years ago CIA technical services tried to build a fake dragonfly? It's in the museum at Langley. It's quite something. A work of art. Equipped with an early miniature video camera, an audio system, a flight mechanism that was revolutionary for the time. And guess what? It didn't work worth squat. The least headwind would send it all over the landscape. But a few years later, the inspiration behind those dragonflies gave us drones. S'all about refinement. Story of life.

"Now, you could say that the AIS is an attempt to build a dragonfly. The Composer project would have worked pretty well. Except for one thing."

"A headwind."

"Exactly! And that'd be you and Detective Sachs. I'll say—this isn't flattery—not many people could have figured out the story we'd put together, the musical kidnapper and all."

Not *many*? Rhyme thought.

"When you raided Charlotte's home, you explained how you figured it all out." A big grin. "We were listening, sure."

Rhyme tipped his head.

"Impressive, Lincoln, Amelia. And hearing you—how you figured out the plan—I got myself an idea."

"Your dragonfly molting into a drone."

"I like that. So. In the world of intelligence gathering, there's HUMINT—that's info from people, assets on the ground. Then there're satellites, computer hacking, wiretapping and video surveillance. That's signals and electronic intelligence. SIGINT, ELINT. But until you took down our dragonfly, Lincoln, it never occurred to me how much intelligence we might learn from . . . evidence. Forensic evidence."

"Really?"

"Oh, we have teams we use, or borrow the Bureau's or army's or somebody's. But it's usually after the fact, when an op goes bad. Get fingerprints or blast signatures or handwriting. We don't use forensic investigation..."

Please don't say proactively.

"...proactively. The way *you* analyze evidence, it's like it talks to you."

Sachs laughed, a clear, ringing sound. "Rhyme, I think he wants to hire us."

Mulbry's pale face betrayed that this was exactly what he was suggesting. "Remember, we're 'Alternative' intelligence gathering. What's more alternative than a forensic team running an espionage op? You consult for the NYPD. Why not for us? You've broken the international barrier. Here you are—*in Italia*! We have private jets too. They're government, so no liquor cabinets. But you can BYOB. Not against the rules. Or not against any rules anyone cares about."

Mulbry's eyes actually shone. "And it occurred to me: What a great cover you'd have! A fabled forensic scientist and his associate. A professor, no less. Yeah, I'll admit I looked you up, Lincoln. Imagine how it would work: You're in Europe assisting local officers in an intractable crime, a serial killer, a cult leader, a master money launderer. Or you're in Singapore to lecture at the criminal justice institute on the latest developments in crime scene techniques. And, in your spare time, you look into whether Natasha Ivanovich has been listening in on conversations she shouldn't, naughty girl. Or Park Jung went shopping for a teeny piece of nuclear trigger he's not supposed to have."

Mulbry eased a glance toward Sachs. "There'd be the issue of your being on the payroll of the NYPD. But that's not insurmountable. They have liaison offices overseas, you know. Or maybe a leave of absence. It's all negotiable."

If Rhyme's torso had been sensate, he suspected he would have been feeling a stirring. Certainly, he was aware that his pulse had increased; this he knew from the rhythm in his temples. Not patriotism, which was a subcategory of sentimentality, an emotion he bluntly rejected. No, what stirred him was the possibility of a whole new set of challenges.

A thought occurred. He said, "EVIDINT."

"Evidence intelligence." Mulbry's lower lip extended and he nodded. "Nice."

"Don't get your hopes up, though," Rhyme muttered. "We're not closing the deal yet."

A nod from Mulbry. "Sure, sure. But say what, just for the fun of it, let me run this by you. Of course, just as an example." The words seemed spontaneous but Rhyme guessed the dangle had been prepared ahead of time, tied like a fly with painstaking care by a fisherman intent on catching a particularly elusive and astute bass.

"Go ahead."

"We have intel that someone connected with the World Criminal Court in The Hague has been targeted for assassination. Not immediately but in the next month. There's a Prague connection. Unfortunately, at this point we have mostly SIGINT—wiretaps and emails, all of which is as vague as the narrator in a Viagra ad. Our people have only one bit of physical evidence related to the plot."

Rhyme lifted an eyebrow.

"A gargoyle's head."

"Gargoyle."

"Apparently a souvenir from, well, wherever one buys gargoyle head souvenirs. It's gray. Plastic. Gargoyley."

"And this is evidence why?" Sachs asked.

"We still use dead drops. A public location where one asset leaves a message for another, usually—"

Sachs said, "I've seen the *Bourne* movies."

"I haven't," Rhyme said. "But I get the idea."

"We received intel that the bad guys had a dead drop in the square by the astronomical clock in Prague, the famous one. We started surveillance."

"'Round the clock?" Sachs asked, a faint smile. Rhyme nodded to acknowledge the pun.

Smiling too, Mulbry said, "That one *did* make the rounds. Anyway, after two days, a man in hat and sunglasses walked past the location and left the gargoyle on a windowsill, the dead drop. It meant something—a go-ahead, we assume. We're still trying to find out more."

"Anyone come by and do something with the gargoyle?"

"Some kids, teen kids, saw it and stole it. But we moved in and got it from them." Mulbry shrugged. "We could show it to you if you like. Maybe you could find something."

"When was this?"

"About a week ago."

Rhyme scoffed, "Too late, too late. All the important evidence is long gone."

"Only the asset and the boy who stole it touched the thing. We couldn't find any note or code inside. The presence of the gargoyle was a message in itself. Like a go-ahead for a prearranged meeting. So, we thought you could take a look at it and—"

"No point."

"It's preserved in plastic. Our people wore gloves. And the dead drop— the windowsill—hasn't been touched. We've been monitoring it."

"The dead drop's not a scene. That's a non-scene. There's another one, one that *would* have been important if you'd moved quickly."

"You mean where he bought the gargoyle?"

"Of course not," Rhyme muttered. "And he didn't buy it. He stole it. Lifted it from a stand nowhere near any CCTV, in gloved fingers. So there'd be minimal transfer of trace. No, the important scene is the one where the other side was sitting with their beer or coffee."

Mulbry's face stilled. "Could you elaborate?"

"If I were a spy putting together an operation in a city like Prague, *my* first job would be to identify the foxes. That is, your people."

"It was another outfit actually. We were working with them."

"Fine. Whoever. Now, the gargoyle served no purpose other than to expose your surveillance team."

Mulbry tilted his head, brow furrowed.

Rhyme continued, "A gargoyle is obvious, it's sure to attract attention. So that your team stayed in place filming anyone who walked by and paid attention to it. The minute those kids copped it, your team was after them. As soon as your people stood up, the bad guys saw and got their IDs, probably followed them. Bugged their homes, scanned their phones. Hm, a plastic toy worth a euro or whatever the denomination is in the Czech Republic took down an entire cell of yours. The table and chairs where the enemy was sitting waiting for you to reveal yourselves would've told us legions. Told *you* legions. But of course furniture's been cleaned, the napkins washed, the bill tossed out, the money in the bank, the cobblestones scrubbed—I'm assuming that's the terrain there—and the CCTV footage overwritten."

Mulbry was completely still for a moment. He whispered, "Goddamn."

Sachs said, "You better tell the team they've been compromised."

Another glance between Rhyme and Sachs. He said to the agent, "We'll talk about your offer. And be in touch."

"I hope you will." Mulbry shook their hands, said goodbye to Thom and climbed from the van, pulling out his phone.

Thom put the gearshift into drive and eased forward. They stopped at the Passport Control and Customs kiosk and handed over documents, which were returned. The van continued on.

Rhyme gave a laugh. "The Czech Republic."

Thom said. "I've been to Prague a couple of times. I'm partial to the česnečka. Garlic soup. Oh, and the fruit dumplings. The best."

"What's the local liquor like?" Rhyme asked.

"Slivovitz. Really potent. At least a hundred proof—fifty percent alcohol."

"You don't say?" Rhyme was intrigued.

They pulled up to the aircraft and Thom began the complicated procedure of lowering the ramp. Sachs climbed out, slung her computer bag over her shoulder. "Spies, Rhyme? Seriously?"

"Stranger things have happened."

His eyes strayed to the copilot, who was completing the pre-flight walk-around.

Everything on the aircraft seemed properly attached and functioning.

The strapping young man—in a suit, white shirt and tie—approached his passengers now. "We're all set, sir. Flight time should be about an hour and a half."

Sachs was frowning. "To New York?"

The copilot's brows furrowed. He glanced toward Rhyme, who said,

"We're not going back to the U.S. just yet. We're meeting some friends in Milan."

"Friends?" She glanced at Thom, who was looking over the airplane as if he himself were about to conduct a second preflight check. And avoiding eye contact. He was, however, smiling.

"Lon Sellitto. Oh, and Ron Pulaski." The young NYPD officer they worked with regularly.

"Rhyme?" Sachs asked slowly. "What's in Milan?"

He frowned and looked at Thom. "What is it again?"

"A *Dichiarazione Giurata*."

"A particularly delicious dinner entrée?"

"Ha. No, it's an affidavit we need to swear to before the consulate general there."

"And why?"

"Obviously. Because we can't get married without it. Ercole and Thom arranged the whole thing. Then we drive to Lake Como. The mayor there'll perform the ceremony. We need to rent the marriage hall—part of the arrangement. It's bigger than we need, I imagine, but that's the way it works. Lon and Ron'll be the witnesses."

"A honeymoon on Lake Como, Rhyme," Sachs said, smiling.

Rhyme tossed a look Thom's way. "He was pretty insistent."

She asked, "And what about Greenland?"

"Maybe our first anniversary," Rhyme said and drove his chair toward the ramp that would take him up to the cabin of the sleek, idling jet.

VOWS

The village of Bellagio, jutting into Italy's Lake Como, has a rich history.

An ambitious Roman co-consul, name of Julius Caesar, sent thousands of colonists here from the south, including many Sicilian Greeks, changing forever the nomenclature and the nature of this far northern region of the country.

Virgil, of *Aeneid* fame, the bane of many a fourth-year Latin student, lived and wrote here, as did Pliny the Younger.

In the Imperial days, the region was never far from war—soldiers defending against barbarians and staging for incursions into Germany. Thousands of legionnaires marched through Bellagio in AD 9, intoxicated by the grandeur and invincibility of the Roman Empire, only to have that attitude readjusted downward, fast and brutally, at the Battle of the Teutoburg Forest.

Bellagio may have a slightly less prominent role in world affairs nowadays, but in one area it excels: it is arguably the best spot in Europe to get married.

As Lincoln Rhyme and Amelia Sachs can confirm.

They are presently sitting and standing, respectively, before the mayor of Bellagio himself, in the commune's ornate town hall, adorned with vases overflowing with blue gentians, from the surrounding hills, and white roses.

Although the couple doesn't generally spend much time on fashion choices, today is different. Sachs is in a floor-length, off-the shoulder dark blue number, trim fitting, with lace at shoulders and hem. And for Rhyme, a dark-gray suit, white shirt and a black silk tie, emblazoned with what appears to be an abstract design but that is, in fact, a gas chromatograph chart of firearm residue—a custom-made present from the students in his criminalistics class.

Behind them are the guests: Thom Reston, of course, Rhyme's aide; Lon Sellitto—Rhyme's partner at the NYPD years ago—and his girl-friend, Rachel; Ron Pulaski, a young patrol officer, who works with Rhyme and Sachs regularly (and who long ago outgrew the status, but not the nickname, Rookie); Sachs's mother, Rose; Mel Cooper—Rhyme's main lab man—and his stunning Scandinavian girlfriend. The final member of the party is Pam Willoughby—the young woman whom Sachs rescued from a clutch of domestic terrorists (headed by the girl's mother, no less), and who is now Sachs's unofficial younger sister.

The mayor, charming and cultured, with a sparkle in his eye, is addressing those assembled, his comments translated by a lean, handsome man of around forty, with a shaved head and a stylish hoop in one ear. The mayor is explaining that Rhyme and Sachs have completed all the proper steps to be married in Italy, adding with some solemnity that he has waived the civil bann requirement—a two-week posting on a wall in the town hall of the intent to marry—because the bride and groom are American citizens. (Rhyme wondered about the requirement. So that former lovers might have a chance to make a better offer? To arrange a duel? A recurrent false-identity issue? These seemed so much more interesting than a concern about an existing impediment to the marriage.)

The mayor now proceeds with the civil ceremony, his rich baritone echoing through the ancient hall.

Rhyme and Sachs considered writing their own vows. He was intrigued with the idea of working the Miranda rights into his—but, clever though this was in theory, it didn't seem appropriate to include "the right to remain silent" and "having an attorney present" in a pledge meant to forge a lasting union.

Besides, he and Sachs are believers, both professionally and personally, in the Occam's-razor principle that simpler is best.

So, in response to the mayor's queries, they settle on the ever popular, and effective, "I do."

The gathering after the ceremony was in the stately Villa Francesco, on the shores of the lake.

Dinner was on a heated balcony—the month was September and in this northern clime, with the ragged spine of mountains dominating the view, the pine-scented air was damp and chilly. The main dishes were fish from the expansive lake and a local specialty—*toc*, a heart-stoppingly rich polenta, served tableside in the cauldron in which it had been made. Rhyme was impressed with the *toc* tradition of using the empty pan to make a spiced wine, *ragell*, after dining. Though the beverage is cooked until the alcohol evaporates, Rhyme had found a workaround: a jolt of grappa added before imbibing.

After the meal, everyone moved to a small banquet room off the balcony, where the air was filled with a tepid cyclone of a mixtape that Thom had assembled. Drinks flowed and the guests, encouraged by Rose Sachs and her daughter, gravitated toward the tiny dance floor.

Rhyme was amused at the spectacle. Sellitto was taking it slow after his recent run-in with a killer. Sachs had enthusiasm but was equally cautious—she'd undergone arthritis surgery not long ago. Rachel had some good moves and she'd orbit past Sellitto occasionally to share some choreography with Pam. But the stars of the dance floor were Cooper and his tall, blond girlfriend, who were competitive ballroom dancers. They weren't showy—hard to foxtrot to Daft Punk (whoever they were, Rhyme had commented)—but it was enjoyable to watch the experts, as in any field.

Rhyme, of course, sat the numbers out.

Which he would've done anyway, even if he'd been mobile.

The evening wore down, and gradually the yellow, white and blue lights reflecting on the glossy surface of Lake Como went silently away.

Rhyme had wanted no toasts, but he smiled when, just before the evening concluded, Rose Sachs stepped to the floor, took a glass of champagne and said to the silent gathering, "I'd like to say a few words. And I mean that literally. Amelia, Lincoln: it's about time."

They raised glasses and she sat once more.

Occam's razor, Rhyme thought, and winked at her.

Theirs was a reverse honeymoon, in a way.

Rhyme's mobility issues made travel difficult, so for the next few days, he and Sachs would stay in Bellagio, while the wedding party would depart temporarily—on a side trip to Courmayeur, a charming ski and resort area in the shadows of Monte Bianco. Everyone except Thom, of course. Ever-present Thom.

So, the next morning, Sachs went downstairs to guide everyone to the Sprinter van waiting at the hotel's arched entryway, while Rhyme stayed in the room. He glanced at the regal mountains, the jewel of the shoreline, the miles of rich blue water.

And turned immediately back to his computer, on which sat the article he was writing for the *Journal of Applied Forensic Science*.

Much better than scenery.

Twenty minutes later he looked up and noted two things: one, it was still morning and too early for a grappa (an opinion held by Thom, the keeper of the bottle, not Rhyme himself, of course). And, two, Sachs had not yet returned. He was merely curious, hardly concerned. A woman who was a veteran NYPD detective and who never went anywhere without a switchblade knife in her hip pocket was rarely at risk.

And this was, after all, Bellagio.

He returned to the article, growing angry with himself because he had accidentally dictated a *which* without the requisite nonrestrictive comma to introduce it.

Ten minutes later Sachs returned. Glancing her way, Rhyme sensed something was on her mind.

Nothing troubling, he noted. In fact, her eye showed a glint. She poured coffee for them both and, with a glance toward where Thom sat at the end of the balcony, reading, she added a dollop of brandy to his.

Hm. Wonder what she wants.

She handed over the coffee and sat next to him. She asked, "You ever thought about doing some private-eye work, Rhyme?"

"Why?"

But she wasn't ready to answer yet.

"Sam Spade, Philip Marlowe."

"Who?"

"Hercule Poirot."

"Oh, I know him. I'm a consultant. Same thing, isn't it?"

"You consult for the police. I mean working, well, *private*. For some joe. Some dame."

After a moment Rhyme asked, "I'll have to look it up."

"Poirot?"

"No. If the 'eye' in private eye refers to E-Y-E, as in spying. Or upper-case 'I,' as in investigator. Why don't you just get to it, Sachs?"

"Okay. I saw everybody off and was coming back to the room but a woman stopped me in the lobby. You might've seen her. She and her husband are staying here. Pretty. Short blond hair, medium height, mid-thirties. American."

One of dozens. The villa was huge. "So, she stopped you."

"She saw us at the wedding yesterday and asked about us. Apparently somebody told her who you are. And she wondered if we could help her."

"Something private-eye-ish?"

"Exactly."

"And since here you are, sharing the story, it suggests you were intrigued."

Sachs said, "I know it's our honeymoon. But you've seen one sight, you seen 'em all, right?"

He nodded outside, with a bored glance toward what anyone else would consider the most beautiful view in all of Italy. His way of saying, I'm with you, Sachs. "Well, what's our next step?"

There was a knock on the door.

"Looks like she's here."

"I'm worried about my husband."

Claire Dunning was sitting on the balcony. She, too, had no particular interest in the view.

Sachs had heard the story and now she said, "Why don't you give Lincoln the background?"

The slim, athletic-looking woman explained that her husband worked for JDZ-Systems, a medical-equipment company, based in Santa Clara, California. Richard, Claire and three employees of JDZ-Sys had come here to supervise the installation of the company's flagship product at a university hospital in Como, about forty minutes away. Claire ran a home decor website and could work anywhere, so she frequently came on business trips with Richard and his assistant, who'd become a good friend. The other company employees were staying at modest hotels closer to the hospital, but since Richard and Claire's anniversary was in a few days, he'd booked a suite here for the two weeks they'd be in Italy.

"But I was telling your wife, Richard's been acting odd lately. Normally, he's so easy-going and open. But..." Her face grew dark and her throat caught. "The other day he said he was going to meet Charlie, the European sales director, and he was away for a couple hours. But I found out later Charlie was in Rome. Richard never told me they didn't get together. And he's gone away a couple of other times, claiming he went to the hospital in Como, but I called and he wasn't there.

"Then he hid getting a text. We were on the couch in the bar and I felt this vibration, no sound. It was his phone. He didn't look at it but a minute later he got up and said he was going to the restroom. Only—have you seen the main hallway?"

Rhyme had. "Mirrors."

"That's right. He didn't know I could see him. He didn't go to the bathroom. He went into the hall and read and sent a text. Then he just came back to the bar and seemed distracted after that."

Claire leaned forward. "Now, obviously a man doesn't bring his wife to Lake Como for their anniversary to cheat on her. I'm worried about something else. JDZ's system is one of the hottest products in medicine now. Basically, it runs most major diagnostic tests in half to a tenth the time most labs do now. Sometimes even less than that. Seconds."

She dug into her purse and pulled out a company brochure. On the cover was depicted a properly demographic mix of medicos—white, black, Asian—contentedly perusing the display on a complicated brushed-steel machine. With his working right hand, Rhyme flipped to a page and glanced at some of the tests the device was capable of.

— Complete blood count (CBC)	— Tests of hypercoagulability
— Reticulocyte count	— Protein C
— Peripheral blood smear	— Protein S
— Erythrocyte sedimentation rate	— Activated protein C resistance
— Motulsky	— Prothrombin mutation
— Fibrin degradation products	— Antithrombin III level
— Levels of clotting proteins	— Factor Xa
— Platelet function	— Circulating anticoagulants
— Bleeding time	— Hemoglobin electrophoresis
— Platelet aggregation	— Heinz bodies

There were dozens more. The list of tests was, to Rhyme, meaningless, though one conclusion was clear: any machine that could run these diagnostic analyses, in record time, had to be a significant development.

"Here's what I'm worried about." She blinked back tears. "When Richard started working for JDZ a few years ago, he told me we had to be careful. Every company he'd worked for before—computers, heating systems, appliances—those were small potatoes compared with medical equipment. The money involved is amazing. He told me that there were spies, industrial spies, working for competitors who'd want to steal the secrets. They'd break into our car, our house." She whispered, in astonishment, "They'd bribe employees for trade secrets or to sabotage the equipment. And even blackmail or physically threaten them. That's what

I'm afraid of. He went to meet somebody and hand over information or get instructions, or something.

"I'm good friends with his assistant, Sharon, and we were in the spa yesterday. Nobody was around. And I asked her about it. She said that, yes, she'd seen him at a conference not too long ago talking with some competitors. But she couldn't believe he'd betray the company. Then she added that, yes, Richard had been acting odd lately. Reclusive, she said." Claire inhaled deeply. "I mean, there's no reason for you to help, but . . ."

Sachs said, "If you go to the police and he is giving up secrets, he'd go to jail."

"Exactly. If I could find out what's going on, I could talk to him. If I have to convince him to quit, I'd do it. We'll get by somehow. He's brilliant. He'd get another job. But if he's doing something wrong and he gets caught . . . that'll be the end of his career." She glanced at Rhyme once and began to cry.

Sachs moved close and put her arm around the woman.

"Sorry, sorry, sorry." Claire shook her head briskly.

"No, it's all right," Sachs said.

Rhyme lost interest in the drama in front of him. He turned his head toward the view beyond the balcony but, as his eyes were pressed shut, he saw none of it. Sachs said something—maybe asking what he thought—but he wasn't paying attention.

He opened his eyes after a minute. "Your husband? Did he take his car to these secret meetings?"

"Yes, one we leased in Milan."

"Where's he now?"

"In the lobby, waiting for Sharon. Or he was a few minutes ago."

"Does he know who I am?"

"Probably just that you were the man . . ." Her sentence ground to a politically correct stop.

"In a wheelchair who got married yesterday."

She blushed and nodded.

"Does he follow the news about crime? I'm in the press some."

A wan smile. "Richard? He's a scientist. Mostly he reads medical newsletters and blogs, things like that."

"We'll have to take the chance. Okay, here's what we're going to do. I'm going to go talk to him."

Sachs was smiling. "Talk to a subject? *You?* Never thought I'd see you fishing for some subtle psychological insight."

Rhyme gave a grunt. "No, what I'm going to do is keep him busy so you two can play spy."

Rhyme wheeled up behind the man and woman walking through the ho-tel lobby, headed toward the doorway. "Excuse me," he called.

They turned. Richard Dunning seemed to Rhyme like a pleasant, distracted history professor, handsome in a dowdy way, sharp eyes, congenial smile. He gave no reaction to the chair, and nodded. "Hello."

"You don't know me, but I met your wife in the lounge."

The assistant—Sharon, Rhyme recalled—said, "You remember, Richard, this is the man who got married here yesterday." Sharon hardly fit the industrial-engineer stereotype. Though she wore a conservative suit and Harry Potter glasses, her hair was long and dipped over one eye, like a movie star's, her perfume was exotic and her makeup might have been applied by a pro.

"Sure. Of course."

"Linc," Rhyme said, reflecting that he'd never referred to himself in that way. He offered a hand and shook Richard's.

Richard said, "And this is Sharon Handler."

She took his hand too.

"I'm sorry to interrupt. But Claire and my wife were talking and she mentioned that you're with a medical-equipment company."

Rhyme glanced past them, into the parking lot, and could see Sachs and Claire opening the door to a car and climbing quickly inside.

Richard said, "That's right. We're in Italy to do an install in Como."

That's not a noun, Rhyme thought. "Install." But he said only, "Claire described the project you're working on. I didn't quite follow but it sounded pretty, well, revolutionary."

Richard nodded. "We think so."

Sharon said, with the enthusiasm of all thirty-year-old assistants, "We've shipped twenty-one units this year. We'll do forty next."

"Congratulations."

Outside, Richard's car door was still open. Rhyme forced himself to stop looking. He said, "You can see I'm a quad."

"C-six?" Sharon asked.

"Four."

"Really? Your mobility is good."

"Some surgery. Some exercise. Anyway, I asked Claire if your company did any spinal-cord injury work. She didn't know."

Richard shook his head. "I'm sorry to say we don't." He paused for a moment. "The medical business...well, it *is* a business. I probably don't need to tell you that. I'm sure you know as much about medicine as a lot of doctors. Companies like ours—we're not one of the big boys—we can only afford to develop treatments or equipment for broad-based conditions. SCI isn't as common as diabetes." A shrug. "Maybe when we're bigger."

"Your wife was saying this device does just about any kind of diagnostic analysis."

"Almost. All in one."

Rhyme said, "Like the unified theory of the universe."

Sharon laughed and glanced toward Richard. "I like that. Maybe we could work it into the ads."

"It's all yours. No royalties necessary." Rhyme glanced past her quickly and saw Claire and Sachs had closed the car door and were walking back to the hotel. He was relieved: he'd depleted his store of small-talk. "Well, thanks for your time."

Sharon was looking around. "Did Claire say she was on her way? I was hoping she could join us for lunch down in Como."

And, in the spirit of the best undercover operatives, who never volunteer information if they can avoid it, Rhyme said, "I don't really know what her plans were."

"Maybe just a touch," Rhyme said to the waiter.

He was ordering grappa. And the limitation on quantity was—thank God—ignored since the server didn't understand it.

Sachs was drinking Coke, which she'd learned to order "*con ghiaccio, senza limone.*" The Italians seemed to like warm Coke with lemon. Not a taste she cared for.

"How did it go?" Rhyme asked.

"Claire would make a terrible cop."

"Nervous?"

"I was going to say Mexican jumping bean, but I'm not sure what those are exactly. So, yeah, nervous. But we got four locations from Richard's GPS that seemed suspicious to her. At the times he'd driven there he was supposed to be in Como, but they're in the opposite direction. I'll go check them out, see what I can find."

She showed him a photo that Claire had printed out in the business center. It was on office paper but the quality wasn't bad. The image was of Richard with his arm around Claire, and the three other employees of JDZ-Systems, the lake behind them. "Sharon, Charlie and Tim." The shot wasn't upload-worthy—Claire's eyes were shut, Charlie was about to sneeze, it seemed, the sun was hitting Sharon fiercely in the face so she was looking to the side with a frown, and Tim was staring behind whoever was taking the picture, with a dark expression. Richard, though, was looking right at the camera. Anyone Sachs showed the picture to could easily recognize him, if they'd seen him before.

Rhyme said to Sachs, "You'll do okay with the Italian?"

"*Certamente, no.*" She laughed. "But private eyes're used to winging it, right?"

"Poirot," Rhyme said.

Richard Dunning's first clandestine destination was about twenty minutes from Bellagio, a small strip mall near a town named Magreglio.

The establishments were a mix of old and new: in addition to two bistros and two bars, there were a traditional grocery, a dusty hardware store, a boutique selling chic clothing and lingerie (Milan, Europe's fashion hub, was not far away), and a pet shop.

The only logical places for him to come were the bars and restaurants, where he might have had a secret meeting, and Sachs now made the rounds, displaying her badge and asking, as best she could, if anyone had seen *questo uomo*. The gold shield, of course, meant nothing legally but the Italians, she'd learned, tended to respect authority. And, more importantly, they had a love of intrigue. An American policewoman—a tall and pretty one, no less!—inquiring about a devious suspect, surely... *Sí, sí*! I will help if I can!

But no one could.

The image of Richard Dunning was met with shaken heads and various versions of "I'm sorry."

Another fifteen minutes down the road, south-east from Bellagio, Richard had stopped at a large variety shop, selling ham, pasta, cheese and wine. It, too, had a restaurant and bar—the likely place for Dunning to stop, but no one inside either recognized him. There was a *tabaccheria* too—one of the ubiquitous tobacco shop/newsstands found throughout Italy. The stores also sold prepaid mobiles and phone cards—perfect for staying in touch with a spy.

But no luck there either.

Back into the rental Toyota, a small car, with a small engine. But at least it had the advantage of a manual transmission, so Sachs got some minor pleasure careening over winding roads in a country where speed limits did not seem to exist (even if suicidal goats and cattle did).

The third stop on her mission as a private eye was different from the first two.

It was outside the town of Lecco, a medium-sized Italian city of about ninety thousand. The address was a small warehouse, amid a number of such small businesses. The one window was dark and the lot was empty. Still, she knocked on the office door. There was, as expected, no response.

Slipping around to the back, she found a rear door, which wasn't locked. She stepped inside and flipped the light on.

The dingy space was filled with wooden crates, a big stack of cut-open cartons and drums of packing material, some automotive parts strapped to pallets. Shelves were stacked with boxes and cans—lubricants, cleaning materials, tools and other items typical of small businesses. She walked to the door of the office and glanced through the blinds. There, unlike in the warehouse itself, she could see a CCTV camera. Her sense was that it hadn't worked for years but why take the chance?

Returning to the center of the warehouse proper, she pulled out her phone and made a call.

"Rhyme?"

"What do you have?"

"Nothing in the first two locations. Now I'm at a warehouse. The back door was open."

"Sachs, don't go to jail over this."

"I got lost looking for *il bagno*."

"You think Richard might've met somebody there?"

"Maybe. It's out of the way. Very out of the way."

"What's inside?"

"Boxes, warehouse stuff. Rats."

"Rats?"

"Dead ones." She was looking at a half-dozen small corpses.

Rhyme grew concerned. "Why're they dead, Sachs? Is there anything you shouldn't be breathing or touching? Think canaries in coal mines. Describe them."

She bent close to one. "Looks like they bled out, though no external wounds. And they frenzied before they died."

"Sounds like inorganic arsenic. Exterminators can't use it in America anymore, but in Italy? I don't know."

"I smell something sweet. It's strong."

Some poisons have a deceptively pleasant aroma. Cyanide smells like almonds, a scent you can enjoy in the few minutes remaining to you before an agonizing death.

Rhyme said, "Arsenic doesn't have an odor, so what you're smelling would be something else. But the place is probably closed because of the fumigation. I'd get out, Sachs."

She took his advice and stepped outside, swinging the door shut. She said, "There might be a legitimate reason Richard stopped here. Can you ask Claire? The name is Magazzino di Arnello."

"I'll check."

They disconnected and she looked around the deserted area, windy and chill and unsettling—the bright sun did nothing to make the place seem more hospitable. In the recent case she and Rhyme had worked, in Naples, she'd carried a Beretta 9mm in her waistband. She missed the comfort of the heavy weapon now.

Five minutes later, she started when her phone drummed.

"Rhyme."

"A dead end—all respect to the rats. Claire looked though Richard's files in the room. She found a memo from Tim—the JDZ employee? It was to the manager of the warehouse. Questions about the security of the place. Anyway, there was a legitimate reason for Richard to be there."

"So far, it's all innocent, Rhyme. One more stop. In downtown Lecco. I should be back in an hour."

They disconnected and Sachs stepped into the grass surrounding the parking lot and shuffled back toward the car to clean her soles. Arsenic didn't seem like a good substance to be tracking around.

Twenty minutes later, following the GPS lady's polite directions, she pulled into a parking garage in downtown Lecco. It was connected to a modest but clean hotel, whose style dated to the sixties.

She walked up to the front desk, smiled and flashed her badge. Then displayed the photo. "*Per favore*, have you seen this man?"

He smiled back, though it was a different genre of smile from hers. "You are not an Italian police officer."

"No, I'm an American police officer."

"Yes, that much I have been able to deduce. I was not asking a

question. If I may enrich our conversation, I will say that Lecco, my
happy town, is in *Italy*. It is not in *America*. So unless you wish to return
with an Italian police officer I will not be able to help you." He turned
and went back to ordering papers that did not seem to require ordering.

She gazed about and stepped into a small bar attached to the hotel.
The thin, mustachioed bartender nodded politely. Instead of the badge
trick she tried a different approach.

"Ah, *sí*," the man said, pocketing the forty euros. "I remember him.
Yes. It was perhaps two, three days ago."

"Did he meet anyone in the bar or the lobby?"

"No, I think they did not."

"They?"

"Yes, yes, that man and his wife."

Sachs frowned. Claire had seen the address from the GPS. Maybe she
wouldn't recognize the location of the warehouse but surely she'd recall
staying in a hotel in Lecco.

Unless...

No. Oh, no. Sachs really hoped she was wrong.

She showed the picture again. "Was this his wife?"

"*Sí*, so beautiful, no?"

He was pointing at the image not of Claire but of Sharon Handler.

Well, they might have come here to meet officials of the company or
the university. Sachs asked, "Are you sure she was his wife, and not just
a business associate having drinks?"

"That I cannot say, but I can tell you when they left, they walked down
that corridor there." He pointed through the glass door into the lobby.
"And that leads only to one place: the hotel rooms."

"And then," Sachs was explaining to Rhyme, in Bellagio, "after Lecco,
I went back to the first two locations. There were some shops I didn't
bother with the first time. A lingerie store and a wine shop. I showed

them the picture. And the clerks remembered them both. Well, they remembered Sharon mostly."

Yes, Rhyme recalled, she was a beautiful woman.

"The first store, Richard bought her a nightgown. 'The sexiest one we had,' the owner told me. And at the wine shop, they got a bottle that Richard told the clerk was very special, very romantic."

"Not espionage," Rhyme said. "An affair."

Obviously a man doesn't bring his wife to Lake Como for their anniversary to cheat on her.

Except, apparently, some do.

Sachs shook her head, seemingly dismayed. "Claire told me they were staying here so they could renew their vows on their anniversary. That's pretty low, Rhyme. Well, I guess the question is, do we tell her?"

We chose to play private eye, he reflected. And he supposed the rules of the game meant you delivered bad news as well as good. "I think we have to."

"You're right." Sighing, Sachs pulled her phone out of her pocket and stared at the screen. "Do you have her number?"

Rhyme was about to find it on his phone but another thought intruded.

No, no, impossible . . .

Or was it?

"Oh, hell!" he snapped.

Sachs and Thom simultaneously blinked in surprise. "Lincoln?" the aide asked. "Are you—"

The criminalist barked to the aide, "Call Ercole Benelli. Now."

"In Naples?"

Rhyme muttered, "How do I know where he is? He might be in Singapore or Chicago. He'll have his mobile. Call. Now!"

Thom sighed and lifted his phone.

"What's going on, Rhyme?" Sachs asked.

"I think we may have a worse problem than infidelity, Sachs."

The phone call was completed: Thom hit speaker and set the unit in front of them.

"Capitano Rhyme!"

Rhyme pictured the tall, lanky, ever-enthusiastic and often-blushing

Forestry Service policeman from Campania. He'd recently helped Rhyme and Sachs close a case in that region of Italy. "Ercole, we need your help."

"Of course, of course. How was the wedding? You must send pictures and—"

"Ercole, there's no time! Do you know any police here in Bellagio?"

A pause.

"Well? *Do* you?"

"Ah, Capitano Rhyme, how I miss your impatience! Now, I will say, no, I do not know any in Bellagio itself. But I do know someone not far away. With the Police of State. He is—"

"Good, good, good," Rhyme barked. "I need an STDP-06 detection kit. I need it now. Brought to our hotel. The Villa Francesco."

"Yes, yes, of course. I recommended the hotel for your wedding, you will recall. I will arrange it now, Capitano Rhyme. But what, may I ask, is this STDP-06?"

"A poison detection kit."

"*Mamma mia!*"

They disconnected.

Sachs said, "Are you getting at what I think you are?"

"A couple having an affair. The husband wants to kill the wife. The husband's work takes him to a facility where he sees—and steals—some very potent rat poison."

"First thing the Scientific Police would look for."

"It's not that easy to detect. Arsenic mimics natural causes. And remember? Claire said Richard, she and Sharon traveled a lot. They might have been biding their time until they came to a small town like this, where police and medical examiners wouldn't be so sophisticated. Or they could arrange it to look like an accident. Plant some in the hotel's kitchen. It spilled and got into Claire's food."

Twenty minutes later the desk clerk called to report that a policeman was downstairs asking for Rhyme.

"Yes, yes, send him up."

The slim uniformed officer, wearing the blue outfit of the Police of State, the main police force in Italy, was in awe that he was meeting Rhyme. "You are so very famous, sir. Il Compositore case! Napoli.

Amazing! I have read all about it. *E mio amico*...Ercole Benelli assisted you. When he called about this..." he handed Sachs a large plastic bag, "...I was delighted, you understand?"

"Yes, thank you," Sachs said.

Rhyme nodded his gratitude, but shot a distracted—and, yes, impatient—glance the man's way.

"What, may I ask, is this for?"

Sachs said, "A research paper he's writing."

"Ah, yes. Such a fine writer. I have a copy of your book. I am reading English, not the best, but some. And I will read your paper. I will look forward to—"

"I really must get to it now," Rhyme said, nodding at the door.

Sachs ushered him out, saying, "We'll send you an autographed copy of his book."

"*Molto bene! Grazie!*"

"*Prego,*" Sachs called, to the closed door.

She took the kit from the bag. The STDP-06 system was easy to use. Samples of suspected poisoned food or beverages were prepared and placed on a detection card. A colored band appeared in a bar if poisons were present. Results were usually ready quickly.

But, of course, you needed those samples.

Rhyme said, "Somehow we've got to search the Dunnings' room."

"How would he administer it?"

"For immediate death it has to be ingested. Medicine capsules maybe. Or food or drinks."

Sachs picked up the house phone. "I'll see if they're out. If so, maybe I can charm or bribe my way in."

She called the front desk and offered a credible story about wanting to deliver a surprise present to the couple.

Her face went still as she listened.

"*Grazie.*"

"What, Sachs?"

"The desk clerk said they probably wouldn't appreciate any disturbances. They were having a romantic dinner in their room tonight in honor of their anniversary. Jesus, he could be poisoning her right now, Rhyme."

Fire alarms in Europe—in Italy at least—don't fool around.

The sound was akin to that made, Rhyme imagined, by a crash-diving submarine's klaxon. It filled the hallways of the Villa Francesco and, within seconds of Thom's pulling the alarm bar on their floor—out of sight of CCTVs—troubled guests were heading out, many covering their ears.

Sachs had been waiting next to the Dunnings' suite, her back to the door, when the alarm went off. As soon as they exited, she leaped forward and, unseen by them, slipped a foot between door and jamb. She waited a moment until they disappeared around the corner, then stepped inside.

They had, she noted, both begun to eat. It was obvious which side of the table Claire sat on—lipstick on the wine glass—but Sachs, in latex gloves, took samples of everything. She made a fast search of the medicine cabinet and found no drugs or over-the-counter products that could be laced with poison, or bottles of beverages that seemed tampered with.

In five minutes she was back in their own suite—just as an announcement came over the loudspeaker in the room, in Italian, English, German and French, that it had been a false alarm.

Sachs stood at the table, hunched over the STDP-06 cards, working furiously. The Dunnings would be back in their suite any moment now and dining once more.

But the tests went quickly and in a matter of minutes they had their answer.

None of the food or beverages was tainted—not the least trace of arsenic or any other poison was present.

Rhyme absolutely hated it when his theories proved false. "All right, maybe murder was a bit imaginative."

"Better safe than sorry."

Rhyme grimaced: he also hated clichés.

Sachs said, "Well, we still have to deliver the message about the hotel room in Lecco."

Rhyme, the least sentimental person on earth, said, "Wait till tomorrow? Let her have tonight, at least? Their last romantic dinner."

Sachs debated. "Why not?"

In the morning, Rhyme and Sachs were sitting on the balcony off the lobby when Claire Dunning approached. She greeted them and sat.

Rhyme looked at Sachs, who'd agreed to deliver the news.

"First, I didn't find any evidence of espionage or blackmail. But..." Sachs took a breath.

Claire held up a hand. "I know, I know. I was going to call you last night but it was late, and I knew we were meeting this morning."

Rhyme glanced her way with curiosity.

"I found out what Richard was up to. His secret drives."

Both Rhyme and Sachs noted her cheerful face and shared confused glances.

Claire continued, "It was for our anniversary."

Sachs was silent for a moment. "How's that?"

"He was shopping, and he got me the most wonderful presents! One of the places on the GPS was..." Claire was blushing "...a lingerie shop. He bought me the cutest little number. Of course, he's a man—so he didn't have a clue what to buy, but Sharon went with him and helped him pick it out. And then he found a store in the area that sold the same wine we had at our wedding in Napa! It's Californian and almost impossible to find here. I think that was the text he got and didn't tell me about. And then—look."

She displayed her phone. It showed a photo of a framed embroidery, a hummingbird hovering over a flower. "One of Sharon's former girlfriends is an artist. Richard commissioned it from her. She took the train all the way from Florence, and Sharon and Richard went to Lecco to get it from her a few days ago."

"At her hotel?"

"Yep. That was one of the directions in the GPS too, I'm sure."

"Girlfriend?" Sachs asked. "Sharon's girlfriend?"

"Oh, yes. Sharon's gay, you know."

Well, Lincoln Rhyme had often thought that misunderstanding and error were very real factors, too often ignored in criminal investigation. And talk about being mistaken . . .

"I'm sorry you had to go on that wild-goose chase," Claire said. "But I'm so grateful." Then she looked past them. "Ah, here she is now. Richard's co-conspirator. Amelia, have you met Sharon?"

"No."

The tall woman joined them and nodded a greeting to Rhyme, then Claire introduced her to Sachs, whom Sharon perused with a smile: one beautiful woman assessing—with approval—another. They brushed cheeks. Sharon sat next to Claire and they embraced too.

"I was just telling Amelia and Lincoln about your friend's embroidery. It's so beautiful."

"And the nightgown? Did you like it?"

"Oh, yes!" Claire blushed.

"I'm sure you looked stunning."

Claire deflected the intimate talk, turning her gaze to the lobby. "You and Richard were meeting for breakfast, weren't you, Sharon?"

"That's right."

"Is he still there? I'll get coffee with him before you leave for Como."

"No, he went back to your room."

Claire sent a text. A moment later her phone chimed and she read the screen. She frowned. "Hm, seems he's not feeling too well. He's gone back to bed."

It was then that Rhyme noticed something curious.

He'd glanced at Sachs and seen her nose flare slightly, her head cocked and her brow furrowed. She looked off slightly, as if trying to place something. A memory was hovering.

A scent memory.

Suddenly, like a blow, Rhyme understood. He whispered, "The warehouse, Sachs."

I smell something sweet. It's strong . . .

"Yes," Sachs replied.

It had been Sharon's perfume that Sachs had smelled in the small building outside Lecco.

Rhyme turned toward a passing busboy and shouted, "We need an ambulance! Doctors!"

"Sir, you are ill?"

"Not me!" he snapped. "The Dunnings' suite. Now! Move!"

The skinny young man hesitated, then ran to the front desk.

"Lincoln," Claire cried. "What is it?"

Sharon knew she'd been found out. She started to rise fast but Sachs lunged forward and pushed her back into the couch, pulling away the woman's purse.

Her dark eyes flared. "You can't do that!"

"Amelia!" Claire gaped. "What's going on?"

Sachs dumped the contents onto the table. In addition to the typical inhabitants of a handbag there were two plastic sacks. One contained a wad of plastic gloves. Another a residue of gray-blue powder.

Rhyme recognized inorganic arsenic.

Sharon again started to rise but Sachs leaned forward and whispered, "Don't move."

Even without a weapon, Amelia Sachs was a formidable woman, one you ignored at your peril.

Richard Dunning's condition wasn't serious.

The poison that Sharon had sprinkled into the smoked salmon at their breakfast table, when he'd looked away, was certainly a lethal dosage but it had not had time to do significant damage before the emergency-room doctors began their treatment. He was at the hospital in Lecco—where, Rhyme supposed, his blood had been analyzed by a competitor's equipment. Claire and the other two employees, Charlie and Tim, were at his side.

Sharon Handler was closer to home: the Bellagio police lockup on via Garibaldi, coincidentally right next to the town hall, where Rhyme and Sachs had been married.

Sitting on the balcony of their room now, looking over the view, Rhyme was reflecting on the close call. He took some solace in the fact that, had this been a proper case, Sachs would have looked more carefully at the players' profiles, what they said and did, and he at the evidence. They might, for instance, have figured out earlier that there was a triangle and that Sharon Handler might have an interest in either Richard or Claire: the three of them traveling for business and becoming "close," as Claire said. And then there was Sharon's frown in the photo Claire had given Sachs: perhaps that was not due to bright sun but reflected her anger at the loving embrace between husband and wife, one of whom she had an obsession with.

It was odd, too, that, though Sharon was staying some distance from Bellagio, she was frequently at the villa.

And as for her attraction to Claire, rather than Richard, well, in the lobby the other day, she'd commented that she hoped Claire was coming to have lunch with them—hardly the words of a woman having an affair with the other woman's husband, but possibly those of someone attracted to his wife. The spa too—possibly at Sharon's suggestion. And Sharon's assessment of Amelia Sachs might have had a subtext.

And knowing that a triangle was a possibility—always a delightful source of carnage—he would have managed samples of the principals' shoes and fingerprints, and searched the warehouse more carefully. Sharon would have been there, of course, to check on the equipment when it arrived via train; she would have seen the dead rats and noted a box of arsenic pesticide. She would have left fibers or friction ridges on the back door, when she taped or jammed the lock open so she could come back for the poison.

Samples of Sharon's clothing, shoes, car and her own hotel room would have revealed easily detected arsenic.

But in the end, Rhyme supposed, it didn't matter much if a psychological profile, deconstruction of suspects' statements and ten-part forensic analysis, or a chance sniff of perfume saved the life of a potential victim.

Results, ultimately, were what mattered. In criminal cases, as in life.

Since the local police were happy to be assisted by the American detective who had helped solve the Compositore case in Naples, Rhyme was given access to most of the evidence. A search of Sharon's room and car did indeed reveal more poison trace, dozens of furtive pictures of Claire, some naked, and a fake email from a European competitor of JDZ-Systems, purportedly expressing anger that Richard Dunning had refused to sell trade secrets and threatening him to keep quiet—a motive for killing him (and a twist coincidentally suggested by Claire herself, when she asked Sharon about the industrial espionage in the spa).

More important for the *procuratore* who would handle the case against her: a diary. In it Sharon wrote poetry about her love for Claire and jotted entries expressing her steadfast belief that she could make Claire love her in return—if only she could get rid of Richard.

It would be good advice, Rhyme decided, for those bent on murder to avoid writing down things like "I vow to kill that son of a bitch."

He chuckled and showed the passage to Sachs.

She, too, laughed. "This is quite the week for vows, isn't it?"

As dusk was descending, the Sprinter returned to the villa with the wedding party. They disembarked and headed into the lobby, where Rhyme and Sachs were waiting to greet them.

Lon Sellitto glanced at the two Police of State squad cars parked in front of the hotel and then, quizzically, at Rhyme, who shrugged in response.

Rose Sachs walked up to her daughter and Rhyme, hugged them both and said, "It was beautiful, Monte Bianco in particular. *Bella*. See, I'm already speaking *italiano*. I took a million pictures. You'll have to see."

"Can't wait, Mom," Sachs said.

The slim woman said, "So, how's your honeymoon been? I was worried that you'd be bored. Bellagio's lovely but it seems so quiet."

"Oh," Rhyme said, "we kept ourselves amused." And turned, guiding everyone into the bar for an *aperitivo*.

ACKNOWLEDGMENTS

With undying gratitude to: Will and Tina Anderson, Cicely Aspinall, Sophie Baker, Felicity Blunt, Penelope Burns, Jane Davis, Julie Deaver, Andy Dodd, Jenna Dolan, Jamie Hodder-Williams, Kerry Hood, Cathy Gleason, Emma Knight, Carolyn Mays, Wes Miller, Claire Nozieres, Hazel Orme, Abby Parsons, Michael Pietsch, Jamie Raab, Betsy Robbins, Lindsey Rose, Katy Rouse, Deborah Schneider, Vivienne Schuster, Louise Swannell, Ruth Tross, Madelyn Warcholik…and especially to my Italian friends: Roberta Bellesini, Giovanna Canton, Andrea Carlo Cappi, Gianrico Carofiglio, Francesca Cinelli, Roberto Costantini, Luca Crovi, Marina Fabbri, Valeria Frasca, Giorgio Gosetti, Michele Giuttari, Paolo Klun, Stefano Magagnoli, Rosanna Paradiso, Roberto and Cecilia Santachiara, Carolina Tinicolo, Luca Ussia, Paolo Zaninoni…and I must note the passing of the wonderful Tecla Dozio, whose mystery bookshop in Milan was always one of the highpoints of my international tours.

ABOUT THE AUTHOR

A former journalist, folksinger and attorney, Jeffery Deaver is an international number one bestselling author. His novels have appeared on bestseller lists around the world, including the *New York Times*, *The Times* of London, Italy's *Corriere della Sera*, the *Sydney Morning Herald* and the *Los Angeles Times*. His books are sold in 150 countries and translated into twenty-five languages.

He currently serves as president of the Mystery Writers of America.

The author of thirty-eight novels, three collections of short stories and a nonfiction law book, and the lyricist of a country-western album, he's received or been shortlisted for dozens of awards.

His *The Bodies Left Behind* was named Novel of the Year by the International Thriller Writers association, and his Lincoln Rhyme thriller *The Broken Window* and a stand-alone, *Edge*, were also nominated for that prize, and one of his recent stories was nominated for ITW's short story of the year. He has been awarded the Steel Dagger and the Short Story Dagger from the British Crime Writers' Association and the Nero Award, and he is a three-time recipient of the Ellery Queen Readers Award for Best Short Story of the Year and a winner of the British Thumping Good Read Award. *Solitude Creek* and *The Cold Moon* were both given the number one ranking by *Kono Misuteri Ga Sugoi* in Japan. *The Cold Moon* was also named the Book of the Year by the Mystery Writers Association of Japan. In addition, the Japanese Adventure Fiction Association awarded *The Cold Moon* and *Carte Blanche* their annual Grand Prix award. His book *The Kill Room* was awarded the Political Thriller of the Year by

Killer Nashville. And his collection of short stories *Trouble in Mind* was nominated for best anthology by that organization, as well.

Deaver has been honored with three lifetime achievement awards: from the Bouchercon World Mystery Convention, the Raymond Chandler Lifetime Achievement Award in Italy, and the *Strand Magazine*.

Deaver has been nominated for seven Edgar Awards from the Mystery Writers of America, an Anthony, a Shamus and a Gumshoe. He was shortlisted for the ITV3 Crime Thriller Award for Best International Author. *Roadside Crosses* was on the shortlist for the Prix Polar International 2013. He contributed to the anthology *In the Company of Sherlock* and *Books to Die For*, which won the Anthony. *Books to Die For* recently won the Agatha, as well.

His most recent novels are *The Steel Kiss*, a Lincoln Rhyme novel, *Solitude Creek*, a Kathryn Dance thriller and *The October List*, a thriller told in reverse. For the Dance novel *XO* Deaver wrote an album of country-western songs, available on iTunes and as a CD; and before that, he wrote *Carte Blanche*, a James Bond continuation novel, a number one international bestseller.

His book *A Maiden's Grave* was made into an HBO movie starring James Garner and Marlee Matlin, and his novel *The Bone Collector* was a feature release from Universal Pictures, starring Denzel Washington and Angelina Jolie. Lifetime aired an adaptation of his *The Devil's Teardrop*. And, yes, the rumors are true: He did appear as a corrupt reporter on his favorite soap opera, *As the World Turns*. He was born outside Chicago and has a bachelor of journalism degree from the University of Missouri and a law degree from Fordham University. Readers can visit his website at www.jefferydeaver.com.